Black

www.penguin.co.uk

Also by Simon Mayo

Mad Blood Stirring
Knife Edge
Tick Tock

Fiction for Younger Readers

Blame
Itchcraft
Itch Rocks
Itch

Black Tag

Simon Mayo

bantam

TRANSWORLD PUBLISHERS
Penguin Random House, One Embassy Gardens,
8 Viaduct Gardens, London SW11 7BW
www.penguin.co.uk

Transworld is part of the Penguin Random House group of companies
whose addresses can be found at global.penguinrandomhouse.com

Penguin
Random House
UK

First published in Great Britain in 2025 by Bantam
an imprint of Transworld Publishers

A CIP catalogue record for this book
is available from the British Library.

ISBNs
9781787636798 (hb)
9781787636804 (tpb)

Typeset in 11.5/16 pt Palladio URW by Jouve (UK), Milton Keynes
Printed and bound in Great Britain by Clays Ltd, Elcograf S.p.A.

The authorized representative in the EEA is Penguin Random House Ireland,
Morrison Chambers, 32 Nassau Street, Dublin D02 YH68.

[Dedication to come]

In the age of fake news and disinformation, we need journalists more than ever to document the unseen and expose the fault lines in our society.

Justice Dhannanjaya Y. Chandrachud,
Judge, Supreme Court of India

1

Sunday

Two cracks, then a shattering. A double strike, then a rupturing.

One brick followed the other and the vast ground-floor window, divided into twenty separate panes by steel runners, splintered at the first, shattered with the second. Gloved fists punched out the remaining daggers of glass, leaving two clean holes in the side of the building. The eighteen remaining panes reflected deep blue sky, elegant trees in blossom and a sea of angry faces. Singing, chanting, cursing. The demonstrators cheered as the glass broke, surged forward. A man in a Puffa jacket tried to haul himself inside but his shoulders were too broad, and the hole too small. He dropped down, waved in a replacement. A smaller figure – dark green beanie hat, grungy black jumper – took hold of the metal runners then slipped through with ease. There was another cheer.

Inside, the demonstrator ran between stands, then stopped to remove two small paintings from a wall, tucked both under one arm, vaulted a turnstile, then sprinted to a staircase that disappeared to a lower floor. Took the steps three at a time. At the bottom, a locked wooden door, a steel handle with a twelve-digit keypad integrated into the locking mechanism. Zero to nine, a hashtag and a 'C' cancel button. The demonstrator punched six numbers with speed and precision, tugged the handle and the door swung open.

The downstairs room was dark, windowless. As the demonstrator stepped inside, the strip lighting flickered on to reveal a classroom-sized basement office with a low ceiling and six desks in two rows of three, each with a computer screen and keyboard. All but the nearest desk had in-trays laden with folders. A grey jacket was draped over one of the chairs. The room looked tidy and organized. Art posters filled the four walls, leaving only a space for a wipe-clean year planner, which was stuck to the far wall. Gunmetal-grey filing cabinets lined two sides of the room.

The demonstrator strode to the nearest desk, placed the paintings on the floor, sat in the revolving chair. A gloved hand punched a key. The screen blinked into life, its wallpaper an art-deco teapot in blues and orange, with the password box in its centre. The demonstrator typed eight letters, one number, and an exclamation mark. The teapot disappeared, replaced by a screenful of files. The demonstrator took a small notepad and a mobile phone from a bum-bag tied under their jumper, placed them together by the computer's mouse. They scanned the files, then started clicking them open. One by one.

As each file opened, the demonstrator read a few lines, scrolled, read some more, then closed it again. Twenty seconds, maybe thirty with each. Eyes flicked to the digital clock in the screen's top right, then back to the next file.

Click open, scan, scroll, scan, click shut.

At the end of the third row, forty-two files down, the demonstrator paused. Took a breath. Clicked on the magnifying-glass search icon, top right of the screen, next to the clock. A 'Spotlight Search' window appeared. Rapid, heavy typing delivered a screenful of results. The demonstrator clicked and leant in.

If the demonstrator had been listening, they would have noticed the sound of the chanting and shouting outside getting louder. If the demonstrator had been listening, they'd have heard more glass breaking, and more boots arriving in the building. If the demonstrator had been listening, they'd have heard those boots descend the staircase. When the demonstrator eventually looked up, it was already too late.

The fire-bomber was a figure in motorcycle leathers, a red scarf tied around their face. They stepped into the room and threw three bottles, one against the left wall, one at the right and the third to the far wall. Each exploded into flame as it hit. The posters caught fast. The smell of petrol enveloped the office. Sprinklers burst into life. A piercing alarm filled the air.

The demonstrator jumped from the chair. Stared aghast. Glanced at the walls, then back to the fire-bomber in time for a fourth bottle to smash on the floor at their feet. The flames caught, enveloping the grungy jumper. They screamed, fell to the floor. The fire-bomber stepped out of the room, shut the door, then took a hammer to the key pad. Six blows and it ruptured, obliterating the 'six', 'seven' and 'zero' digits. The fire-bomber tried the handle. It swung down but the door stayed locked.

From the other side, a hammering fist.

2

The fire was confined for twenty-two minutes. The flames climbed the walls, then scurried across the ceiling.

After six minutes, the computers popped and cracked. After ten the chairs melted, till just the metal frames remained. The tables were ablaze. By the door, the demonstrator was alight, hair to shoes. The locked door blistered.

The sprinklers had failed. Too much of the fire was out of their reach. The fire clung to the ceiling, like Christmas decorations. The water turned into steam. As the ceiling burnt, the sprinklers dropped to the floor.

After twelve minutes, eight firefighters were congregating around the door. Three ran around the outside of the gallery, each glancing up at the three storeys as they went. At the broken window one stopped, smelt the air, spoke sharply into his radio.

At fourteen minutes, a well-dressed woman in black arrived at the front door, breathless and trembling. She produced keys, opened up. She stepped aside, the firefighters ran in. The tallest, light gold uniform, yellow helmet, showed the woman a tablet screen. Together they raced to the centre of a lobby, then through an open door.

The ground floor was one long open-plan room with temporary partitions dividing the space into smaller areas. Paintings hung on the walls. Left and right, illustrated stands carried potted histories of the paintings and artists. The air shimmered with the heat. The smell of petrol was unmistakable.

At sixteen minutes, the tall firefighter bellowed instructions, pointing right. His team began removing the pictures. The woman pointed at the screen, shook her head then pointed again. More instructions. More paintings taken down. One, gold-framed, caught the sunlight, glittered as it was tucked under a firefighter's arm.

At eighteen minutes, a firefighter ran up a central flight of stairs to the first floor. The tall one watched him go, then shouted after him.

At nineteen minutes he returned, a small painting in browns and whites under his arm.

At twenty minutes the wooden floor began to smoke, patches turning black.

At twenty-one minutes, the tall firefighter ordered an evacuation.

At twenty-two minutes the floor began to burn. Flames appeared simultaneously across the area, three partitions ignited. The door from the basement office burnt through. A ball of flame shot up the stairs, a caged monster released.

At twenty-three minutes, the West End Gallery of Granary Square, London, was on fire.

3

Famie Madden chose Mozart over Max Richter, Sauvignon over Coke. She stared at her laptop, then at her garden, and came back to her laptop. Twenty-seven posts since lunch. It was the most she could remember. Her heart sank.

'So much shit,' she said aloud. 'Just so much.' She closed her eyes. Had it always been this bad and she hadn't been paying attention? Or was it the case that every month, every year was demonstrably worse than the one before? She felt sure it was the latter. Took a mouthful of wine. Read more posts.

A new message appeared, the chime of the notification clashing with the music. Then another. And another. Same author, someone who identified on the site as KT. Reported mainly from Turkey, occasionally Syria and Afghanistan. The posts were brief, hurried, uncorrected.

> AGENSTS IN HOUSE DOOR KICKED IN, SZ
> IM WAITING OUTISE. NOT CALLING POLICE.
> THEYVE BEEN TROLLING FOR DAYS. DIDNT
>   THINK THEYD COME.

Famie sat up straight. Killed the music. Watched the screen. She waited for more, holding her breath. She opened another screen, looked for KT's details on her login. It gave an email, and a phone number with a +90 prefix. 'Editor' was written next to both. She waited for another post. After a minute, she lost patience and called the number. It rang four times, then clicked to a message in what Famie assumed was Turkish. She didn't speak.

Famie scrolled KT's previous posts. They seemed to concentrate on human trafficking and forced labour, following routes that started in Syria. She shook her head. As front lines go, KT had certainly picked one of the most dangerous. War zones, drug gangs and poverty would always be a lethal combination. Writing about them, as Famie had discovered in Pakistan a decade ago, could be just as dangerous. She was relieved to be out. She emailed the given address, alerting whoever saw it to the danger KT might be in, and went back to watching the screen.

The Mozart finished, her glass was empty. She poured more, then replaced the bottle in the fridge. She was heading back to her laptop when a combination of the bell ringing and a hammering at her front door made her jump.

It was Charlie, her daughter, which was good, but a frightened Charlie, which definitely wasn't. Her eyes were as wild as her brown curls. 'Charlie! What on earth . . .' Famie pulled her inside before she could reply. She locked and bolted the door, re-engaged the chain, steered her to the table in the kitchen and sat down next to her. 'You smell of burning,' she said, concern rising.

Charlie was breathing hard, sweat running into her eyes. She wiped them with a hand, then peeled off her old university sweatshirt and used it as a towel. 'You know the gallery Lena works at, the one her dad owns?' She pulled at her T-shirt where it had stuck to her skin.

'Sure,' said Famie. 'I went there once.'

'Well, that's what's burning,' said Charlie. She got up, poured a glass of water at the sink.

Famie sat bolt upright. 'What?' she said. 'Some of it? All of it?'

7

Charlie downed the glass, poured again. 'Don't know. It was the first floor when I left, but it looked bad, Mum. I heard the main fireman, the one I spoke to, say, "Make pumps ten," into his radio. I guess that's ten fire engines he was after. Anyway, I ran straight here.'

'Not to your place?'

'Fire brigade had closed off access to it.'

'My God,' said Famie. 'Was anyone inside the gallery?

Charlie shook her head. 'All shut up. The protest, remember?'

Famie didn't, and frowned.

'Lena was on it,' said Charlie. 'So was I. Another anti-capitalist march at King's Cross.'

Famie held up her hand. 'Wait,' she said, astonished. 'Definitely wait. Lena Nash, your flatmate, posh Lena, who is part of the Nash empire, who actually works at the West End Gallery, she was on the anti-capitalist march that torched her own family's property?'

'The march was literally next to our flat, Mum. We could see it all happening. Of course we were on it.'

Famie was incredulous. 'But she's so smart. I like her, Charlie! But, good God, what a fool.' Famie shook her head.

Now Charlie was irate. 'She *is* smart, Mum. You really can't say that. Just because her family's loaded doesn't mean she can't have a conscience.'

'Sure. But she was demonstrating outside her family's own gallery—'

'We live next door!' interrupted Charlie. 'And we went as far as the Google building by Pancras Square and stopped. Some idiot threw a fire-bomb and we thought it was time to bail out.'

'You think?' said Famie.

'We pulled back, stepped away from the crowd. We were just heading back towards King's Cross when Lena got a call from

8

the fire brigade. She just froze. They said the gallery was burning and her name was top of their list of contacts. She looked shit scared, Mum. But we ran back to the gallery. The fire brigade was there. Lena went inside with them. I came here.'

'Lena went in with them? Into the fire?'

'I think it was just in the basement at that point. There was this smoky haze. There weren't any flames, but you could smell the burning.'

Now Famie stood, leant against the table. She had met Lena many times, always liked her. An entitled Bristol arts graduate for sure, but unlike most of them, she knew it. And she actually was 'entitled'. The Nash family sponsored and supported scores of charitable organizations, mostly in the arts. She 'understood her privilege' was what Charlie said, and tried to do something about it. The flat they shared was always buzzing. A social hub. Lena was generous with her money and her time. Charlie loved sharing with her. She felt secure, she said, which, after the last few years, was quite something. They were two twenty-three-year-olds living in one of the old King's Cross gasholders, one of London's most sought-after apartments. The canal, shops and cafés always attracted an international crowd. No wonder Charlie had said she was living in some kind of dreamland.

Famie remembered Charlie and Lena's particular excitement – exclusive perhaps to two English and art graduates – at discovering the nearby church had once employed Thomas Hardy and the churchyard contained the grave of Mary Wollstonecraft. The new homes cost millions but Lena's father had taken care of the finance. Famie had paid for the coffee machine.

'Have you heard from her?' said Famie. 'Do you know if she's okay?'

'Wait,' said Charlie, head cocked. She walked to the folding doors that opened to a long garden, with grass and paving stones.

She paused by the door, then pushed the handle. As it swung open, the sound of sirens floated in with the breeze. Charlie stepped out, and Famie joined her. They stood by some black metal chairs, heads tilted up. A plume of black smoke rose above the houses opposite.

'Is that it?' said Famie.

Charlie nodded. 'Must be.'

'Where is she, Charlie? Where's Lena now?'

Charlie didn't take her eyes from the sky. 'She went to get her dad,' she said.

4

Michael Nash watched his gallery burn. Rigid with shock, he had said nothing since his arrival. His daughter, Lena, slipped a supportive arm through his. His eyes flicked left and right, sometimes following a firefighter, a shifting hydraulic ladder or a running policeman, but now he'd seen enough. He turned his back on the devastation. He was forty-three, but walked as if he was ninety, holding Lena with a grim determination. They were the same height, five feet nine, he in a dark Crombie coat, blue suit and tie, she in a black dress, buttoned-up cream cardigan and DMs.

The police hadn't allowed him to cross the Regent's Canal and he hadn't argued. The heat rolled over the water, grass banks and tarmac paths; a hundred metres away was quite close enough. They had told him that the fire had spread to all three floors and that although the fire brigade thought the walls would hold, most of the interior would be damaged or destroyed. A few paintings had been saved but most would perish. The cost was incalculable.

He slumped onto a bench. Lena lowered herself next to him, head craned to the inferno. Round face, brown eyes, she had black smudges on her nose and cheeks. She smelt of smoke.

Michael removed his heavy-framed black glasses, wiped his eyes with a handkerchief. 'It's the most terrible thing, Lena,' he croaked. 'The most terrible . . . How can I even . . .' His voice trailed away. He folded his glasses, then slid them into his coat's top pocket. 'Tell me what's happening,' he said. 'Tell me what you can see. I can't bear to look any more.' He straightened his tie, placed his hands in his lap and closed his eyes.

Lena stood, turned to face the fire. Twisted her shoulder-length black hair into a loose bun. 'Well,' she said, voice tight. She hesitated, gave a quick glance to her father. He had always been gaunt, but now, without his glasses, he seemed positively haunted.

She surveyed her family's gallery. The building had been a nineteenth-century warehouse, restored and refurbished with the rest of the King's Cross area. It had survived the Blitz but it wouldn't survive this. Her vantage point showed her the southern end of the gallery and its front. The light and dark brown patchwork of bricks seemed solid enough but the massive windows of the ground and first floors were gone. Where the glass had blown, huge flames roared through the breach. Thick black smoke billowed high into the air, then rolled slowly south, high above King's Cross station. The air was acrid. Ash blew around them like blossom.

'Lena?' he prompted.

'It's about as bad as you can imagine,' she said eventually. She paused, cleared her throat. 'So. Those trees in front of the steps have just caught. They'll be done pretty quickly, I would think.' The four pear trees were burning furiously, a wall of blue and orange flame crackling and spitting. 'Another fire engine has just arrived,' she said. 'The first two still have their ladders above the roof, hosing it down. The others have their water jets aimed at the windows on the ground and first floors.'

'Not working, though, is it?'

'Not really.'

'And the second floor?' asked Michael.

'Fully ablaze,' she said softly. She put a hand on his shoulder. 'It's all going, Dad. I'm so sorry.'

There was a silence between them as Lena watched and Michael listened. Firefighters yelled over the hum and hiss of their engines. More sirens nearby, more glass windows exploding, the hi-hat of the panes splintering over the bass roar of the inferno. With each blast, Michael recoiled as if he'd been punched in the chest. Blow after blow. Eventually he folded, put his head into his hands.

'Tell me what happened,' he said, 'when you got there.'

Lena sat down next to her father. She took a breath. 'I had the keys. I always have the keys.' She pushed her hands deep into her dress's pockets and pulled out four keys and a black leather fob hanging from a metal ring. Michael didn't look up. She put them back into her pocket, stared ahead. 'Most of the crowd, the demonstrators, had gone by then, I think. As soon as the fire brigade turned up, that was pretty much that. There was one fire engine by the steps, another arriving through the square. Maybe two more. Not sure. Ten or so firemen were at the front door tooled up, ready to go in. One said I was now the incident coordinator or something like that. They asked if anyone was inside. I said we'd been closed for the day. Then I opened up and they ran in.' She paused as if to get her thoughts into the right order. 'You could smell it straight away, Dad. No flames. Not then anyway. Just this weird heat haze. Everything . . . shimmered. And there was this thick smell of everything burning.'

'You knew that, then?' said Michael, through his fingers.

'Well, I wanted to go into the office to get the grab list, but they stopped me. Said that was where the fire was. That the door was the only thing keeping the fire at bay. That they had electronic copies of the list anyway. And we had seconds to retrieve anything that was on it. One guy called out names from the list, I pointed at where each item was. We got everything out from the ground floor . . .'

Michael glanced up. 'Including the Gerstein?'

'Including the Gerstein,' said Lena. Michael nodded.

'One of the firemen made it to the first floor,' said Lena, 'but I was pushed out before I saw him again. Don't know if he got anything.'

He waited for more. None came. 'Is . . . that it?' he said.

Lena folded and unfolded her arms. 'I thought I could smell petrol, Dad. In fact I'm sure I did.'

Michael shuddered, slumped forward again. He was silent awhile, then whispered, 'So how many saved?'

'The list had eight on the ground floor,' she said. 'But maybe more if they got to the first floor in time.'

'Eight,' he said, his voice thin, 'from all of it, just eight.'

'Eight for certain, yes,' said Lena. 'I'll open the strong room as soon as I get back.'

'Were there flames,' he said, 'when you were inside? Could you see flames?'

'No, but I could hear the roaring,' she said. 'There was smoke coming from somewhere. And we were running out when the fire broke through the office door.' Lena swallowed. 'Everything seemed to go at once,' she said.

Lena started to stand up but Michael pulled her back. A gentle tug on her arm. 'You were there when it started?' he said.

'Yes and no,' said Lena. 'Me and Charlie Madden were at the rally, as you know . . .'

'Rally or riot?'

'Rally, Dad. It was a demonstration. You know what it was.'

'I can see what it turned into.'

Lena didn't respond. Michael hung his head. When he looked up, Lena was crying. He reached for her hand, she let him take it. 'It was peaceful,' said Lena.

'Until it wasn't,' said Michael.

Lena conceded the point. 'Until it wasn't,' she said. 'Obviously.' She wiped her eyes with her sleeve.

'You're sure there was no one inside?' he said.

'We were closed, if you remember,' she said. 'We warned all the other stores what was going to happen. They said they'd heard nothing from the police.'

'Right,' said Michael, flatly.

'Most got bricked,' said Lena, 'so just as well they were shut.'

'Police said the Google building got fire-bombed too. Is that right?'

'Yes', said Lena, 'and that fancy studio-café round the corner in Stable Street.'

Michael looked up, caught Lena's eye. 'I don't see them burning, though,' he said. 'Or any of the big research labs. Or the data science places. They seem fine.'

Lena said nothing. There was nothing to say. The gallery was the only building alight, all the others, by comparison, merely damaged. The Google fire-bomb had sprayed burning petrol across the entrance but had been put out without further carnage. Every clothes shop had broken windows. Waitrose had been sprayed with paint: 'CAPITALISM IS KILLING YOU' in quickly written green letters. 'FUCK YOUR JOBS' was written on the walls of the Central Saint Martins art school. Same colour, same handwriting.

Granary Square was strewn with overturned tables, chairs

and smashed-up advertising hoardings. Specialist food stands had been thrown into the canal.

'It's just us, Lena, just us burning,' said Michael. 'Just my West End Gallery, see? Nothing else.' He hauled himself to his feet, took one last look at the blaze and turned away. 'I'm going home.'

WEST END GALLERY
SALVAGE GRAB SHEET

ITEM
Claustrophobia/David Gerstein

LOCATION/CLOSEUP LOCATION, FLOOR PLAN
Ground floor. Stand 10. Top painting of 3

PRIORITY
One

DESCRIPTION
Acrylic on canvas.
Blue car, grey driver
162cms x 130cms

INVENTORY NUMBER
236

WEIGHT
1.3 kilos

ACCESS
Direct from ground floor

REMOVAL
Gloves needed. Two-person removal

5

After Charlie had left, Famie returned to her laptop. The wine had given way to a cafetière of coffee, the Richter for Mozart's Grand Mass. Its solemnity matched her mood. There was nothing new from KT and no reply from whoever the email had reached. If it had reached anyone.

The latest post came from one of her Indian followers, who called herself Nita, and detailed a Hindu nationalist attack on an Indian Muslim home in West Bengal. Nita had heard local politicians follow up with verbal attacks on local journalists. These had become actual physical assaults when two of the journalists had gone to work. Both had been stabbed. One was dead, the other critical.

'Dear God,' muttered Famie.

Next came posts from Bolivia, the Philippines and Hong Kong. Each was anonymous, the writers using pseudonyms to tell their story. The front page of the site was a world map showing where the reports had come from. It formed an at-a-glance guide to where press freedom was under attack. Even the most cursory glance suggested the answer was 'pretty much everywhere'.

Famie had only set up the Howl website eighteen months ago. She and her old news-agency colleague Sam Carter had quickly established its reputation as one of the primary campaigning sites for journalistic freedom. After the Russian-led terror attacks four years ago that had killed so many of her

18

colleagues, Famie had been lost. She had written a bestselling book about it with the man they had rescued, Hari Roy. It turned out the world wanted to know their story and she had been happy to tell it, but then the world wanted more, her publisher certainly. Famie wanted less.

She turned down the option of a second book, and a return to her old job at the IPS news agency. She had turned down everything.

The royalties had kept her going but she knew she wanted to work. With Charlie out of university and making her own way, Famie craved the return of routine. She wanted to wake up in the morning and know what she had to do. If she wasn't running a newsroom or a student daughter, she needed something else.

The last of the day's sunshine lit the end of the garden. Tall grass and potted plants lined a high wall. Three ancient silver birches grew on the other side, hiding Famie from her neighbours. Her eyes drifted higher. Black smoke still floated into the darkening sky. That's some fire, she thought, then wondered again why she hadn't gone back with Charlie to find out more. 'Because you don't work for the agency now,' she said aloud. 'That's why.' She poured more coffee, tried again.

In the top right corner of her screen, a small rectangular frame showed images from her front-door camera: a narrow cobbled street and number twelve's garage door opposite. The occasional pedestrian wandered past, sometimes a slow-moving car trying a shortcut. In the top left of her screen, an identical frame showed the wide-angle images from her garden camera: a small paved area, then uncut grass and bushes to the high wall. Out of habit, her eyes flicked between them, then back to her words.

Howl had been Charlie's idea. And, like all the best ideas, it had seemed so obvious. A perfect fit. They had been at a curry house with Sam and his police-officer wife, Jo. Sam had been horrified by an attack on a newsroom in Pakistan. Three journalists had been killed. He and Famie had known one, a former IPS man. They had raised a glass to him. Then Charlie had said, 'You always say that if there's anything you believe in, Mum, it's journalists being journalists without being intimidated. Well, you guys should do something. Run a website, maybe. A campaigning site. Make it like Bellingcat, with followers around the world, watching out for journalists. Maybe it could help.'

Famie had looked at Sam, who had said, 'I recognize that smile, Fames. And I haven't seen it for quite a while.'

So Howl was born. Her fame as 'the journalist at the cathedral', the woman who had exposed a murderous terror plot, then helped to stop it inside Coventry Cathedral, guaranteed that everyone took notice when they launched. Howl built a respectable following, backing up its website with social media. A global collection of collaborators, sleuths and fact-checkers followed the fortunes of journalists, what they wrote and what they broadcast. Sam had been there too, but he was happy to let Famie take the lead. 'It was always your story really,' he said, 'plus I don't look like a hard-shell Jessica Chastain.'

Famie had frowned. 'Neither do I,' she said.

'Actually, you do,' said Charlie, smiling and grabbing her mother's arm. 'A hard-shell, world-weary Jessica Chastain who could do with an espresso.'

She was slow today, she knew. It had been bad enough before Charlie's visit, but now, with the still-open garden door leaking a constant wail of emergency sirens, Famie couldn't concentrate. Charlie had already been gone an hour, but the gallery fire at

Coal Drops Yard was clearly a major incident. She might not be a news journalist any more, but instinct said, 'Go.' She closed her laptop.

In the utility room, she found her running kit and swapped her jeans and jumper for vest, shorts and tracksuit. She grabbed her phone, set the house alarm and locked up.

6

She stuck to the main roads. There were shorter routes to get her to Charlie's flat but she never fancied the side-streets or canal paths. 'Major roads or nothing,' had been Charlie's demand and she'd happily agreed. It wasn't just that the attacks in Coventry had been terrifying, but her website now regularly filled with anonymous reports from journalists and media workers in trouble around the world. Every day brought eyewitness reports of intimidation, beatings, imprisonment and murder. Most came from Russia, China, Syria and Iran, but increasingly Famie had been reading posts from India, Sri Lanka, Myanmar, Israel, Gaza, Mexico and, occasionally, the UK. The site often incurred the wrath of a ragbag assortment of thuggish governments, politicians, pressure groups and militias. Famie checked both ways, ran along Agar Grove, took the right-side pavement ready for the turn to King's Cross. I used to piss people off just at work, she thought, but now I piss them off all over the world. Well done, me. A great career move.

She kept a steady pace along a deserted pavement, fighting the urge to sprint through Agar Grove's seedier parts. It had once been known as the foulest slum in London, and Famie thought it had never quite shaken off the tag. She was suspicious of everyone anyway, but here she assumed every car, every motorcycle, every food-delivery bike was driven by a criminal. Two joggers appeared from a side road ahead of her. They ran on the left pavement, Famie still on the right. She slowed to increase the distance between them. Two men, she thought, serious runners, at a serious pace.

Occasionally she missed the Northamptonshire cottage the security services had arranged for her after Coventry, which she had tolerated for eight months. The roads were certainly quieter, the views prettier. But no job, no Charlie and no London had been unbearable. When the Camden mews flat had appeared on the market, she hadn't hesitated. She also hadn't told anyone, knowing they would advise her to stay put. By the time anyone found out, it was too late. Her friends had been furious for a while, but Famie loved it. She loved the sole use of the garden, the brand-new kitchen and the thunderous shower. She also loved the busyness, the hustle and the anonymity. No one in the street cared who their new neighbour was. Plus Charlie was a twenty-five-minute walk away, twelve if she ran. Even if it was through bloody Agar Grove.

The two runners turned left. A hundred metres further back, Famie shrugged. Of course they weren't interested in her. She turned right, running downhill.

Now she could see the smoke from the gallery, high and black in the windless sky, then diffusing into a grey cloud and drifting south. On the bridge above her, a hissing blue and yellow Eurostar train eased its way towards its terminus at St Pancras. She heard its rhythmic clattering on the tracks as it passed above her. 'Never run with headphones,' her security guy had said. 'You need to hear everything going on around you.' He had shadowed her every move until IPS decided their debt had been paid, and she was on her own. Northamptonshire's tranquillity had, at a stroke, become more threatening. The move back to London had seemed the most obvious choice.

Famie cut right as soon as she reached the King's Cross development, running past the shiny towers of apartments and fashionable shops. The smoke column was now a beacon that guided her in. She knew she was heading for Charlie's apartment but the soot and vapour loomed large as she got closer. She could taste it too. She had covered many fires as a reporter. Each one was different but the house fire's acrid smell was always particularly nasty.

The undercover market that led directly to the gallery was sealed off, full of fire engines, flashing blue lights and billowing smoke. Famie ran right, looping round the boarded-up and vandalized shops. She skipped around an obstacle course of tipped-over bins, overturned café chairs and wooden benches. Her trainers crunched broken glass with every step. Tins of fruit lay scattered across her path. Some had burst open and Famie slowed to a walk. The syrupy peaches, pears and apricots had been flung wide on impact making this a treacherous path. Looted weaponry was her best guess.

Four hundred metres to her right, she saw the canal-side gas cooling towers, with the redeveloped flats in the middle. Charlie and Lena's was number 22. She'd be there soon enough. Famie turned left into Granary Square.

7

It had become one of her favourite places in London. A wide-open space the size of Trafalgar Square, but with rows of intricate coloured fountains instead of a column. Cafés and the new Central St Martins art school hemmed one end, the canal and the vast new Google building the other. But now it was closed and the fountains were off. The square was filled with fire engines and police cars, their emergency lights still flickering.

Famie watched two firefighters in gold PPE run from their truck holding what appeared to be a large red fan on wheels. They pushed it at speed across the square, then disappeared around the far corner.

Red and white tape allowed her only a few metres along the periphery of the square. Famie went as far as she could, then ducked under it and took a few more steps. The gallery was still out of sight, but the column of smoke above the art-school buildings pinpointed it precisely.

The nearest firefighter shouted at her, waving her back. She couldn't make out the words – they were lost in his mask – but the meaning was clear. Famie took a few steps back. The firefighter still wasn't happy. Four strides and he was in her face. 'Behind the bloody tape!' he yelled. 'What do you think it's there for?'

Famie did as she was told. 'I'm so sorry,' she said. 'I'm from the flats over there, by the canal. The Gasholders?' She pointed at Charlie's building in the cooling tower. 'I was concerned the fire might spread. Is it under control?' Famie thought she sounded more like a reporter than a concerned resident. The firefighter seemed to think so too. He undid the straps of his mask, let it hang from its tube. He was wreathed in sweat, wiped a hand across his eyes. She saw him looking at her running kit, felt her lie exposed in an instant.

'The tape here,' he said, his voice harsh and dry, says, "Fire, Do Not Cross," for a reason.' Londoner, mid-twenties. 'And that reason is that you might die if you cross it. Okay?'

Even though she knew he was right, Famie bridled at his tone. He couldn't have been much older than Charlie. She fought the impulse to snap back and smiled. 'Understood,' she said, 'but should we evacuate? If it's under control, obviously we can stay.'

'It's under control.'

'So we can stay.'

Another firefighter ran up, her oxygen tank bouncing on her back. 'Persons reported!' she shouted. The firefighter in front of Famie spun round.

A voice squawked through his radio. 'Make it a persons-reported fire. Basement.' Without looking back, he ran off, the second firefighter close behind.

Famie watched them go, then ducked under the tape again. She noticed the strange combination of dread and adrenaline she hadn't felt for years. A newsroom speciality. As she walked around the edge of the square, one end of the West End Gallery came into view. Thick yellow hoses snaked from three fire engines, water cascading into the building. Two extended ladders topped with firefighters aimed more water onto its roof. The only flames she could see were shooting from a second-floor window. Smoke enveloped the building, but the fire seemed contained in the gallery. It wasn't spreading. The firefighters were methodical: they seemed in control.

But she knew what 'persons reported' meant, remembered it from her years of ringing the fire departments of the world, chasing a story. American crews called it a 'black tag' but 'persons reported' was the understated British way. Somewhere in the basement of the gallery, the London Fire Brigade had found a body. At least one. Charlie had said the gallery was closed. So either it hadn't been or an arsonist had been caught in their own flames. Famie took one last look at the gallery, then walked back along the square and ducked beneath the tape. She began the walk to Charlie's flat, realizing that, for the first time in four years, she missed being a journalist.

WEST END GALLERY
SALVAGE GRAB SHEET

ITEM
Tomato/Laura Takishenko

LOCATION/CLOSE UP LOCATION, FLOOR PLAN
Ground floor. Stand 2. Opposite main entrance

PRIORITY
One

DESCRIPTION
Oil on Canvas.
Modern literalist.
A flattened tomato. Silver scalpel

INVENTORY NUMBER
129

WEIGHT
1.7 kilos

ACCESS
Direct from ground floor

REMOVAL
Gloves needed. Two-person removal

8

Charlie let her mother into the flat and chained the door after her. Famie kicked off her shoes. Lena was sprawled on a low grey sofa, hugging a cushion. She scrambled to her feet as Famie walked in, embraced her as though she was her own mother. She reeked of smoke – obviously hadn't changed or showered. Famie caught Charlie's eye and they raised an eyebrow. 'I'm so sorry, Lena,' she murmured. For a fleeting moment, she felt like the mother of two girls.

The view was second floor, south-facing across the canal. Floor-to-ceiling windows with a herringbone timber floor. The grey sofa was part of a suite of furnishings that Famie knew had been extremely expensive and, from experience, were uniquely uncomfortable. There were potted ferns in the corners of the room and framed art filled the walls. A curved wooden table held two half-drunk mugs of tea. One, Famie recognized, was Charlie's old 'GRL PWR' mug she had had since school – the only bit of her daughter in the whole room, she thought.

Lena slumped back onto the sofa, pulled a blue and green rug over her legs and hugged the cushion again. Famie could hear Charlie in the kitchen. She eased her way onto one of the chairs and sat facing Lena.

'Tea or coffee?' called Charlie.

'Coffee is good,' said Famie, 'thanks.'

'How close did you get?' said Charlie.

'Close enough for the fire brigade to get cross,' Famie replied.

'Of course you did,' said Charlie.

The coffee machine buzzed. Famie looked at Lena, who was staring out of the window. Charlie appeared with a small mug, which she placed on the table next to hers, then sat at Lena's feet. 'You didn't have to come,' she said. 'Nice to see you and everything but we're okay.'

Lena seemed dazed. 'I'm sure,' Famie said, sceptical. She reached for her coffee, sipped twice. 'But there's something you should know, Lena.' Lena turned, Famie's tone letting her know she wasn't about to hear good news. 'Charlie said the gallery was closed today. Is that right?' Lena nodded. Famie continued: 'So, no one was inside?'

'We were closed,' said Lena, 'so obviously no.'

'Mum?' said Charlie. 'What are you saying?'

'Well,' Famie said, 'when I was in the square just now, being moved on, I heard some of the fire brigade's radio chatter. And, well, it sounded like . . . it sounded like they'd found at least one body inside the gallery.'

Lena swung her legs off the sofa, lost the cushion. 'What?'

'It's just what I heard,' began Famie. 'Not confirmed yet.' She looked from Lena to Charlie. 'I'm sorry, but I thought you should know.'

'But that's not possible . . .' muttered Lena. 'I know it was locked. I unlocked it for the fire brigade.'

'Might someone have let themselves in, then locked the main door behind them?' asked Famie.

'No,' said Lena. Then, 'Well, yes. I suppose so. But only four of us have keys.'

Charlie stood, walked to a small table by a corner fern. She picked up a phone, handed it to Lena and sat next to Famie. 'You've got all the staff numbers,' she said. 'Ring everyone. Won't take long.'

'Right,' said Lena, scrolling.

'How many?' said Famie.

'Eleven altogether,' said Lena.

Famie and Charlie sat in silence as Lena called her colleagues one by one. They shared the dread of no answer. Eight picked up, three rang to answerphone. Lena left the same message on each. 'It's Lena Nash. Please call me back urgently. I need to know you're safe. There's been a fire at the gallery.'

When she was done, she looked to Charlie. 'Brandon, Katerina and Nick,' she said.

'Not answering?' said Charlie.

Lena nodded. 'And you're sure the fire brigade found someone, Famie? In the gallery?' 'Sorry, Lena, but yes.'

Lena's phone rang. Everyone jumped. 'Katerina! Thank God,' said Lena. They heard a high-pitched, unintelligible stream of words from her phone. She said goodbye, ended the call. 'Katerina,' she said. 'And Nick is with her. So that's just Brandon unaccounted for.'

Lena dropped her head, her hair falling like a curtain. Charlie draped an arm around her.

'Who is Brandon?' Famie asked.

Lena swept her hair out of her eyes with both hands. 'Brandon Richards, finance manager. Friend of my dad's.'

'The guy with wandering hands?' said Charlie.

'The same,' said Lena. 'And I'm giving him three minutes before I call Dad.'

'Is he a key holder?' asked Famie.

'Yup.'

They fell silent. From where they were sitting, looking southwest towards Regent's Park, everything was clear and quiet. No hint of the inferno behind them had drifted into their view. If Famie listened intently, she could just about make out the shouts

31

of the firefighters, the clatter and bang of their work. Otherwise it was a peaceful London spring evening.

'Why would he want to get into the gallery when it's shut? said Charlie.

Lena shrugged. 'He wouldn't,' she said. She looked at her phone. 'One minute.'

Famie stirred. 'Presumably he worked in the office, not on the gallery floor?' she said.

'Yup,' said Lena.

'And that was downstairs?'

'Yup.'

Lena was watching the clock on her phone. Eventually she took a deep breath. 'Okay. I'm calling my father.' She selected 'Phone' then 'Favourites'.

And then her phone buzzed. Lit up.

'Huh,' said Lena. 'It's Dad. Says he's outside.'

9

Famie's first thought was that Michael Nash was blind. He appeared in the doorway of the lounge, his arm through Lena's. He wore dark glasses, and seemed unsteady on his feet, uncertain in his manner.

'Come in, Dad, sit down,' said Lena. Famie stood, though she wasn't sure why. Sympathy, maybe, for a man who had lost everything. Lena steered her father to the sofa, eased him down. He muttered his thanks, removed his dark glasses, and dried damp eyes with a white handkerchief, which he folded, then put back into his jacket pocket. Not blind, thought Famie, just distressed. She sat down again and waited for him to realize she was there. Charlie hovered behind her.

Michael retrieved his clear glasses from an inside pocket, put them on, and glanced around the room. His gaze settled on Famie.

'Mr Nash, I'm Charlie's mother. I'm so sorry about the gallery. You must be devastated.'

His eyes filled, the lenses magnifying the tears. 'Thank you.'

Lena appeared with a mug of tea and a packet of biscuits. She put them on the coffee-table, then sat next to him.

'Dad, we think the fire brigade have found a body,' she said. 'In the gallery.'

Michael's jaw slackened. 'But we were shut!' He sat back and closed his eyes. A man on the ropes.

'I've been through the staff list,' said Lena. 'Only Brandon is unaccounted for.'

He opened his eyes, swivelled to look at her. 'Brandon?' he said, his voice cracking. 'You think it's him?'

Lena shrugged. 'Who knows?' she said. 'He's the one we can't find. Could be all kinds of reasons.'

'But why would he be in there?' he said.

'We don't know it's him, Dad.'

Michael shook his head. 'My God,' he said.

'It could be anyone, Dad,'

'But Brandon is missing?'

'He's just not answering his phone.' Lena was patient, Famie thought. And loving.

'I understand,' he said, sounding as though he didn't.

'Would you like a bite to eat, Dad?'

'A small something would be lovely, if it's not too much trouble. Just not a biscuit, sorry.'

'Of course,' said Lena, who disappeared into the kitchen. Charlie followed.

Famie and Michael glanced at each other.

'I'm so sorry,' Famie said again. 'I can't imagine how you're feeling.'

'Do you know the gallery?' he said. 'Have you visited?'

Famie was relieved to be able to say that she had. 'Yes,' she said, 'just after Lena and Charlie moved in here. To the Gasholders.' She smiled. 'Although all I remember is that the Bach Variations were playing over your sound system. That impressed me. And the Gerstein.'

'Of course,' said Michael, nodding. 'That's safe at least.' He looked away, seemingly lost again.

Famie tried to reel him back from wherever he was. 'Is it yours?'

'The Gerstein?' He frowned.

'The gallery. Is it yours?'

'Yes. Er, yes. It's mine. I run it.'

'I see,' she said, and paused. 'That's not quite the same.'

'The family own it. I run it and I'm family. So, I think that probably is the same.'

'Sure. I'm sorry. Just getting it clear. They must be devastated.'

'Who?'

'Your family.'

'Oh. Yes. I suppose.'

'Do they know?'

'Yes, of course.' Michael was sounding a little bewildered. Famie pushed on regardless.

'So that's your brother and sister?'

'Yes.'

'Will they be visiting?'

'I'm sorry?' he said.

'Will they be visiting the gallery,' said Famie, 'to see what's happened?'

'Good God, no. Why should they do that?'

'Because it's their gallery?'

In the uncomfortable silence, Famie realized she'd gone too far. 'I'm sorry, Mr Nash. I was a journalist once. Old habits and all that.' Michael didn't appear resentful or hostile, just sad. Bereft. He stared motionless into the middle distance, hands clasped around his mug. Famie wasn't sure he'd taken in a word she'd said. She had seen her fair share of trauma over the years and it was possible he had PTSD on top of his grief.

She changed tack. 'Lena's tough,' she said. 'Charlie admires her very much.'

He came to. 'Really?' He managed the briefest smile. 'That's good to hear.' He sipped his tea. Charlie and Lena returned.

'Pasta in five minutes. I hope that's okay,' Lena said, and returned to the sofa. Charlie sat next to Famie. Lena put a hand on her father's knee, just as her phone pinged. She hauled it out of her jeans back pocket, read the message and sighed deeply. 'Brandon's fine,' she said, smiling. 'His phone was on silent. That's all.'

'Okay,' said Michael. 'Thank God for that. Yes.' He took a deep breath. 'So whoever it is, it isn't one of ours . . . but some- one died in there.'

'Presumably someone who shouldn't have been there,' said Lena.

'A rioter,' said Michael. 'It must be.'

Famie was sure Lena was about to object to the 'rioter' tag, but held back. She smiled inwardly, admiring Lena's self-control, then stood up. She had stayed long enough. This was a matter for the Nash family. 'I need to get back before it's totally dark,' she said.

'Call an Uber, Mum,' said Charlie. 'You're not running back now.'

Famie shook her head. 'They won't get here,' she said, 'not even close. Not with the fire. I'll be fine.' Charlie rolled her eyes.

Famie nodded at Lena and Michael. 'Good night and, again, I'm so sorry about the gallery.'

As she emerged from the Gasholder flats, Famie eased into a slow, sloping run. Sorry about the gallery? What kind of half-witted thing to say was that? She lengthened her stride, started the timer on her watch. You're a moron, Famie Madden.

*

At the far end of Granary Square, by the police barriers, a small crowd watched the still burning gallery. The only person who noticed Famie go was a man in motorcycle leathers and a red scarf.

WEST END GALLERY
SALVAGE GRAB SHEET

ITEM
Green Salvo/Johann Morris

LOCATION/CLOSE UP LOCATION, FLOOR PLAN
Ground floor. Stand 10. Top painting of 3

PRIORITY
One

DESCRIPTION
Oil on canvas.
Impressionistic images of a Californian harvest.
Blues and yellows.
220cms x 150cms

INVENTORY NUMBER
236

WEIGHT
1.3 kilos

ACCESS
Direct from ground floor. No restrictions

REMOVAL
Gloves needed. Two-person removal

10

Monday

Famie was back at her laptop in a T-shirt, sloppy jumper, jogging pants. It was nine a.m. and sunshine lit the garden. An almost empty cafetière stood in the middle of a battered kitchen table. She had been intending to run, but her website was too busy and she needed caffeine. She considered calling Charlie, decided no. She'd get her fix of gallery-fire news online.

Most of the sites had similar images and video from Coal Drops Yard, with estimates of the damage. The *Times* art critic wrote of her recent visit and her informed guess as to what might have been lost. Famie knew none of the artists mentioned, apart from William Makepeace Thackeray, whom she had thought just a writer. All the papers listed the family's charity donations and their obsession with secrecy. The *Sun* reported that 'Owner Michael Nash was taken to hospital, overwhelmed by the loss.' She messaged Charlie with a screenshot of the article.

The reply was immediate: *Not true. Not in hospital. But GP told him to stay at home for as many days as he can bear.* Then a second message: *Overwhelmed is absolutely right.*

'Poor man,' she said.

None of the reports mentioned the discovery of a body. They all said the gallery had been closed and left it there. She knew no one from the gallery was missing. So maybe she had heard wrong. Maybe the firefighters had been wrong.

Or maybe something else was happening. Famie considered how many people would know of the body in the West End Gallery. She concluded that, other than the London Fire Brigade, there would appear to be just one. Her. Her flesh prickled.

The porch cam on her laptop showed a 4x4 trundling slowly past her door, followed by a familiar face. Close-up, full screen. She saw her visitor reach for the intercom. Her laptop buzzed. Famie leant in. 'I hope you've brought pastries,' she said. The figure in the screen held up a paper bag. She smiled. 'Sam Carter, I love you more every day.' She walked along the short hall to the front door, unbolted top and bottom, unhooked the chain and released the dead lock. A dishevelled man in supermarket jeans, polo shirt and gilet grinned, handing her the bag.

'All right, Fames?' he said.

She took the bag. 'If it wasn't for your annoyingly beautiful and talented wife,' she said, 'who is also annoyingly a copper, I'd suggest you marry me right away.' She waved him inside, clocking a black Range Rover silently leaving the mews, turning right.

'Was that your Uber?' She pointed in the direction of where the car had been.

'No,' Sam said. 'Walked from the tube at Camden. There's a new bakery. Just opened. And I was feeling weak.' He followed her into the kitchen. 'As long as you have the coffee.' He spied the almost empty cafetière. 'Oh.'

Famie filled the kettle. 'More on the way,' she said. 'So . . .' She pulled up a chair, ripped open the pastry bag. She chose a plain croissant. Sam declined. They sat next to each other facing her laptop. She typed, accessed Howl.com.

'Speaking of marriages destined to fail,' said Sam, 'Jacob

40

messaged me about the fire. Asked if you were okay.' He pulled a pained expression. 'I said I'd mention it. Sorry.'

Famie's eyes didn't leave the screen. 'I never reply to his emails,' she said, 'his texts or WhatsApps. If he had ever been seriously interested in me or my welfare, the time to show it was when we were married. You know this.'

Famie knew Sam would only have mentioned her ex-husband under sufferance. They both knew that the mere mention of his name would always sour any conversation. She understood why Jacob kept in touch with old friends and, occasionally, their daughter, but she resented every breach of the Jacob-free world she had fashioned.

'Don't you communicate with loads of people you detest?' said Sam.

'On a daily basis,' said Famie.

'Well, why don't you just add Jacob to that list?' he said. 'Because it would definitely make things easier if you did.'

'For you?'

'Yes. For me. I can't speak for Charlie.'

'No shit, Sherlock.'

They sat in silence. Famie pretended to scroll her site. She was surprised Sam had pushed her on this. It was unlike him. She was about to loosen her intransigence when a memory fired.

'When May twenty-second happened,' she said, her voice quieter, slower, 'when our colleagues were slaughtered, one by one, I messaged him to say I was okay. Do you know how long it took him to reply?' She didn't wait for an answer – Sam knew it. 'Four days, Sam. Four fucking days.' Louder, faster now. 'So there's Jacob's answer. It was him who fucked off. It was him who fucked that publisher. It was him who fucked our lives over.'

'Famie, I—'

'And,' she added, 'you were quite right to tell me.' She

41

reached across, took his hand. 'You're my best friend, Sam. No one else would have told me, so thank you.' He looked relieved. Surprised too. 'Just never mention the fucker again,' Famie said. They laughed. She removed her hand. 'So where were we?' she said.

They each scrolled the site daily, but this was their weekly catch-up. They had a network of volunteers but a small hardcore, an inner circle who trawled the internet, monitored their journalists. Sam had set up an online workspace where everyone could collaborate remotely on a private message board, uploading articles and images. It was the closest either of them got to the buzz of a newsroom.

As journalists at the agency, they had always groaned when another campaigning press release arrived in their inbox. It would always demand coverage for the latest 'outrage' with suggested 'talking points' and 'plans for action'. Now that Famie and Sam were the writers of the press releases, they strove to make sure they didn't fall into the same traps. They knew they were targeting experienced journalists. They didn't patronize, didn't sensationalize. They kept track of their correspondents. When they had a good story, they wrote about it. Their weekly communications were brief, restrained, targeted.

'I think Nita could be in trouble,' said Sam. He highlighted her last post. 'The Hindu nationalists are making her life hell.'

'And will go to any extreme to terrorize her into silence,' said Famie. 'It's the funeral of the murdered journalist tomorrow. We should put something on the front page. If Nita can't write it, we should. Plus KT seems to have disappeared. Nothing from her editor either. We should write that up too.'

Sam looked at Famie.

'What?' she said. He shrugged. Famie thought he seemed a little crestfallen. Always pale, even after a summer holiday, today Sam seemed particularly pasty. 'What is it, Sam? I did apologize . . .'

He shook his head. 'It's not that.' He sighed. 'I mean, I can write it for sure,' he said. 'I just wonder if it'll make any difference, that's all. We can write a the-world-is-watching piece, but it really isn't, is it? The world is worried about a thousand other things before it worries about some local journalist in West Bengal or Turkey. We've written them before, remember?' He rocked back on his chair. 'I always get the feeling that governments, police, security services, whatever, are laughing at us.'

The kettle had boiled. Famie got up to make the coffee. 'Sam, there's not many of us,' she said. 'Same as it ever was. We can do nothing, other than shout a bit. Make a fuss. But you've always known that. And we're getting pretty good at it. So, yes, they might be laughing at us sometimes, but when they stop, they go straight back to threatening us again. We make a difference.'

'Do we, though?' said Sam. He stood, walked to the garden doors and stared through the blinds, hands clasped behind his back. 'On the home page,' he said, 'how many journalist deaths this year?'

Famie knew without looking. So did Sam. 'Eighty-seven,' she said.

'And imprisoned?' he asked.

'Seven hundred and six,' she said. 'And why are you asking when you know the answers?' She was annoyed now. 'And you know what I think, Sam? If we weren't running this site, maybe those numbers would be even higher.' She brought the fresh pot of coffee to the table, banged it onto the mat with the mug for Sam. 'You know if we had no correspondents, if we weren't constantly being reminded how shit it is to be a journalist, if the site traffic was declining, maybe you'd have a point. But it isn't and you don't.'

Sam hadn't moved or spoken.

'Unless this isn't about the site at all,' she said. She poured the coffees, both black. 'Have some caffeine, eat a Danish. You bought them, for Christ's sake. You can't expect me to run off three of these buggers.'

Sam turned, managed a hint of a smile. 'The old Famie charm,' he said, and sipped some coffee. 'It's true times are tough. Jo is earning fine. I'm not. I need to bring in more.' He looked sheepish now, stared at the floor. 'I wasn't going to mention it this week but I've been thinking I'd do some freelance work. Back at the agency. At IPS.' And before Famie could react, he added, 'Jo wants me to. And I think she's right.'

Famie wasn't surprised. They had quit the agency after eight of their colleagues had been slain in the terror attack of May the twenty second, but their lives had been very different since then. After she had published her book, Famie had become famous,travelling the world and talking about it. Sam had been asked to write a few articles on journalistic freedom, then struggled for work. The website could keep him busy, but it couldn't keep him solvent.

'I think that's fair,' she said. 'I get it.' Sam exhaled slowly. 'Really I do,' she continued. 'Journalism breaks your heart. I know that's true and so do you.' A thought: 'Do you want to quit the site altogether, Sam? It can take over your life if you let it. When my heart is broken it makes me somehow more adventurous. But that may not be the same for you.'

She knew for certain it wasn't him. Sam's eyes scanned the room, as though looking for answers on the fridge, the ceiling and the spice rack. Eventually he said, 'Maybe. Probably. Yes, I think so. At the moment, I don't think I can. Not yet. I can't forget all these people we have writing for us.' He drank some more coffee, then reached for a *pain au chocolat*.

'Thank God for that,' muttered Famie.

'I worry about them,' he said, 'worry they're breaking cover by posting. Worry that we're making things worse. That the funeral tomorrow will attract violence, because they know it will be reported. Three of our regulars haven't posted for a week, five for a month.' He ate half the pastry in two mouthfuls. 'In time I'll want to quit, but I can't let that go just yet.'

'Okay,' said Famie. 'Let's make a list of them. The missing.'

'I have already,' said Sam. 'I'll send it to you.' He hit some buttons.

Famie's laptop and phone buzzed simultaneously. She read out the names: 'Green, Flakes, M907, Meeracat, HIX, Junkheart, Kula and Zebedee.' She looked up from her screen. 'All silent?'

Sam nodded. 'Yup,' he said. 'The first five have been gone longest.'

'Okay,' said Famie, 'and we need to follow up with KT, who was clearly worried that she'd had police or agents in her house. Do we specifically ask them to post?'

'I think we do.' Sam sat back at the table, clicked through to the home page. 'And we put it here.' He tapped the screen with a fingernail. 'Right at the top. And we ask all our correspondents to stay in touch. To post anything. If they don't post, if they disappear for a week, they're on the list.' He finished the *pain au chocolat*. 'Agreed? Famie?'

But Famie was distracted. Head half turned to the front door. Cocked. Suddenly alert. She raised a finger in the air. Hold that thought. She was listening. In the time she had been in the house she had learnt to identify cars by engine sound and sometimes by the noise of their tyres. Heavy cars made a splattering sound as they moved over the cobbles of the mews. And splattering

45

was what she heard now. Rubber on stone. No engine. So a high end, plug-in hybrid SUV would be a pretty decent guess. She pointed at the porch cam image just as a blacked-out Range Rover trundled past her door again.

'Shit,' she said. She grabbed her phone and ran for the door.

11

Famie flung the front door wide and ran outside. She pointed her phone at the disappearing SUV, took four shots. Then it was gone. Sam hurried out after her, looking up and down the street. She stood, breathing hard. Checked her images. The first had the number plate, clear as day. She realized she was barefoot and went inside.

'Could just have been lost,' said Sam. 'Loads of expensive cars drive around here. You live in a north London mews, Famie. A passing car is way more likely to be an SUV than a Honda Civic, no?' They stood by the table watching the door cam on her laptop.

'Maybe,' she said. 'And maybe not.' They stared at the cam some more. A Deliveroo cyclist went up the street as a man delivering leaflets came down it. Her letterbox rattled, the clatter sounding unnecessarily loud. Sam retrieved a folded flyer. 'Estate agents,' he said. 'Apparently you live in one of London's most sought-after addresses and they'd be happy to sell it for you.'

'I bet they bloody would,' she said.

Famie felt unsettled. Even jumpy. She paced the kitchen, grateful for Sam's presence and their shared history. 'Doesn't take much, does it?' she said.

'Nope,' said Sam. 'And it shouldn't. These bastards have long memories. They're prepared to wait.'

'You think that was suspicious?'

'Probably not. But that doesn't mean you're wrong,' he said.

'Send the licence plate to that copper who stayed in touch. See what she says.'

Channing Hunter had been the DCI stabbed in the Coventry Cathedral attack and then helped expose the terror gang involved. She had stayed interested in Famie's work and in the threats she and Sam received.

'Good call,' said Famie. She emailed the photos from her phone, with a note of explanation. She felt relieved to have done something. 'Will you tell Jo about this? A low-paid job with death threats isn't an easy sell. Least of all to your wife.'

Sam shrugged. 'Not much to say, really,' he said, 'so probably not.'

Famie sat at her table, glanced between the webcams. 'So how long do I have you for? It would be good to know.' She removed her glasses, polished each lens with the hem of her T-shirt, hooked them back on and regarded Sam.

'Let's get this list on the front page,' he said, 'follow our reporters, find the lost ones. See what's happening.'

Famie smiled. 'So if I assumed I had you till the end of the summer,' she said, 'might that be about right?'

Sam didn't return the smile. 'Sounds about right.'

Over the next week they followed and chased the Howl reporters who worried them most. They currently had 270 active correspondents, fourteen were quiet. Or missing. Or dead. Who knew? From the original list Green, Flakes, M907 and Meeracat were still silent, but HIX, Junkheart, Kula and Zebedee had resurfaced. Famie and Sam divided up the others, with Famie, mindful of Sam's comments, taking the lion's share. She posted personal messages to her eight reporters. There was one in the UK and the rest were all in Mexico and the USA. The UK correspondent was named Flint Hill. The Mexicans were Bo, Leon,

Patria F and Luna C, the Americans Maya, Chico and Slam. Famie used all the means of confidential communication the reporters had shared. An email generated a reply from Leon and Chico. A WhatsApp found Slam. A friendly editor accounted for Maya.

The front page of Howl showed the given names of the remaining missing and the length of time they had been silent. Sam had found two from his list, which left twelve. Famie knew they might all be fine – on holiday, undercover or even given up. But Famie doubted it. The twelve had been reporting on corporate and government corruption, gangs and drugs, Mafia-style families and police illegality. Any 'disappearance' needed an explanation.

Howl was her operation. She owed them.

WEST END GALLERY
SALVAGE GRAB SHEET

ITEM
Wipers and Solvent/Cecilia Mo

LOCATION/CLOSE-UP LOCATION, FLOOR PLAN
Ground floor. Stand 4. Bottom painting of 3

PRIORITY
One

DESCRIPTION
Acrylic on canvas.
Black and white stripes.
Melting from the top
120cms x 100cms

INVENTORY NUMBER
231

WEIGHT
1 kilo

ACCESS
Direct from ground floor

REMOVAL
Gloves needed. One-person removal.

12

The three Nash siblings hadn't sat together for a decade but now here they were, brought together by fire and devastation, arson and death. Also by extravagant, and as yet uncalculated, financial loss. Michael, in grey suit and black tie, sat at the head of a long, stylishly battered table, hands in his lap, a glass of iced water on a small coaster in front of him. Helen, mid-fifties, sharp suntanned face, lay flat on a sofa, her untied shoulder-length auburn hair splayed over a small cushion. She clasped a phone to her chest with one hand, leaving the other to drape over the sofa back. Her eyes were closed. Robert Nash, late fifties, was the eldest and shortest of the three. Five foot nine, round tortoiseshell glasses, fitted dark blue shirt. He was pressing buttons on a coffee machine without getting any coffee. He slapped one of its black and chrome sides, then gave up, walked to the large double windows and stared at the view. No one had spoken for a while, not since Helen and Robert had arrived. As though they were out of practice. Or couldn't remember their lines.

Robert broke first. 'Not a bad view, I suppose,' he said eventually. It didn't need a reply and didn't get one. He continued: 'And Lena's just one floor down, you said?' A gravelly smoker's voice.

'I did say that.' Then, as though he realized more was needed, Michael added, 'That's how I heard about . . . this place.' He gestured with both hands, as though blessing the room. 'The man

51

who owns it is away for three months. He likes the gallery. Likes it very much. He heard about the fire and that I was looking for a temporary office. He said it was the least he could do.'

Robert reached into his shirt's breast pocket, produced an open packet of Marlboro. He played with it in one hand. 'A stroke of luck, really,' he said. He pulled out a cigarette.

Michael snorted. 'Really?' he said. 'You think anything about this catastrophe is *lucky*?' He spat the word.

Robert held up his hands. 'I misspoke,' he said. 'I just meant it was a kind offer.' He put the cigarette into his mouth.

Helen, from the sofa, waved her free arm. 'You know what he meant, Michael.' The flat's decor was minimalist, the lack of furnishings giving the room a bright, harsh acoustic. Helen's words bounced off the walls. 'Don't be so touchy, for Christ's sake.'

'I'll bear that in mind, Helen, as I survey the wreckage of the gallery,' said Michael. He muttered something under his breath, sipped some water.

The three returned to their silent routines. Michael looked at his glass. Helen looked at the ceiling. Robert looked at the view.

The third-floor Gasholder flat had the same outlook as Lena's, elevated by twelve metres: the deep brown of the canal, the ancient stones of St Pancras Old Church and, in the distance, a slash of green from Regent's Park. The interior was a large, open kitchen diner and lounge, which shone with chrome and polish and smelt of beeswax.

Helen studied her blue-painted nails. 'So,' she said, 'what have we lost? In pounds, not paintings.'

'We've lost the gallery,' said Michael, his voice small and exhausted. 'Fifteen million. And most of the contents,– so . . . so maybe another twenty mill. Insurance will cover some. Maybe most. Their inspectors are back tomorrow.'

Robert removed the unlit cigarette, turned his head to him.

'Most of it?' he said. Michael looked puzzled. 'You said most of the contents were lost,' said Robert. 'So some were saved. I've read the press but maybe you could be more specific.'

'Yes,' said Michael. 'Of course. All of the ground floor was saved, so that's the Gerstein, thank God. And one from the first floor, so that'll be the Thackeray. They're all in the St Martin's strong room. I'm going there later.'

'So you don't know?' Helen sounded incredulous. 'You haven't checked?' Her words were sharp. The room gave them extra edge.

For a moment it seemed Michael wasn't going to answer or hadn't heard. He shifted in his seat, then folded his arms. 'Someone lost their life in there,' he said. 'The police think the dental record check will be complete soon. Then they'll contact next of kin. And they'll announce it.'

'But to be clear,' said Robert, 'you haven't checked the saved paintings?'

'As you know, I've been unwell,' said Michael.

'Not that unwell,' said Helen.

Michael blinked a number of times.

Robert put the cigarette back between his lips. 'Howard should handle this,' he said.

'There's no need,' said Michael.

'There's every need,' said Robert. The cigarette, stuck to his lower lip, bounced as he spoke.

'He doesn't speak for the gallery,' said Michael.

'But he speaks for the family,' said Helen. She swung her legs from the sofa, pivoted to face Michael, then pulled at her dress until it covered her knees. 'When it gets big,' she said, 'when reporters are talking about the family – and they are – it's time for Howard. Even you know this.'

Michael was deathly white. Whatever blood had been in his

face seemed to have drained away. 'He's a total shit,' he said. 'And loathed by everybody he meets.' He looked at his sister. 'Even you know this.'

Helen's eyes narrowed. 'Of course I do, and of course he's a shit. But he's our shit. Our *consigliere*.' Her voice was louder now, as though she was addressing a classroom of rowdy pupils. 'He gets things done. We need to be alert to the dangers. He'll protect us as he always has done.'

Robert removed a silver lighter from his trouser pocket. 'I agree with Helen.'

'Of course you agree with Helen. You always fucking agree with Helen,' Michael snapped, exasperated. He stabbed a finger at the lighter. 'And obviously don't fucking smoke in someone else's fucking house. What are you, some kind of child?' Robert froze with the lighter a few centimetres from the end of the cigarette. He stared at his brother, then lit the cigarette. He inhaled deeply, blowing the smoke against the window.

Below, a brightly coloured narrowboat eased its way passed the Gasholder flats. Michael stormed out of number 302, slamming the door behind him.

13

It had been a while since Famie had seen someone quite so angry. She hadn't intended to drop in on Charlie and Lena but the end of her run had taken her close to St Pancras so here she was. She had been standing with Charlie at the marble and stone sink when the fusillade of knocking hit the front door. When Lena let her father in, Michael was shaking with fury.

'This fucking family!' he said. He paced to the middle of the room, then to the large windows, then back to the middle. The contrast with the quiet, controlled man she had met previously was astounding.

'Dad?' said Lena. She took his arm. 'Dad, what is it? What's happened?' Michael sat down suddenly at the kitchen table. Famie was convinced he hadn't seen her or Charlie, and felt like an intruder in a private row. He placed his hands on the table, palms down, and took several steadying breaths.

'They've called in Howard Taylor,' he said. He sounded defeated.

'Ah,' said Lena, pulling up a chair next to him.

'Your esteemed aunt and uncle at work. God almighty.'

Now it was Lena's turn to look outraged. 'But Robert's never been involved in the gallery.'

'Of course he hasn't!' said Michael. 'Why should he ever have taken an interest in proper art? Or, for that matter, anything of beauty. But it's different now because apparently "people are talking about the family".'

'You should just refuse.'

'I have. But I'm outvoted. Two of them, one of me. Always the same. Robert and Helen on one side, me on the other. It's a permanent fucking majority against me. We aren't equals. We never have been. I'm merely an inconvenience. My guess is they'd already agreed to call Taylor before our meeting. When your grandfather was alive, at least he was some kind of check on them, would sometimes even say no to them.'

'Not often, Dad,' said Lena. 'I don't remember you ever saying he supported you. I used to dread you coming back from Brighton.' She touched his arm lightly. 'You were always in a bad mood. Did he ever take your side? It never felt like it to me.'

Famie and Charlie exchanged looks. Famie mouthed, 'Should I leave?' She jerked her thumb at the door. Charlie shook her head.

Michael was on his feet again. 'I need to speak first,' he said. 'I'll speak for the gallery. Taylor can say what he likes, but he's not speaking for me.' His pacing now took him close to Famie and Charlie. 'We could put out a press release,' he said to Lena, 'with my email on it. Get ahead of the game.'

'Saying what?' said Lena. 'We haven't got anything to announce, have we?'

She glanced at Famie. Is she wanting me to say something? thought Famie. Or suggesting I leave? She put her hands into her pockets. 'I really should be getting on,' she said, 'and this feels like a family matter.'

Michael raised a hand. 'It does and it is,' he said. 'However, you used to be a journalist and I imagine you write or have written a press release or two in your time. May I ask you what you think?'

She shifted uneasily against the sink. Keep out of this mess, Famie, she thought. It's nothing to do with you. She pulled a face. 'Not this kind of press release,' she said. 'Who does your comms?'

Lena raised a hand. 'Usually me,' she said. 'But I don't do that much. The family doesn't really do comms as such.'

'Well,' Famie said, 'just do the obvious, really. You could tweet or instagram some exterior shots of the gallery now, with a few words promising updates on the website as soon as possible. Maybe a quote from you, Michael.' She shrugged. 'Sorry I can't be more help.' And that's your lot, she thought.

Michael hadn't responded. He stood motionless, one hand on a kitchen chair.

'Dad? What do you think?' Lena waited. 'Dad?'

Michael opened his mouth but made no sound. He swayed slightly. A light sheen of sweat had appeared on his forehead. He closed his eyes. Lena jumped up. Charlie and Famie both took a step forward. Michael's right knee gave way and his body crumpled. His head caught the table edge as he fell. There was a sharp crack, and then a thud.

14

After a brief examination, the ambulance paramedics stretchered Michael, then wheeled him to the lift. Lena, Charlie and Famie took the stairs, arriving on the ground floor first.

A large man in an expensive-looking double-breasted suit stood in front of the lift doors, reading something on his phone. He glanced up as he heard their steps. He had a well-fed face with a thatch of white hair and half-moon glasses resting on the end of his nose. He glanced up, frowned. 'Lena?'

'Mr Taylor.' Lena's reply was cold, her tone flat. She was not inviting a conversation. The women walked towards him.

He glanced at Charlie and Famie as they all stood by the lift. He looked confused. 'I'm so sorry about the gallery . . .' he began.

The lift doors opened. Two male paramedics stood at either side of a wheeled stretcher, Michael strapped and blanketed on it. Eyes closed.

'Michael!' Taylor was clearly flabbergasted.

The medics pushed the stretcher into the lobby, Taylor shuffling out of their way. 'What the hell happened?' He glanced first at the medics, then Lena.

'He fell, cracked his head on the table,' she said, following the stretcher to the lobby doors.

'Is there anything I can do?' Taylor called after her.

'Sure,' said Lena. 'Stay away.' She disappeared.

In the lobby the lift doors closed. Taylor looked between Charlie and Famie. If he was expecting more detail on what had befallen Michael Nash, he was disappointed. He pressed the lift call button. The doors opened immediately. 'Going back up?' he said. He stood aside as if to wave them in.

'Nah,' said Famie. 'We're good.' The Madden women headed for the stairs. Famie felt Taylor's eyes follow them up, then heard the lift clatter shut. They walked in silence till they were back in the flat. Charlie chained the door.

'You can just tell,' said Famie, a pronounced edge to her voice. She walked back to the kitchen table, sat down.

Charlie made more tea. 'You certainly can,' she said. 'What was it this time do you think?' She placed two mugs on the table, sat next to her mother.

Famie inhaled the steam, took the mug in both hands. 'I don't really know,' she said. 'It's the whole package really.' She sipped gingerly. 'Corporate. Corpulent. Monied. Entitled. Threatening. Seen it so many times before,' she said. Famie knew she was fitting Howard Taylor into the mould of all the upper-echelon management she had always hated and always fought, but she had seen the effect his name had had on Michael. 'Has Lena mentioned him before?'

'No,' said Charlie. 'But if she wants him to stay away, that's really all I need to know.'

In front of Gasholders, its port-side now flush with the towpath, the brightly coloured narrowboat had come to a stop, its engine idling.

15

Five minutes later and two floors up, Howard Taylor was taking notes. He had explained what he had seen downstairs but neither Robert nor Helen Nash seemed overly concerned. 'He was always so dramatic,' Helen said. 'He has a history of fainting. He was never a strong boy.'

The siblings sat on the sofa, Taylor at the table. He had squeezed uncomfortably into one of the chairs and was now leaning forward, pen in hand, writing fast. His considerable stomach rested on his thighs, shirt buttons straining. His double-breasted jacket was undone. He chewed a thin lip as he wrote. 'So what's he going to do next then,' he said, 'this brother of yours? Once he's back.' Taylor spoke with the hint of a South African accent. Like something he might have tried to lose at law school but slipped out when he was distracted. 'Because I'll need to be working on this immediately. Need to shape where the media are going to put it. Frame it so that it's a law-and-order story, vandals or arson.'

'But it is a law-and-order story,' said Robert. 'It is an arson story. What else would it be?'

'Well, it was us that were burnt out,' said Taylor. 'Google wasn't. Waitrose wasn't. The gallery was. Why, do you think?' His words were clipped, his tone combative.

'We're the victims,' said Helen.

'Correct,' said Taylor. 'We're victims of a wild anti-capitalist mob. And when the police identify the body, we'll have our arsonist. But why us and not Google? It's not like they haven't made a few enemies in their time.' Taylor looked between Helen and Robert, his eyebrows raised.

Robert leant forward. 'You're over-complicating it, Howard,' he said. 'There doesn't need to be a reason. It was a mob. The gallery had bigger windows. It didn't have the same security as one of the biggest tech companies in the world. And that's it.'

Taylor smiled. 'You're right, of course. We were a soft target. And globally there have been many other attacks on prestige ventures such as ours over the years. Seattle, Berlin, Paris.' He waved his arms. 'London is just the latest in a trend.' He tapped his pad with his pen. 'Your father was always alert to the threat. We'd be wise to follow his example.'

Robert and Helen shifted uncomfortably on the sofa. Robert raised his hand, palm towards Taylor. 'Stop,' he said. 'We never need be lectured about our father's legacy,' he said. 'Don't bring him into it.'

Helen touched her brother's arm. 'Of course,' she said. 'Howard knows that.' Her tone was emollient. 'But if the Nash name is being traduced, Robert, we have to be fierce in our rebuttal. It's bad enough with bloody Lena draping herself over every fashionable cause that comes her way. We certainly don't need any more attention.'

Taylor raised his hand. 'If I may,' he said, glancing at Robert as if asking for permission to speak, 'you should know that, as I understand it, Lena was on the march. The march that became a riot. The riot that burnt down her own gallery.'

'Our own gallery,' snapped Robert. 'For fuck's sake, Howard. It's a Nash gallery. Michael runs it, with Lena and for us. Jesus. It gives them something to do, you know that.' He stood, retrieved his cigarettes, then walked to the balcony windows.

He shook out a Marlboro, placed it between his lips. 'We're always grateful, Helen and I, for what you do and what you've done. Our father also. Above and beyond,' he said. Then he turned to face Taylor, pointed the cigarette packet at him. 'But you are not a Nash.' He held the pose like a darts player taking aim. 'Well-connected, yes. Contacts, yes. Membership of every club, library and society, yes. Feared and loathed, yes. But still not a Nash.'

He slid open the window, stepped onto the balcony, slid it shut. Helen watched him light up, sending a puff of smoke towards the canal.

'Lena was on the march?' she said, keeping her eyes on her brother.

Taylor nodded. 'She was,' he said. 'And the *Mail Online* has a photo. At least one.'

Helen sighed deeply. 'Of course,' she said. 'Anything you can do?'

'I'm working on it,' he said. 'But this is bad, Helen. Very bad. You and Robert need to understand that. Keeping enquiries away is difficult enough at the best of times, but now?' He spread his arms. 'With the fire and with Lena, it'll be impossible.'

Helen stood, smoothed her dress. 'In that case,' she said, 'control it.'

Taylor nodded. 'And Michael? I'll need a steer. When he resurfaces . . . you know.'

Helen wafted him away. 'Robert and I will deal with it,' she said. 'It's a family matter. It's always been a family matter.'

'As you wish,' he said again. He sounded unconvinced. She raised her eyebrows. He held her gaze for a moment, then left the room.

16

Tuesday

The next day, Famie returned to Coal Drops Yard. The Waitrose store was open again and already clear of graffiti. Google was cleaned up, business as usual. Just a few of the damaged smaller shops were still closed. The post-riot detritus had largely disappeared but the fountains were still turned off.

The West End Gallery was disappearing behind tarpaulin and scaffolding. Famie stopped to watch. The ground floor was hidden already, white and green sheets wrapped around ten-metre metal poles. A wooden platform ran around the gallery, level with the ground-floor windows. Men in yellow jackets and hard hats bolted, hammered and shouted to each other. They were working fast, the urgency, Famie assumed, triggered by rapidly approaching storm clouds. She zipped up her fleece.

The gallery's brickwork was scorched black, all the windows had blown and there was a gaping hole where one set of chimneys had been, but the building was still standing. She was no architect but it looked solid to her. Maybe the West End Gallery would survive after all.

Four police cars and a van were parked prominently in Granary Square, forming a line by the fountains. A declaration, thought Famie, that all was not well. The riot might be over, the fires might be out, but the uncertainty, maybe the threat, was still present. A few people wandered in and out of the art college but it was quiet. She walked to a small coffee stall near the canal. The young, bearded man standing by the chrome apparatus looked pleased to see her. 'What can I get you?' he said, beaming.

'A large black coffee and a flat white, please,' said Famie.

'Awesome,' said the man, and reached for some cardboard cups in livid colours.

Famie glanced at the police cars. 'Still work for them to do, then?' she said.

'Yup. And while they're around, my customers are going somewhere else.' He ground some beans, shouted over the noise, 'The only people I'm serving are coppers. You're the most normal person I've seen today. No offence.'

Famie smiled. 'They tell you how long they'll be here?' she said.

The man filled a large and a small cup with coffee, steamed some milk. 'Press conference today, one said.' He poured the milk, put lids on both cups. 'They promised me some journalists as customers to make up the numbers.' He handed her the cups.

'They say anything else?'

'Nope,' said coffee man. 'You a journalist or something?'

'Just nosy,' said Famie.

'From around here?'

'Kinda.'

He shrugged. 'Five pounds twenty.'

'Thanks,' she said, and tapped her card.

'Awesome,' he said.

Famie called Charlie, who had messaged to say Lena was visiting her father in hospital. He was in 'a stable condition', which, Famie thought, meant everything and nothing. He could get

64

worse, he could get better. He could die, he could live. Whatever the hospital meant, Famie interpreted Charlie's text as saying she would like company. And Famie was happy to oblige.

By the time she reached Gasholders, Charlie, in tartan pyjamas, was standing by the lift. Famie handed her the flat white. 'You look tense,' she said.

'Nice to see you too,' said Charlie. 'Thanks for the coffee. Saved me talking to Seb.'

They rode to the second floor. 'The coffee guy?' said Famie. 'Seemed nice enough. A bit hairy maybe. Too hipster for you?'

'Too chatty,' said Charlie, opening the door. 'Just too interested. I want coffee, not a conversation about the state of the world. Or to know that my blouse is missing a button. Or that I'm looking tired.'

'Or tense?'

'And that.'

Famie smiled. It all sounded very familiar. She pulled her laptop from her rucksack, placed it on the low table. She needed to work but she needed Charlie to be okay too. 'So what's Lena saying?'

Charlie sat at the kitchen table, coffee in her left hand, phone in her right. She put both on the table. 'Lena is very quiet,' she said. 'And very jumpy.'

'Understandable,' said Famie. She drank some coffee. Seb might be annoying but he certainly knew how to do his job. 'Are you worried about her?' Charlie nodded, but said nothing. Famie let the silence continue. Eventually she said, 'Has Michael regained consciousness?'

Charlie shook her head, eyes on the table, the loose pyjamas hanging off her angular frame. She gestured at Famie's laptop. 'You can work here, Mum, if you like. The Wi-Fi is good.' She stood. 'I'll get dressed.'

'One thing,' said Famie. She shifted her weight in the chair. 'Has . . . has your dad been in touch?'

Charlie looked astonished. 'I don't think you've ever asked me that before,' she said.

'I know. So, here I am asking.'

'Yesterday,' said Charlie. 'He wanted to know how I was. How you were.'

'And what did you say?'

'I haven't got round to it yet,' said Charlie.

Famie smiled. That was everything she needed to know. 'Okay,' she said.

Charlie disappeared to her bedroom. Famie opened her laptop. The Howl homepage was still the map of the world. It still gave a running total of journalists killed and imprisoned since the start of the year, but now there was an addition: a small white rectangle with black type. It listed the quiet journalists, the ones causing the most concern. Since Famie's conversation with Sam, Patria F, one of the Mexican correspondents had posted, M907 had messaged to say all was well and Mexican Bo had left journalism to become a teacher.

So, the box had five names: Green, Flakes, Meeracat, Flint Hill and Luna C. It was captioned 'Still missing' at the top and 'Please post if safe' at the bottom. Her work message board had photos and maps uploaded to it. Colleagues and friends of the missing had shared information to Howl, some of which they had posted on social media. The citizen investigators, the digital sleuths, were posting anything they thought important. One was clearly wearing a GOPRO HD camera as they went from door to door in a Mexico City suburb, holding up a photo of 'Luna C' and being told to go away. Famie always thought the more noise they made the better. It was harder to intimidate journalists or make them disappear if everyone knew who was trying to stop them. She watched the Mexican video play out. No news.

Her phone buzzed, offered her a news update. Police investigating the fire at the West End Gallery, London, are holding a press conference. Follow live.

Famie clicked the link, called Charlie.

17

The live feed from the press conference was streaming on the news channels, even if nothing had actually happened. The screen showed a long table, with a number of microphones clumped in the middle and two chairs behind. Famie turned down the sound. They've gone too early, she thought, the journalist of old surfacing again. Classic mistake. She allowed a moment's pity for the poor reporters who even now were having to 'fill', talking to camera with every remembered fact about the fire, the riot and the neighbourhood. And all without looking terrified. Charlie walked in, glanced at Famie's laptop, walked out again. 'Call me when they start,' she said.

Famie lost patience with the live feed, returned to Howl. The GOPRO was back, more footage. This time it was a street altercation around an orange car, a thirty-second clip that Famie failed to understand. Except that everyone appeared to be furious with everyone else. Then Sam posted, 'KT is back,' and Famie smiled. Thank Christ for that! She clicked through to the right page, read the report. KT explained she had been working on a human trafficking and slavery story involving three prominent Turkish families. Two had links to the government, one to the judiciary. She wrote that she had pushed too hard and local police (or men dressed as local police) had smashed up her place.

Charlie walked back into the room, put the press conference on the television.

The screen on the wall showed two people sitting at the table with the microphones. A uniformed policeman sat next to a suited woman. The man was speaking. Famie went back to KT's post, marvelled again at her bravery. She explained that while her flat was being vandalized she had hidden behind a neighbour's bins. When the men had gone she had waited an hour before calling a friend. 'I shall hide for a while,' she wrote. 'I have disappeared.'

The TV sound shot up. 'Here we go,' said Charlie.

The uniformed man had just handed to the suited woman, who was rustling papers. 'You know the broadcasters only cover press conferences because they have to,' Famie said. 'They have hours to fill so of course they take every last detail.'

'I know,' said Charlie. 'I believe you've told me before.'

'And you never learn anything.' Famie waved at the TV. 'And because the sound is so shite.' Despite the bundle of microphones on the table and under the woman's chin, her words were lost. She sounded miles away but carried on regardless. 'Someone find the right mic, for Christ's sake,' muttered Famie.

While the TV behind her relayed the live stream from Coal Drops Yard, the laptop screen filled with images, maps and words from Turkey. She tried to follow both but Turkey was winning. A video posted by KT seemed to show a black saloon driving quickly past her hiding place. On X a small group of Howl supporters were trying to identify the car, matching it with images from recent Turkish demonstrations. State thugs had taken to wading into crowds in Istanbul, Ankara and Izmir and if – it seemed to Famie a very big if – they could match vehicles, it would be another awkward question for the authorities.

From the TV behind her: '. . . and we are appealing to all Londoners who may have information . . .'

Any light Howl and its supporters could shine on what appeared to Famie to be a clear-cut case of state-sanctioned brutality helped the cause. 'We see you,' she said aloud. 'And we know what you're doing.'

'. . . only extinguished by the extraordinary bravery of our colleagues in the Fire Brigade . . .'

More Turkish photos were being posted now, six in the last thirty seconds. They seemed to Famie to be random and inconclusive images of cars and crowds. She highlighted one, zoomed in. She clicked each in turn. And there was nothing.

'. . . just the one casualty. We can now confirm . . .'

Three more photos, three more cars. Famie leant in.

'. . . has been identified as Jamie Nelson, aged twenty-nine, from the Flint Hill area of Dorking, Surrey.'

Famie spun round in her chair. 'Flint Hill?' she said. 'What the hell?'

18

Thursday

Famie resisted for twenty-four hours, then took a train for Dorking. She had no idea if the gallery fire had just become a Howl story, but there seemed no point in staying in London. Charlie had offered to come too. They sat opposite each other, table between them. Two coffees. Two phones. Famie's Ray-Bans. Her rucksack with her laptop inside it was on the floor, between her legs.

The bleak drudgery of south London was only slightly improved by a cloudless blue sky but neither woman was looking. The carriage was sparsely populated but they spoke quietly, leaning in till their heads nearly touched.

'Well, the papers have already decided,' said Charlie. 'An easy hit for them, really.'

'Yup,' said Famie, 'police too. And you can see why.' They had scrolled the online coverage. Most sites had shared the same photo of Jamie Nelson, who looked around sixteen, dark skin, cropped hair, soft smile. Maybe a sports top of some kind. Perhaps taken at school. 'If these facts are right, that you're a political activist, campaigner, demonstrator and, apparently, when it came to it, a rioter and an arsonist, that's not a lot of wriggle room.'

'If those "facts" are right,' said Charlie.

71

'Always,' said Famie. 'Always and for ever.' She sighed. 'Instagram account look authentic to you?'

'Barely anything to go on,' said Charlie. 'A private account.' She swiped and tapped her phone, spun it on the table. 'See here.'

The account page showed an image of an old tree where the portrait image usually went. 'Huh,' said Famie. 'A hundred and fifty-six posts. Eighty followers. And following just one.' Famie handed back the phone, stared out of the window. 'Who goes on Instagram, then follows only one person?' she said.

'Egotistical wankers for the most part,' said Charlie. 'Comedians. Footballers. Celebs. Fake accounts. Even then, they normally follow a handful of accounts for appearances' sake.' Famie had never liked social media, had left it altogether when people tried to kill her, and refused point blank her publishers' polite but desperate requests for her to rejoin. To 'tell your story'. To 'connect with your audience'. Famie was having none of it. Charlie told her anything she needed to know.

'But Jamie Nelson wasn't a celebrity, a footballer or a comedian so far as we know,' said Famie. 'So it must be the politics. I reckon if we could see who his followers are, we'd find campaigners and activists like him.'

A brief silence.

'And you think he's your Flint Hill, don't you?' said Charlie.

What did she think? 'It's more than a a hunch,' Famie said. 'And a hunch is fine. It's instinct informed by experience and I would follow that for sure, but Flint Hill hasn't posted since before the fire and, if it is Jamie Nelson, he posted quite regularly.'

'What sort of thing?' asked Charlie.

'Way more enigmatic than most correspondents,' said Famie. 'Vague, but angry. Fight the power stuff, you know?' Famie had trawled the Howl archive as soon as the press conference had finished, finding every post 'Flint Hill' had written. 'Often they were comments on what other reporters were posting,' she said. 'Small encouragements, really. The only clue to what he was doing would be "long journey today" or "heading north again". Some made no obvious sense. Or were in German. He uses Roman numerals quite a lot. Occasionally it was overtly political, referenced Extinction Rebellion, Just Stop Oil, that kind of thing. I guess he may have joined their activities as they moved around the country.'

Charlie glanced through the window. 'Not surprising to find him on an anti-capitalist march.'

'If it is him, then no. Not surprising at all.'

'Maps or images of any kind?'

'None. I've sent everything to Sam to look at.'

The train slowed, stopped. Five passengers off, three on. Two sat on the other side of the aisle. Famie and Charlie leant back. Charlie picked up her phone. Famie drank the remains of the cold coffee. She had programmed Flint Hill's only given contact number into her phone and called it many times: no rings, no answerphone. Texted many times: no reply. There was no email, no publication or editor details. Just an address and a phone number.

Famie's turn to stare out of the window. She hadn't called her police contact, wasn't sure if there was any point. She'd see what Dorking turned up, if anything. Ray-Bans on.

From the station, the walk to Flint Hill was forty minutes. Famie navigated on her phone. The midday sun had given some real warmth to the spring sunshine. 'Shirtsleeve order', her dad would have called it and she marvelled at the mind's ability to recover phrases lost for decades. They took a path alongside a dual carriageway to a high street. 'Left at the end of the shops,' she said. 'After Waitrose.'

'And I'm guessing this one won't have "Down with capitalism" sprayed on the doors,' said Charlie.

Famie laughed. 'I don't think they do that kind of thing here,' she said.

'Flint Hill might have,' said Charlie.

Famie nodded. 'I guess.'

They walked up a raised, well-kept path with tall evergreens on their left, and a ferociously busy road on their right. 'Horsham Road. It becomes Flint Hill up here somewhere,' said Famie, phone in hand.

'And when we get there?' said Charlie.

'No idea,' said Famie. 'Haven't done this for a while.'

'What's the address?'

'Flint Hill Close. Other side of the hill.'

Famie hoped that the Jamie Nelson named in the press conference was not her Flint Hill. That all of this was a coincidence. That a new post from him or her would drop. That she was overreacting terribly. She knew she wasn't responsible for her reporters – how could she be when most of them were so far away? – but she felt it. They had all signed up to her site. They all posted knowing they were speaking to their peers and, presumably, hoping it provided them with some degree of cover. And while she couldn't travel to Turkey or India all the time, she could certainly make it to Surrey.

Flint Hill Close was a quiet street, lined with unremarkable cars and unremarkable1950s houses. Many were substantial, detached, with driveways. But a few were drab and run down with overflowing bins. 'Unless twenty-five-year-old Jamie Nelson is still living with his parents,' said Charlie, 'it'll be one of the sad houses we're looking for.'

'Well, here comes the answer,' said Famie. A broadcast van branded 'OBS, Outside Broadcast Surrey' swept into the road, passed Famie and Charlie, stopped fifty metres away outside one of the 'sad houses'. Famie and Charlie leant against a lamppost to watch.

Passenger got out, a woman, mid-forties, trouser suit, walked to a front door. Driver stayed at the wheel. Front door opened. Man, mid-twenties, tracksuit. The visitor might have had time to say a brief sentence before the door was closed again. The visitor hesitated, then returned to the van.

'That went well,' said Charlie.

'How many housemates in a place like that?' said Famie.

Charlie frowned. 'You what?'

'How many housemates—'

'No, I heard. But what are you asking?'

'I'm assuming it's three. Or four at a pinch.'

The woman in the trouser suit was back in the passenger seat and on her phone.

'The tracksuit guy clearly doesn't want to talk,' said Famie. 'That leaves two, maybe three others who might.'

'Or might not,' said Charlie, 'because they all hate the press. Hate the mainstream media. And hate the fascist state and its client journalists.' She pointed at the van. 'That's them and it's you.'

Famie smiled. 'You've been on too many demos.'

Charlie shook her head. 'If Jamie Nelson was a far-left agitator and wannabe arsonist, he's quite likely to live with people who agree with him. Who see the world in the same way.'

The van was moving: the occupants were giving up. 'The press is the press, Mum. You're all scum. You'll get the same treatment. No exceptions.'

Famie knew that was right, and if all the residents refused to speak to her, she understood. They weren't his family; they had no reason to explain their fallen comrade to anyone. She'd had refusals like this all her life. One more wouldn't be a problem. The van drove past, the woman staring at them. A proper head-turn stare.

'Someone's read your book,' said Charlie. She watched the van leave Flint Hill Close. When she turned back, Famie was striding towards the house, rucksack swinging in her hand.

'Mum?' She hurried to catch up. 'Mum, wait!' Famie had reached the front door recently vacated by the other woman. 'You sure about this?' said Charlie, at her shoulder.

'Not really,' said Famie, extracting her laptop from the rucksack. 'Not at all, actually. But here goes nothing.'

Sunglasses off. Famie rang the bell. A two-tone chime. She took three steps back.

19

Famie opened the laptop. The Howl website home page lit up. She turned the screen towards the door and held it up. Like it was her ID card. She realized her hands were trembling.

There was movement behind the door. Charlie fidgeted. Famie held her breath.

The door opened. Famie went first, spoke fast. 'Hi. My name is Famie Madden. I run the Howl website.' She held the laptop higher, stepped forward. 'This one.'

A woman stood at the door, dressing-gown over pyjamas, bleary-eyed, long black hair, late twenties. She opened her mouth, then closed it again. Peered at the screen, frowned. Famie thought she'd take her chance. 'Jamie might have mentioned Howl?' she said. She watched the woman's eyes dart around the map of the world, then settle on the number box that showed the total of journalist deaths that year. 'I know it says eighty-seven,' said Famie. 'But was thinking it should be eighty-eight.'

The woman bit her lip, her eyes filled, and Famie knew she had it right. Her heart sank. Flint Hill was Jamie Nelson. And Jamie Nelson had burnt to death in the West End Gallery. 'I'm very sorry for your loss,' she said. 'This is my daughter Charlie. We were just passing so we thought we'd pay our respects.'

The woman glanced over her shoulder, stepped outside, pulled the door almost shut behind her, wiped her eyes with her dressing-gown sleeve. 'You can't come in,' she said. 'They wouldn't like it. None of them. But I know Jamie . . .' She pushed her hands deep into her dressing-gown pockets, raised her eyes to the sky and forced out the words. 'I know Jamie liked your site. So. Thank you.'

Famie folded her laptop, tucked it under her arm. 'Maybe we could speak some other time,' she said.

The woman shook her head. 'Probably not,' she said.

'I understand,' Famie said. She produced a small embossed card, handed it the woman. 'Just in case. How to contact me at Howl.' The woman took the card without looking at it and put it into her pocket. 'Well,' said Famie, 'we'll be going. Thank you for talking to us.' She turned. Then, as an afterthought: 'Can I ask your name? Would that be okay?'

'No, it wouldn't,' said the woman. 'You can fuck off now.' She stepped inside, shut and locked the door.

'Could have been worse,' said Famie, turning away. 'At least the fuck-off came at the end of the conversation.'

She and Charlie walked up the road. The OBS van was back, parked by the lamppost, exactly where Famie and Charlie had stood to watch the trouser-suited woman fail.

'Okay,' said Famie, quietly. 'Someone in the house may well be watching. We don't speak to these guys. In fact, we cross the street – obviously, theatrically – to ignore them.' She and Charlie walked into the road and along the kerb. The van's passenger window was already down.

'Excuse me,' the trouser-suited woman called. 'Famie Madden? Jane Boskin, TV South. I see you got further than I did! Was that Nelson's girlfriend?'

Famie and Charlie kept walking. 'I've no idea, I'm sorry,' said Famie, eyes on the kerb.

'Can we speak?' called the woman.

'No, that's your lot,' muttered Famie.

'Famie, please?' She sounded desperate and annoyed.

'No. Fuck off.'

'Way to go, Mum,' said Charlie, as they left-turned back onto Flint Hill. 'Safe to talk?'

'Safe to talk,' said Famie.

'That. Was. Impressive,' said Charlie. 'My God!'

'Why, thank you,' said Famie. How satisfying, she thought, to be able to impress your daughter at the age of forty-five.

'The card was a bit cringe, though,' said Charlie. 'No one does that.'

'You think?'

'Yup.'

'And when she, whoever she is, gets in touch to talk about her friend, when she thinks it's safe to speak because her housemates are out, or she is, and we find out more about what Jamie was up to, what will you say then?'

Charlie laughed. 'I'll stop cringing,' she said. 'But not till then.'

Famie glanced at her phone screen. Twenty-five minutes to the station, the next train was in thirty.

'Maybe she's the one person he followed on Instagram,' said Charlie.

'I was thinking that,' said Famie. 'I'll remember to ask her when she gets in touch.'

'You do that,' said Charlie. 'Oh, and that was a proper upper-class fuck-off at the end, didn't you think? I'd say southern counties, educated.'

'One of your own, then,' said Famie.

'Ha!' laughed Charlie. 'Probably fair. Though she was more graceful in her grief than I've ever managed.'

They walked down Flint Hill till it became Horsham Road and the trees turned again to houses and care homes. Charlie was right about the woman's dignity. Her poise had been striking. Famie knew she had been right to give the woman her card. Because she needed her to get in touch. The papers would doubtless discover more about Jamie Nelson's life, but she guessed it wouldn't be from their dressing-gown revolutionary. She'd give her three days. Then she'd need to be back on Flint Hill.

20

Saturday

The call came in two days. Eight a.m. Number withheld.

'You can call me Sara,' was how it started.

Famie pulled on a T-shirt, raced to the kitchen, grabbed a pen and her cafetière. She knew immediately whom she was talking to. They'd exchanged just a few words, but there was no doubting who this was. 'Right. Sara. Yes. Thanks so much for calling. I call you Sara because you are Sara or you just want to be called Sara?'

'I wasn't going to ring,' said Sara, ignoring the question. 'But there's so much shit being written about Jamie I couldn't just sit here on my arse.'

'Can I record this conversation?' asked Famie. 'Just for my own records?' She knew as soon as she had said it aloud that it was all wrong. She winced. Gritted her teeth.

'No,' said Sara. 'Can't you use shorthand or something? But absolutely no recording.'

Famie knew she wouldn't get another chance. 'Understood. Completely understood,' she said. 'What was it you wanted to—'

Sara jumped in. Like a dam bursting. 'First up, there is no way Jamie lit that fire. No. Fucking. Way. I don't know who did and I wasn't there but the way he's being written about . . . Christ, it makes me sick. Makes it sound like he's Guy fucking

Fawkes. I haven't spoken to anyone, and no one in the house has either. You need to get that out there.'

She was speaking fast and at high volume. Obviously on her own, Famie thought, or outside somewhere. 'Of course,' she said.

'He's been one of the few pacifists in my life,' said Sara. 'Like, a proper pacifist. Most of us say we are, but we're quite happy to chuck a brick if we need to. Not Jamie. He was a radical for sure. Press got that right. Eco-warrior is right. Activist is right.. He might glue himself to an oil tanker or something, but no violence, no way, man.'

Famie hadn't written so fast for years. 'Why was he inside the gallery?' she said.

Sara sighed. 'The only possibility I've come up with is that maybe he was going to damage a painting or something. Or he was planning some kind of stunt. That's been done in the big galleries. He certainly thought direct action was justified.'

'Had he ever done that before?' asked Famie.

'Not as far as I know.'

'How long have you known Jamie?'

'Long enough to tell you he didn't burn down the gallery, okay? Also, and this is the other thing, long enough to know that he would have been incensed by the way the press went after his father. Someone needs to be saying that was a fucking disgrace.'

Famie had seen this. Brian Nelson lived in Kingston, Jamaica. He had been on the receiving end of mindless aggressive questioning outside his house. Famie shared Sara's opinion. 'A fucking disgrace is right,' said Famie. 'He must be traumatized. Did you ever meet him?'

'No.'

'Did Jamie mention his parents at all?'

'For sure. Of course.'

'Did they know about Howl, do you think?'

'His mother died. And I have no idea about his father.'

'So, I have a problem' said Famie. She stood up, walked around the kitchen, smoothing her T-shirt as she talked. 'You and I are the only ones who know that Jamie posted as Flint Hill on Howl. I'd like to say that on the site. Pay him a kind of tribute, even if I didn't know him. Then, at the end, a clear condemnation of the treatment of Jamie's father.'

'Huh,' said Sara.

'Would Jamie want that?' said Famie. 'Do you think it's okay?'

'You're making me sound like next of kin,' said Sara. The quietest words she had spoken. 'I'm not comfortable with that.'

'No,' said Famie. 'I'm asking you as his friend.'

'It would make him number eighty-eight on your screen,' said Sara.

Shit, she remembered, thought Famie. 'It would, yes,' she said.

'I think you should do it,' said Sara.

Famie felt surprisingly moved by her. 'This might seem a weird question,' she said, 'but do you know if Jamie spoke German?'

'What?'

'He wrote a couple of posts on Howl in German. Pretty basic but I was wondering—'

Sara cut in: 'Yes, probably. He liked languages. He travelled a lot. Seemed to have contacts in Europe. So. That'll be him.'

'Okay,' said Famie. 'And have you heard anything about the funeral arrangements?'

'No.'

'Would you go?'

'Of course.'

'Maybe we could meet.'

'Maybe.'

'Is there any way of my staying in touch with you?' said Famie, sensing the end of the conversation.

'If I call you, yes.'

'One more thing, Sara.' Famie thought she knew the answer to the next question, but went with it anyway: 'On Jamie's Instagram he follows just one person. Do you know who that might be?' From her phone, Famie could hear traffic noise and birds singing but there was silence from Sara. 'Maybe it's you,' she added.

The phone went dead.

21

Famie fired a message to Sam, summarizing the call, and cc'd Charlie. In the shower, she composed some thoughts about Jamie Nelson. By midday the Howl website had updated. Its front page announced the new total of journalists who had died that year. A hyperlink took the reader to a list of the deceased. Jamie Nelson/Flint Hill was now at the top.

Famie had kept it simple: she had not known Jamie or what he had been working on. Those who knew him believed him incapable of the arson at Coal Drops Yard, and the treatment of his father in Jamaica was inexcusable.

Famie considered her conversation with Sara. Her suggestion of some kind of publicity stunt that had gone wrong seemed implausible but it was a line of enquiry worth considering. If that had been Jamie's intention, would he have chosen pictures at random? Or might there have been particular paintings to target to maximize the publicity?

Lena would know, and Charlie might be with her. Famie invited herself back to Gasholders.

From Jamie Nelson's Instagram

Well, that's one way of looking at it. This is what I have. Here's the view from my window. I'm going for the cluttered, shabby and shitty vibe. Looks good, no? Thinking of a massive planting operation if I can get the others to pay something. No one seems interested. Have you ever seen a Poui tree? They are incredible. The fiercest yellow you have seen! They make me smile. Also nervous at the same time. When the Poui blooms, we all know exams are just around the corner.

Missing the colours of home. Can't believe everything is so drab and washed out here. Send me photos of any COLOURS!

22

Seb was standing behind his kiosk, hands pushed deep into his apron pockets. He nodded, smiled as Famie approached and raised a hand in salute. 'Hello again!' he said. 'Charlie's mum, isn't it? Heard you call her last time.'

Famie's frown was hidden behind her sunglasses. Too familiar, too many assumptions. One of the reasons she preferred independent sellers was the anonymity. No one asked your name, no one asked you to say it again, no one spelt it wrong. 'A large black coffee and a flat white, please,' she said. She had not returned the smile.

'Awesome,' he said. 'Though Charlie and Lena have already got their coffees. They're down by the canal if you want them. On the steps.'

Famie bristled. She hated being 'of interest'. She hated being seen, hated that her daughter's movements had been spotted. Even if it was by the apparently benevolent Seb. 'A large black coffee and a flat white, please,' she repeated, her words sufficiently slowed for Seb to get the message.

'Right you are,' he said. 'Awesome.'

Famie crossed Granary Square, glanced left at the now fully shrouded West End Gallery. She stopped. If she'd been religious she might have crossed herself, bowed or genuflected. She felt the need to do something. Jamie Nelson, one of her own, had died in there, an agonized, terrifying death for which he was being blamed. Without any new information, and despite Sara's fervent protestations, Famie knew that was the story that would stick. Crazed arsonist kills himself, takes the gallery with him.

'What were you doing in there?' she said aloud. 'You poor, poor bastard.'

She took a breath, walked towards the canal. Green plastic grass covered a stepped seating area that led down to the water. Two longboats moored opposite, another easing its way past the onlookers. A hundred or so were enjoying the spring sunshine. Famie hesitated at the top step, then spotted Charlie's corkscrew hair. She made her way down, coffees balanced in a cardboard tray.

'Hey,' she called, as she got close. Charlie and Lena both turned, waved. 'Your gnomic, all-seeing coffee man told me you were here. Irritating sod, isn't he?'

'Told you,' said Charlie.

'You did,' said Famie. She offered the coffees.

'But you haven't got one,' objected Lena, oversized black-framed sunglasses perched on her head. She shuffled away from Charlie, and Famie sat in the gap between them.

'Well, I'd ordered before Mr Google Maps over there told me you two were here. And I was buggered if I was about to change it.' Lena took the black coffee, Charlie the flat white.

'How's your father, Lena?' said Famie.

Lena hesitated, tucked a thick strand of hair behind an ear. 'He's in the King Edward VII Hospital,' she said. 'He has concussion, shock, PTSD, exhaustion, anxiety. They want to keep him in for observation.' She shuffled slippers on the fake grass. Famie realized she was wearing what might be pyjamas: sloppy grey sweatshirt and sweatpants. 'And that's fine with me,' said Lena. 'Don't want him at home on his own. Not yet anyway.' Tinny jazz played from a boat moored on the far side. 'He cried for most of the time I was there.'

'So who's running things?' asked Famie. 'Is that you?'

'Not really. Dad has an assistant who handles the grants and applications. Kate Rivers is the woman there. She and Dad pretty much deal with that side of things.'

'So, the famous benevolence of the Nash family,' said Famie. 'Is that all your father's doing?'

'It is now,' said Lena. 'My grandfather set it up ages ago. Back in the eighties. But my aunt and uncle don't show much interest in it so my dad runs it. By default, really.'

Famie expected more, but Lena had finished. She sounded exhausted.

'I just updated Lena,' said Charlie. 'Read her your email about Jamie and Sara.'

The sun disappeared behind grey cloud, and Famie buttoned her jacket. 'Sara mentioned the possibility of a targeted protest,' she said. 'That maybe Jamie had been planning to damage a particular painting. Or paintings. Can't see it, really, given how things ended up, but thought you'd know what art was on the ground floor.'

Lena hesitated, then reached for her phone. 'Sure,' she said, tapping the screen. 'Mainly it was contemporary British artists. Beagles and Ramsey. Sonia Boyce. Kaye Donachie. That kind of thing.'

Famie shook her head. 'No idea, no clue,' she said. 'Enlighten me.'

Lena scrolled, then put down her phone. She laced her fingers together as if in prayer. 'We mostly deal with art by living painters,' she said, 'particularly those who create large, colourful canvases. Paintings with what my dad calls "wall power". They demand attention. Catch the eye, you know?' Famie supposed she did. 'We have older works, too, of course. Just as long as they have wall power.'

'Understood,' said Famie.

Lena folded her arms. 'But what's interesting about what you're saying,' she said, 'is that, according to the Fire Brigade, two paintings might be missing.'

'What?' said Famie.

'I didn't know . . .' began Charlie. Mother and daughter shared an identical look of astonishment.

'I went to see the guys who fought the fire,' said Lena. 'I wanted to thank them. And, well, this might be all wrong, of course, but one of the firefighters said they'd removed what they could – the art that was on the list – but he noticed two empty spaces. That there were two mounted captions with information about the art and the artist but no paintings.' A pause. Lena took a breath. Above the canal, a slow-moving queue of taxis heading for King's Cross hooted each other.

'Do you know which paintings he meant?' said Famie.

'Not for certain,' said Lena. 'Quite a lot on the ground floor wasn't on the list – and certainly these two weren't – but the fireman said he thought both captions were orange.'

'Is that significant?'

'Well, there weren't any all-orange captions but two had orange borders. They were left over from a Pop Art exhibition we ran last month. Famous ads for Fanta. They were like exploding Fanta bottles with waves of orange everywhere.' Lena spread her arms, waggled her fingers.

'And that's Pop Art?' said Famie.

'Yes,' said Lena, 'as used in advertising.'

'And that's Fanta, as owned by Coca-Cola,' said Famie.

'Yes,' said Lena, 'and created in Nazi Germany. During the war. It was an alternative to Coke because they couldn't get the syrup from America.'

Famie stood up. She slid her sunglasses to the top of her head and pushed her hands into her jeans' back pockets. This might be making sense now, she thought. 'So, at an anti-capitalist riot,' she said, 'a man we know was an anti-capitalist breaks into the gallery. We don't know why. He ended up in the basement. Again, we don't know why. But on the way there he passed, or may have passed, two technicolour ads for a product famously owned by one of the biggest corporate companies in the world. And that might have been enough, really, but these have a Nazi heritage.' She turned to Lena. 'Correct?' Lena nodded. 'So if you were intending to "make a statement",' Famie mimed the quote marks, 'these Fanta ads, this Pop Art, would be precisely the ones you'd pick, no?'

Lena nodded again, more slowly this time. 'I guess,' she said.

'I guess too,' said Famie. She sat down again.

They were silent for a while. Famie's head filled with Jamie Nelson's final minutes. The demonstration that had turned violent. The broken window. The climb inside the gallery. The Fanta artwork. All of that made sense. If he'd stopped there, if he'd defaced the painting, vandalized or even stolen it, she would have understood. He might even have had public opinion on his side. But what was left of him was found in the basement, the building torched. And no one understood that.

'Why would he go into the basement, Lena?' she said. 'Remind me. What would be the point? What's down there?'

'Nothing really,' said Lena. 'It was admin. Planning. Rotas. Accounts.'

'Anything else?'

Lena shook her head. 'Stationery. Personal bits and pieces. That kind of thing. We all had a drawer we could lock. Coffee- and tea-making stuff for when you couldn't afford Seb's rip-off prices.' She stood, brushed herself down. 'I'll talk to my dad about the Fanta paintings,' she said, and edged past Famie and Charlie.

'Ask him why they were still there,' said Famie. 'Why the Fanta images had been left behind.'

'Will do,' said Lena. 'See ya.' She hoisted a small bag over her shoulder. Famie and Charlie watched her go back up the steps to Granary Square.

'She okay, do you think?' said Famie.

'Not really, no,' said Charlie. 'She was crying this morning. She only does it when she thinks no one's looking.'

'Seemed in a hurry,' said Famie.

'Seemed fucked-up,' said Charlie.

23

Michael Nash was propped up in bed, four pillows at his back. His eyes were closed, his breathing shallow. Lena sat at his side, leant forward on a plastic chair. She held his hands in hers. 'Me again, Dad,' she whispered.

It was a small room off a small ward, no windows, standard light blue paint. Monitors on trolleys and drips on wheels hemmed the bed on two sides. Lena sat on the third. The monitors beeped occasionally, displayed red numbers on their screens. Lena didn't glance at them. She was scanning her father's face. The bruising from his fall had discoloured his forehead, a purple shadow emerging from his hairline and reaching his left eyebrow. His mousy-blond hair, always immaculately swept back and waxed into place, had fallen forward. With one hand, she pushed it back and stroked it flat. 'I was just passing,' she said. 'I brought you a sandwich in case you fancied it. Ploughman's, I think.' Michael didn't stir. 'I can bring more things tomorrow.' She unclasped his hands to wipe her eyes. When her hands began to shake, she held her father's again. 'God, what a state I'm in,' she muttered.

The light in the room changed slightly and Lena turned to see a nurse standing in the doorway, black hair tied up high. Mid-thirties. She didn't smile. 'How is he doing?' she said.

'I was going to ask you the same thing,' said Lena. 'Do you need to come in?' She stood up but the nurse shook her head.

'No, I'll come back when he wakes,' she said. 'Sleep and rest are good.' And she was gone.

'You don't say,' said Lena, sitting down again. Michael stirred and licked his lips. Lena turned to the small bedside cabinet next to her. Flowers in a vase, a plastic tumbler of water and Michael's glasses. She reached for the water. 'Got a drink here, Dad,' she said. He opened his eyes, managed a smile.

'Yes, please,' he croaked. She handed him the tumbler, he took a few sips, handed it back. 'You're back again,' he said. 'Lovely to see you.' He cleared his throat. 'Is something up?'

Lena managed a small laugh. 'You mean apart from everything?' she said.

'Yes, I suppose. Apart from everything.'

'Then everything else is fine.' She took one of his hands again. 'Mainly you need to rest, recover from the concussion. That bruise is a shocker.'

He stared at her, as if judging what to say. 'Did they tell you I fainted this morning? When I got up?'

Lena looked shocked. 'No, they did not! What happened?'

'Well, I just wanted to get up,' Michael said. 'I felt okay. The next thing I was flat on my back, three or four doctors and nurses helping me up.'

'Good God, Dad. And presumably telling you not to try such a stupid thing again?'

'Something like that.'

Lena was exasperated. 'You really can't afford to fall again! You know that!'

'I do.' He tried to smile. 'Learned my lesson, love, honest.' He pushed back against the pillows.

'Okay,' she said. Then hesitated.

Now father studied daughter. 'You want to ask me something,' he said. 'It's probably to do with the fire, so you're not

94

sure whether to burden me with it. Am I right?' Lena smiled. 'Nothing wrong with my paternal instinct then,' he said.

'I went to thank the firefighters,' Lena said. 'They did what they could, saved what they could save.'

'Nice idea,' said Michael.

'Anyway, one of the guys said two paintings on the ground floor were missing from their stands. And I'm pretty sure it was the two Fanta Pop Art pictures.'

'Because?'

'Because he said the captions were orange. I know they were both left over from the Pop Art exhibition last month.'

Michael nodded. 'The ones Robert bought and hadn't got round to picking up.'

Lena straightened in the chair. She looked past Michael. Her eyes narrowed. 'You once told me Uncle Robert had a . . . I think you said "challenging taste" when it came to art. I remember because you seemed very uncomfortable at the time. Then I saw all the nudes in his flat. I suppose some were Pop Art but mainly it was creepy.'

Michael stretched his fingers, inspected his nails. The silence ran for a long time. Lena waited, watched her father thinking.

'So,' he said eventually. 'My brother has always liked nudes. When he buys art, normally there'll be someone naked at the heart of it.' Michael paused. There was obviously more to say, if he could find a way of saying it. He glanced at Lena. 'The effect is accumulative. It appears to be tasteful at first. A Rubens, a Freud. Incredible art. But then you realize that's pretty much all there is. Nude after nude. Paintings, sketches, photos, more paintings. It's faintly amusing to begin with. Then it becomes distasteful. And then . . . then you can't wait to leave. To escape.'

Lena took a breath. 'All legal?' she said.

Michael winced. 'What you can see, yes. Of course. Scrupulously so.'

Lena nodded. Message understood. 'What does Helen think?' she asked.

Michael closed his eyes. 'I don't know,' he said. 'And I've never wanted to know. They're from another time, another place, Lena. Your aunt and uncle. She's fourteen years older than me. He's nearly sixteen years older. That's almost a generation. We're . . .' Michael shook his head in wonder. 'It's like we're centuries apart. Galaxies, even.'

She waited for more. None came.

'Some other time maybe,' he said.

'When you're stronger,' said Lena.

'Agreed,' her father whispered. 'But, Lena, honey, have you been to check the paintings? The ones the firemen did save?' Michael's eyes were still closed, but he was squeezing her hand again.

'They're safe, Dad,' Lena said, squeezing back. 'In the college's strong room. As agreed.'

'But I worry . . .'

'Of course you do. I'll go and check tonight, report back tomorrow.'

He mouthed, 'Thank you.'

Lena gathered her things together, checked her emails. 'Sorry. One more thing, Dad. It looks like Howard Taylor wants to meet me.' Her father's wince told her everything she needed to know. 'He just sent an email. Why would that be?'

'Nothing good,' he said.

From Jamie Nelson's Instagram

Housemates cooked this yesterday. Probably the best lasagne I've ever tasted. Sara says it's the Worcester sauce. That's the third Jack Daniel's you can see. Don't judge me. Last day at the Halls tomorrow. And feeling sad already. They've been good people. But it's right to go. You know I have things to do. Proper things. Proper work. I can feel the flame going out here. Watching films all the time is a great way to go numb. Don't want that. More flames! More feeling!

24

Sam Carter was waiting for Famie at her front door, rucksack in one hand, black waterproof in the other. 'No coffee, no pastries. Apologies,' he said.

'You're slipping,' Famie said. She opened up, keyed numbers into an alarm pad. He followed her inside. Music played loudly from the kitchen. She found a remote control, and the music faded.

'You always leave that on?' said Sam.

'Yup,' said Famie. 'Another security fetish I've acquired.' She opened her laptop, keyed a digit. The screen lit up.

'Of course,' said Sam. 'Because no one would break into a house playing Vivaldi. Not the done thing.' He grinned at her.

'It was Mozart, actually,' she said, eyebrows raised. 'One of the piano concertos. You really are such a disappointment, Sam Carter. I've clearly taught you nothing.' She sat at the kitchen table. Sam sat opposite. Famie positioned the laptop at right angles so they could both see its screen. Top right the street cam; top left, the garden cam; green lights beneath both.

'You've taught me many things, Famie Madden,' he said, 'but a love of, or any interest in, classical music is not one of them.' He removed a laptop from his bag. 'And before you give up on me altogether, I have some questions.' He opened the laptop. 'I've been working through the posts from Flint Hill you sent me. Or Jamie Nelson.' He looked up. 'What shall we . . .'

'Let's call him Jamie Nelson from now on,' said Famie.

Sam nodded. 'Okay. Jamie's use of the Roman numeral for thirteen is intriguing.' He found the page Famie had sent him and scrolled down. 'So these are mostly from around August '22.' He indicated the posts: 'XIII full of surprises'. Then 'Still with XIII'. And the final one: 'XIII support'. 'They don't really mean anything or take us anywhere.'

'Tea?' offered Famie.

Sam shook his head. 'Also in August,' he continued, 'the first German post. "*Mit vorsicht folgen*", which Google Translate tells me means "following with caution". The other German posts are later in the year. December, I think.'

Famie allowed herself the briefest smile. She knew Sam was excited about something, knew this was going to lead to a denouement of some kind.

'So here's a thought,' he said, 'even if it's a bit out there.'

Here we go, thought Famie.

He tapped the keyboard, checked the screen. 'In my misspent youth I played a lot of video games.'

'Yes,' said Famie. 'I remember your wife mentioning that a few times.'

Sam grimaced. 'Still a bone of contention, if truth be told,' he said. 'But, anyway, I used to play this game.' He spun the laptop. The screen showed a video-game cover in claret and yellow. 'XIII' was in heavy white type. The main image was an illustration of a man's head and the barrel of a large pistol.

Famie leant in. 'It looks shit,' she said.

'This is twenty years old,' said Sam. 'It was a great game actually, huge fun. Wasted way too much time on it. Then it got remade and that was shit.' He looked up.

'Go on,' said Famie. 'Do your reveal.'

'And it was launched at the GamesCom convention in

August '22. In Cologne, Germany.' He half smiled, sat back. 'Just a thought.'

'Well, if he's a gamer, it makes sense,' said Famie. 'But that's one of many things we don't know about him. Those lines with the numeral would make a bit more sense, but why would he post about a game he was playing on Howl?' That's what you'd put on Instagram to friends who played the same game. To other people who cared.'

'Maybe he did that too,' said Sam. 'We don't know and can't check.'

It didn't sound much of a theory to Famie, but she didn't have anything else to go on. She'd play with it. 'What happens in the game?' she said. 'I'm assuming you wander around shooting things. Mainly people. Yes?'

Sam rolled his eyes. 'Yes and no,' he said. 'There's thirteen chapters, thirty-four missions. It's based around a Belgian graphic novel, same name in the same Roman numerals. You play a guy who's lost his memory. Washed up on a beach somewhere. Brooklyn, I think. He's got the numerals tattooed on his right shoulder. Turns out he's killed the President of America.'

Famie's eyebrows were up. Sam slowed down. 'He's also fallen in with conspiracy theorists.' His shoulders slumped. 'And I can tell I've lost you.' He managed a smile. 'And, to be honest, I was losing myself as I said the words out loud. Forget it.' Sam closed his laptop, deflated.

Famie had been about to laugh at the ludicrousness of what Sam was saying, but held back. Partly because she didn't want to offend him but also she had felt his words snag on a truth somewhere. She had no idea what it was but had learnt not to ignore these moments when they came. The preposterous-sounding game had shifted something.

'What are the other German phrases?' she said. 'The later

ones?' Sam opened the laptop scrolled again. '*Voller überraschungen,*' he said, 'meaning "full of surprises", dated December the fifteenth. And *Alle einkäufe in Deutschland* on the sixteenth. ' "All shopping in Germany".'

Famie shook her head. 'He can't have been Christmas shopping surely?' she said. 'In Cologne or anywhere else. What would a British radical leftist be doing in Germany, autumn and winter of 2022? Were there demonstrations he could have been on?'

Sam sat up straight, alert again.

Jamie and demonstrations.

'Always,' said Sam. 'Take your pick. Most of the arguments back then were over how much support to give Ukraine after the Russian invasion. The Die Linke party pretty much tore itself apart over it.'

Russia, thought Famie. 'Far left, yes?'

'Most definitely.'

Of course Russia.

Famie stood, paced the room. 'Fuck it, Sam, why had we not given Ukraine or Russia any thought? Us! For Christ's sake, we were actually targeted by Russians in Coventry!' She walked the length of the kitchen, back and forth. 'And Israeli or Jewish art? What about that? I need to message Lena.' She typed as she moved.

'Famie, this has nothing to do with us,' said Sam. 'Why should it have anything to do with international politics?'

'Maybe it hasn't.'

She typed: *Lena, was there any Russian, Ukrainian, Israeli or Palestinian art at the gallery. Lost or saved?* 'Just asking Lena. These conflicts, Sam, these wars have many fronts. They have ways of spreading, overlapping.' She stared at her phone. Nothing. 'Big crowds can do terrible things. We know that. And we also know

101

the Russians have plenty of agents in London capable of burning down a gallery. And killing Jamie Nelson in the process.'

Sam sat with his hands in his lap, eyes on Famie. 'Which would make this a very different story,' he said. 'It would make it a targeted kill on a Howl journalist. Who "works" for the famous Famie Madden.'

Outside the light was fading. The shadow of her neighbours' silver birches stretched close to her back door. Famie closed the wooden shutters, switched on the lights. Her phone buzzed. She scanned the text, read out: 'David Gerstein is Israeli, born in Jerusalem. No Palestinian art. Two Russian artists who escaped the war had paintings on floor three. They pulled out of the Venice Biennale, because of the invasion of Ukraine. Call me.'

Famie and Sam stared at each other. 'It's possible,' said Famie.

'It's a theory,' said Sam, his tone measured.

'And we don't have many,' said Famie. 'But we're looking for a spark, Sam. And God knows some raging infernos out there can catch over here. So, yes, it's a theory. And, yes, it's possible.'

25

Lena put her phone on the sofa arm. 'Remind me to call your mum when Happy Howard's gone.' She and Charlie sat on their sofa in the Gasholders flat. Lena wore a baggy green sweatshirt and her oldest jeans, Charlie a blue granddad shirt buttoned up to the neck, with old jeans rescued from her dirty-washing pile.

'Dress rough,' Lena had said. 'Goblin mode. If you're showing any curve, or any flesh, Howard Taylor's eyes will be on stalks. And he'll be here for ever. Go drab and we might kick him out in ten minutes.'

'I feel disgusting,' said Charlie.

'And you smell,' said Lena. 'Excellent work.'

'He'll hate us,' said Charlie.

'I wouldn't bet on it,' said Lena.

The intercom buzzed.

'Well, let's see quite how revolting we are,' said Charlie. She left the door ajar and went back to the sofa.

A single knock and Howard Taylor was in. He raised a hand in greeting. 'Hello, girls.' He struggled out of a beige raincoat and made a show of placing it over a kitchen chair. He removed a folded brown A4 envelope from an inside pocket, walked to an armchair and eased his way down. He glanced from Lena to Charlie and back. Lena shuffled nervously. Taylor scowled. 'I know you said Charlie would be here,' he said, 'but I must repeat, this is Nash business, Lena. Family business. She should go.' He pointed at Charlie.

'I asked her to stay,' Lena said. She managed a smile. 'So that's that, really. What did you want to see me for?'

Taylor played with the envelope, turning it round end to end. 'Like I said—' he began.

Lena cut in: 'Say what you have to say, Mr Taylor,' she said. 'Charlie and I both live here and I tell her everything anyway.' Still Taylor hesitated. Lena pointed at the front door. 'Or feel free to leave anytime.' Taylor stared at Lena. He sat taller in the chair. Her words had changed something. A switch had been flicked. Taylor was suddenly motionless, alert, threatened.

'Very well,' he said. He pushed himself forward in the chair, slid two large photographs from the envelope. He separated them, looked at both, offered them to Lena.

She didn't move. 'What are they?' she said.

He flourished them, inviting her to get up and retrieve them. Lena still didn't move. 'What are they?' she repeated. Charlie made to get up but Lena tugged her sleeve and she sat down again.

Taylor offered the photos again. When neither Lena nor Charlie moved, he dropped them onto the floor. He stared at Lena as though reassessing her. 'Okay,' he said. 'And be very careful now. Try really hard not to fuck this up, any more than you have already. These are two of the photographs sent to the *Daily Mail*.' His voice was quieter, angrier. 'They both show you, Lena, at the heart of the riot that burnt down your own gallery. I believe there are others, and the *Mail* are going to print them. Run the whole story. Headline something like "Millionaire heiress burns down her own gallery". Or maybe "Man dies as heiress torches her own gallery". How do you like that?'

Lena said nothing, stared at her hands. 'Well?' said Taylor. 'When these go public,' he stabbed a finger at the photos on the floor, 'this becomes a global story. You do realize that? You and the family go from victims to villains. Overnight.'

Lena clasped her hands together. She looked at Taylor. 'I was on a march. That's all.' She took a breath. 'I didn't burn anything. As you well know.' She stood, crouched to pick up the images, retreated to the sofa and shared the pictures with Charlie. In a sea of faces massed outside the West End Gallery's front door, a clear side view of Lena, mouth open, hand raised as if in greeting. Next to her, though partially obscured by the hand, was Charlie.

'Yes, that's you there also, Miss Madden,' he said. '"The daughter of famous journalist Famie Madden" will obviously add spice to the story. And ensure a global interest.'

'Actually,' said Charlie, 'I don't think anyone will care.'

Taylor seemed to inflate. He glowered at Charlie. 'Really?' he said. 'With all your experience of the law and the press, that's your conclusion? No wonder Lena's in trouble if that's the wise counsel she gets.' His volume kicked up a notch. 'Let me make this clear. Quite apart from the shame and humiliation that are coming, the gallery's insurers will be paying very close attention to this.' He shifted in the chair, pushing himself to its edge, hands on his knees. 'Because if they suspect that you, Lena, are complicit in the riot that led to the arson, and therefore the death of the gentleman who was inside, there will be no payout. No rebuild. No gallery. Nothing. *Nada*.' He sat came back for one more shot. Softer now. 'The reputational damage to the Nash name is incalculable,' he said.

There was silence in the flat. Charlie, arms folded, head down, Lena, hand over mouth, staring into the distance. Taylor surveyed the damage, studied both women.

Lena sat forward. 'Unless,' she said.

Taylor frowned. 'Unless what?'

'That's what you've come here to say, isn't it?' said Lena. 'That there is a way of keeping this out of the papers. That these,' she waved the photos, 'will be printed, unless I do something. Say something. And you will take great pleasure in telling me what that something is.' She returned Taylor's gaze.

His eyes narrowed. His words were delivered with quiet menace. 'Oh, I think it's too late for that,' he said. 'Don't you?' He hauled himself to his feet and walked towards Lena, towering over her. He folded his arms. 'If you think of something that could . . .' he searched for the word '. . . distract the press, do let me know.' The hint of a smile. 'And I will let you decide how and when to tell your father. I wouldn't want to . . . hinder his recovery.'

Lena bristled. 'Like you care,' she said.

'It seems that I care for the Nash reputation considerably more than you do,' he said, recovering his coat.

'So they'll print these whatever?' said Charlie.

Taylor replied without turning. 'As far as I'm concerned, Miss Madden, you are not here,' he said. 'This is Nash business, not yours.' He folded the coat over his arm.

'So they'll print these whatever?' This time it was Lena.

Taylor turned now. 'I think so,' he said. 'I'm still talking to their lawyers but I'm not hopeful. They seem determined to run with what they say is an important story.'

Lena stepped towards the departing Taylor. 'What did you mean by "distract"?'

He walked to the front door. 'I'll see myself out.'

The door clicked shut. Lena exhaled slowly. 'And that's who we're dealing with,' she said.

Charlie waited till she was sure Howard Taylor had caught the lift. 'Well, what *did* he mean by "distract"?'

'What do you think?' said Lena.

Charlie frowned. 'I have no idea.' Then the penny dropped. 'You don't mean some kind of sexy photo shoot?'

'One hundred per cent,' said Lena. 'That's the way he works. It's why we dressed like tramps.'

Charlie shook her head in disbelief. 'Does he think this is the nineteen eighties or something? That some kind of pathetic titillation piece will trump those photos? He really is a dick.' She got to her feet, walked to the kitchen table. 'Terrifying. But still a dick.' She stood still. Staring into the distance.

'You all right?' said Lena.

'I've just had the most ridiculous idea,' said Charlie.

From Jamie Nelson's Instagram

Here's everyone saying goodbye. That's Clio at the end, with the hair! They said I can have the job back if I change my mind. Here's what I'm writing, title page. Reckon I have 4 weeks tops before I run out of funds. Will have to move fast and break things. (Was that Zuckerberg? God, I hope not).

Needed a walk. Took this. It's not exactly 7 Mile Beach but the Downs are doing their best to cheer me up. 2 hour walk to get this view. Saw no one. Perfect. Thought you might like it.

26

Two hundred metres from Famie's mews, the garage on Camden Road was busy. The sun had set, but the air was still warm and heavy with fumes. Inside the garage's shop, the aircon clattered noisily but struggled. A few customers bought petrol, but most wanted food and alcohol. The queue for the tills snaked around counters of cheap chocolate and outsized bags of sweets. Eighth from the front, a tall man, black hoodie. In his hands, two red plastic bottles of barbecue fuel hidden in a rolled-up newspaper. He stared straight ahead, shuffling forward as the queue moved. Two tills processed the purchases, each customer waved forward as sales were completed.

Three from the front, the man stooped, dropped his head. His black-and-white image was now showing on one of the CCTV screens behind the cashier. None of his face was visible. In front of him, a man in shorts, a woman with a baby. He held the newspaper in front of him, in both hands. As he was called forward, he unrolled the paper, handed all three items to the cashier. He paid in cash. He didn't look at the cashier. She didn't look at him. He rolled the bottles back into the paper.

Outside the garage, the man walked to the main road, turned left. On the corner he handed the newspaper to another man. He, too, wore a black hoodie, the hood pulled low over his face. He was the shorter of the two and he twitched with a nervous energy. 'Çok yaşa,' he said, as took the package.

'*Heb beraber,*' replied the first, not breaking stride, not looking back. The shorter man scurried away, disappearing down a dark alley. Famie's house was just over a hundred metres away.

27

When Charlie and Lena's Uber arrived, Famie was ready. They had messaged from the car, knowing her dislike of unannounced guests. When her phone buzzed again, they were outside. Famie deactivated the street cam and opened the door. She embraced Charlie, then Lena. 'A phone call would have been fine,' she said, ushering them inside. 'And, Lena Nash, this is Sam Carter. He's with me at Howl but I don't think you've met.'

Sam stood, shook Lena's hand. An earnest smile. 'Actually, we met briefly at the gallery,' he said. 'Way back. I'm so sorry for what happened. I hope your father's getting better now.'

'Thank you. It's a slow process but he'll be okay, I think.' Lena turned to Famie. Slightly flustered. 'I'm ... I'm so sorry, Famie. I didn't know you had a guest here. We'll do this another time.'

Sam shook his head. 'No worries at all. And I was just wrapping up.' He reached for his waterproof.

Famie touched Lena's arm. 'So two Russians and one Israeli were exhibiting at the gallery.'

Lena nodded. 'Mainly the painters are British, American, Canadian. Also Japanese and Korean.' She stared at Famie. 'But, yes, there were two Russians and an Israeli.'

'Do you really think there's a link between them and the fire?' Lena asked. She and Charlie sat down at the kitchen table, while Sam leant against a small kitchen island. Famie boiled the kettle.

'Who knows?' said Famie. 'It's certainly possible. Could you get in touch with the artists for me? Pass on some questions?'

'I think so,' said Lena. 'My dad will have the contact details.'

Famie bustled with mugs, milk and tea bags. 'It's just a theory,' she said.

'No, it isn't,' said Charlie. 'It's way more than that. You spend your life reading and responding to Howl members in conflict areas around the world. You're just playing it down for us. None of this stuff happens in a vacuum. You always say that! Your seven IPS colleagues who were murdered and the carnage at Coventry Cathedral happened because your boss had been corrupted by the Russians and his reporting in Chechnya. So, if the West End Gallery was targeted because it displayed work by a Jewish painter, you tell the police. If Russians are targeting the gallery because it displayed art from Russian dissidents, you need to tell the police. That policewoman from the Coventry attacks, for example, she'd be interested.'

Famie sipped. 'She would.' She sat at the table, eyes flicking to her laptop screen, and reactivated the street cam.

'Channing Hunter,' said Sam. 'She stayed in touch for a while. She's still in the Met. I'll message her.'

Famie looked between Charlie and Lena. 'I assume that's why you came?'

Lena looked at Charlie, who took a breath. Famie was intrigued. 'Well, all of a sudden, there's tension in the air,' she said. 'Hit me with whatever you have.'

'Should I . . .' Sam pointed at the front door.

Famie shook her head. 'No, stay. It's fine, I'm sure. Carry on, Charlie.'

Charlie explained about their meeting with Howard Taylor.

When she got to the photos from the demonstration, Famie put her head into her hands and groaned.

Lena put down her mug, adjusted the coaster. She looked dejected. 'My family have always been very private,' she said. 'They do some good stuff, as you know, but are also pretty fucked up, as you also know. Taylor made it clear this fire is going to mess with everything. My aunt and uncle are horrified at the prospect of the photos going public. Never mind the insurers. If the "rich riot girl" story gets out, we'll be on every front page.' She sighed long and hard. 'God knows what that'll do to my dad. Anyway. We had an idea.'

'Also, Mum, I'm in the picture,' said Charlie. 'Behind Lena's hand, but it's me. No one would know but you should know.'

Famie felt the familiar sense of dread in her stomach. She could barely speak. Where to start? 'So when the "rich riot girl" story has run its course,' she said, ' "terror-victim riot girl" can take over. Genius! Well done, you two.'

'You know we didn't do anything wrong,' said Charlie, voice raised. Before Famie could respond, Charlie retreated, raised her hands in surrender. 'But we are where we are. Which is, we agree, a bit of a shit show.'

Famie waited. She looked between Charlie and Lena. 'And so?' she said.

'Grubby pig that he is,' said Charlie, 'he talked about "distracting" the *Mail*.'

'Which means,' said Lena, 'in Howard Taylor-speak, a fleshy photo-shoot of some sort.'

Famie shook her head. 'Of course it does. Dear God.' More silence. More awkward shuffling. 'Obviously you're not doing it, so why the hesitation here?'

Lena cued Charlie.

'I wondered if it was even worth suggesting . . .' Charlie broke off, laughed nervously.

'Just tell me, Charlie, for Christ's sake!' Famie couldn't remember the last time she had seen Charlie so diffident, so unsure.

'Okay,' said Charlie. Now she spoke fast. Getting it out of the way. 'I was wondering if you'd consider writing a profile of the Nash family for the *Mail*. "Britain's most secret family", that kind of thing.' Charlie and Lena watched Famie's face closely. 'It might serve as the distraction Taylor wants,' Charlie continued. 'I know you don't write that kind of piece and that the *Mail* isn't exactly your favourite paper. I haven't mentioned this to anyone, apart from Lena, obviously.'

Famie was flabbergasted. Where had that idea come from? 'What the fuck?' she said. 'Really?' Charlie and Lena recoiled. 'Charlie, I've never written pieces like that. I've never written celeb pieces and you know it. And I've never written for the utterly toxic *Mail* either.' Famie was agitated. She stood because she needed to move. 'Are you saying it's me writing a hideous suck piece on the Nashs, or you and Lena going all Kardashian? Is that the choice?'

Lena made to speak but Charlie got in first. 'Well, yes, pretty much,' she said. 'Or they print the photos. I shouldn't have mentioned it. Sorry, Mum.' Charlie's voice was smaller. 'Just couldn't think of anything else, really.' She raised a hand to Sam. 'And sorry, Sam, that wasn't very edifying.'

Sam was looking embarrassed. 'No, no, don't worry about me,' he said.

That appeared to be that, thought Famie. If they'd come to ask her to write for the *Mail*, they had their answer.

Charlie and Lena appeared to have reached the same conclusion. Lena tapped Charlie's knee. 'We should . . .' She made to get up.

'Yeah, of course,' said Charlie. They both stood. 'Sorry to have had such a crap idea,' she said. They walked to the front door. Deflated, in a hurry to leave.

'Charlie, wait,' said Famie. 'There must be something else. Some other option.'

'Nope,' said Charlie. 'Don't think so.'

'Hey.' Sam put his hand up. 'Were the Russian artists Kirill Savchenkov and Alexandra Sukhareva?' He was looking at Lena. 'The ones who lost their work in the fire. Is that them?'

Lena nodded. 'Yes. I'll forward the details when I get them.'

And they were gone. Sam pulled on his jacket. 'It's late and I'm needed at home,' he said.

'Tell me I'm right,' said Famie, putting mugs into the dishwasher.

'Most of me says you're right,' he said. 'If that helps.'

'What's the rest of you say?'

Sam laughed. 'That it would be one amazing piece.'

'Bye, Sam,' said Famie.

On Famie's laptop, the garden cam light popped red.

WEST END GALLERY
SALVAGE GRAB SHEET

ITEM
Fireworks and Gunpowder/Kirill Savchenkov

LOCATION/CLOSE UP LOCATION, FLOOR PLAN
Ground floor. Stand 10. Top painting of 3

PRIORITY
One

DESCRIPTION
Metallography on aluminium.
Typed poetry with line drawings. Black-and-white
47cm x 20cm x 2cm

INVENTORY NUMBER
236

WEIGHT
0.5 kilos

ACCESS
Direct from ground floor. No restrictions

REMOVAL
Gloves needed. One-person removal

WEST END GALLERY
SALVAGE GRAB SHEET

ITEM
The case of a bestial boredom/Alexandra Sukhareva

LOCATION/CLOSE-UP LOCATION, FLOOR PLAN
Ground floor. Stand 18

PRIORITY
One

DESCRIPTION
Chlorine applications on canvas.
Beige canvas, brown lines
230cm x 350cm

INVENTORY NUMBER
415

WEIGHT
0.5 kilos

ACCESS
Direct from ground floor. No restrictions

REMOVAL
Gloves needed. Two-person removal

28

From under Famie's stairs, the intruder alarm wailed, filling the house with an ear-splitting noise. Famie dropped a mug, which shattered on the kitchen floor. She ran to the screen, keyed two digits. The garden cam image now filled the screen. Sam was at her side. The rear garden was flooded with light, all the way to the end. 'There!' said Famie, pointing at the top of the wall.

'What?' said Sam, staring at the screen, eyes flicking left and right. 'What? I can't see anything.'

'Someone dropped down the other side of the wall,' she said. 'Just caught some movement.'

Sam glanced at the shuttered windows, now framed with the electric light from the garden. 'What's the routine?' he yelled. 'Do we check outside?'

Top right of Famie's screen, the street cam window dropped. Now its light was red too. A second alarm fired, higher, more urgent. The cacophony was deafening, immobilizing.

'What the fuck?' shouted Famie, eyes flicking from garden to street.

'Is this an attack?' yelled Sam. 'Do we call the police?'

'They'll know already,' shouted Famie. Two figures appeared in the street cam screen. Both turned their faces to the camera: Charlie and Lena. Famie was both relieved and scared to see them back. She ran to the front door, herded them inside.

They screwed up their faces as they ran past the alarms in the hall.

Charlie held up her phone. Its screen was flashing red. 'It's the app you set up!' she said. 'We'd only got to the end of the street. What's happened?'

'Intruder, back garden,' said Famie. 'Scared off, I think.' Talking felt impossible. 'Wait,' she mimed. They all watched the laptop image of the rear garden until first one alarm, then the other stopped.

'Thank God for that,' said Sam.

Famie's ears were ringing, her heart hammering, but her focus was the screen. 'I'll scroll it back in a minute,' she said. 'Once I'm sure this is okay.' They all studied the screen. The garden was still floodlit. It showed the wall, the grass and the paving. Nothing moved.

'That dark area of the wall is new,' said Famie, pointing at the screen, her voice louder than she'd intended. 'What the fuck?' She peered through the window. The floodlights switched off, the screen went dark. Four long exhaled breaths. 'I'll scroll back,' she said.

Famie clicked a rewind icon, pressed again for double speed. Four faces edged closer to the screen. A bird landed backwards. A shadow appeared at the top of the wall. Famie hit stop. 'Gotcha.' She rewound to just before the lights kicked on.

In the gathering gloom, a figure in silhouette appears on the top of the wall. Head and shoulders. He hauls himself to a straddle, swings to a sitting position, then jumps. He lands in a crouch, hands to the ground. The floodlights power on, filling the garden with intense white light. Every detail is picked out. The intruder is now in hi-res. He turns, dazzled. Black jeans, black hoodie and cap.

'Literally caught in the headlights,' said Famie. The figure hesitates, looks down the garden, side to side, then back to the wall. He removes a red bottle from his jacket, sprays the wall with fluid, then struggles with a cigarette lighter. When it doesn't spark, he takes a few steps, turns, runs at the wall, then leaps, hands finding the coping stone. One heave, another straddle, and he's gone. Famie rolled the images back, froze the picture as the intruder stood.

'Male,' she said. 'Five ten, maybe six foot. Wearing gloves. A cap plus hood so not much face. But what we can see is light brown skin, unshaven. Twenties, thirties maybe. And he was going to burn us out. Another fucking arsonist.'

'Or the same one,' said Sam.

Famie looked at him blankly. 'My God,' she muttered.

'And he was agile,' said Charlie. 'Got up that wall in no time.'

'Small rucksack on his back,' said Sam. 'Swung a little as he climbed. So I'd guess not very heavy. Maybe more fuel.'

'Enough to set fire to this place for sure,' said Famie.

'And either very clean or very new trainers,' said Charlie, peering at the screen. 'New Nike brand. Expensive.'

Famie's phone rang. She checked the screen and took the call. 'DI Hunter,' she said. 'I somehow thought it would be you.'

29

Detective Inspector Channing Hunter arrived twenty minutes after the first police car. She had already viewed the video Famie had sent her. They stood at the foot of the garden wall. The thick, sweet smell of lighter fuel hung in the air. The garden floodlights were back on, casting two enormous shadows against the orange and brown brick. Where the fuel had been splashed, the tones were darker, the brick still damp with ethanol. Hunter, hands deep in her jacket pockets, looked up at the top of the wall. 'Well, I couldn't climb it,' she said. She raised both hands till they were parallel with the coping stone. 'Can't even reach the top.' She was five foot five, cherubic face, high-waisted dark blue trousers, white shirt. 'So he's young and athletic for sure. An amateur is my guess. A chancer. Looks like he had no idea about your security and no plan once the lights came on, so he just squirted the wall with fuel and ran away. Back wherever he came from.'

Voices from the other side of the wall. 'Ma'am?' called one. 'Sending you a photo.'

'What of?' said Hunter

'Graffiti, ma'am.'

'Saying?'

'Wouldn't like to guess, ma'am.'

'Message it.'

Her phone buzzed. She tapped the image on the screen of

the wall from the other side. Brown and orange bricks, now with large black letters sprayed across the base. Famie peered over her shoulder. '*Turkiye de yapaldi,*' she said.

'Made in Turkey, apparently, ma'am,' called the voice from the other side. 'According to the internet anyway. Man in the house this side says it's new. He's quite annoyed, actually, but didn't see who did it.'

Hunter looked at Famie. 'Let's go inside.' They walked in silence along the path. Yellow poppies and crimson pansies ran alongside the neighbours' fence, freshly cut grass everywhere else.

'You have any of your bloggers in Turkey?' Hunter said, sitting at the kitchen table, her back to the garden.

'Of course,' said Famie.

'Have you upset anyone in Turkey?'

'Looks like it.' Famie sat next to Hunter. 'But I upset people everywhere. You know that.'

Hunter smiled. 'You got that right,' she said. 'It's your superpower. Play me the video again. Don't pause it. Real time.'

They watched the footage of the intruder again. From his shadowy first appearance above the wall to his floodlit disappearance, it lasted nineteen seconds. Famie was about to stop it but Hunter held up her hand. 'Wait,' she said. They watched the wall till the lights went out. Ninety seconds.

'Okay?' said Famie. Hunter nodded.

After she had stopped the video, they sat in silence both staring at the final darkened image of the garden. Now Famie felt the fear return. It wasn't the run-and-hide fear she had experienced before, more a growing sense of dread that she was, once again, a target. She had been threatened hundreds of times. Mostly it was online, where endless numbers of keyboard warriors lined up to denounce her, wish her dead.

Occasionally on her book tour she had been shouted and sworn at, but in each case, security had swiftly ejected the protesters. After the knife attack on Salman Rushdie in 2022, her publishers had taken no risks, hiring bodyguards and protection teams at all venues. She didn't recall being scared once. But now, sitting in her kitchen, with Sam, Charlie and Lena gone and just Channing Hunter for company, she felt exposed. The world knew where she lived after all. She folded her arms to stop her hands shaking.

'You okay?' said Hunter.

'No,' snapped Famie. 'I'm really not.' She kept her voice steady but it was a struggle. Her head had filled with images of the conflagration at the gallery. Flames, smoke and ash. Ambulances, police cars and a body bag. 'It's fire again, Channing,' said Famie. 'The West End Gallery is still smouldering. Jesus, there's probably still some smoke coming from it somewhere, and now this?' She stabbed a finger at the garden. 'The fact this bastard's lighter failed is irrelevant. His intention was arson. He wanted to burn me out.' She placed both hands flat on the table and looked Hunter in the eye. 'I've never believed in coincidences, Channing. Not when they happen to other people. And not when they happen to me.'

Hunter's face was impassive. It was her work face and Famie, in spite of herself, found it both familiar and reassuring. Hunter returned Famie's gaze. 'I understand all of that,' she said. 'And you may be right. Of course you may. If it were anyone else, I'd be as convinced as you are. But just pull back a bit. I don't think it has happened to you. There has been one botched, amateurish attack on your house. Due to your very wise safety precautions, it failed. There has also been one attack on the West End Gallery. Which was devastatingly, murderously successful. But it wasn't an attack on you. You have become involved in the story because of Charlie. And Lena. After the fact. And also because . . .' She paused.

'I am fantastically annoying?' said Famie.

Hunter smiled. 'No, because you're Famie Madden,' she said. 'And I know you have many enemies, Famie. State actors. Big players.' She raised both hands. 'Whole governments, for Christ's sake. If there were more attacks on you or your house, no one should be surprised.' She clasped Famie's hand. 'Yes, they both involved a fire accelerant. One ignited, the other didn't. But, really, these two crimes don't feel necessarily connected to me. Not at this point in time.'

Famie squeezed Hunter's hand, then pulled away. Her friend was right, of course she was. 'If you say so,' she said. She slumped in her chair, managed a smile. 'Sorry,' she said. She reached out, closed her laptop. 'So should I be encouraged or depressed by the amateurishness of it all?' she said.

Hunter chewed her lip. 'Okay,' she said. 'That is the right question.'

'Well done, me,' said Famie. 'The bastard wrote "Made in Turkey" on the wall, Channing. So he was claiming responsibility for something. Even if he never managed to do it. There was clearly something that was going to be "Made in Turkey". Presumably burning my house down. God knows how much fuel was in his bag.' Famie got up, paced the room, worried all over again. 'And Charlie was here. Maybe she's in danger too. Christ, what a mess. This is attempted murder!'

Hunter swivelled to follow Famie. 'The first question you asked—'

'Should I move again?' said Famie, interrupting. 'Because I could if I needed to.'

Hunter put up her hand, like a child in school. She waited.

Famie didn't notice. 'No one wanted me to move to this

124

house in the first place but I'd just had it with the bloody countryside. But now maybe . . .' She noticed Hunter's hand, stopped pacing. 'Okay, sorry.' She sat down again at the table.

Hunter leant towards her. 'The first question you asked was whether you should be encouraged or discouraged by this ill-thought-out . . .' Hunter searched for the right word '. . . this ill-thought-out trespass. And attempted arson. So the answer, I'm afraid, is discouraged. There is evidence from across Europe of local gangs being used for dirty work by foreign governments. Instead of sending highly trained agents, they use unattributable, small-time, part-time, petty crooks. In Germany last year, police in Munich stopped a pizza guy killing a Hungarian businessman who had fallen out with the wrong people back in Belgrade. He'd been hired locally. A thousand euros was all he was paid. It failed, but next time?' Hunter made a who-knows expression. 'It's risk-free assassination.' She jerked a thumb over her shoulder. 'If I were you, I'd take your presumably Turkish visitor very seriously indeed.' Hunter sat back. 'And maybe, yes, you should move out. I know you won't. But that's my advice.'

Famie was wide-eyed, said nothing. Hunter waited for a response. 'Well?' she said.

'You mentioned Germany,' Famie said.

125

30

Famie walked DI Hunter through the Jamie Nelson/Flint Hill story, his German visits and posts on Howl, then the Jewish artist whose work had been saved and the Russian dissident artists whose work had burnt with the gallery. Hunter made notes, face impassive. When Famie had finished, she exhaled theatrically. 'That's all you got?' she said.

'For now,' said Famie. 'Thought it might be useful.'

Hunter put away her notes. 'And I'm guessing you haven't told this to anyone actually working the gallery-fire case?'

Famie shrugged. 'I only talk to you, Channing. You know that.' The two women exchanged smiles. 'And if you've found someone you trust in the Metropolitan Police,' said Famie, 'you should probably stick with them.'

'Well, in the spirit of cooperation,' said Hunter, 'did you know Jamie Nelson's father is arriving in the country tomorrow? He's receiving his son's remains. I don't know the details. I do know that the team are convinced that Jamie Nelson was the arsonist.'

'Of course they are,' said Famie. 'Case closed.'

Hunter pulled a face. 'I didn't say that. You know I didn't.'

Famie spread her arms. 'Whatever,' she said. 'Sure. Let's see. But, yes, that's interesting about Jamie's father. Could I meet him?'

Hunter was ready to go, jacket fastened, bag over her shoulder. 'He can meet whoever he wants, of course. Whether he wants to meet you is another matter. I know he's asked to visit Coal Drops Yard. If I find out when, I'll message you.'

Hunter left. The house was quiet. Famie poured wine. She considered Hunter's words about moving. She hadn't wanted to discuss the matter but knew there was sound reasoning behind the DI's advice. But move where? Charlie would probably offer but Famie didn't want to put her in any more danger. Ditto Sam. She could afford a hotel for a while but that could only be a temporary fix. And if Hunter was right, that the local pizza-delivery men were all secret assassins, was anywhere safe?

Famie topped up, watched the condensation run down her glass. 'Fuck it,' she said.

She got up, went to the back door, unlocked it. The bolt clicked open. She felt the dread bloom again, so moved quickly. Opening the door wide, she strode to the nearest garden chair. She found some Chopin on her phone, played it as loudly as the speaker could tolerate. The night was still warm. Increasing cloud had kept most of the day's heat. If she'd thought about it, she'd have pulled on some shorts, but to go back in now seemed a compromise. A victory for Turkey. Her eyes ran to the end of the garden. She stared at the wall, still visible in the gloom.

'I don't think I'm going anywhere,' she said.

From Jamie Nelson's Instagram

Sending you some words. Been trying to write something good enough for the site I mentioned. These journalists are heroes. You should read the piece from Rafah. Here's the link. I hope I can write like this one day. I'm in awe of these people! I try to write like them. To be clear like them. So much pressure, so much danger but great writing. I wonder if anyone else cares. Who steps up when these souls are gone? Intimidation works and everyone knows it. The truth is exhausting.

31

Monday

Brian Nelson's visit to the site of his son's death was appropriately discreet. Famie watched from a seat on the other side of the canal. Two police officers in uniform, one male, one female, escorted a tall, mid-fifties Jamaican man in a dark blue suit with cropped white hair to what had been the gallery's entrance. Five bunches of flowers had been laid against the white tarpaulin and steel scaffolding. Just five, thought Famie. Hardly an outpouring of public grief. The police had decided Jamie had burnt the place down, and so, it would appear, had everyone else. Self-immolation and serve him right.

And maybe it would turn out that they were correct. Occam's Razor and all that. The simplest explanation is the best one. But Famie had heard that before, usually as an excuse for police laziness or sloppy thinking. Nothing had altered the fact that Jamie had posted on her site and, consequently, Famie owed him. There had obviously been something about Howl that had pulled him in. And the only reason for anyone to sign up was a belief in journalistic freedom and security. Maybe his father would know what his son had been working on. She thought it unlikely, but she'd be crazy not to ask.

Famie watched as the police waved Brian Nelson forward. He took a few uncertain steps, then stooped to lay his flowers. A small wreath of white lilies on a concrete slab. An altar centrepiece. He knelt in front of them, one hand to the ground for support, bowed his head. Around Coal Drops Yard, life carried on. Shoppers trundled their trolleys; late breakfasts and early lunches were served at elegant, sun-lit tables. But for Brian Nelson, time had stopped. He had travelled thousands of miles on this desperate pilgrimage, and his devotions were unhurried. His head moved occasionally. Famie assumed he was praying or maybe just talking to his dead son. She wiped tears from her face.

After what she guessed was at least five minutes, the man hauled himself to his feet. He brushed his knees free of dirt and dust, stood to attention, hands by his sides. One final nod and he walked back to the police officers. Famie walked across the bridge, watching them. She had no idea what Brian Nelson was doing next or how long he would be in the country, but she knew it was now or, probably, never. She waited for what looked like a break in the conversation, then walked over.

Nelson had his back to her, and both police officers saw her coming. She addressed them both, smiling broadly. 'Excuse me, Officers, my name is Famie Madden, I'm a journalist.' She stood alongside Nelson, who had turned when she spoke. 'Mr Nelson, my condolences. I'm so sorry for your loss.' She offered her hand, which he took. A quizzical face. His brow furrowed. He said nothing. 'I run the Howl website,' she said. 'There's a chance Jamie might have mentioned it.'

A light in his exhausted eyes. 'That's you?' he said. His face softened.

'That's me,' said Famie, smiling again. This conversation just got easier.

'I would like to speak with you,' he said.

Famie turned to the police. 'Is it okay if we . . . ?' She pointed at an empty bench nearby.

130

'Go ahead,' said the policewoman. 'We're finished here. Completed the formalities yesterday. He's all yours.'

Famie and Brian Nelson walked to a slatted wooden bench. They sat together, stared across the canal to the high-end shops and glittering offices.

Nelson spoke first. 'I haven't been to London before,' he said. He spoke softly, his Jamaican accent strong. She noticed a white cotton handkerchief balled in his hand.

'It's not all like this,' said Famie. 'This is all new. Last few years.' Stop now, she thought. You're not a tour guide.

Nelson turned slightly to look at her. 'You said you ran the website,' he said. 'So did Jamie work for you?'

'Not exactly,' said Famie. 'Not at all, really. He commented sometimes on other journalists' work, but there wasn't much, I'm afraid. He used the name Flint Hill, after the place where he lived. It's about twenty miles away. South London.'

'I didn't know that,' said Nelson. He placed his hands in his lap and stared ahead. 'I looked sometimes on your site, but I could never see anything from him.'

'He didn't tell you he was using the name Flint Hill?'

'He did not.'

'Did he stay in touch?'

'He did. To begin with.'

Famie waited for more, but he had stopped. She sensed his obvious reluctance to give too much away. She would start at the beginning. 'Tell me about Jamie,' she said. 'What kind of a boy was he?'

There was a pause, then the saddest smile she had seen. Nelson's eyes brimmed. He blinked twice, then dabbed with the handkerchief. 'Oh,' he said, 'he was a grand boy.' He sighed deeply. 'Do you know the term "duppy conqueror", Miss Madden? Do you know it?'

Famie shook her head. 'No, I'm sorry I don't.'

Nelson nodded. 'A duppy is a ghost. Back home, everyone believe in God and everyone believe in ghosts. If you're a duppy conqueror, you're a ghost conqueror, a fearless person. That was our Jamie. He was our duppy conqueror. Right from when he was small. He stood up for what he thought was right.'

'Did you think he was right?' said Famie.

'Most of the time, Miss Madden, most of the time. How familiar are you with Jamaican politics?'

Famie shrugged. 'All I know comes from my website, I'm afraid. I have two or three reporters who write about Jamaican politics. From memory, the high levels of criminal and gang violence concern them the most. Would that be fair?'

Nelson didn't answer. Famie wondered if he was calibrating his answer. Cautious again.

'Our Jamie was a righteous man, Miss Madden. His mother saw to that, may she rest in peace. When he saw trouble, he stood up. He stood straight. When he saw an injustice, he spoke up. I would have been quiet. But Jamie . . .' He dabbed again. 'Sometimes that kind of thing can get you noticed.' He turned to Famie, his eyes narrowed. 'You understand me, Miss Madden?'

Famie nodded. 'I do. Yes. And, please, call me Famie.' She wasn't sure if he would be comfortable with the informality, so added, 'If that feels comfortable, of course.' She also wasn't sure he was listening to her.

He spoke when he was ready. 'I encouraged him to come to England,' he said. 'It was me. I thought he would do well here. Away from the gangs.' He let the sentence hang.

She trod carefully. 'Are they still a problem back home?' she said. He nodded.

'Mr Nelson,' said Famie, 'do you think gangs might have been involved in your son's death?'

Nelson brushed imaginary crumbs from his thighs. Rolled his shoulders. Clenched and unclenched his hands. 'What I do know Miss Madden,' he said, 'is that my son would never do that.' He pointed behind them at the wrecked gallery. 'Never. A demonstration, yes. Absolutely. But burn a building to the ground? No. No. No.'

Famie watched a taxi stop, drop two people at the bridge, fifty metres away. A woman and a man. She recognized them. Her stomach tightened. She turned to Nelson, her back to the hack and her photographer who would pass them in twenty seconds. She hoped she was shielding him enough. 'Mr Nelson,' she said, 'we need to go.'

From Jamie Nelson's Instagram

Research day. Came across this letter from a church here. An open letter about the killing of George Floyd. It's all too full of Jesus for me (my ma would have loved it) but see the highlighted bits! 'Tragic pattern of abuse of power' and 'this prejudice is visibly and invisibly manifest in our communities' is spot on.

I'll let you know if I start singing hymns.

32

Most of the coverage of the gallery fire and Jamie Nelson had appalled Famie. He was a 'lone-wolf' far-left rioter, who had caused his own death. His 'violent hatred' of capitalism had pushed him into 'one last desperate gesture'. One journalist – the woman Famie had just seen jump from a cab – had implied he was, in effect, 'a suicide bomber against Western civilization'. If Famie could protect Brian Nelson from her clutches, she would.

'Go where?' he said.

'That woman who ran past?' she said. 'She's from the *Daily Mail*. So is the photographer behind her.' She saw his eyes widen. 'Anywhere but here is the answer. We have maybe twenty seconds before they turn and see us.' He stood up, and Famie steered him from the square, over the canal, then the zebra crossing. On the down slope to King's Cross, they dipped inside a clothes shop. Famie glanced back. 'Think we're okay,' she said, still peering back up to the square. 'She's a terrible, terrible woman, Mr Nelson. She wrote about Jamie . . .'

'I know, I read it,' said Nelson, 'and thank you. I might have struggled with her.' He leant on a circular rack of extravagant summer shirts.

A salesman approached, topknot, tattoos. Famie was about to wave him away, then reconsidered. 'Do you have any hats?' she said.

'Baseball caps,' said the salesman. 'That's all. Just over there.' He pointed to the tills and was gone.

'Mr Nelson,' said Famie, 'when do you fly home?' She steered him away from the shirts.

'Tomorrow morning,' he said. 'What are we doing, Ms Madden?'

'Would you like to see where Jamie lived?' she said. 'We could catch the train there. St Pancras is ten minutes from here, then it's about ninety minutes to his house.' He considered her suggestion. Famie took two hats from a shelf, one blue with NY in gold letters, the other black with a gold sun embroidered on the front. She paid for both, offered them to Nelson. He took the gold sun.

'I would like to see where he lived,' said Nelson. 'If that can be arranged.'

Caps on, they sat opposite each other on the train to Dorking. Famie's back to the driver's cab. No one took the seats alongside them. The nearest passengers were facing Famie, a few metres away, pensioners with newspapers, eating sandwiches from a Tupperware box. Nelson seemed on edge, regularly glancing at their fellow travellers. He folded and unfolded his arms, checked his watch.

'We're okay, Mr Nelson,' Famie said. 'No one is interested in us. Trust me, I've learnt to be watchful. I can't be certain about everyone, of course, but it's mainly old folk and mums with babies here.'

Nelson exhaled. 'Thank you,' he said. 'I'm a little overwhelmed.'

While he stared out of the window, she watched the passengers. There were no doors between the carriages so when

136

the track was straight she could see the entire length of the train. She felt it unlikely that any journalists or pizza-delivery assassins were on board, but she wasn't as certain as she had led Nelson to believe. She did, however, need to be honest with him.

'Mr Nelson, I can't guarantee Jamie's housemates will be in,' she said. 'I've only met one of them, a woman called Sara, but with luck . . .'

He continued to stare at the passing trackside houses. 'You have been there?' he said.

'Just the once,' she said.

'I would like to see it.'

Famie wasn't sure how much she could ask, but knew that tomorrow he was gone.'Could I ask when you last heard from Jamie?'

He didn't answer for a while. She wasn't sure he had heard. Eventually he said, 'Around two months ago.' She waited. One of the pensioners snapped the sandwich box shut, stowed it in a carrier bag on the floor. 'Jamie emailed me,' he said. 'It is what he did.'

'That's how he communicated?'

'It was.'

'Not Instagram?'

'Not Instagram.' The one follower on Jamie's account wasn't his father, then.

'And how did he seem when he emailed?'

Nelson shrugged, palms turned up. 'How can you ever tell?' he said. 'He told me things he thought I'd want to hear. Things that had gone well for him, never anything that had gone badly. He didn't want to worry me, you see.'

'What sort of things were going well?' asked Famie.

137

He paused. 'I think he liked his friends,' he said. 'He was working. And he travelled a lot. He would send photos sometimes.'

Famie leant in. 'Where from?' she said.

The train stopped. They fell silent, and Famie sat back. The pensioners got off, leaving their newspaper and a paper coffee cup behind. New passengers joined two carriages down. The train jerked, pulled away from the station.

'Mainly different places in the UK,' he said. 'He liked his photography, Miss Madden. He sent me images of England he thought I'd like. Fields, trees, phone boxes, crowds. You know?'

'Crowds?' asked Famie.

'Yes, crowds,' said Nelson. 'Football sometimes. I think he went to see Crystal Palace play a few times. And politics, that was all the time. Marches, campaigns, all of that.' Brian Nelson spoke to the window, his words steaming the glass. 'Sometimes I didn't understand his protest, but he wrote with such conviction that even I was persuaded.' He allowed himself a small smile.

'And you said all of that came from his mother?' said Famie, aware she was sailing close to the wind.

The smile broadened. 'Ah, yes,' he said. 'My Alice was a firebrand for sure.' He looked at Famie now. 'She was a teacher, Miss Madden, and briefly, a deputy head in her school. She could quote the Holy Bible better than any preacher. She understood Jamaican law better than any judge. She was beautiful, you know. Even when the cancer took her, inside and outside, she was the most beautiful woman I ever saw. I have a photograph . . .' He pulled a wallet from his jacket pocket, then produced a small Polaroid, offered it to Famie.

Like it's the 1960s, she thought. She took the image. The woman in the photo had short-cut black hair, silver-rimmed glasses, and an embarrassed half-smile. Behind her, a scarlet banner with words in gold type. 'She's stunning, Mr Nelson,' said Famie. 'What is written here?' She pointed to the top of the photo.

'That's a Bible verse. Micah, chapter six, verse eight,' he said. '"Do justice, love mercy and walk humbly with God" or something like it. It's the only one I can remember because it was Alice's favourite. Do justice, Miss Madden. Love mercy. That's what Alice always did. And it's what Jamie wanted to do. And now . . .' He swallowed hard. 'Well.'

And now they're both gone, thought Famie. She handed the photo back. He slid it carefully into his wallet.

'Have you been to Jamaica, Miss Madden?' he said.

'I'm afraid I haven't,' she said. And then, because she couldn't think of anything else to say, she added, 'Whereabouts in Jamaica are you from, Mr Nelson?'

'The most beautiful part,' he said. 'Negril. Far west of the island.' The hint of a smile. He offered no further information and Famie didn't ask. The train was slowing through green fields and rows of vines. Dorking next stop. She hoped for a cab. And for Sara to be at home.

'This is our stop,' she said.

'One question, Miss Madden,' said Nelson. 'Might the press be at Jamie's house when we get there? Because I said nothing when they came to me at home. In Negril. And I will say nothing here also.'

Famie was off the boil. Of course, the hounds of the press would be there. What was she thinking? If they knew Jamie's father was in the country, and they did, and if they knew Jamie's address, and they did, they would be camping out in Flint Hill Close for sure. And when Brian Nelson, 'father of the arsonist', turned up with Famie Madden, 'best-selling journalist', all hell would break loose.

They got off the train. Three other passengers alighted, and Famie watched them disappear down stone steps. Her phone buzzed. Number withheld. 'Huh.' She answered the call.

The irate voice at the other end was Sara's. 'Is this your doing?' she shouted.

33

The minicab dropped Famie and Brian Nelson round the corner from Jamie's house on Flint Hill Close. It was too late to change anything now. She had committed to Brian Nelson, and she wasn't going to leave him. Hell, he wouldn't even be here if she hadn't suggested it. She had explained in the cab that there would be a press gauntlet to run, that she would lead the way and that Sara would open the front door as they approached. He would see his son's room, maybe learn from Sara more of how he had lived, then get the minicab back. He would be in his hotel by the evening and on the plane home to Jamaica by tomorrow lunchtime.

She had spent most of the short ride from the station pacifying Brian. They sat side by side in the back. Nelson's anxiety radiated in waves, his agitation so severe that his seatbelt tightened as if responding to a crash. The driver glanced in his mirror. 'You all right, mate?' he said.

Famie leant forward. 'He'll be fine,' she said. 'Had a rough day.' She held Nelson's arm with both hands. 'You follow me, Mr Nelson. You don't say anything. Let me do the talking. And I apologize in advance for any bad language I might use.' He nodded. 'Here we go, then.'

They got out of the car and Famie threaded her arm through Nelson's. They had twenty metres to walk before they were visible to anyone outside Jamie's house. She dictated the pace. 'We keep going, Mr Nelson. You hold onto me and we keep going.

There'll be lots of shouting. And jostling probably. Keep your head down or look at me. We walk with confidence, okay? And, Mr Nelson?' She stopped, he stopped. He looked at her. 'We're doing this for Jamie.'

He squinted slightly, stood taller and led the way.

34

Famie counted five steps before they were spotted.

'There!'

'That's him!'

'Shit! Go!'

A dozen or so reporters ran towards them. Phones held high. Two men shouldered large cameras.

'Mr Nelson!'

'Brian, can we have a word?'

'Why was your son an arsonist, Mr Nelson?'

Famie pulled Nelson closer. 'Ignore them. Ignore them all. Walk fast.'

They lengthened their strides. The first reporters reached them, shoved phones and microphones at them. 'Excuse me!' Famie yelled. 'Excuse me and get out of our fucking way.' She turned her shoulder to the scrum and pushed. Brian Nelson held tight to her arm, tucked in closely. He said nothing. It was a rolling maul, all the way to the front door. Two phones came too close. Famie batted them away. They cracked together, fell to the tarmac. She trod on one, kicked the other. Their owners howled.

Nelson was now in lockstep behind her. Bodyguard and celebrity. Prison guard and convict. She locked her eyes on the red front door, three metres away. She prayed Sara was watching the melee, that the door would open and slam closed behind them.

'Brian, tell us why you're here!'

'Have you come to apologize, Mr Nelson?'

'Why are you supporting terror, Famie?'

Famie hated every one of them. They weren't her crowd, never had been, and these were the worst. She felt her jacket pulled sharply, then a restraining hand on her arm. She twisted, the hand fell away.

'Mr Nelson, why won't you speak to us?'

Two metres away.

'Mr Nelson, you owe us a statement!'

One metre away.

A red-faced man pushed his way between Famie and the door. 'Thought you cared about journalists, Famie Madden!' he shouted. She felt spittle on her face.

'When you are one, let me know. Now fuck off!' she shouted back. Then, to the door, 'And now would be good, Sara!'

Famie heard a bolt slide and keys rattle. The door opened half a metre. Sara reached out, grabbed Famie and pulled hard. Other hands reached for Nelson. The two of them collapsed inside, Nelson falling on top of Famie before rolling swiftly away. The door slammed shut. The hammering began.

35

Famie sat up. Nelson, already on his feet, offered her his hand, which she took. She looked around. A dilapidated hall, distressed carpet, stairs leading to the first floor. Unopened post on the bottom step. Unironed clothes on the second. A smell of damp and boiled pasta.

Sara stood, hands on hips, khaki shirt, black pencil skirt, DMs, two men next to her, both taller than her, both late twenties. Famie recognized the T-shirt one was wearing. Red, black and green vertical stripes, crossed with the words 'Roti Kapra aur Makan'. She pointed at the man's chest. 'Bread, cloth and house,' she said.

The man looked startled, then smiled. 'You've been to Pakistan?' he said.

'I was stationed there for two years. Long enough to spot a PPP T-shirt for sure.'

She was aware of Nelson, hands held in front of him, head down. 'I'm Famie Madden. This is Brian Nelson. Jamie's father. He wanted to see this house before he returned to Jamaica. Thank you, Sara, for opening the door. And sorry for the shitty people outside making your life so miserable.'

Sara held back. The two men stepped forward. The PPP man offered his hand. 'My name is Ali,' he said. 'Jamie was my friend, and I am very sorry for what happened.'

Nelson, stiff-backed now, shook his hand. 'Thank you,' he said.

The hammering continued.

The second man shuffled forward. Sandals, shorts, collarless white shirt. 'I am Fahad,' he said. 'We are all so sad about Jamie. He was a great guy.' Fahad retreated.

Sara placed both hands over her heart and took a deep breath. 'I have no words, Mr Nelson. That is the truth of it. I miss your son every day. I will always miss him.' Her eyes brimmed with tears, but she held Nelson's gaze. 'He was our warrior.'

Nelson nodded twice. 'He was,' he said. 'You knew him well.'

Sara wiped her eyes with a hand, and Famie wondered again about any relationship between Sara and Jamie. Lovers? Comrades? Her words suggested that both were possible.

'We have a few of his things that the police didn't take,' Sara said. 'I don't know how much you can manage, of course. Would you like to see his room? We put everything in there.'

'Thank you,' said Nelson. Sara led the way. Famie gestured for Nelson to follow.

Nelson held the banister, which shifted slightly under his weight. He removed his hand, then resumed his climb, hands at his sides. A small, carpeted landing, four closed doors. One had a small plastic green, black and gold Jamaican flag stuck on it.

'Jamie's room, obviously,' said Sara, pushing open the door. She went inside, Nelson and Famie following. It was a sunny room, a double-glazed window wedged open with a magazine, and below it, a cheap, three-shelf bookcase. A small built-in cupboard bore three unframed black-and-white photos stuck to its door, three faces in close-up. A single bed, no bedding. On the mattress, a supermarket carrier bag.

'His clothes are in the cupboard, Mr Nelson,' said Sara. 'I don't know if you . . . what you can . . .'

She's all at sea, Famie thought. 'Maybe we should leave you for a moment, Mr Nelson,' she said.

'Thank you, yes,' he said.

'Of course,' said Sara. They filed out, closing the door gently behind them.

The hammering stopped. 'Thank Christ for that,' said Famie.

The two women stood on the landing facing each other. Sara had her hair tied up loosely on top of her head. Exhausted, mournful eyes. She leant against the wall, hands behind her back.

'What did the police take?' said Famie, keeping her voice respectfully low.

'A laptop and a camera,' said Sara. 'That's all, we think.'

'Phone?' said Famie.

'Had it with him,' said Sara. 'Well, he did when he left.'

'What's in the carrier bag?'

'Some photos he took. And an old camera.'

'Did the police not want that?'

'They didn't know about it.' Famie felt a sudden tug, deep in her gut. She raised an eyebrow.

'He said it was his fun camera,' said Sara. 'The one he took walking. It's pretty battered.'

'How old is it? Does it use film?'

'No,' said Sara. 'Early digital.'

'So the photos would be on the laptop the police took?'

Sara took a beat, seemingly unsure. 'Some, yes,' she said.

'Meaning?'

Another beat. Famie assumed Sara was working out how far to trust her. As she had been since that first meeting with Charlie.

'The laptop had been full for years,' Sara said. 'He hadn't used it for ages.'

147

'So where did he download his new photographs?' said Famie.

'The SD cards are in that bag. The images are on my laptop.'

Famie's mind was racing. 'Forgive me, but were you—'

'We used to be,' Sara interrupted. 'Briefly. But it was still fine between us, so he carried on using it. He didn't keep many photos, deleted most.'

'How many are there?'

'Two hundred or so,' said Sara. 'About that.'

'Could I see them?'

Sara considered, then nodded. 'I think Jamie would have said yes. I mean, they're not very interesting. Just rural stuff really. The crowds and protest pictures he kept off the cloud. That's why he's kept the SD cards.'

Famie tucked two strands of hair behind her ears, folded, then unfolded her arms, paced the landing. There was no doubting the charge of adrenaline the news of the camera had provided. If she had a window into Jamie's work, the Flint Hill side of him, she might be able to piece together why he was in the West End Gallery in the first place.

'Is there an SD card in the camera?' she asked.

'There is,' Sara said. 'Quite a new one, I think.'

Famie's heart kicked up a notch. 'Have you looked at the images?'

'I have,' said Sara. Then added, as though in justification, 'I thought they might explain what happened to him.'

'And?'

Sara pushed herself off the wall. 'Maybe they'll make sense to you,' she said.

From Jamie Nelson's Instagram

You asked about my family. Well, here's a favourite photo of Fada. That's his favourite hat! He's had it for years. This must have been seven or eight years ago. I'm just out of school and we're heading for food somewhere. The expectation of food is always worth smiling about. Just caught him right, I think.

I miss Mother every day. I never appreciated her, you know? When she went, the house lost its anchor. We just drifted, Fada and me. We had no direction, but two captains who thought they knew what they were doing. We steered in different directions. One of us had to go. I think he's okay without me. I hope so. I email sometimes but writing this makes me realize it is not enough.

No brothers, no sisters. I think they tried. I asked sometimes but they were always uncomfortable. So I left it alone. We were happy! We worked well as a three.

36

When they re-entered Jamie's room, they found his father sitting on the bed. He was holding the camera, but he was looking at the photos. Actually, Famie realized, he was studying them. There were five A4-size black-and-white prints laid out on the bed. A row of two and a row of three. Even upside down, she could tell they were family portraits. Brian was top left, ten years younger maybe, wearing a fisherman's cap and smiling broadly. A woman Famie assumed was his late wife came next. Older than she was in the photo she had seen on the train but still clearly of her. She had her hands in the air and a face full of wonder, as though she had just seen the greatest magic trick. Then there were two of the Nelson family together around a table and one of a baby in a cot. Famie guessed Brian Nelson hadn't seen these photos for a long time. He hadn't noticed Famie and Sara's return. The photos had cast a spell. The women waited.

'These photos,' he said, without looking up. 'I would like these photos. And this football shirt.' He indicated a neatly folded claret and blue one at the end of the bed. 'Nothing else.'

'Of course,' said Sara. 'We kept the books and clothes. Just in case, you know . . .'

'I have my books,' he said. 'I have my clothes. I have no need of any more. But these pictures . . .' He put the camera down, gathered the photos, held them to his chest and closed his eyes. 'This is who we were,' he said.

Famie felt as if she was intruding. She scanned the bookshelves for anything on video games, saw nothing but took a picture anyway. She perched on the corner of the bed. 'Mr Nelson,' she said, 'I was wondering if I could have a look at the camera, maybe see some of the images.'

He kept his eyes closed. 'Take it, Miss Madden. And if you could leave me for a few minutes? Maybe then I'll be ready to leave.'

Sara led Famie back down the stairs. Jamie's camera looked like the type everyone had had at the turn of the millennium. It was a small silver Konica. No case, no strap. It could have fitted in the palm of one hand but Famie held it in both. Like a holy relic. It had in-built flash top right, the word Revio top left and a zoom lens covered with a sliding metal cover. At the foot of the stairs, she pressed the 'on' button. The cover slid away, the lens whirred forward. 'Jesus,' Famie muttered. She sat on the bottom step and flipped the camera over. A large LED screen sat below the viewfinder eyepiece.

Sara leant over, pointed. Famie smelt citrus and chewing gum. 'If you press "play",' she said, 'it shows you the last photo taken.'

Famie's hands were clammy – she wiped each palm on her jeans. She had no idea what to expect, other than that Sara had seemed nonplussed by her viewing. She pressed the play icon. The screen lit up. A single tree filled the screen: a cherry tree in full blossom. It was an impressive photo of an impressive tree but not what Famie had hoped for.

'You'll get a lot of those,' said Sara. 'He loved trees.' She leant over Famie's shoulder again. 'You can tap these arrows to go forward and back.' Famie tapped. The sequence of trees ended eventually. Then came a run of crowd shots, a protest of some kind, a woman gluing herself and an older man to a fence. Three figures prostrate on a road. A muddied policewoman grabbing a man by his hair. The screen counter showed there were ninety-seven more images on the card. Famie tapped, pausing occasionally.

The door hammering resumed, then stopped again. Sara stood up, stepped over Famie. 'Tea or gin?' she said.

'Wine,' said Famie. 'Or, failing that, gin. Thanks.' She scrolled through everything. More people, more trees. She didn't slow down till she reached the last three. Ornate gates and a gravel drive in one. A blurred image of what look like a flowerbed in another. And then a woman in a doorway. Poorly framed, her face was partially obscured by curtains and her raised arm. She wore a full-length orange dress and trainers. Light brown hair tied back. Middle-aged probably, maybe older.

Famie got up and walked to where she thought Sara had gone. She found her in a small cluttered kitchen. The source of the smell: a pan of drained pasta sat on an electric hob. Sara sat at a wooden table, set with two empty tumblers and two bottles. 'Neat gin or with some flat lemonade?'

'Flat lemonade is my favourite,' Famie said. She held up the camera's screen. 'Who's this?'

Sara glanced at the woman in the orange dress. 'No idea,' she said. 'I wondered that myself. She's not on any of the other images that I could see.'

Famie placed the camera on the table and sipped her drink. It was disgusting. 'He's not going to take just three pictures somewhere, is he?' she said. 'He takes twenty or thirty at least. This must be the end of something.' She looked at Sara. 'We need the previous SD card.'

Sara left the kitchen, climbed the stairs, and Famie heard her knock on the door of Jamie's room. A brief, muffled conversation and she was back, with a small plastic box in her hand, a silver laptop under her arm. 'They're numbered,' she said. She showed Famie a Tupperware box full of SD cards and tipped them onto the table.

Famie flattened the pile with her hand, spreading the cards like Scrabble tiles. She turned them all number-side up. The highest was twenty-seven. 'So let's assume that's twenty-eight in the camera,' she said. She picked up twenty-seven and gave it to Sara. 'Go on, then,' she said.

37

Secure Digital Card twenty-seven began with the last image taken. The woman in the orange dress was still in the doorway, still with her arm raised but she wasn't partially obscured by the curtains. She looked furious, her face screwed up as though she was about to spit at Jamie. Maybe she was.

Famie touched the back arrow. The preceding photos were all of the same woman. Seen in reverse, the anger came late. The earliest images of her appeared to have been taken without her knowledge. Back to the camera. Lighting a cigarette. On her phone. A few indicated a reasonable conversation – in one she was even smiling. Then the anger, and the apparently swift departure.

'Any the wiser?' said Sara.

'Nope,' said Famie. She carried on scrolling back. More shots of Orange Woman's house and grounds, then a jump to a black front door. A small silver 26 above the letterbox. A Georgian townhouse. Very expensive. Now a man appeared at the door. Just the one image. Tall, muscular, cropped hair, neck tattoos under a white shirt and suit. Then wider shots of the street.

'Kensington,' said Sara.

Famie smiled. Charlie had observed after their first encounter with Sara how southern counties she had sounded, how 'properly' educated she had appeared.

'Your stamping ground?' Famie said.

'Hardly,' said Sara. 'But I worked in a clinic there for a year.

154

That's near Kensington High Street, I think. Cadogan Street possibly.'

'Well, let's try something,' said Famie. On her phone she googled '26 Cadogan Street London'. She got 'Mirabelle Holdings Ltd', and called Sam.

'Hey, it's me,' she said. 'Can you look up who owns Mirabelle Holdings, please? Offices in Cadogan Street, Kensington.'

'Sure. Hang on,' Sam said. A clattering from a keyboard. 'How's it going with Mr Nelson?'

'Good,' said Famie. 'Fill you in when I'm back.'

A brief silence, then a 'Ha!' from Sam.

'What?' said Famie.

'Like you don't know?'

'Sam! Just tell me!'

'Mirabelle Holdings is a property-development company owned by the Nash family. Helen Nash is the CEO. That what you wanted?'

The adrenaline kicked in faster than the gin.

'Well-well,' said Famie. 'Thanks, Sam, talk later.' She sat back on her chair, drank some more gin, googled 'Helen Nash' and 'Images'.

'Show me,' said Sara. Famie held up her phone. 'So the woman in the orange dress being doorstepped by Jamie was Helen Nash. That Helen Nash.'

'He having previously been at her company headquarters,' said Famie. She stared at her gin. She knew she and Sara were thinking the same thing. And a few days later, Jamie dies in the family's gallery.

But why would Jamie have been chasing Helen Nash? Famie wondered. At her work, then at her house. Or one of her houses. 'Can we keep the SD cards?' she asked.

Sara nodded. 'I don't think Mr Nelson is interested.' She

opened her laptop, then a file. Scores of photos appeared. 'And I don't think you'll be interested in these. Jamie's pastoral shots were the ones he separated out. No faces, no people.'

Famie agreed with Sara's assessment. But she had seen too many images now, knew she'd need another go at these. 'Is there some way we can keep in touch?' she said. 'I understand your reluctance before, but there will be . . . matters arising from all of this.'

Sara looked at her long and hard. Famie held her gaze. Sara's face softened slightly, and she held out her hand. 'Phone,' she said. Famie placed it in her hand. Sara typed a number, pressed send, then cancel. 'There you go,' she muttered.

Famie sighed. 'Thank you,' she whispered.

They heard Brian Nelson's cautious steps on the stairs. Famie needed a taxi and a swift return to London. She called Charlie.

'You know that really shitty idea you and Lena had,' she said, 'about me writing a Nash family profile in the *Mail*?'

Charlie's voice was caution itself. 'Yes,' she said, elongating the word considerably. 'I do remember that. And it didn't go well from my point of view.'

'Well, I've changed my mind,' said Famie. 'It's actually quite a good idea. And I've decided I'm doing it. If Mr Taylor is still interested, that is.'

Before they left Flint Hill Close, before the taxi that had to slalom through the press mob, Famie popped her head round the door of the front room. Ali and Fahad were both on laptops. The curtains were closed, and the room was sweaty and musty. In the far corner, a TV was freeze-framed on a zombie show. Two games consoles were stowed underneath. They looked up as she entered.

'Sorry to disturb you,' she said. 'I see you have some games there.' She pointed at the PlayStation and Switch consoles. 'Was Jamie into gaming at all? Did you all play together?' Both men laughed.

'He never got it,' said Ali. 'Never understood why we loved them so much. So, no. He never joined in.'

Famie nodded. 'Okay, thanks,' she said. 'And have you ever played a game called Thirteen? That's roman numerals. An X and three Is.'

They shook their heads. 'Heard of it,' said Fahad, 'not played it. Sorry.'

Famie smiled. 'Not a problem. Thanks again.'

From Jamie Nelson's Instagram

Okay, well, since you asked. I'd say this woman. Queen Nanny! Granny Nanny! Nanny of the Maroons. She fought the British. The first Maroon War was 1728. And here she is on our 500-dollar note. That's a fierce face. You want to look at our history? Start with Nanny.

And check out 'Red Gold and Green' by Kabaka Pyramid, or Chronixx and Protoje. Pivotal voices! Also 'Downpresser Man' by Peter Tosh. It's ancient for sure. My dad loves it. But that bass is something else. No one understands bass here.

38

The man with the red scarf sat on a creaking khaki canvas chair. His legs were crossed at the ankle, his arms folded, his eyes closed. The chair and the man rocked slightly as another narrowboat eased its way past the mooring. He didn't open his eyes. The Regent's Canal was always busy, particularly at weekends. The towpaths were rammed with cyclists, walkers and joggers, and the canal was as hectic as a canal can get. But he showed no interest in the boats. He showed no interest in the passers-by at all.

He sat with his back to a thin sliding door, which separated the cramped single bedroom from the rest of the boat. Twelve metres long, it was unremarkable in every way. Inside, a kitchen unit, a toilet, two benches with four cushions and a table. Everything smelt of diesel and dust. Outside, no ornamentation, no trimmings, no style. Black hull, dark blue box cabin, grey curtains at every window. It was by some measure the least interesting narrowboat on the canal. In a world where outlandish colour and decoration were the norm, the *Hilversum* was almost invisible. Which suited him just fine.

He wore loose-fitting jeans and a black T-shirt. The red scarf and a battered black leather jacket hung from the back of the chair. A Manurhin MR 73 revolver lay at his feet. At arm's reach, on the sink surround, a small glass of tap water and a phone. Every few minutes he reached for the phone, checked the screen, put it back and shut his eyes again. He was in his late forties, with long, wavy, rapidly greying hair, two days of white beard. His name was André Visser. His few friends called him Kenny Rogers. His employers called him City Boy.

His phone rang as he was falling asleep. He answered after one ring. 'Yes,' he said. He listened, reached for the water, emptied the glass. 'I know how this works,' he said. 'Tell me when you're ready.'

He hung up, replaced the phone. Refolded his arms, closed his eyes. Another passing narrowboat caused *Hilversum* to roll slightly. City Boy fell asleep.

39

Tuesday

Famie was early for her meeting with Howard Taylor, but she ran there anyway. She needed the thinking time and Ubers weren't much quicker. She had a water bottle in her hand, rucksack, with a change of clothes, on her back. She had no intention of meeting the man in her running vest and leggings. Charlie's warning had been clear: 'If you want this creep to look at your face, dress loose, dress unflattering.' She had met Taylor's type before of course but this had to be different. She needed him on-side. She needed to reassure him. She needed him to trust her. If Taylor wanted a flattering, nothing-to-see-here, rose-tinted art-icle on the Nash family, she had to persuade him that that was precisely what she would write.

Game on.

This morning was warmer. Too warm for spring, Famie thought. The kind of premature heat that makes you worried for summer. Agar Grove had smelt even shittier than usual. She hopped, skipped and jumped over discarded takeaway contain-ers, empty cans and pools of vomit. She exhaled heavily as she took the right towards the Eurostar bridge.

Yesterday's events and conversations ran over and over in her head. Brian Nelson's quiet grief and quieter dignity. His request for just the four photos. Sara producing Jamie's camera. The sight of Jamie visiting Helen Nash at home and at Mirabelle

Holdings. Sara's laptop stash of his other images. Quite a day. She had left Brian Nelson at Victoria Station with directions on how to find his hotel. He had shaken her hand and said he hoped she would be a 'duppy conqueror' for his son. She had said she would try.

At Gasholders she ran up the stairs, Lena let her into the flat – sky blue cropped trousers, white T-shirt, saddle-leather cross-body bag. She was on her way out. She looked surprised, 'Oh, hi, Famie,' she said. 'Charlie's just popped out . . .'

Famie grimaced. 'Ah. Well. No worries. You look amazing,' she said, dripping sweat on the carpet. 'And I look like shit. Charlie said I could have a quick shower before I meet Taylor upstairs.'

'Let me get you a towel.' Lena glanced back at Famie as they walked to the bathroom, smiled. 'If you went in like that, you could convince him of anything.'

Famie laughed. 'I intend to convince him, but dressed as an old maid,' she said. 'You going anywhere nice?'

Lena shrugged. 'Nah. Just the West End. To see Dad.'

Famie frowned. 'He's in the West End? I thought . . .'

'It's the King Edward VII Hospital,' said Lena. 'It's in the West End.' Lena reached into a cupboard, produced a thick white towel. 'He prefers it there.'

'I'm sure he does,' said Famie. 'And I've never thought about that before. Why is it the West End Gallery when it's not in the West End?'

Lena handed the towel to her. 'Not sure. Dad will know. I think it's because his grandparents had a house on Piccadilly or something like that. When you interview him for this piece – and thanks for doing it by the way – you should ask him.'

A few moments later Famie stood under the shower, the water pounding her head and neck. She thought her way through

162

the Taylor meeting. She had no intention of writing anything for the *Mail*, and nothing in her CV suggested she would. Taylor was smart. He would need to be convinced. She assumed he would hate her but his world was full of people he hated. One more wouldn't be a problem as long as she did as she was told. Which had never been her strong point. If she wasn't careful, she'd end up with nothing. And there was no question she needed officially sanctioned access to this weird, fucked-up family.

So, for now at least, she would play nicely.

40

In the Gasholders flat above Lena's, Famie sat across the table from Howard Taylor. They both had coffee and water in front of them. Famie had a notepad in her lap, a pen in her hand. She was wearing black balloon trousers, elasticated waist, and the largest hoodie she could find. It was grey and had the word 'House' in black letters across her chest. It had been a freebie picked up on her book tour. She had no idea what 'House' referred to and didn't care. It wasn't exactly old maid, but it was close enough and might mean she got through the meeting without punching Taylor.

Famie was convinced he was wearing exactly the same outfit as he had the last time they'd met: tired double-breasted grey suit, undone jacket, a straining white shirt and a red tie. His half-moon glasses were on his nose. He was looking at her face. 'You changed your mind, then,' he said.

Famie had expected more, but none came. Her turn. 'Well, Charlie told me about the photos.' She sighed deeply. 'And my first reaction was anger, Mr Taylor, I have to be honest. What a bloody stupid thing to do. To go on a march against your own family! I was cross with Charlie but furious with Lena. A girl like her should realize what a privileged position she holds.' Another sigh. 'I was surprised I have to say. Do you have children, Mr Taylor?' She was trying for a small win. An unexpected question. It didn't work.

'That's irrelevant,' he said. His expression was set. He was waiting for more.

'I decided,' said Famie, 'on reflection, that if I could help my daughter and her friend, why wouldn't I? What did the *Mail* say to you?'

Taylor leant forward. He produced an A4 envelope, spread some prints on the table. Famie peered at them. They were as bad as Charlie had told her.

'They said they had these photos and were planning to run them with a "spoilt rich girl" story,' he said. 'You know where it all goes from there, Ms Madden. "What we don't know about Britain's richest family" and all of that bullshit. It would be open season on the Nashs. And that is what I want to stop. What I will stop.'

Famie indicated for him to carry on.

'They are considering my suggestion of something racy for their online readers. The "sidebar of shame". I'm sure you know it. Two friends who live together, swim together . . .' Both hands moved in rolling circles in front of him. The implication was clear. 'You've seen the kind of thing they do,' he said. Then, as an afterthought, 'It would be classy, of course.'

'Naturally,' said Famie, gritting her teeth. She knew she was struggling. 'Just a – just a hint of tits and arse as opposed to all of it,' she said. Taylor's eyes were cold but his mouth was smiling. She found the disconnect deeply troubling. His was a cruel face. Her mouth had dried. She sipped her water.

'That's about it,' he said.

Famie wondered if she had been slow on the uptake. Taylor wasn't just a lecherous old lawyer, wasn't just an old-time wheeler-dealer with one hand down his pants. Taylor was dangerous. A danger to her, to her daughter and her daughter's friend. But, still, she had to play. Famie forced the words. They came slowly. 'But classier still,' she said, 'and crucially more tempting for their sales and marketing, if we offered an exclusive look into the private world of the Nashs . . .' she made herself repeat his words '. . . Britain's richest family.' God, she hated this. 'And all of it controlled by you.' And if he doesn't go for that, she thought, I have nothing left.

He clasped his hands together. The cogs were turning. 'Maybe,' he said. 'Within certain parameters I could make that work,' he said. 'Actually, just one parameter. Absolute copy and image approval. That's it. Not a word, not a photo that hasn't been sanctioned. And all of it will be Nash family copyright, including the photos you don't use. If you go off-piste in any way, we sue your arse for everything you have. And ruin your name.' He folded his arms. 'All right so far?' She nodded. 'One interview with each of them, no longer than thirty minutes. Three thousand words. You can live with that?'

Famie nodded, not trusting herself to speak.

Taylor leant forwards. He was sweating in spite of the aircon. 'And also,' he said, interlocking his fingers and tapping his praying hands on the table, 'I would strongly advise you to be as vague as possible about all finances and personal relationships. Avoid childhood stories. Sober but friendly photos.'

No tits and arse, then, Famie thought. 'But, of course,' was what she said.

41

Lena Nash had stood in the lobby of the Gasholder flats for ten minutes. Sunglasses on top of her head, she had tucked her hair behind both ears, adjusted the bag strap across her chest, checked her phone. When it had rung, she had answered and left the building. She paused briefly to lower her sunglasses.

The path to Granary Square took her past the smarter clothes shops, the kind that are still closed at ten fifteen in the morning, then the smarter Indian restaurants, the kind that are open for breakfast. She checked her appearance in one of the windows, adjusted the bag strap, turned left into the square. On a day like today, the fountains would normally have been overrun by children racing in and out of the jets of water. But there were no fountains, no children. The square might be open again, but it was not that open. The lightest of breezes still brought small eddies of ash dancing round the café tables. The smell of smoke and cinders came with them. The students and office workers were back but the walk-through shoppers were walking through other shops. Somewhere there wasn't a floating, drifting, grey-and-white reminder that a man and a building had been incinerated.

Lena kept close to the tables, strode confidently to the art-college entrance. She went inside, placing her sunglasses back on top of her head. She raised her hand to greet the receptionist. 'Hey, Daisy,' she said.

The woman stood when she saw Lena, rising from behind a high counter. She looked stricken, reached for Lena with both hands, then burst into tears. 'I'm so sorry. So, so sorry,' she managed, then put both hands over her mouth. Lena pulled her into an awkward, across-the-desk hug, then broke away.

The receptionist, cropped blonde hair, early twenties, produced a packet of tissues. She offered one to Lena, who took it. 'How's your dad?' said Daisy. 'I heard he was in hospital.'

'He's okay,' said Lena. 'I'm going there next. As soon as I'm done with the insurance guy. I'll need the keys to the storage rooms, please.'

'Of course,' said Daisy, ducking behind the counter. Lena heard a small metal cupboard being unlocked.

'I mean he's not really okay,' said Lena. She waited till Daisy reappeared above the counter. 'He's in shock. In mourning. And he's fallen a couple of times too, which is why he's still under hospital observation.' Daisy handed over two keys on a brass fob. They clanked in Lena's hand. The keys opened the storage rooms. Inside, the strong room was accessed only via one of two master keys that Michael and Lena held.

'Sign here,' said Daisy. Lena signed the key log, or 'key movement register', as it was labelled. She had also signed the previous entry on the night of the fire. The night the firefighters brought the grab-list paintings to storage. Or the ones they could reach before everything burnt. 'I was wondering when you'd come in,' said Daisy. She leant in conspiratorially. 'How many did you rescue? How many were saved?'

'I can't remember exactly' said Lena, 'but not many. Not many at all.'

Daisy looked away, distracted. Lena turned. Behind her she

saw a short man in his sixties, open-necked shirt and chinos. One hand held a suitcase, the other was extended in greeting. 'Malcolm Harper' he said, 'Addington Loss Adjusters. I think you were expecting me.'

42

Lena unlocked the strong room, two locks, two keys with a ten-centimetre shank. Top and bottom. She stretched for the first, crouched for the second. The door swung open. Cool, conditioned air rolled into the room. Malcolm Harper stooped and stepped inside. Lena popped the lights. Six strips of neon flickered, then steadied. They revealed a small windowless room, steel walls, and floor to low ceiling racked storage. Yellow and blue metal adjustable upright frames, wooden shelves. Harper blinked theatrically. '*Fiat lux*,' he muttered.

'I'm sorry?' said Lena. She shivered in the temperature-controlled atmosphere.

'Let there be light,' he said, looking around. 'Apologies, old habits.' The storage units were three shelves high and full of paintings, framed and unframed. Some were stacked three or four deep.

'All yours?' he said.

'All ours,' she said. 'Some just arrived, some going back. Some we can't work out what to do with.' She shrugged. 'You know how it is.'

Harper turned to her. 'Which of these are salvage?'

'Far wall,' Lena said. 'Everything on the lowest level is salvage. All that was rescued from the list. It really isn't very much, I'm afraid. Everything else is storage. Waiting to be moved on. Or rehung. Back from when there was actually somewhere to hang them.'

Harper removed a file and disposable gloves from a suitcase, followed by a camera and a torch. He dropped to his haunches. He looked along the line. 'This is really it?' he said.

Lena bristled. 'You know the answer to that,' she said, her voice low. 'Yes, that's all that's left of my family's gallery. You have a record of what was hung at the time of the fire. Subtract these eight . . .'

'It's ten actually.'

'Okay, subtract these ten from the total. Everything else is gone.'

'Right you are,' said Harper. He pulled on the gloves. Lena watched as he scuttled along the row of paintings, all of which were covered with a square of grey fabric. He lifted each one as if it was a sheet in a morgue. He picked up each survivor, inspected it, smelt it, photographed it, then placed it back on the row. He switched on his torch, shone an ultraviolet light in a tight beam over every centimetre, replaced the fabric and wrote in his file.

After thirty minutes, his work was done. He stood, peeled off his gloves. 'There is no visible smoke or fire damage,' he said. 'Some chipping on three frames. That's my initial assessment. I'll need to come back obviously. You know how the art markets insist on pristine condition for everything. They'll need a lot of reassurance here, particularly after the fire.'

Lena nodded. 'Yes, of course,' she said.

He shoved the gloves into a trouser pocket. 'Is it your understanding that the fire and smoke detectors worked, Ms Nash? Did they do the job they were installed to do?'

Lena folded her arms. 'Yes I believe so,' she said. 'You'd have to check with the fire brigade. Certainly all the alarms were ringing when I got there.'

Harper wrote on his pad. 'And they were well maintained?'

She pulled a face. 'We have a service agreement with an alarm company. So I assume yes. I'll forward the details to you.'

He smiled. 'Appreciated,' he said. 'And one more if I may. When were gallery staff last present inside the building?' His pen was poised again.

'The day before,' said Lena. 'Then we closed for twenty-four hours. Because of the, well, the demonstration.'

Harper wrote some more. 'Were they all in?' he said. 'Were any staff absent?'

Lena shifted her balance from one foot to the other. 'I'll check the rotas,' she said. 'I can't remember, I'm afraid. Most of us were in, I think.'

Harper lost the smile. 'I'll need that information obviously,' he said. 'And you'll get that service agreement and the staff rotas to me today?'

'Sure.'

'I've appointed a disaster-management company to assist with the clear-up,' said Harper. 'I'm sure they'll have questions of their own.'

'Understood.'

'And I'm very sorry about your gallery, Ms Nash. A terrible loss.' He picked up his suitcase, exited the strong room. Lena hesitated, glanced again at the row of ten. She walked to the first painting, removed the fabric, took a photo on her phone and replaced it. She repeated the process with each of the ten, then followed Harper out. Double-locked the door.

43

Jamie Nelson's SD cards contained, in total, 2,027 images. Famie, Charlie and Sam studied each one until one of them said, 'Yes,' or 'No.' They were speaking to Sam's tech guy, an earnest Frenchman called Benoit. His face appeared on a laptop, one of four on Famie's kitchen table. He was curating a 'yes' file and a 'no' file. If there was anything on any of the images that one of them considered worthy of investigation it was a yes. As they weren't sure what they were looking for, there were many more yeses than nos. They had been at it since nine a.m.

The remains of their lunch had been cleared to the sink, the table not big enough to accommodate food and laptops. The door to the garden was open, a light breeze replacing the smell of pizza and sweat with wisteria and roses. No one noticed.

At around the five hundred mark, a run of ten images featured a smiling Sara. They appeared suddenly, then stopped. Sara had said they were an item 'briefly'. Famie guessed these photos chronicled the beginning and end of the relationship.

'Can you put those together, Benoit?' said Famie. We should send them to Sara.'

'Of course,' he said. 'Are we interested also?'

'I don't think so.' Famie stood, stretched. 'I know this is vague but somewhere in these photos there must be clues to what Jamie was working on, who he was investigating. We know he was interested in Helen Nash, but we haven't found any more of her.'

'Unless she's in one of the crowd shots,' said Sam, 'or big group photos. The face recognition software can only work relatively close up.' He looked at Famie. 'Can we look at the dates he was in Germany?' His tone was hesitant.

'Of course!' she said. 'GamesCom '22. And what are we looking for?'

Sam shrugged. 'Well, we know he was in Germany in August. If there's anything with the Thirteen game, that would be interesting. Even if everyone else thinks it's a mad idea.' Sam explained the game and the possible link to Charlie and Benoit. The Frenchman didn't react.

Charlie smiled. 'When you said out loud assassinated the President of America,' she said, 'I wasn't sure whether to laugh or cry. I think mainly I'm laughing.'

Benoit was scrolling back through the images. 'August one' he said. 'Here you are.' He clicked through the file. The images were coming up on all their screens.

Famie leant in to hers. 'Dorking, Dorking, don't know but probably Surrey. More Surrey. Food. Looks like the kitchen in Flint Hill Close maybe.' Benoit clicked on.

'Stop,' said Sam.

The image on-screen was a cobbled market square, tall, elegant houses on two sides, black spired church.

'Not Dorking,' said Famie.

'Not England,' said Benoit. He zoomed in on the road signs. '*Voilà*' he said. '*Willkommen*. Welcome to Germany.'

'Geolocation time,' said Charlie.

'Where in Germany are we looking? asked Benoit.

'Try the Cologne area,' said Sam. 'Radius of, say, fifty miles.'

This was one of Benoit's specialities. He had shown Famie how to use the basic tools of geolocation and explained how it had revolutionized their research. Google Earth now gave anyone views that had previously been available only to governments and their intelligence services.

They watched him work. On a page called OpenStreetMap, he clicked on the tabs marked 'recognizable features'. Church. Square. Three-storey buildings. Four-storey buildings. Then a sliding bar. 'Maximum distance between features': he left it on the default '100 metres'. He scrolled, then adjusted the map to roughly fifty miles around Cologne. Hit the search button. They watched a blue bar scroll across the screen.

'I think it is too big a search area,' said Benoit. A minute later he was proved right. 'No results' appeared on the screen. 'We need more information.'

He went back to the roll of Jamie's images. Moved on from the market square. Click. Click. Click. More of the square. Click. A change. This one was half water, half town on a hill. The water-side properties were painted cream and red. Not especially grand, municipal even. Behind them, a steep slope and what appeared to be ruins of some kind.

'That's more like it,' said Sam, his nose almost touching the screen. 'Could that be a castle?'

'Enough for you to use, Benoit?' said Famie.

'On it,' said the Frenchman. He added the new information, searched again. 'No results.' A groan from everyone, bar Benoit. 'This is not magic, you know,' he said. 'I just need more information.'

Click. Click. Click.

Another street view, two cars parked in front of a gathering of around twenty people. Well-dressed, well-heeled. But he wasn't looking at the people.

'THL,' he said. He scrolled back through the photographs to the square.

'TH what?' said Charlie.

Benoit had zoomed in on the three closest parked cars. The first three digits on two of the registration plates were THL. More rapid typing. 'The first letters of the registration plate show where the cars are from,' said Benoit. 'And these cars are all from Thuringia. Central Germany. Near Bavaria.'

'Which is a small enough area to search?' said Famie.

Benoit said nothing. He was reframing the search map.

'And not near Cologne. At all,' muttered Sam.

'Three hundred and seventy kilometres,' said Benoit. 'Approximately.'

'Thanks, Benoit,' said Sam, defeated.

Three boxes appeared under the map.

'We have three hits,' said Benoit. He clicked on the coordinates under the first box. A small street map appeared. He switched to the satellite image. 'And there we are,' he said.

Famie, Sam and Charlie leant in. Then Famie stood up. 'So on August the thirteenth, 2022,' she said, 'Jamie was in a town called Bad Lobenstein. In the state of Thuringia, central Germany.'

'Bad what?' exclaimed Charlie.

'*Bad* means spa in German,' said Benoit. 'So it's Lobenstein Spa. Like Leamington Spa.'

'Understood,' said Famie. 'Thanks. But what the fuck was he doing there?'

44

The answer was not long coming. The next six images were of an elaborate church-like building. Its windows and central door were arched. Two stone lions sat at either side of the entrance steps. Painted white, it had a central tower crowned with battlements, and underneath,, a massive antlered stag's head. A twelve-pointer.

'Typical German neo-Gothic shit,' said Benoit.

'Yes,' said Famie. 'And a hunting lodge by the look of it.'

'Jagdschloss Waidmannsheil,' said Benoit, reading from his screen.

Sam was on the same page. 'Jesus Christ,' he said.

'Are you translating or exclaiming?' said Famie.

Sam had gone white. He swallowed twice. 'Jagdschloss Waidmannsheil,' he said, speaking slowly, as though he couldn't believe what he was reading, 'belongs to Heinrich Reuss, a German real-estate developer. His full name is Heinrich XIII Prinz Reuss.' Famie had caught up now.

'That fucker? The guy who was planning a coup?' she said.

Sam read on. 'Reuss is a far-right activist. A member of the Reichsbürger movement. A follower of anti-Semitic conspiracy theories.'

'Inevitably,' said Famie.

'He was arrested,' said Sam, 'by German Federal Police, when more than three thousand police launched dawn raids on

December the seventh, 2022.' They were all standing now. Sam paced to the garden door, then turned.

'And there's the Thirteen Jamie was talking about,' he said. 'It's not a video game. It's a fascist group. Jamie was tracking the German far right.' Famie was buzzing. This was now starting to make sense. There was a story here. She had no idea where it was heading but at last a piece of the jigsaw had fallen into place. She hadn't had such an adrenaline kick since Coventry.

'Benoit, keep scrolling through the pictures,' said Famie. 'The coup attempt was December. This is August. Did he know ahead of time? Keep going.' Benoit clicked through the roll.

'Stop!' called Famie. 'Back one.'

Click.

The market square again, this time with some kind of festival going on. Brass bands, marquees, street-food vendors.

'Forward one,' said Famie.

Click.

A white-haired man has his raised hand in front of a video camera. The operator and a man next to him are recoiling.

'Next one.'

Click.

The camera man and his friend are on the cobbles. Both appear to be in pain.

Charlie put up her hand. 'Got this!' she said, voice raised. 'Local journalist wrote it up. Dude with the white hair is the town's mayor. He's just been filmed in conversation with our Heinrich the fucking Thirteenth and a member of the far-right AfD. He attacks the journalists and one of them ends up in hospital.'

'Okay, so go back one,' said Famie.

Click.

'There he is, at the table with the mayor,' she said. The image

178

showed an older man, lime green suit, greying wavy hair, standing with a younger man, short brown hair, blue suit.

'Guy in the green suit. That's him,' said Famie. 'Hello, Heinrich. How's prison going?'

'Found the footage,' called Benoit, from his screen. 'It's still on X.'

Their screens switched to a letterbox format. When Benoit pressed play, they followed the action from a slightly different angle. They watched as the mayor set about the journalists. Famie stared at the screen. Her heart kicked up another notch. 'Play that again,' she said. Something in her tone made Charlie and Sam stare at her. The video played. 'Stop!' Famie yelled. 'There! Over the shoulder of the AfD guy!' The freeze-frame showed a man and a woman. Younger man, with an older woman. She had long hair, tied back. Orange dress, white trainers. Sam gasped. Charlie put a hand in front of her mouth.

'Well, well,' said Famie. 'Helen Nash.' She leant in close. There was no doubt. 'And *sieg* fucking *heil* to you too.'

From Jamie Nelson's Instagram

I'm on the German trail. Can't decide about these Reichsbürgers. So fringe. So old and hilarious. Hard to see them as a threat. But did Weimar journalists write about the NSDWP and the DAP like that? Fringe until it wasn't. And by then it was too late.

So XIII is a lunatic. And HN enjoys his company. That's all you need to know. The fight in the tent was nothing really. Apart from how quickly it turned nasty. I assume you've seen it. If not here's a link. Until the punch, I was afraid that I would be the centre of attention. There's about 100 in the tent and 99 are white. Not just white, but far-right white. That's a wholly different shade of stupid. But XIII is old money. Land, castle, all of it. If I had money to invest in the new Reich, I'm not sure these people would be on the list. But maybe they said that about the Deutsche Arbeiterpartei and the Nationsozialistische Deutsche Arbeiterpartei. And obviously HN sees it differently.

But these people are everywhere. So we need to fight them everywhere.

45

The December photos were less revealing. Jamie had taken versions of pictures Famie had already seen. There were around twenty of Heinrich Reuss in orange corduroy trousers, green jacket and handcuffs being escorted from his house by police in balaclavas and all-black commando uniforms. Others showed similarly clad officers removing cases, computers and boxes. Jamie's photos were, in truth, less revealing than those online and only showed Reuss's arrest. No Helen Nash present that Famie could see.

Benoit signed off, and Sam summoned an Uber. Famie and Charlie took cups of tea into the garden. The late afternoon was cloudier, the air heavier. Famie's shirt had stuck to her back. She pulled at the cotton, eased it away from her skin. 'I think I smell,' she said. 'Do I?'

Charlie leant close. 'Nah. Not much anyway.' She dragged two grey metal garden chairs together. They sat facing the far wall. 'Does it still say "Made in Turkey" on the other side?' she asked.

Famie shrugged. 'Remarkably, I'm not being updated on the council's anti-vandalism activities,' she said, 'but my guess is yes. The other side of that wall still bears the mark of the bastard who was planning God knows what for me. Then ran away.' She sipped her tea. 'I'd actually forgotten about him for the moment,' she said.

'Sorry,' said Charlie.

Famie shook her head. 'Not a problem. Reminds me what I need to be thinking about. What I should be thinking about. Whoever climbed over that wall, it wasn't Heinrich the Thirteenth.'

'That would have been a surprise!' said Charlie, laughing.

Famie kept silent. Truth was, Charlie was right. The wall climber, whoever it was, might return. That was the big threat. She should be working on the Turkish invader, not the German pretender.

But it was Jamie's work that had captured her attention. His father Brian's dignity was part of it. His flatmate and former lover Sara's loyalty was also part of it. But seeing the footage of Helen Nash at the fascist fair, at the table next to the man who was currently in prison for insurrection, was too good to leave alone.

'You're working out your questions for Fräulein Nash, aren't you?' said Charlie.

Famie smiled. 'Not exactly,' she said, 'but I'm getting there. Somehow Jamie had discovered that Helen Nash was involved with the far right in Germany. Maybe elsewhere as well.'

'Do we know that?' said Charlie. 'They could just have been having an affair or something.'

'They could,' said Famie. 'Of course they could. She might be the kind of woman who goes for a man in orange trousers. But Jamie had found something that took him to her house, then all the way to Germany a few times. And then to the gallery. Which burns down as soon as he's inside.' She swatted at a mosquito, missed.

'Did Sara tell you anything more about Jamie? Feels like we need to know about him if we're going to . . .' asked Charlie.

Of course, thought Famie. She jumped up, ran inside the house.

'Mum?' said Charlie, calling after her.

Famie grabbed her phone off the charger, ran outside and slumped back into the chair. 'I took a photo of his bookcase just before I left. Look.' She swiped through some photos of the press scrum outside the Dorking house and two she had taken of Brian Nelson at the station. Then it was the bookcase. She enlarged the image. 'Here.' She leant over to Charlie. The phone's screen showed a tired bookcase. It held three shelves, each one jammed with books. The top shelf seemed to be full of works by photographers.

Charlie called out the titles, head tilted. '*Photographs Not Taken* by Will Steacy,' she said. '*The Social Photo* by Nathan someone.' She squinted at a big red book with black and white letters along its spine. '*New York* by William Klein.' She looked at Famie. 'None the wiser so far.'

Famie's eyes were darting ahead. She saw novels next, nothing exciting or startling she thought. Bottom row. Left to right. 'Here we go,' muttered Famie. 'Look at these.' She stabbed her finger at the screen as she read. '*The Radical Right in Germany, Germanic Tribes, the Gods and the German Far Right, White Supremacy in Western Europe, The Politics of Fear*, and so on.' Famie stared down the garden. 'Who knows what we'll find?' she said. 'But Jamie clearly thought Helen Nash was a white supremacist.'

Charlie had her phone out. 'Mum, look at the last book,' said Charlie. She pointed at the phone. Famie enlarged again. Black cover, red letters. 'I've just looked it up.'

'*The Grey Wolves of Turkey*,' Famie read. Her skin was prickling. She looked at Charlie. 'Go on, then, tell me,' she said.

' "The grey wolf salute is a Turkish hand symbol," ' read Charlie, ' "thumb holding down the third and fourth fingers. It is often compared to the Nazi salute." '

Famie closed her eyes. 'So,' she said. 'Made in Turkey.'

46

Thursday

Two days later, Famie got the call from Howard Taylor. Helen Nash would be at her Soho club that afternoon between three and four. He would sit in, record the conversation. He reminded Famie of the rules. She said there was no need.

She took half the journey by tube, then walked. Noise-cancelling headphones played Bach. It slowed her pace, eased her impatience. The solo piano was as stately as it was delicate. Famie allowed herself to walk at tourist speed. Baker Street, Madame Tussaud's, Harley Street, Oxford Street. Queues, shoppers, hawkers, beggars. Famie was oblivious to it all. She played the meeting in her head. Visualized the contest. There was little doubt that Helen Nash had the advantage. Her club, her consigliere and his rules.

This interview, Famie thought, was almost certainly Taylor's idea. She didn't think for a moment that she would find an eager-to-please interviewee. She had found no interviews with Helen Nash in the last ten years and precious few before that. There were a few magazine profiles and photos from when she had made a stab at being a pop star. A 1989 photo shoot showed her with big hair, tiny shorts and Madonna levels of jewellery. The copy beneath declared breathlessly that her debut album 'would send pulses racing'. Famie had found no evidence for that. On the contrary, it seemed to have disappeared without trace. She concluded that Nash had clearly been a rich girl playing at being a star. When that hadn't fallen into her lap, she'd given up. Her brief Wikipedia entry suggested she had become fully involved in the family businesses soon after. It linked to her father Harry Nash, who seemed to have run the company until he had died two years previously. There was mention of her mother's suicide in 1981. It said her full name was Helen Marion Nash and that she was fifty-seven. No partners, no children.

And that was it. There was no Nash family website. There was no mention of her on the West End Gallery's site. She had no social-media presence. This was a woman who did not court attention. Famie knew she had her work cut out.

She turned down Greek Street in Soho and found the club between a coffee shop and a high-end restaurant. A discreet black front door, a small brass plaque, 'The Pothunters', in etched letters. A single bell on the frame. Famie took a breath. She hated private clubs. Hated the dress codes, hated the smugness, hated the barely suppressed masculinity. She pressed the button. 'This could be a fucking car crash,' she muttered.

47

A woman in a silver grey cocktail dress opened the door, smiled, stepped aside. 'Welcome to the Pothunters,' she said. Edinburgh accent. 'Who are you meeting today?'

'Helen Nash,' said Famie, catching the woman's glance at her outfit. Yes, I am bloody smart enough, thought Famie. A dark green jumpsuit with a white T-shirt was as smart as she was prepared to get for anyone. Charlie had approved, and that was good enough for her. The woman consulted her screen. 'Second floor, turn right. Miss Nash and Mr Taylor are in the grey booth. Just by the entrance to the library.'

When the doors of the lift had closed, Famie shook her head. 'Of course they have a fucking library,' she breathed. 'Where else would you go to borrow a book?' The lift slowed. 'Best behaviour, Famie,' she warned herself. 'Best behaviour.'

The lift door opened, she turned right. Swing doors led to a large, tennis-court-sized room with high ceilings and low sofas. Laptops were open, business was being conducted, and small plates of food were being served. She smelt citrus and leather.

Around two sides of the room, small booths offered more privacy. The decor of each was different, and only one was grey. Famie could see Taylor talking animatedly, presumably to Nash, who was hidden by the grey wall. Next to their booth, through open double doors, there were shelves of books.

Famie was nervous. This was uncharted territory. She would be having a conversation that had to be trivial yet deadly serious.

Gossipy and discreet. Jamie Nelson's pursuit of Helen Nash had cost him his life. You need to get your shit together, she told herself.

She followed the booths around the room, taking the long route to Taylor and Nash. Eight on each side, all busy. She caught snatches of conversation as she passed, all sotto voce, except one. Helen Nash she could hear from across the room, jumping in on a conversation, disagreeing loudly with Taylor. Maybe she's losing her hearing. Famie hoped their conversation would be quieter.

One booth away, Nash was still holding forth. Famie took a breath and walked into their view. Taylor reacted first, briefly trying to stand. A baseball-capped Helen Nash carried on talking and finished her sentence. 'I think that's the problem, Howard,' she said. 'You need to fix it.' She turned to Famie. A killer smile. 'Famie Madden. How wonderful to meet you.' She offered her hand. Famie shook it. Silver rings on her thumb and forefinger. Three silver bands around her wrist. Her face said mid-forties. Her hands told the truth. 'Come in, sit next to me,' she said, patting the seat. 'I'm so much nicer than Howard.' The smile again, a brief laugh from Taylor.

Famie sat. Nash also smelt nicer than Taylor, thought Famie. Her side of the booth was like a high-end perfume shop. 'Thanks,' she said. She nodded at Taylor. 'Hi,' she said.

'Good afternoon, Ms Madden,' he said, his manner brisk.

'I read your book,' said Nash. 'What a story!'

'Oh,' said Famie, surprised. 'Thank you. Yes, it was a scary few days for sure.' She twisted so she could look at Nash rather than Taylor. She guessed she had only just read it. Preparation for this interview, she thought, doubtless suggested by Taylor.

He leant forward, placing both hands on the table. His words were for Nash, but he looked at Famie. 'Ms Madden has agreed to all the terms,' he said, his voice low. 'We have a maximum of thirty minutes together. Less if that is possible.' He made a show of starting a timer on his phone, then placed it in the middle of the table.

Helen Nash touched Famie's arm. 'My understanding is that this is going to be a nice piece,' she said. 'A warm piece. To take the heat off your daughter and my wayward niece. Is that how you see it?' Another smile, and she removed her hand.

Someone is taking control, thought Famie. And her quiet voice was scarier than her normal one. 'That's the plan,' said Famie, producing a pad and pen from her bag. 'Charlie is very grateful to you. And your brothers.' She found a recording app on her phone. 'This is just a back-up,' she said.

'I'm recording it also,' said Taylor. 'Just so we're all clear.'

Famie kept her eyes on Nash. Let's start easy, she thought.

48

'Tell me how you see your role in the company,' said Famie.

Helen Nash sipped a cup of Earl Grey. She adjusted the shoulders of her white linen blouse. Picked at a seam in her jeans. She smiled again, then squinted at Famie. She spoke softly, catching Famie by surprise. 'Well, Famie, that question is as dull as ditchwater,' she said. 'Who cares what I do? Try something else.'

Famie forced a smile, considered her options. 'My job here is to write a revealing article that actually isn't revealing at all,' she said. 'I think we agree on that.' A small nod from Nash, nothing from Taylor. 'So let me put it like this. How do you and your brothers divide the responsibilities of running the West End empire?'

Helen Nash's face was impassive. For a moment Famie thought she would stonewall again. Then she nodded. The question had passed muster. 'Oh, well, Michael is the dreamer, the artist if you like. Robert is the numbers guy. Future projects usually come from him. And I sort of flit between them. Helping out where I can.' A ditzy smile.

Okay, well, this is all bullshit, thought Famie. I know you have your own companies. That's why poor Jamie followed the trail to your offices. But I'll follow where you lead.

'Of course, you were a pop star for a while. Back in the eighties.' Famie noticed a brief Taylor smile and nod. Maybe this was what he wanted more of. 'I imagine it must have been difficult to force your way in after that.'

'Precisely right,' she said, smacking the table. 'They'd stitched the whole thing up without me!' She laughed loudly. The volume was back. 'I was the blowsy, gobby girl who'd tarted herself around the studios and clubs. They thought they wouldn't need me but I worked my way in eventually.'

'Was that fun? Being a pop star?'

Nash sat up straight. 'Are you kidding?' she said, 'My God, it was amazing!' Famie had her back to the room but she guessed everyone could hear Nash now. 'I had the best time. Being any kind of pop star in the late eighties was amazing. Concerts, studios, the clothes, the TV, the drugs, you name it.'

'Why did you stop?'

A beat. 'Lawyers,' said Nash. 'Lawyers screwed my contract. If you have the wrong kind of lawyers, you're fucked. I never knew that before.' Taylor fidgeted, suddenly uncomfortable.

The wrong-lawyers' remark was interesting and Famie was about to follow up but held back. Taylor would jump all over it. She tried a different tack. 'Could you have carried on?' she asked.

'I wasn't very good, of course,' said Nash. 'That's the truth. I know that now. But if I could have avoided the snakes and cowards in the record industry? Sure. Who knows? If I had had Howard here, back in '87, it might have worked for me. Once he's stopped staring at your tits, he does a scarily effective job.' She had emphasized the word 'scarily' with briefly wide eyes.

Taylor tapped a finger on the table. 'Moving on maybe,' he said. He wound a finger in a circular motion.

'Sure,' said Famie. Maybe he was feeling it. Maybe she was listening out for it, but Nash's finger-pointing and bitterness ran deep. It sounded like an anti-Semitic attack to her. The kind that had got singers into trouble before. Particularly the lazy, dumb or just racist ones. But moving on.

'What did you learn from your parents?' she asked.

Nash looked surprised. 'Oh, interesting,' she said. A few seconds of silence. 'I suppose we all learnt how to run a business, my brothers and I. We saw my father's drive, his attention to detail, his focus.' Famie waited for more. 'When my mother died,' Nash said, 'he thought about selling everything you know. The whole group. He wasn't sure he wanted to carry on.' Nash's voice was softer now. 'She had been ill for a while. But I guess she'd had enough pain.'

Famie stole a glance at Taylor. He seemed placid enough. She'd try pushing. 'Michael was just a baby then,' she said. 'Have I got that right?'

'He was the final straw, I'm afraid,' Nash said.

Taylor raised a hand. 'Maybe rephrase that, Helen?' he said.

A flash of irritation, then Nash relented. 'You're quite right,' she said. 'What I mean is, her post-natal depression was the last straw.' She glanced at Taylor. He nodded, then pointed at Famie.

Back to me, she thought. 'And what values did they instil in you?' she said.

'Traditional,' Nash shot back. 'No question. Respect. Decency. That kind of thing. They were old-fashioned like that. Throne and empire, Crown and country. That kind of thing.'

Famie felt the little snagging hook again. 'Are they your values now?'

'They are. For sure. This company goes back a long way. We adapt, of course, take on new ideas when we need them, but we're proud of what we've built.'

'How far back can you trace the history?'

'Oh, Robert's the historian, not me. Ask him. Have you

spoken to him yet?' Famie shook her head. 'Well, he'll know,' said Nash.

'You must all have been devastated by the gallery fire,' said Famie. 'How much of a blow was that to the West End Group?'

Taylor shifted his weight. Played with his pen.

'Devastated is right,' said Nash. 'The accountants and insurers will do the numbers, of course, sort everything out. But it made me look at my own stuff in a different way.'

'How so?'

'Well, what would I save? If that happened to me, at my house, what would I grab? Isn't that what everyone's thinking?'

Famie knew she was being played, deflected from her line of questions, but it was a skilful move. She almost admired the precision of it. Some of the coverage of the gallery fire had played with the grab-list idea. Some papers had printed their own cut-out-and-keep forms for readers to fill with their valuables, ranking them in order of importance.

'And what was the answer?' Famie said. 'What would you save?'

Nash looked sheepish. 'Well, I have a painting of my first dog, Max. He was a black Schnauzer and I loved him so much. So I would grab that. My brothers will think that's ridiculous, but that's the answer.'

'What do your brothers think of you?'

'That I'm a bit of a crank. A new-age crank.'

'And are they right?'

'Well, I don't accept the mainstream narratives, if that's what you mean.'

Another tug. Famie needed to listen back to all of this as soon as possible. 'Do you have any heroes? Anyone you look up to?

'Anyone who doesn't accept the mainstream narrative.'

'Like who?'

'Anyone.'

193

Taylor's hand rose again. 'We'll send you a name,' he said.

Helen sat back. The smile was gone. Time for a rescue. 'And what do you enjoy most about your job?' said Famie, hating herself for asking such a limp question.

Nash spotted her discomfort. 'How very *Smash Hits* of you, Famie,' she said. 'But let's see. I suppose I like travelling. I get to travel a lot.'

'Favourite places?'

'Sweden and Norway for sure. Italy, Spain. And Germany. There's always a thrill visiting Germany.'

49

Famie speed-walked out of Soho, zigzagging north across Oxford Street and Great Portland Street to Euston Road. Where the pavements were full, she walked in the road. Cap and aviators on, she had a head full of Helen Nash. Famie felt energized. Whatever doubts she had about the 'article' had vanished. She drop-boxed the interview audio to Sam and Charlie, messaged, *Call you in twenty. Listen double speed?*

Most of the Nash conversation was not what Famie had expected. Nash had been more likeable, more open. Occasionally even bearable. But there was no doubt in Famie's mind that she was a far-right sympathizer. She used traditional conservative language most of the time, but her use of the 'mainstream narrative' phrase pushed her rightwards. Her blaming 'the wrong kind of lawyers' for her stalled music career probably took into her into anti-Semitic territory. 'The wrong kind of lawyers', in Famie's experience, was usually code for Jewish lawyers.

She walked into Regent's Park, still moving at a sweat-inducing pace. The paths were busy, the green spaces studded with picnickers, sunbathers and impromptu games of football. She looked for somewhere to talk to Sam and Charlie. A few hundred metres away, under a large oak, she watched a family gather their things and leave. Famie jogged there, then dropped to the grass. Notebook and phone in her lap, she took a breath.

Why had Jamie taken photos at Nash's house? Was he hoping

for a *mea culpa*? Did he think she'd confess? Had she recognized him from the tent in Bad Lobenstein? Famie checked her watch. Sam and Charlie should have listened to most of the interview by now. Earbuds in, she conference-called both. Sam picked up first, Charlie a few moments later.

'Mike Green and Danny Friedman,' said Charlie.

'Is that instead of hello?' said Famie.

'That's the answer to your first question,' said Charlie. 'The wrong lawyers. I just found them. There's even pictures of a very young Helen Nash with them. Signing a contract by the look of it. I'll send it to you.'

'Are you on headphones, Charlie?'

'Yup. I'm in the flat but Lena's not here,' she said.

'"Wrong lawyers" is quite a tell,' said Sam. 'That puts her with the rapper who said Jews ran the record business. What was his name?'

'That was Wiley,' said Charlie. 'A few years ago. Called Jews cowards and snakes. Stuff like that.'

Famie whistled.

'Got something else,' said Sam.

'And that's your excited voice again,' said Famie. 'Let's hear it.'

'She used a phrase that sounded weird to me. When she was talking about her parents' values.' Famie realized she knew what Sam was about to say. It had jarred with her too.

'"Throne and empire",' continued Sam. 'She said "throne and empire". You heard that anywhere before?'

'No,' said Charlie.

'Don't think so,' said Famie. 'Another of your video games?'

'You're hilarious,' said Sam. 'I'll send you a document. Then you can say, "Thank you, Sam."'

Her phone vibrated, she clicked on the pdf icon. Felt her

pulse quicken. The page was headed 'Heil Dir Im Siegerkranz' and in brackets below 'Hail to thee the victor's crown.'

'What is this, Sam?' asked Charlie.

'It's the imperial anthem of the German Empire,' he said. 'The Kaiser hymn. Look at the third verse.'

Famie scanned the text, the English translation alongside the German.

Holy flame, glow,
Glow expire not,
For the Fatherland!
Then we shall all stand,
Valiant for one man,
Fighting and bleeding gladly,
For Throne and Empire.

Famie read it again, checked the German: *Für Thron und Reich.* She cleared her throat. 'Well. Thank you, Sam. And the case for the prosecution rests,' she said. 'Throne and Empire. Capital T, capital E.' Famie laughed. 'Holy shit.'

'Capital H capital S,' said Charlie. 'And never mind that all national anthems are terrible – "bleeding gladly", for Christ's sake. Whoever bled gladly, even in the deluded nineteenth century? But "throne and empire" as a phrase was obviously so much part of her vocabulary, her *lingua franca*, that she didn't realize what she was saying.'

'Unless she did and she didn't care,' said Sam. 'Did Taylor flinch when she said it?'

Famie thought about it. 'Not that I recall. But you heard him when Helen said that Michael was the "last straw". Weird way to talk about your brother.'

'You haven't got a brother,' said Sam. ' I can imagine my brother saying precisely that about me.'

Famie watched two men in suits sit on a bench ten metres away. One produced a carrier bag and sandwiches. She stood and walked round to the other side of the tree.

'I thought the "new-age crank" stuff was interesting too,' said Charlie.

'And followed by the old "mainstream narrative" bullshit,' said Famie.

'Are we in QAnon territory here?' asked Sam.

'It's quite possible,' said Famie. 'Which would plug the Nashs into a whole new level of batshit craziness.'

'There's some of that down at Camden Market now,' said Charlie. 'The stalls with the new-age hippie stuff. It used to be peace and love, beads and candles. That kind of thing. Now, it's mixed up with the anti-vaxxers, nine/eleven truthers and all that bollocks. Lena was talking about going to the market later. Maybe I should go with her. Have a poke around.'

Famie glanced around the tree at the two men on a bench. They were still eating sandwiches and hadn't looked at her. She told herself to stop being paranoid.

From Jamie Nelson's Instagram

The Reichsbürgers are well into this book. English title is *Regime Change* by some guy at the University of Notre Dame called Patrick Deneen. Don't buy it! I have a copy I stole from a far-right book fair (which was very satisfying. Imagine not noticing the only Black customer to visit their stall). Says the current elite need to be replaced with 'a better aristocracy brought about by muscular populism'. This is the way Mussolini spoke, for Christ's sake! These bastards are getting organized. This 'muscular populism' is an infection. Hungary has it, France has it, Israel has it, America (obviously) so the UK will follow. Back home we've had guns in our politics for a long, long time. Nothing good comes from this.

50

Charlie and Lena looked at home in Camden Market. Twenty-somethings, bright colours, sunglasses. The early-afternoon Sunday crowd jostled and queued, shouted and vaped. Street stalls traded tacos, samosas and bowls of katsu. The air felt drenched with dope and fried chicken. Music from everywhere played everywhere.

Charlie ate Korean from a carton; Lena had a wrap in a bag. They steered away from the old warehouses, where the permanent stalls were, towards the jewellery and clothing stands. These were the ones that would fold and disappear come sunset. Local vendors, homemade craft. The sellers all dressed the same. Big shirts, loose-fitting trousers, wide smiles.

On the walk from Gasholders, Charlie had told Lena the salient points of her aunt's interview with Famie and the possibility of some kind of drift towards the far-right.

'Wouldn't surprise me,' Lena said. 'She's always been something of a crystal stroker. But when she talks about "big pharma", climate change lies and her anti-vaxx bullshit, it feels to me as though she's drifted somewhere else entirely.' Lena pointed at a number of stalls they were approaching. 'And she's drifted here. Tin Hat Central.'

There were five stalls, all under one awning. An array of trestle tables displayed cheap watch straps and phone covers all with angel and serpent designs. There were incense cones, candles of all sizes and a selection of what could only be called wands. A handwritten sign declared, 'These are not toys. Handle with care.' Green quartz 'tumblestones' in jars 'relieve anxiety', rose quartz 'purifies your heart and promotes inner healing'. One stand devoted to what looked like tambourines with hanging tassels was labelled 'Dreamcatchers'.

'I mean, where to start?' muttered Charlie.

Lena pointed at a pile of newspapers. 'I'd start right there,' she said.

Two neat piles of tabloids sat in the middle of two of the tables. *The Truth* was writ large in a red box at the top of the cover page. 'Find out the whole story' was the strap line underneath. This edition's headline was 'The Lies They Tell Us'. A well-drawn illustration in blacks and browns showed cowed men and women in chains, a large fist hovering above them. On the other side of the table, a middle-aged woman, jeans and T-shirt, looked up from her phone.

'Help yourself, dear,' she said, pointing at the papers. 'First is free. It'll open your eyes for sure.'

Charlie hesitated. Lena stepped up. 'I'll take one, thanks,' she said. 'What will it open my eyes to exactly?'

The woman leant in, as though for a private word. 'You'll just know the questions to ask,' she said. 'Let's leave it there, shall we?'

'Okay, thanks,' said Lena, enthusiastically. 'Can my friend have one too? She always has loads of questions.'

'Help yourselves,' said the woman. She handed a paper to Lena and another to Charlie. 'Come back if your friends would like one.'

'Oh, we will,' said Lena. 'Thanks so much.'

They left the woman, both opening the pages of *The Truth* as they walked.

'Wow,' said Charlie. 'And I don't think she realized you were taking the piss.'

'Too much incense,' said Lena. 'Rots the brain.'

They ordered coffees from a converted black taxi by the canal, then perched on a low wall, facing the water.

'Okay,' said Charlie, 'so let's say you had to spend a weekend with either your aunt Helen or your uncle Robert, which would you choose?'

Lena's head dropped. She sipped her coffee. 'Really?' she said. 'They're the only options?'

'That's the choice,' said Charlie.

Lena stared at her feet. Swirled her coffee, sipped some more. Shifted her balance on the wall. 'Shit, Charlie. What a question,' she said. She swallowed twice. Clearly she was struggling.

'Hey, no worries, Lena,' said Charlie. She draped an arm over her friend's shoulder. 'It was just a joke really. Forget it.' Tears ran from under Lena's sunglasses. Charlie pulled her closer. 'Hey,' she said.

Lena rested her head briefly on Charlie's shoulder, then sat up and wiped her face with a hand. 'No, it's fine,' she said. 'Because it's the kind of question a lot of families would struggle with. But for very different reasons. Like, how do you choose when they're both so lovely?' Lena swallowed again, then continued more slowly: 'But for me, it's not quite like that.' Then, in a whisper, 'Not quite like that at all.' She started to shake. Charlie put a supportive hand on her thigh. Lena hadn't finished. 'But here's the answer to your question. If I had to choose, I'd rather stay with Aunt Helen because at least she hasn't got paintings of naked women on every available wall.'

'Fair,' said Charlie. 'You've seen his place, then?'

Lena nodded. 'One of them. And that's enough,' she said.

They both watched an extravagantly painted longboat chug slowly past.

Charlie sighed. 'What can your father think? How does he cope?'

There was a long silence. Lena stood up, brushed herself down. 'He doesn't,' she said. 'Not really. He pretends, of course. He's been pretending for years. It's just that I now realize he's pretending.' She sat down again. 'Maybe it's more obvious since Grandpa died. Maybe the pretence was for him.'

'Why would he pretend for his father?' said Charlie.

'Doesn't everyone?' said Lena. Charlie said nothing. 'My dad says his father was a difficult man,' said Lena. A silence fell between them. Lena shuffled on the wall. 'His wife, my grand-mother, took her own life. Soon after Dad was born.'

'How terrible,' said Charlie. 'Poor woman.'

'Post-natal depression,' said Lena. 'Apparently.'

'Apparently?'

'Dad doesn't remember, of course, but that's what Robert and Helen say. According to Dad, they kinda blamed him for their mother's death.'

'What?'

'Just when he was young,' said Lena. 'Robert and Helen were teenagers. Sixteen and thirteen. Bad time to lose your mum.'

'Weren't you . . .' began Charlie.

'Sixteen when my mother walked out?' said Lena. 'Damn right.' She drained what was left of her coffee. Charlie followed suit. They stood to leave. Lena hesitated, looked as though she had more to say.

'What?' said Charlie.

'Let's walk,' said Lena.

51

The smiling jeans-and-T-shirt woman had three new visitors to her stall. All men, all mid-thirties, each unremarkable. Two wore light chinos and dark golf shirts. The third was in jeans and a claret hoodie. The men stood around the woman while she talked, leaning in to catch every word. She looked angry, her words punctuated with stabbing fingers. Occasionally her eyes drifted towards where Charlie and Lena were sitting. A few seconds later, the men's heads turned in the same direction. She called them back, resumed her lecture.

As Lena stood, T-shirt Woman held up her phone to the men. They studied the screen, nodded and walked away. Claret Hoodie Man glanced at the departing women. He smiled briefly, lit a cigarette, then joined his colleagues.

They took no interest in the stall.

52

Charlie and Lena walked the canal path back to Gasholders. It was a slow journey, their every step obstructed by joggers and cyclists, but it was busily anonymous. They frequently stopped altogether, backing against the towpath wall to let everyone pass. Charlie took to walking half a step behind Lena, single file often the easiest option.

For ten minutes, neither spoke. Charlie watched Lena, and Lena watched where she was going. Then, around a bend in the canal, the Gasholder flats came into view. Lena began talking. Charlie tried to keep up.

'My family do a lot of good,' she said. 'The Nash Foundation and other charities they support hand out millions every year, usually to places where the government has given up. The arts in particular. Most theatre companies, dance companies and opera companies have benefited. Some wouldn't exist without Nash money.' Lena stopped to allow two cyclists to go by. Charlie pulled up behind her. They waited for a runner with a baby buggy to pass, and then they were off again. Lena picked up her family résumé.

'And it was Harry Nash, my grandfather, who started the philanthropy. Who knows why? He never really liked concerts or going to the theatre. Maybe it was guilt at all the money he'd made, I don't know.' A few more paces. Charlie stayed on her shoulder. Lena was concentrating. Measuring each word.

'Maybe it was guilt about Janet,' she said, 'his wife. That's what my father thinks.'

'Why would he feel guilty?' asked Charlie.

Lena shrugged. 'Maybe that's standard after a suicide,' she said, 'feeling you should have known what was happening. Feeling you could have stopped it.'

'I suppose,' said Charlie. 'Do you have any photographs of her?'

'On my laptop, I think. My dad has one framed. She's at the launch of some show or movie. Incredibly glamorous.'

'So she was the arty one.'

'I think so.'

They came to a short, moss-encrusted tunnel over the canal. The temperature dropped, and two children shouted to enjoy the echo. Charlie and Lena said nothing till they were on the other side, back in the sunshine.

'I know you've told me before,' said Charlie, 'but was it your granddad who made all the money?'

'Not exactly,' said Lena. 'From what Dad's told me, he refocused the company. He had less time for what he saw as the reckless endeavours of the past.'

'What were they?'

'Good question. He called his parents "cavalier". Old Harry pulled it all back together after the war.'

'Built an empire,' said Charlie, 'but lost his wife somewhere along the way.'

'That's pretty much it.'

'And without him, we wouldn't be staying here.' Charlie pointed at the looming Gasholders flats dead ahead. 'So thank you, Old Harry.'

Lena frowned. Charlie missed it.

Fifty metres behind them, just approaching the tunnel, a man in a claret hoodie lit a cigarette. He sent a text message.

53

At the kitchen table in Lena's flat, Famie, Sam and Charlie were poring over the pages of *The Truth*. Taken apart, there were eight sheets, printed on both sides. One copy covered the table. The other they spread on the floor. Each was anchored by a mug or cup. A breeze blew in from the balcony's open door. The loose pages flapped against the weights.

'It really is a spectacularly bad publication,' said Sam. He stood at the far side of the table, facing Famie and Charlie, back to the view. The sun was setting in a sky full of high wispy clouds. It turned the room orange. Sam cast a long shadow. 'Half of it is hokey, home-spun, harmless stuff. "How to make your own trousers", that kind of thing. Then, on the next page, "Was Mussolini Right?" It's pretty unhinged, really.'

'"We're only asking questions" is what Lena's aunt Helen would say,' said Charlie.

'Which is bullshit, of course,' said Famie, moving to the pages on the floor. 'They know precisely what they're doing. By merely "asking the question", you raise the tiniest possibility that it might be true. It's the oldest trick in journalism. "Did the archbishop shag his secretary?" The answer is no but the question mark does all the work. One, it gets you out of legal trouble. Two, it spreads the gossip. Job done. Total bastards.'

'But if your working assumption' said Sam, eyes till scanning the newsprint, 'is that you're being lied to, either by the "mainstream media", the "deep state", the "Zionist lobby" or whichever secret cabal you might think is controlling everything, then of course the archbishop has been shagging his secretary. So the fact that this story is only in *The Truth* isn't proof that it's cobblers. It's proof that it's true.'

Outside Gasholders, Claret Hoodie Man sat on a bench. He nursed his cigarette in cupped hands. When Lena Nash left the building, en route to the hospital, he watched her walk. When she was twenty metres away, he stood. And followed.

'I've counted fifteen adverts in total,' said Charlie. 'How much revenue would that bring in?'

'Not enough,' said Famie. 'Not considering the quality of the paper. By which I mean,' she added quickly, 'its overall aesthetic. The photographic quality. Not the content.' She pointed at a page near her on the table. 'There's a box, what you might loosely call an editorial, that says it's funded by donations from "readers and fellow truth-seekers around the world".' She crab-walked over to a page on her top row. 'Small box here. Page ten. "With thanks to the Always Ready Foundation". That's it. Never heard of them.'

'On it,' said Sam. He hit keys on his laptop, started reading. His eyes flitted across the screen. 'Okay, no surprises, really. Looks like a fundamentalist church in south London, off-shoot of a mega-church in Texas.'

'Is that mega or MAGA?' said Charlie.

'Er, both, I'd say' said Sam. He tapped some more. 'Also this from a pro-Democrat news site. It says that Always Ready Trust has become one of the most influential channellers of funds in republican and far-right circles. Last year they're thought to have accumulated three hundred and sixty million dollars. That's according to a tax filing they've seen.' Sam skim-read some more. 'Donor identities can be kept private, it says. And it's been called "a virtual ATM for dark money organizations".'

'Can they fund groups here?' asked Charlie.

'Can't tell you that,' said Sam. 'Not yet anyway.'

Famie stood up, stretched her shoulders and arched her back. 'If we could see the donors, what do you reckon are the chances that our Helen Nash would be up there?' Charlie and Sam looked up. Famie met their gaze. She smiled. '"Pretty high" is the answer.'

Claret Hoodie Man followed Lena along the underground walkways that led to the Metropolitan and City Line. He almost lost her in the throng of two-way, fast-walking passengers but just caught her left turn to the down escalator. By the time he was on its top step, she was just twenty metres away.

Charlie brewed more tea, brought the pot and three cups to the table.

'Which leaves us where?' said Sam. 'How does this affect the piece you're writing, or not writing, for the *Mail*?'

Famie had been pondering precisely those questions. 'I think I have to write a virtual *Mail* piece. Something I can show Taylor if he asks. And we may well need it to stop them writing about Lena and Charlie. Something soft and sugary. But the piece I'd like to write would be something else. Something harder. Something that our "Flint Hill" would approve of.'

Charlie poured the tea. Sam massaged his forehead. 'And what happened to him, Famie? I'm sure he was working on something he approved of. Something harder. And now he's dead.' He took a breath. 'There's a point we get to – maybe we're there already – when our personal security needs to be

209

considered. You, me and Charlie. We're beginning to see who we're up against. If the Reichsbürger movement were happily planning a coup, they or their comrades will be more than happy bashing a few Brits if they need to. And maybe there's a connection with the Turkey graffiti at your place, Famie. We don't know. But somewhere in all this, Jamie Nelson was murdered and the West End Gallery was burnt down. These are violent people.' He stood, paced to the large window and talked to the glass. 'I realize I'm going to sound like a total coward now but we need to proceed carefully here.' He turned, eyes on Famie. 'If you want to accuse someone in a very wealthy and powerful organization of financing far-right terror, you'd better be bloody sure of your proof. And have sufficient evidence when you get to court. We don't have a legal department but we'll definitely need one if we get this wrong.'

Lena travelled three stops to Baker Street. Her carriage was half full. She perched at the end by the door, read her phone. She didn't look up. Eight seats away, Claret Hoodie Man read a free newspaper and watched her reflection in the window.

Famie had bitten down on her immediate reaction, which was indeed to challenge Sam's bravery. But she caught Charlie's side glance at her and knew that wasn't right. Not for the first time, her daughter had caused her to reconsider. And a moment was all it took.

Famie screwed up her face. 'Okay, you're right,' she said. 'I'm just charging forward because I've got the scent of these bastards. But I need you both on-side. So . . .'

'So what is the story you want to write?' said Charlie.

'Until I've spoken to Robert and Michael Nash, I don't know. Maybe there won't be one because the evidence won't be sufficient. Or the threat level is too great. Or both. In which case, maybe it'll be just the *Mail* puff piece after all. Which would be a bitch but there it is. Maybe the other two Nashs are as sweet as candy and raging liberals. Who knows?

'Although one of those sweet liberals also buys Pop Art with a distinct Nazi heritage,' said Sam.

A buzz from Charlie's phone. She stood and walked away from the table.

'Lena, hi,' was as far as she got before the yelling from her phone's speaker cut her off.

54

At the bottom of the escalator out of Baker Street, Lena noticed the man in the claret hoodie. He was three metres away. He was looking straight at her, making no attempt to hide. Thirties, unshaven. A shade over six feet. Jeans and scruffy trainers. He held his phone in front of him, clearly filming. She looked startled, started to climb. The man climbed too. He caught her up in three seconds.

'Can I ask you some questions?' he said. Lena ignored him, took two steps of the escalator at a time. 'I just want to ask you some questions,' said the man, his voice raised now, phone still in his outstretched hand.

'Go away!' said Lena. Heads turned above her.

'It'll take thirty seconds,' called the man.

'Fuck off!' she shouted. Taking three steps at a time now, Lena reached the top of the escalator, then ran to the ticket barrier. A heavy-set man in the blue and red uniform of London Underground staff stood, arms folded, watching the to-and-fro. Lena ran to him, turned and pointed. 'That man is following me,' she said, fighting breathlessness. 'Can you call the police?'

The Underground man reached for his radio. 'Sure, love. This bloke here?' The man in the hoodie strode over to them. The Underground staff member pushed Lena behind him. 'This woman says you're following her. I'm calling the Transport Police. Go away. Right now.' Lena was on her phone.

Claret Hoodie Man looked annoyed and continued to film.

'I'm not following anyone. I've never seen her before we were on the escalator just now.' He sounded indignant, strong Belfast accent.

'All the way!' shouted Lena, over the Underground man's shoulder. 'He's followed me all the way from King's Cross!' A stream of passengers flowed through the barriers, a few pausing to watch the shouting, phones out. More Underground staff appeared.

'She can't just make accusations like that!' yelled Claret Hoodie Man. 'What a bitch! We're just on the same route. That's all.'

'Why are you filming this?' asked the Underground man.

'It's for a documentary,' said Claret Hoodie Man. 'About who really runs the country.'

'Really?' said the Underground man. 'Well, the police will be here in thirty seconds. You can film them, too, as they arrest you. Then you'll know precisely who really runs the country. Now why don't you leave? Through that barrier. And right now.'

Claret Hoodie Man stepped closer. 'I just want to ask her some questions. Is that a crime?'

'Yes,' said the Underground man. 'And I thought you said you were "just on the same route"?' His radio crackled with code words. 'Police here in ten seconds. Why don't you argue with them?' Claret Hoodie Man made a lunge for Lena, catching hold of her shirtsleeve. He pulled hard. Lena screamed. Three Underground staff grabbed him and pulled him away. He stumbled, they let him fall. He cracked his head on the floor and dropped his phone. Two Transport Police officers appeared, vaulted the barrier, cuffed him.

Lena sat on the steps of Baker Street tube station. One of the officers stood with her. They both watched Claret Hoodie Man being bundled into a police car with its lights flashing.

'What a piece of work he is,' said Lena.

'Do you know him?' asked the officer. She was about Lena's age, blonde hair pinned neatly under her cap.

Lena shook her head.

'Any idea why he targeted you?'

'No. Not really.'

'Not really?'

'I don't know,' said Lena. 'He was outside my flat at King's Cross. Maybe he'd seen me before. I didn't recognize him.'

'But he knows where you live.'

'Presumably.' Lena sounded exhausted.

The police officer checked her notes. 'Are you one of the Nashs from that gallery?' she said. 'The one that went up in smoke?'

Lena's head dropped. 'Yes.'

'Might the man who followed you know that?'

'It's quite possible. I didn't get round to having a chat with him.'

'Of course.' The police officer flushed slightly. 'Will you be okay? I can get you dropped somewhere.'

'I'll be fine, thanks. Just visiting my father in hospital, actually.'

'Okay. We'll be in touch soon. Thank you for your cooperation.'

Lena watched as she walked to the police car. She stayed on the steps till Charlie, Famie and Sam ran out of the station.

55

They took a table at the back of the first coffee shop they found. As far as Famie could determine, they were the only group speaking English. Stock photos of Sherlock Holmes on the wall. Overpriced coffee, tired pastries, indifferent, inattentive staff. It suited them just fine.

Famie sat with her back to the far wall. She could see all the tables, the front door and the street. She watched Lena as she recounted her ordeal. She seemed remarkably composed, considering she'd been followed, yelled at and assaulted. Maybe it was breeding, Famie thought. Maybe the monied classes were just calmer than the rest of us. Lena's story unfolded to gasps from Charlie, studied concern from Sam. The fact that the man had been waiting for her outside Gasholders was what worried Famie most. This wasn't a random incident. If the flat there wasn't safe, Lena and Charlie would have to move.

'Did he follow you from the market?' asked Sam. 'That seems most likely to me.'

'No idea,' said Lena. 'We certainly didn't spot anyone, did we?' She looked at Charlie, who shook her head. 'But if he did, he can't know for sure that I'm living there. I could just have been visiting.'

'We have to assume he knows,' said Famie. 'It's not difficult to check this stuff. So then the question is just whether you're safe there or not.' Charlie and Lena exchanged glances.

'Your place is hardly a sanctuary, Mum,' said Charlie.

Famie sighed. 'I'm afraid that's true.'

Sam looked sheepish. 'I would suggest ours but really—'

Lena interrupted. 'Guys,' she said, 'we're fine, I think. Let's see what the police say. If we need to move, we'll find somewhere anonymous.'

'Like Claridge's,' said Charlie. They all laughed, drank some coffee.

'Will you tell your dad what happened?' said Charlie.

'Don't think it'll speed his recovery,' said Lena, 'so probably not.'

Famie looked around the café. A school trip, families of tourists, pensioner couples with guidebooks. A toilet to the left of them, a fire exit. She checked their location on the CityMapper app. The fire exit would lead to a side-street.

'Mum? What are you up to?'

Famie realized what she'd been doing. 'Sorry. Old habits.'

'Well, precisely,' said Sam. 'We had just been discussing our personal security when you, er, called. We absolutely need to keep this under review. Even if we assume this was a crank, a loner with conspiracies running wild in his head, it's a warning. If you stamp on a wasps' nest, don't be surprised when you get stung.'

Famie wondered again about Sam's commitment. He had said he wanted out, and she knew it wouldn't take much to push him over the edge. But she was still annoyed. 'Meaning what, Sam?' she said. 'What should we do next?'

He sat back, staring away from their table. 'Meaning we need to be careful,' he said. 'That's all. Just more careful than we have been. If we assume the wasps are aggravated, that they're looking for someone to attack, believe they're being threatened, we'll take the right precautions.'

Everyone nodded.

'Totally fair,' said Famie. They finished their coffees. At the counter, a middle-aged man spoke in German to another. Famie looked up, the others turned.

'What did he say?' said Sam, a note of urgency in his voice.

'He asked if he could borrow a handkerchief,' said Famie. She smiled.

'Huh,' said Sam. 'Once a Berlin correspondent . . .'

'You got that right,' said Famie. 'And it's time to go. We'll walk you to the hospital, Lena.'

Lena started to protest, then smiled. 'Actually, that would be great.'

They left the café, crossed Baker Street in single file. Like an army reconnaissance unit on patrol, thought Famie.

56

Lena hesitated outside her father's room, her hand against the door frame. She glanced around, pulled out her phone, put it away again. She took three steps, stopped and turned back. Mind made up, she slipped into the room and walked on the edges of her feet, her shoes silenced. She eased herself into the chair.

Michael Nash's eyes were closed. He looked peaceful. At his side, Lena looked anxious. She leant forward, hands in her lap. Her fingers locked and unlocked. Her right leg bounced. There were no tubes in him now, no wires connected, no electronic beeps. The only noise was from the other side of the door: trundling, clattering, shouting. On her side of the door, there were just Michael's breathing and Lena's creaking chair. A black glass vase on a cantilevered table held a bouquet of fresh tulips. His glasses and a framed photo of Lena on her twenty-first birthday were by his bedside next to a jug of water and a half-full plastic beaker. She leant forward then back, forward then back, rocking gently, as though in time to some silent prayer. She glanced at the door. Decided something.

She stood up. He stirred and opened his eyes. 'Hi, love,' he said.

She sat down again. 'Hi, Dad.' He drank some water, then slumped back on his pillows. 'Good to see you.' He smiled.

'You're a sight for sore eyes, all right,' he said. He let out a long sigh. Reached for his glasses, slipped them on. Pushed fingers through his hair.

'I hope you've stopped falling over,' said Lena. She held his hand. 'How are you today?'

A crease appeared down the middle of his forehead. 'I keep thinking I'm better,' he said. 'Then I get out of bed and everything spins again.' His free hand drew imaginary circles in the air. 'And because I live on my own, they're recommending I stay here until the balance comes back.'

Lena played with the collar on her shirt. 'When do they think . . .'

Michael shrugged. 'They don't know seems to be the answer. I had been thinking . . .' He pressed his lips together. The line on his forehead appeared again. 'And do say if this is a problem, but apparently we – the family – have use of a flat above yours. I got a message from Robert, quite out of the blue, really.'

'He is your brother and you are in hospital,' said Lena, 'so not that out of the blue.' She watched her father. 'But, yes, I understand the point you're making.'

'Well, quite,' said Michael. He paused, stared ahead, eyes on the middle distance. Lost for the moment. She waited. His eyes filled. 'Sorry,' he said. 'A thousand memories, all at once.' He sounded exhausted. 'Hospital can do that.' He pulled himself together. 'Anyway. What I was thinking was that maybe I could stay temporarily – very temporarily – above you at Gasholders. Then I could discharge myself from here. And maybe you could pop up every now and again. Just to check on an old man.' He smiled weakly.

Lena did not return the smile. 'Is that wise, Dad? I mean, yes, of course, but what if you wanted to get out of bed in the night?

Or I was out and you fell?' She squeezed his hand. 'Have you thought of that?'

Michael nodded slowly, his eyes downcast. 'I had, of course,' he said. 'And I think I'd need a carer of some kind, don't you? Just until I was safe on my pins.' He watched Lena, squinting slightly. 'Embarrassing, really. Feels like I'm bloody ancient.' Lena didn't reply. 'You all right, love? You look as though you have the cares of the world on your shoulders.'

She managed a half-smile. 'I have the cares of the gallery and a father in hospital on my shoulders,' she said. 'Plus Famie Madden is writing this article . . .'

'Yes, I heard.'

'Is she coming here to talk to you?'

'No,' said Michael, 'I said I'd do it when I'm out. I think being here . . .' he took a beat, smoothed his bedclothes '. . . being here inclines one to too much confessional conversation.' He raised his eyebrows. 'Final last words and all that. I'd like to be more business-like.'

Lena nodded. 'Of course. I'm sure that'll be fine.'

Michael pushed himself up higher. 'Now,' he said, 'show me the paintings. I think I know everything about the survivors but I need to see for myself.'

'Sure.' Lena took an iPad from her bag, tapped and swiped, then placed the tablet on her father's lap. 'Still just the ten,' she said, 'from a hundred and sixty-three. So not good.'

He looked through her photographs. He took his time. He studied each surviving painting as though he was seeing it for the first time. Occasionally he would gasp. Occasionally he would zoom in, pressing his fingers on the screen.

'You look like you're touching holy relics, Dad,' Lena said.

Michael took his hand away, stared at her and forced a laugh. 'I guess I do and maybe I am,' he said. 'Perhaps we can rebuild from here. Use these ten as the foundation. Add some from storage. Although the Thackeray goes back to Boston, of course.'

'Not till the end of the year,' said Lena. 'In theory. They might want it back immediately now that we don't have anywhere to display it.'

'And you don't like it anyway,' said Michael.

'Which is not the point, of course,' said Lena. 'But being down to nine certainly is.'

He turned the iPad over, screen down, handed it back to Lena. 'I know you're hurting too,' he said. 'We've lost so much, you and I.' He reached for her hand. 'And it was all a deliberate act. That's what's so appalling! If it had been an accident it would have been awful but to know someone took all this from us on purpose.' He had raised his hands into the air, clenched both into fists. 'I swear I cannot comprehend that, really I can't.'

Lena said nothing. They sat with their thoughts. Eventually Michael cleared his throat. 'What was the name of bastard who did it?' he said. 'I've been told but I've forgotten.'

Lena clasped her hands together. 'The man who died was called Jamie Nelson,' she said. Her voice was matter-of fact. His had been impassioned.

'That's the bugger,' he said. 'Do we know why?'

'Maybe,' Lena said. 'You know I told you about the two Fanta paintings that were missing. There's a theory that he picked on them because of their Nazi links. That maybe he intended to burn them, or was going to deface them in some way. Make a big statement. Then it all went wrong.'

Michael Nash looked as though he was going to say more, then changed his mind. He nodded.

Lena stood up. 'Well,' she said, 'I have to go. Just don't

discharge yourself or anything mad. We want you at home but you have to be in better shape than you are now.' She bent down and kissed his forehead.

He offered a pained smile. 'I'm so sorry it came to this, Lena. So, so sorry.'

57

Famie was on the down escalator at Baker Street, Lena and Charlie three steps ahead. Sam had jumped into a cab, saying he was meeting his wife. A brief phone conversation with DI Hunter had led them all to conclude that Gasholders plus extra vigilance was still, for the moment, the sanest option for Lena and Charlie. They were discussing quite what that meant as they descended to the District and Circle Lines.

She watched Charlie and Lena deep in conversation. Their rapid-fire talk was something to behold. Their words overlapped with each other, then one paused to let the other finish. They had an instinctive mutual understanding. Famie felt grateful.

Side by side on the same step, Charlie was a good three inches taller than Lena, her curls accentuating the difference. The hair and height she got from her father. Famie was happy with that because the trade-off seemed to be that she didn't have any of his spite or selfishness. In fact, it was her generous nature and kindness that defined Charlie. And Famie loved her more than she had ever thought possible. She could barely remember a time when she hadn't been fearful of putting her daughter in danger and here they were riding to who knows where, doing it all again. But Charlie had embraced it, choosing to stay involved. If Sam left Howl, Famie knew she'd be in trouble. If Charlie walked, she wondered if she'd have the heart to carry on.

Her phone rang as she stepped off the escalator. She stood

still to take the call, surprised the signal had reached so far down, and that the caller was Sara. She sounded scared, spoke fast.

'Famie, thank Christ you answered. I need to see you but you can't come to Dorking. I'm heading to London on a train. Now. I could meet you at London Bridge or Blackfriars.' Famie hesitated, waved at Charlie and Lena to wait. 'Actually,' said Sara, 'I just realized it also stops at St Pancras. You have to meet me, Famie.'

Charlie, now alongside her mother, mouthed, 'Who is it?'

'Sara, I'll see you off the train at St Pancras. Look for me. I'll be there.'

'It arrives in about twenty-five minutes. I'm three carriages from the front.'

'I'll be there.'

'Okay, bye.'

Charlie and Lena looked at Famie. 'Posh Sara from Dorking?' said Charlie.

'The same,' said Famie. 'She sounded pretty frantic. Meeting her at St Pancras in twenty-five minutes. I was going to come back to yours . . .'

'We'll come,' said Charlie. 'We'll wait.'

Lena seemed unsure. 'She might not want to meet a Nash,' she said. 'Particularly the one from the gallery.'

'It's a long platform' said Famie. 'No one has to meet anyone.'

They took the three stops to King's Cross St Pancras, then walked the labyrinthine tunnels to get to Sara's platform. Famie, Charlie and Lena sat on a metal bench. Two long platforms faced each other, southbound trains on platform A, northbound on B. High ceilings, polished grey stone floors.

'This is the weirdest bloody station,' said Lena. 'An Underground platform for Overground trains.'

'Tunnels start after Blackfriars,' said Famie, checking the arrivals screen. 'Saved knocking half of London down. And Sara is here in two minutes. Why don't you both move a couple of benches in case she freaks out because it's not just me?' They did so, and Famie stood in the middle of the platform. She guessed there were possibly a hundred other passengers waiting for trains. Short of standing on a bench and waving her arms, she couldn't think how to make herself more visible. She felt on-view and didn't like it. Three men in sports shirts wandered past, then stood too close. Famie moved away a few paces. A woman with a baby in a buggy and a phone to her ear strode past, talking loudly.

Across the tracks, a train arrived making the loudest screeching sound Famie had heard. Two children near her put their fingers in their ears. She'd heard it before, but it still surprised her.

One minute till Sara's train. Why had she said Famie couldn't go to Dorking? Sara had seemed grounded and, as far as Famie could tell, pretty unflappable. Clearly something had happened to disturb that equilibrium. The screeching train stopped. It was filled with passengers heading towards Brighton. Famie checked left. Charlie and Lena were thirty metres away. Charlie raised a hand. Famie nodded.

More screeching announced the arrival of Sara's train. The passenger board said it had sixteen carriages, first class at the front. Famie positioned herself near to where she imagined carriage three would stop. She was out by one, walked back a few metres. Famie peered though the carriage windows, saw no one she recognized, checked left. Charlie raised a hand again.

Sara was the last passenger off. She stepped out, looking as if she might have the wrong stop and would step straight back on. Famie raised a hand. Sara nodded. Denim jacket over a lime green shirt and black linen trousers. Grey rucksack over both shoulders. Her hair was tied up in a loose bun. Famie stayed where she was, and Sara walked to her.

'Not here,' she said, and went past her to a free bench, the last on the platform. Four along from Charlie and Lena. She sat, rucksack now between her legs, one hand on a strap. Famie sat next to her. Sara fidgeted in her seat her brown eyes darting everywhere.

'Hi,' said Famie. She thought she'd leave it at that and see what happened. Hear what Sara had to say. But she said nothing. 'We can go somewhere if you're—'

'No, here is fine,' she said. In front of them her train left, pulling out of the station, engine straining. On the far side, more screeching from a new arrival. The bedlam gave Sara the confidence to speak. Famie leant in close to catch what she was saying.

'Thank you for meeting me. I'm going to give you my laptop and you're going to take it away. My login password is Bangalore seventy-six, all lower case. You remember the photos you looked at, all of trees? Jamie had downloaded them. Do you remember?'

Famie nodded. 'Of course,' she said, trying not to shout.

'I do computer tech,' said Sara. 'It's not my job but it's what I studied. When you left our house, the page of tree photos was still up. The document title Jamie had given it was "All about the roots". It was one of the things he always used to say. He thought where you came from was really important. Also you can lay down new roots and so on.'

The squealing train had stopped, disembarking passengers flooding the far platform. Sara blinked. She looked around, spoke more quietly. 'It was his laptop login as well. "All about the roots". The last photo in the sequence is a close-up of a tree's roots. You might not have noticed but it is there.'

She swallowed. 'So. Yesterday a package arrived for Jamie. It

226

was obviously a book he'd ordered. I was pissed so I opened it. It's also in here.' She patted her rucksack. 'It's called *Steganography*, Edition Six'. He already had the previous two on his shelves. I went to put the new one in his room and there they were. I'd never seen them before.' She looked directly at Famie. 'Does that mean anything to you?'

'Absolutely nothing,' said Famie. 'Stenography, yes, steganography, no.' She realized she was clenching the edge of the metal bench. She peeled away her fingers.

'Steganography,' said Sara, 'is hiding data in plain sight. It's concealing something secret in something that is not secret. In this case, I think there's a good chance that Jamie hid some data in that last photograph. The roots one. I don't have the kit to find it. And I'm fucking terrified anyway, because if they killed him and burnt down a gallery they won't think twice about me or my place. So I'm giving it to you.' She lifted an orange Sainsbury's bag from her rucksack. 'Because,' she said, 'I think Jamie would approve.'

Famie hadn't moved, head spinning, heart thumping. 'Take the bag, Famie,' Sara hissed.

She took it. It was heavy. Laptop and hardback-book heavy. Sara stood.

Famie looked up at her. 'Wait! What if it's nothing?' she said. 'It won't be nothing,' said Sara.

'Why don't you just send me the picture? 'said Famie.

Sara shook her head. 'No, no, no. It's safer this way. I'm decontaminating. And I never want to see it again. I've wiped everything apart from that file, so it's a gift.' She picked up her rucksack, hooked the straps over her shoulders. 'But it won't be nothing.'

'And who else knows about this file?' said Famie 'This roots photo.'

'Just me,' said Sara. 'And now just us.' She bent down to whisper in Famie's ear. 'But do not delay one fucking minute. If it's what I think it is, some scary bastards are going to be pretty pissed off.' She straightened up.

'And what do you think it is?' said Famie.

'You saw his bookshelf,' said Sara. She looked along the platform. The flicker of a smile. And she was gone.

58

Friday

By the time Famie had corralled Sam and Benoit onto the same screen, it was after midnight. At Gasholders, Famie and Charlie were sitting at the kitchen table. Lena was making coffee. All blinds were drawn, windows closed. Two laptops lay on the table. One was open – Sam and Benoit peered out of a split screen. The other was Sara's and was still closed. Famie had explained everything that had happened at St Pancras.

'It's a MacBook Air,' said Famie. 'Pretty good condition by the look of it. It's plugged in, should be ready to go. Everybody okay?' Nods from the screen.

'Yup,' said Charlie.

Famie felt drained but the thrill of acquiring Sara's laptop had kept her buzzing all evening. She had been tempted, albeit briefly, to open it up as soon as they'd got back to Lena and Charlie's, but the fear of somehow messing up the photo had kept it closed. Until now.

Famie lifted the lid of the laptop, pressed the on button. It played the single tone as it started up. A screensaver of blue sea appeared, followed by a login box. Famie typed the password Sara had given, then hit enter. The blue sea disappeared and was replaced with a file titled, as Sara had said, 'All about the roots'. It was studded with photo thumbnail icons.

'Can you see this, Benoit? I know we're screen-sharing but I want you to see exactly what I'm seeing.'

The Frenchman nodded. 'Yes, all clear. Scroll down?' Famie down-arrowed till the icons stopped. The last sat on its own line. Where all the other images were clearly trees in greens and light browns, this was dark, almost black.

'There it is,' said Famie.

'Double click,' said Benoit. Famie heard Charlie hold her breath, and double-clicked. The screen filled with the image of an ancient tree-trunk base and an extensive root system. The tree's bark was cracked and split with age. A girdle of moss had bloomed around its girth. Three large feeder roots were visible, adjoining the trunk like a claw. Two of the roots had buried themselves in the ground within a metre of the tree. The largest had a life of its own, twisting its way into the foreground of the photo and out of the frame. Where it left the trunk, it appeared to have a deep cavity running along its side. A natural opening in the wood, maybe a foot in length.

'Zoom in on that big root,' said Charlie, 'where it looks like it's been cut.'

Sam nodded. 'That's where my eyes are drawn for sure.'

Magnified many times, it was a blistering from within the root, splitting the bark with raised ridges along both sides.

'Am I supposed to be able to see something?' said Sam.

'No,' said Benoit. 'Sometimes yes, but usually no. We'll need the software to see if anything's hidden. We're talking about altering a single pixel here. Each pixel has red, green and blue values. Jamie will have modified these slightly to represent the information he's hiding.'

They all continued to stare at the tree. 'If he has altered anything,' said Benoit, 'I agree the slit in the main root is the first place to look. Airdrop it to your phone, Famie, then send to me.'

'Is that safe?' she said. Benoit smiled. Famie did as she had been told.

'I have it,' said Benoit. 'Disconnect Sara's laptop now. Switch it off. Now I'll share my screen.' He tapped at his keyboard. Benoit and Sam disappeared from the other screen, replaced by the roots image. He talked and tapped, pausing occasionally to allow the laptop to catch up. 'So now I copy the image into a safe place. Highlight the split root. Open a new tab, run the steganography software, upload our image. Now I click on decode.' After a few seconds, a box appeared above the tree image. It filled with hundreds, maybe thousands of letters, symbols and signs. All of them meaningless.

Famie's head dropped. 'What's that?' she said.

Benoit carried on working. 'Well, it's not plain text,' he said. 'So I'm opening the image in Notepad. The message is encoded.'

Famie's heart was racing. 'So . . . so there is something?'

Charlie grinned.

'For sure,' said Benoit, his voice emotionless. 'There is definitely something there.'

Now the symbols flew up the screen, then slowed, then stopped. 'You see this line?' He bounced his cursor on some letters. 'That's what we're looking for. This is in Base Sixty-four. If you copy the message, then click on decode on a new tab . . .' The screen went green with a white box in the middle. Benoit's cursor flew across the screen, highlighting, clicking. The words appeared in the white box. 'And there is your message,' he said.

59

Famie thought her heart was going to explode. She leant into the screen and spoke, her voice higher than normal. 'Nash. Arrow. MKN Global Fiduciaries Ltd. Arrow. CitizenYES. Arrow. Family First.' She said it again. Then, 'What the fuck is that?' Rapid typing sounds came from all around.

Sam spoke first. 'I know Family First, I think. Far-right pressure group out of Italy. Catholic. Anti-woke, all of that. Hang on . . .' More keyboard sounds. 'Used to have Russians on board. When they peeled away after Ukraine, found money harder to come by. New funders were sought. Their youth wing seems to like flags and uniforms quite a lot. Offices in Spain, France and Holland.'

Charlie raised a hand. 'I've got CitizenYes!, all one word and an exclamation mark.'

'Hate them already,' muttered Famie.

'They are an evangelical Christian campaigning organization seeking to support patriotic attitudes,' said Charlie. 'Originated in Texas. Now they coordinate with movements across Europe and say they can get around campaign finance laws. Pump unlimited funds from proxy groups into domestic political races. That kind of shit.'

Famie stood, put her hands on her head. 'Wait, wait,' she said. 'This is no good.' She was trying to think straight, exhaustion and adrenaline fighting for control. 'This is all too legit,' she said. 'Horrible, of course, but standard Trumpian man-oeuvring. I don't see what was worth the cloak-and-dagger here. Unless . . .' she studied the screen '. . . unless MKN Global Fiduciaries are actually in league with Satan, we must be missing something.'

'Next to nothing on them,' said Sam. 'Based in Malta, by the look of it. A shell company, I assume. So the Nash money goes into MKN and from there to CitizenYes! and Family First. That's still a good story, Fames. Britain's benevolent, arts-funding Nash family secretly funding the new right in Europe.'

'It *is* a good story, Sam. You're right.' She looked at the Sam/Benoit laptop. 'Can we see you guys? Lose the steganography.' Sam and Benoit reappeared on a split screen. 'Thanks. Still gorgeous, not tired at all. So.' She gathered her thoughts. 'This is not evidence. There are no accounts, no documents proving anything. Just what I imagine is the sum of Jamie Nelson's work. He's given us the bottom line. His conclusion. But he hasn't shared his working.' Famie stretched, massaged her neck. 'Maybe we should pick this up again tomorrow.'

Lena had been standing back from the kitchen table, cradling a mug of tea. From a cupboard she produced a biscuit tin, removed the lid. 'In case sugar is needed,' she said. Famie had almost forgotten she was there.

'Do I need to go?' Famie said.

'Stay, Mum,' said Charlie. 'You're not going back now. The couch is pretty decent. Even for middle-aged women.' Famie play-punched Charlie's arm. She was relieved, happy neither to run home nor wait for an Uber.

'Of course stay,' said Lena. She bent to the Sam/Benoit laptop. 'This might be a dumb question,' she said, 'but is that the

233

only hidden message? From the pixels in the root? Would the scan you ran have picked up everything?'

'It would,' said a tired-sounding Benoit. 'I'm searching for text that appears different from the symbols. The double equals sign was what I was looking for.' He shared the screen again, highlighted the text he had decoded. 'I think that was the only one but let me do another trawl.'

The screen filled again with the mystifying array of signs and symbols. 'These are the usual Base Sixty-four special characters.' Benoit scrolled. 'This is where our message was.' He bounced his cursor on the double-equals sign. 'But of course let's check for more.' The scroll resumed, slower this time. Famie's eyes scanned the lines, not really knowing what she was looking for. The scroll stopped. 'That's the end of it, the last line,' he said. 'Ah. *C'est beau*. Look at that.'

Numbers, letters, symbols. And two equals. 'There's more?' she said.

Benoit said nothing, just ran the same decoding sequence. Green screen, white box. And one small black-and-white photograph. He enlarged the image. It showed four people, one woman and three men, sitting around a table set for a formal dinner. Tablecloth, silver cutlery and decorated plates. Champagne flutes and wine glasses. Possibly a restaurant or club. The woman was mid-twenties, short crimped hair, dark dress with buttons at the neckline, and next to her a man, early thirties, rakish, legs crossed, white dinner jacket and black bow-tie. The two other men were older, mid to late fifties, formally dressed. One sported a turned-up moustache and round glasses, and the other was almost bald with a heavier moustache and trimmed beard. All four were smoking cigarettes, the youngest man's held high, level with his right ear. None was smiling.

'Now, what have we here?' said Famie. She leant in closer. There was handwriting on the white border. She read aloud: 'J and M with Petrie and Y-B.' She leant back. 'Any takers?'

'Yes,' said Lena. 'The couple on the left are my great-grandparents.'

60

Famie and Charlie turned to look at Lena, who was still staring at the screen. 'J and M will be James and Marion. Must be the 1930s by the look of them. Don't know the others, I'm afraid.' She pursed her lips, pensive. 'And I don't think I've seen this photo before.'

'More to the point,' said Charlie, 'what is Jamie Nelson doing with it, then encoding it in this document?'

Sam jumped in. 'He's telling us they're up to no good. And that somehow the two hidden messages are linked. The family in the thirties and the family now.' Everyone had woken up again. Another shot of adrenaline.

'This looks like a private photo from a private collection,' said Charlie. 'Maybe he stole it at Helen's place.'

'How would that happen?' asked Sam.

Charlie shrugged. 'It's just a thought.'

'If you google "1930s Petrie",' said Charlie, 'first up you get Sir Flinders Petrie, explorer, but he was born in 1853 so it's not him. And next it's Sir Charles Petrie, third baronet, historian. Wrote loads about Charles the First. And, in the 1930s, flirted with the far right. A fan of Mussolini and Oswald Mosley. In 1934 he joined the January Club.'

'Which was?' asked Sam.

'"A discussion group,"' read Charlie, '"founded by Oswald Mosley to attract the Establishment to the British Union of Fascists."' She looked up from her phone and pointed at the photo.

'This must be a January Club dinner,' she said. The sound of rapid typing from the laptop.

'In which case,' said Sam, 'Y-B is Francis Yeats-Brown.' He read ahead, then summarized. 'Army officer, author of a book called *The Lives of a Bengal Lancer* and various articles in praise of Spain's General Franco and Hitler.'

Famie was pacing the room. 'What a table,' she said. 'A getting-to-know-you session with your friendly local fascists. Christ, what are we in here?' She turned to Lena, now sitting at the table, head in hands. 'So, for clarity,' said Famie, 'so everyone knows. Lena, please correct anything I get wrong. James and Marion Nash, your great-grandparents, have a son, Harry. He marries Janet. Harry and Janet have three children, Robert, Helen and Michael. Michael is your father. After your father is born, Janet commits suicide.'

'Died by suicide,' corrected Charlie.

Famie put her hands in the air. A surrender gesture. 'She kills herself. Is that okay?' she said. 'So then neither Helen nor Robert has children.'

'As far as we know,' said Lena.

'As far as we know,' agreed Famie. 'So you are the youngest Nash and therefore the heir to the Nash estate.'

There was silence in the flat and from the Sam/Benoit laptop. Charlie looked at her mother. 'I'm not sure that came out the way you intended,' she said.

Famie considered. 'You're right,' she said. 'It sounded like a massive accusation. I'm sorry, Lena. I was just trying to be factual.'

Lena raised her head, her eyes bloodshot. 'Look. We're a shitty family, okay? What can I say?' She wiped her nose with a tissue. 'But I like to think it stopped with Dad and me.'

Charlie shuffled her chair over and put an arm around her.

'No question of that,' she said. 'We know you and we love you.' Lena wrapped both arms around her and sobbed.

'For a shitty family, you certainly give a lot of money to some very good causes,' said Famie.

'Of course, yes,' said Lena, weary now. 'Yes, we do. I choose a lot of the projects. Often with Dad. He takes it seriously.'

'To compensate for his siblings?' asked Famie.

'That'll be some of it, of course,' said Lena. 'Compensation. Misdirection. It's a family game, you know.'

A notifications ping from Sam/Benoit, closely followed by the same from Famie's phone. 'Who is emailing at one in the bloody morning?' She read the email. 'Oh, do fuck off,' she said. 'It's Howard Taylor. Interview with Robert Nash tomorrow. Ten a.m.'

From Jamie Nelson's Instagram

LOOK at these pictures! I told you about Queen
Nanny of the Maroons. The one with the fierce face?
Well, check this link. One of my photography heroes is
Renee Cox, Jamaican/American superstar. She's done
a whole study on Queen Nanny, posing for it herself!
There are NO officially recognized Jamaican heroines
apart from Nanny, all the others are men.
She is retelling and recasting history.

Also here, look at Vanley Burke - he's the godfather of
Black British photography. And he's from St Thomas,
Jamaica (way out east). He photographs what he sees.
It is what I do also. You laughed when I told you I walk
to visit trees. But it is true. They are magical. They are
mystical. They have so many stories. Roots in the soil.
Messaging to each other, reliant on each other.

I'll send you some of my favourites.

61

Famie had, inevitably, slept terribly on the couch, partly because her head was swimming with Nazis and coffee but mainly because it was a terrible couch. Six thirty-five in the morning, three hours' sleep and not enough time to prep for good old erotica fan Robert Nash. Who would, of course, come with the personal attentions of resident pervert Howard Taylor. What a treat. So, on the plus side, looking shabby would not be a problem today. And had its advantages. She undressed, showered briefly, then pulled on the same clothes. You're a class act, Famie Madden, she thought.

She made coffee, triple shot. Read a 3 a.m. email from Sam. Short and to the point. *Absolutely no other record of any Nash family involvement in the January Club. No other pictures that I could find. Tread carefully. Good luck today.* She sipped her coffee, enjoying the burn. If the Nashs had been a family of the far right, they had kept their secret remarkably well. Jamie Nelson really had been delving deep.

Famie tried to concentrate on how to handle Robert Nash. She could stick to the questions she'd asked his sister. Of course she could. She had to keep reminding herself that this was not an interview. Not in any meaningful sense. She would not be robustly challenging his ideas and company policy. She would not mention his playboy lifestyle and certainly not raise questions about the family's funding of the far-right parties in Europe. Nice and easy would have to do it. It wasn't her style but this time it was all she had. Howard Taylor had to believe that all she wanted was to get Charlie and Lena off the ludicrous hook they had got themselves caught on. Famie 2.0. She didn't believe it but Nash and Taylor had to. Forget the January Club, forget CitizenYes! with the stupid exclamation mark, forget the Fanta paintings. She would smile and simper. As though her life depended on it.

Crossing Granary Square, she glanced unthinkingly at the wraps around the West End Gallery. She was considering whether to brave rush-hour on the Tube or take a taxi to Robert Nash's Chelsea flat when she pulled up short and turned again to look at the shrouded gallery. A solitary figure was standing in its shadow with the aid of a stick, hunched, and dressed, despite the morning's warmth, in an anorak. It was Michael Nash. Famie hurried over. 'Mr Nash! Hello. It's Famie Madden, I don't know if you remember . . .'

He turned to look at her, then back to the gallery. 'Good morning, Ms Madden,' he said. He coughed, cleared his throat. 'My apologies. You're only the second person I've spoken to today. I sound a little gruff.'

'Who was the first?' said Famie.

'The man in the clothing store over there.' He pointed towards the shops on King's Boulevard, running down to King's Cross. 'Sold me this coat. I was feeling cold.' The anorak swamped him. He looked lost.

'Have you just come from the hospital?' Famie asked.

'I have.'

'And Lena doesn't know you're here, does she?'

'She does not. She would not be happy. Best not say anything, eh?'

'Of course.'

They stood quietly together. Famie knew she was going to be

late if she stayed more than ten minutes but this opportunity wouldn't come again. A Nash sibling with no Howard Taylor. She would take her chances.

'I'll return to the hospital in due course,' he said. 'I know I'm not yet fully recovered. But I had to come, you see.'

'Of course you did,' said Famie.

'I want to see the paintings that were saved,' he said. 'Lena has shown me the photos, of course.' He turned now to face Famie. 'But it's not the same. I have to feel them. In my hands. Do you understand, Ms Madden?'

No, I do not, she thought. 'Yes, yes, I do,' she said. 'And please call me Famie.'

'In which case, Famie, would you have time to escort me to the vault? I feel I might need someone to lean on.'

In all likelihood, she would lose the whole of the Robert Nash interview but this was a good trade. 'I'd be honoured,' she said. 'Lead the way.' With her right hand, she supported Nash. With her left, she selected her phone's voice-recording app and pressed the mic button.

62

Famie had taken the strong-room keys from an evidently surprised, thrilled and nametagged Daisy on the college's reception desk. ('Our secret if you don't mind,' Michael Nash had said.) Now he stood in front of the strong-room door, leaning against Famie, cane held firmly. He was clearly anxious. He had stopped walking but was still moving. A hand brushed his hair back, then played with his belt. He flexed his shoulders, altered his balance, licked his lips. He spoke as though there were others in the room but he wanted only Famie to hear.

'It took me many years to build the gallery,' he said. 'I knew how big it could be with the right support. I just knew. The others weren't interested, really. Let me get on with it.'

'You mean your siblings?' said Famie.

'I do,' he said. 'And I'm wondering whether I'll be able to build it again. Whether I'll have the nerve. The energy.' He paused. 'Or the money.' He sighed, and let go of Famie. She wondered if he might bail on this completely. If it was all too much. Maybe it wouldn't be too late for the Robert Nash interview after all.

Then he gathered himself. 'So,' he said, 'I know which paintings survived. I've seen the photos. I wrote the list. But there were so, so many others on it. All floor two gone, so that's the Amouzou images, the Claudette Johnson and the Susan Hiller. Everything on one, bar the Thackeray.' He swallowed twice. 'My, my.'

Nash was clearly still reluctant to go into the vault. Famie was happy to wait. 'What gets on the grab list?' she asked. 'How do you decide?'

Nash stared ahead. For a moment she thought he wasn't going to reply. Maybe it was a dumb question. He shifted his balance again. 'How would you decide?' he said.

'If I ran a gallery, you mean? Highest-value items, I suppose. The most famous. I'd start there.'

'And what about your house?' he said. 'How would you decide what to save there?'

Famie laughed. 'Well, there's nothing of value, so it would be sentimental stuff, I suppose.'

Nash nodded. 'And there's your answer. That's what I do, too. Mainly value-based. Sometimes items on loan. And the occasional sentimental choice. The Takishenko *Tomato* is one of those. That was on the ground floor. That was saved. The Gerstein painting I love. That was saved.'

'They have wall power?' said Famie.

Nash smiled. 'You've been speaking to Lena. And, yes, wall power in abundance.' Still he stood facing the door.

'And what do the other Nashs think should happen to the gallery?' she said.

Another lick of the lips. And a mind finally made up. 'Shall we go in now?' he said. 'Would you do the honours?' He gestured to the steel door. Famie unlocked top and bottom, pushed it open. She felt the temperature drop as they stepped inside. Famie gazed at the rows of shelving. She waited for Michael's guidance.

'To the left, I think,' he said. She took his arm, steered him, row by row, to the far wall. Felt him pull back briefly as they approached. Then they shuffled forward. When the first of the ten shrouded paintings came into view, Michael gasped. When he saw all ten, he wept. 'All that's left,' he whispered.

Well, not quite, Famie thought. You have a fortune and a big house on Hampstead Heath. 'And you have a beautiful daughter,' she said.

'Yes,' he whispered. 'We're both lucky to have loving daughters.'

Famie walked to the first painting. 'Would you like me to, er, unwrap them for you?' she said.

Nash considered that. 'I don't really know,' he said. 'Isn't that feeble? He played with his cane, tapping it a few times on the tiled floor. 'Okay. Yes, please. Why don't we make a start?'

She crouched, picked away the thick cotton cloth that covered the first painting. Vivid blues and greens, heavy gold frame. Famie guessed it was sky and fields but wouldn't have bet on it. She continued along the row. Unwrapping, unfolding. She glanced at each painting as it was revealed. A solitary black figure on a bench, a tomato and a scalpel, a blurred car and driver. She moved on, crab-like. The smallest package, not much bigger than a paperback, contained words, poetry maybe, embossed on metal. Then some Black women and children in a room. Then an exploding gun, some orange clouds and a canvas of melting stripes. The last was the largest, about the size of a door. A vivid yellow top half, an electric blue lower half. Either a beach scene or a Ukrainian flag, Famie wasn't sure. She liked the poetry one and the tomato one, but the rest seemed unremarkable. They were all on the gallery's grab list, though, so what did she know?

Famie stood, glanced at Nash. His eyes were as round as coins. One hand covered his mouth, the other trembled on his cane. He looked horrified. Swayed slightly. She ran to his side, took his free arm. 'Is something wrong?' she said. 'Mr Nash?'

His mouth was moving before the words came. 'Where are the others?' he murmured.

Famie frowned, studied his face. It seemed contorted with pain. 'This is it, Mr Nash,' she said. 'This is what the Fire Brigade rescued. There is nothing else.'

'So where's the Thackeray?' He turned to Famie. His skin was like paper. 'If this is it, then where is the Thackeray?'

Famie looked along the line of paintings. 'Forgive my ignorance, Mr Nash, but are none of these by Thackeray?'

He looked at her glassy-eyed. Then, faster than she thought possible, he turned and walked for the door. 'It's the wrong list!' he said, his voice no more than a croak. 'They saved the wrong fucking list!'

246

63

Famie rode a cab with Nash back to the hospital. His eyes were closed, his breathing shallow. He said nothing. She had peppered him with questions. He had answered none. Eventually she stopped talking, let the ride go by in silence. Up front, the driver took calls, played an oldies station on the radio, cursed at everyone. Euston Road did its worst: a ten-minute journey would take thirty.

They were both on the back seat, Nash behind the driver. Famie messaged Howard Taylor again. Apologized again. Wondered if she could be an hour late. Or maybe ninety minutes. She wasn't hopeful. A red light at the top of her phone screen reminded her that it was still recording. The strong-room conversation was good, devastating even. Everything since was a waste of time.

They had saved the wrong paintings. How was that even possible? Was that the Fire Brigade's fault? Or were they working from an incorrect list? Nash's precise words had been 'They saved the wrong list', which suggested there must have been more than one. And were all the paintings wrong or some of them? Or just one?

Nash had mentioned the tomato painting as a favourite and that was in the vault. So at least one was correct. But the others? And at what stage in the unwrapping process had he pulled that desperate face? Nash could answer all of those questions but he wasn't playing. Presumably Lena was the only other person who could help. And maybe Famie should tell him so.

She turned to Nash, spoke softly: 'I'll run all these questions by Lena,' she said, 'so you rest. I'll call her later.'

Nash opened his eyes, looked out of the window. 'I worry about her,' he said.

A response at least. Famie nodded. 'We all worry about our kids. And it never stops, does it? Just because they're grown-up it doesn't mean they actually know anything. God knows I worry about Charlie all the time.' She took a beat. 'Which is, of course, why I'm writing this piece for the bloody *Mail*. I'll need to come and have a chat with you. When you're feeling up to it.'

They stopped at traffic lights, left lane. The hospital was a few minutes away. Famie was still looking at Nash. Nash was still looking out of the taxi window. 'But I worry about her,' he said again.

'I know,' said Famie. The silence between them ran on. The taxi made the left turn. She had maybe ninety seconds to get anything else from him. Her phone buzzed. Howard Taylor said two p.m. at Chelsea Harbour. The two Nash brothers in one day. What a treat, she thought. 'I'm seeing your brother later,' she said.

Nash said nothing.

'I've already spoken to your sister.' Nash kept his hands on his knees. 'She said you both think of her as a bit of a crank.'

Still no reaction from Nash. Famie could see the hospital ahead. The taxi slowed. Nash zipped his jacket. 'I'm sorry you had such an upsetting morning,' she said. 'The paintings in the vault must have been quite a shock.'

Then she remembered their conversation in the square. 'Although, wait, didn't you say you'd seen them – the paintings – in photos Lena sent you? I'm sure that's what you said.'

The taxi stopped; the driver tapped the meter. 'Forty-two twenty, please, mate,' said the driver.

Next to Nash the card reader illuminated. He fumbled in his trouser pocket, found a slim leather wallet.

'Did Lena show you the wrong photos, maybe?' said Famie. 'Is that why you were shocked?'

Nash tapped his wallet against the card reader.

'Was the Thackeray painting in her photos?'

Nash reached for the door.

'Why do you worry about Lena, Mr Nash? Is she safe?'

Famie knew she had pushed far enough. Maybe too far. Nash froze, fingers around the door handle, glanced at her. 'Tread carefully from here, Ms Madden,' he said. He opened the door and walked slowly back into the hospital. Was that a warning? wondered Famie. Or a threat?

64

The first coffee shop with seats available was a Starbucks near Bond Street. Famie ordered a black filter and, in need of sugar, some kind of muffin. She slumped into a faux-leather armchair. She had maybe forty minutes before she left for Chelsea Harbour and she had to prep for Robert Nash, but another name was running through her head.

She felt she needed to know something about William Makepeace Thackeray before she moved back to the Nash story. Michael Nash had been particularly distraught about the absence of a Thackeray in the saved paintings. On her phone, she accessed the West End Gallery's website. Unaltered since the fire, it gave Famie what she wanted. The art in question turned out to be an album of twenty-six original drawings in pen and ink by Thackeray called *Adventures of a French Count* and was on loan from the collection of his cousin, Eyre Crowe. It was, according to the website, one of the finest Thackeray items in existence.

'Not any more,' muttered Famie. She scanned the rest of the information. The site added that he was mainly known for being a satirical novelist, and that in his time he was regarded as the equal of Charles Dickens. He was born in Calcutta in 1811, and died in London in 1863. And that was it. She clicked off her phone, drank some coffee, decided she didn't want the muffin. If there was a significance to the Thackeray, it was lost on her.

She sent the audio to Sam, then messaged Lena: *What's the big deal with Thackeray?*

That was enough art, she decided. She accessed the Notes app on her phone. Typed 'Robert Nash'.

65

The address in Chelsea Harbour was not, as Famie had thought, a Robert Nash apartment. From the outside, all polished chrome and sparkling glass, it was as expected. From the inside, however, after she had been buzzed through, it was a small, bright ground-floor office. There was a sharp citrus smell. Recently applied perfume, thought Famie. One main room with a view of hedges and flowers, and a side room with smoked glass. Door closed. Framed prints on three walls. In front of her, two women sat at desks facing each other; a third escorted her to a small sofa. She was late twenties, white-blonde, strikingly beautiful. She was also wearing the baggiest shirt and trousers Famie had ever seen. She glanced at the other two. They wore shapeless dresses, one with a thin cardigan.

'Nice outfits,' said Famie, smiling. 'I got that memo also.'

A flash of understanding from the woman. A small nod. 'Thank you,' she said. 'I'm Kate Rivers. Mr Nash and Mr Taylor will be with you shortly. Can I get you a drink? Tea, coffee and water are easy. Most other drinks are gettable.'

The scent, Famie realized, was hers. 'Some water would be fine,' she said. 'But tell me, where am I? I was expecting a private flat but this is clearly an office. There was no sign on the door. Unless I missed it?'

Rivers nodded. 'This is the main office for the Nash Foundation. We don't advertise our existence so you didn't miss anything. I'm the director. These are Toni and Harper, assistants to me and to

Michael Nash when he's on Trust business.' She indicated the other two, sitting in front of laptops and surrounded by box files and paperwork. They smiled, and Famie raised a hand in reply. The prints on the wall, now she studied them, were certificates, press cuttings and smiling photos of Michael Nash.

'Is it normal for Robert to work from here? To have meetings here?' asked Famie.

Rivers smiled briefly. 'Let me get that drink for you,' she said.

Famie watched her walk into the side room, then reappear with a frosted-glass bottle of mineral water and a tumbler, which she placed on a small wooden table in front of her. 'Can I ask you anything about how the Foundation does its work? Who decides who gets the grants? Or are you going to defer everything to Nash and Taylor?'

A raised eyebrow from Rivers. 'I think you know the answer to that question, Ms Madden,' she said.

Famie held her hands up. 'I get it, really I do,' she said. 'I'll wait here, keep quiet.'

Rivers went back to the third desk, put on a headset and tapped her keyboard.

Famie checked her phone. No reply from Lena on Thackeray. She tried another message:

Should I avoid any reference to suicide? Talking to your uncle soon.

This time there was an instant response: *I think you can go there.*

Famie thought of asking the Thackeray question again but the office door opened and she forgot about it.

66

Robert Nash came in first, followed by Howard Taylor. Neither spoke nor looked up. They walked straight between the desks to the side room, closed the door. Behind the smoked glass, Famie watched them as two grey shapes walked around a table, then sat, Taylor on the left, Nash on the right. She heard muffled voices. Then Taylor put his head out of the door. He looked at Rivers, who whipped off her headset. 'Send her in in two minutes,' he said, pointing at Famie, then disappeared again.

What a charmless fucker you are, Famie thought. The idea of being in the same room as Taylor and Robert Nash made her shrink slightly. She wondered what the turnover of staff at the Nash Foundation might be. A question that would have to wait until she spoke to Michael again. If she spoke to Michael again.

The three Nash Foundation women worked in silence. The only sound in the room was the rapid tapping on keyboards. Famie noticed them glance at each other a few times. An office code, maybe. She was sure they were messaging each other. There was undoubted strength in numbers and she was glad there were three of them.

Famie selected her phone's voice recorder and pressed record, then slipped the phone back into her pocket. After two minutes, Rivers rose from her desk, smiled at Famie and knocked on the smoked door.

'Yup,' called Taylor. Famie was waved in. She tried to read Rivers's immaculate face as she passed. She failed. Both Taylor

254

and Nash stood as she entered. Both smiled, both offered hands to shake.

Famie shook and sat opposite Nash. 'Thank you so much for being flexible,' she gushed. 'I'm sorry about the delay. One of my correspondents was in danger. Needed some instant advice.'

Robert Nash leant forward, frowning. 'Oh dear' he said. 'That sounds serious. Is everything okay now?' Tobacco fumes rolled across the table..

'I hope so,' Famie said. 'Time will tell, of course.' She placed her notepad and phone on the table. And when you guys find out I was actually talking to Michael Nash, she thought, you'll go apeshit.

Taylor pulled at the two sides of his jacket, as though he was going to button it. 'So part two of our family chats,' he said. 'Same rules as before, as we all know.' He placed his phone between them, ostentatiously pressed record. Famie retrieved her already-recording phone, made a play of finding the right app, then placed it next to Taylor's.

'Weapons drawn,' said Nash, smiling. 'Fire away, Ms Madden. I'm all yours.' White shirt, dark blue tapered chinos. A preacher's smile. 'Where shall we start?' Up close his skin was freckled with sun damage, his face developing deep lines around the jaw.

'Maybe you could explain where you fit into the Nash organization,' she said. 'What are your main areas of focus?'

'Sure,' Nash said. 'Well. We work as a team, of course, Helen, Michael and me. It's a good fit, I think. Our father ran the company for a long time. He had big shoes. Between the three of us, we do our best to fill them. My main responsibility is the property and building side. So that's West End Roche Limited. We offer a range of services across twenty-six countries. Mainly we work in ground engineering, foundations, infrastructure,

255

commercial and residential property. That kind of thing. And some leisure and retail activities as well, of course.' He leant forward, clasped his hands on the table. Two watches, Famie noted. 'I could send you a prospectus,' he said, 'but it is, I'm afraid, a little dull. Full of men and women in yellow helmets pointing at buildings. That kind of thing.'

'I'll take one for sure,' said Famie. 'It might have some detail I can use.'

Nash nodded at Taylor, who made a note on a pad.

'We employ close to eight thousand people around the world,' Nash said. 'We date back to 1866 and we have, I think, a reputation as one of the leading general contractors in the construction industry.' He unclasped his hands. 'Is that the kind of thing you want? I wasn't sure.'

Famie nodded. 'Good background,' she said. 'And pre-tax profits last year end of eighty million pounds. Have I remembered that right?'

'You have,' said Nash, 'and revenue up above four billion. Which is why,' he spread his arms wide, 'we can run the foundation here the way we do. Six hundred grant applications a year, four hundred payouts. I think we totalled sixty million pounds in the last three years. You can see some of the grateful recipients in these pictures.' He gesticulated around the room. There were six framed photos, each with smiling men and women in smart evening wear. Five featured Michael, one included all three Nash siblings. 'These are all big grant winners,' he said. 'Art-gallery extensions, school orchestras, ceramic studios. All built with Nash money. They literally wouldn't exist without the grants.'

'It's very impressive,' said Famie, glancing around the room. She wondered if the photo with all the Nashs was a last-minute addition. To give Robert some kind of presence here. 'Is the Foundation mainly Michael's work, would you say?' she said.

Nash shrugged. 'Yeah, I guess,' he said. 'We all contribute, of course, but Michael does . . .' He waved a hand in the air, conjuring the words he was looking for. 'He seems to be able to devote more of his time to it. And well done him, I say.'

Famie looked at her notepad. If he was this condescending about his brother to a stranger, Christ knew what he must say to his face. 'Where did it start? The philanthropy. Whose idea was it?' Nash and Taylor smiled at the same time.

'Old Harry usually gets the credit,' said Nash. 'My father, of course. And he certainly put rocket boosters under the fundraising. But really it started with his father James and his grandfather Anthony Nash. We're talking the 1860s now. It's been going for a long, long time.'

The image of James and Marion Nash at the fascist fundraising dinner came to Famie. 'Were they society people?' she asked. 'They were a successful and prosperous family. They must have been courted. Sought after. Businessmen. Scroungers. Politicians. They would all have wanted to be close.'

Nash laughed. 'All three!' he said. 'Absolutely yes to that.'

Famie knew she was nodding a lot. She knew it was going fine, that Nash and Taylor would be quite happy. And she hated it. A question formed in her mind. Tell me about the Fanta paintings. And the nudes.

67

Famie didn't ask it. 'What's with the watches?' she said.

'I'm sorry?' said Robert.

'You wear two watches,' she said. 'I was . . . intrigued.'

'Old and new,' he said, and raised his left hand. 'Classic time-piece. A Breitling I inherited from my father.' He raised his right hand. 'Smart watch. Measures my heart. Tells me if I'm getting into trouble.'

'And do you? Get into trouble?'

'Always,' he said. He smiled.

Famie knew she was supposed to find his gurning roguish. Instead she found it revolting. She had met 'rogues' before. Men whose behaviour you might condemn, but you had to smile while doing so. The old arched eyebrow. The knowing no-harm-done shrug. And every rogue had been a shit. Famie knew what she was talking about. She had been married to one. She saw no reason to change her mind now.

'Your father was clearly an impressive figure,' she said. 'Made a big impression on you and your siblings. But can I ask about your mother? What did you learn from her?' Let's see where this takes us, she thought. Nash sat back in his chair, peered at the ceiling. Taylor stared at Famie.

'She was the heart of the family,' said Nash. He spoke more slowly now. 'The centre of my father's life. What did I learn from her?' A long exhalation. 'Well, she was tender, quiet, thoughtful. Bookish, you might say.' He dropped his eyes from the ceiling to the table. 'She was a big supporter of the Foundation. She loved it. So maybe I learnt that caring mattered. This sort of stuff.' He pointed at the photos around the room. Now he looked at Famie. 'Also that caring costs money. We build a music room for a school or a new wing for a gallery because we have built a deep-tunnel sewerage system in Malaysia. It's all connected.'

Famie wrote some words, took a breath. 'It must have been a terrible shock to lose your mother like that.'

'It was,' he said. Jaw clenched.

'And forgive me,' said Famie, 'this is obviously difficult for you. I'm just trying to give some depth to my article. To make people understand this . . . extraordinary family of yours.' Taylor was clearly uncomfortable. He fidgeted – tapped his leg, bit his lip. But he deferred to Robert. Unlike the Helen interview, Famie thought. Nash had his hands in his lap. He seemed calm. 'I imagine it was a total shock,' she said.

'At the time,' Nash said, 'I was sixteen. And, yes, it was. Looking back now, though, I think there was a history of depression there. And after Michael was born, she sank pretty deep.' He adjusted his glasses. 'Can we move on?'

'Of course,' said Famie, 'of course. Just this maybe. Would you say the Foundation could be seen as her legacy?'

'Not really, no,' Nash said. His voice had hardened. 'The Foundation is a family legacy. A Nash family legacy.' He leant forward again, palms flat on the table. 'We date back to the early nineteenth century, Ms Madden. We've been part of the fabric of this country for hundreds of years. We have built it, shaped it, paid attention to it. Our own land. You understand? British resources, British wealth. We mind Britain's business. That's what we do.' He banged the table with one hand. 'Now move on.' He glanced at Taylor.

'Last question,' Taylor said.

'But half an hour was the agreement . . .'

'It was,' said Taylor. 'Last question.'

Bastards, thought Famie. 'Okay,' she said. 'Your sister said to ask you this, as you're the family historian. Why "West End" as the company name? It's the prefix for all of your companies. You mentioned "West End Roche" earlier. Where did it come from?'

Nash removed his glasses, wiped the lenses on a cloth from his pocket. 'Interesting question at last,' he said. 'Anthony Nash's father, John Nash, owned a house in Piccadilly. It was near where Fortnum & Mason is now. This is around 1830, something like that.' He put on his glasses. 'A lot of the early Nash business started there and the term "West End" began doing the rounds about then. So "West End" stuck. The "Roche" name, as I understand it, was chosen completely at random to give the construction wing a definitive presence.'

He sat back, produced the flirty smile again. 'And that's it,' he said. Taylor picked up his phone, pressed stop.

Famie picked up hers, left the recorder running. 'Thank you,' she said. 'I can work with that, I'm sure. Any news about the gallery? Will you rebuild?'

'Yes, I think so,' Nash said, as he stood. 'It's such a shame what happened. But we'll go again.'

Now Famie got up, brushed herself down. 'Your sister asked me what I would save from my house if it was on fire. It was an interesting question. She said the fire made her look at her own stuff in a different way.'

'Did she now?' said Nash.

'She said she'd save a painting of her dog.'

Nash rolled his eyes. 'Of course she did.'

'What would you save, Mr Nash?'

'I'm not playing your stupid games, Ms Madden.'

'Did you lose any paintings in the fire?' she asked.

The tiniest hesitation. 'No,' he said. 'That's all Michael's area.'

'Ah, right,' she said. 'I thought you'd bought the two Fanta paintings. I must have got that wrong.' She held her breath.

Nash and Taylor were by the door. Nash turned. 'You will learn, Ms Madden, that my niece is . . . how shall I put this? . . . an unreliable witness. You understand me?'

Famie's stomach tightened. Too much, too soon. 'Actually it was the London Fire Brigade,' she lied. 'They told me about the missing paintings.'

'And they told you who had bought them too?' He looked imperious now, sure of his ground. 'Is that why you're here, Miss Madden?' He took a step towards Famie. The genial flirt was long gone. His mouth was a thin line.

Famie retreated. 'My mistake,' she said. 'I'm sorry. I obviously got the wrong end of the stick. I won't take any more of your time.' She forced a smile.

Taylor held open the door for Nash.

'The lovely Kate will show you out,' Nash said.

She watched as both men hovered around Kate Rivers. Nash draped an arm over her shoulders, pulled her in.

Famie stepped out. 'Don't forget that prospectus, Mr Taylor, will you?' she said. 'And apparently you can show me out, Ms Rivers.'

Nash removed his arm, and both men left the office. Both women stared at the door. Rivers exhaled slowly. Eventually Famie produced one of her cards and handed it to her. 'You just never know when you might remember something.'

68

Famie took an Uber home. The journey lasted forty minutes. She saw none of it. The driver tried a conversation. She heard none of it. She realized she was scared. She realized she had fucked up. She was sure she was in danger. The more she thought about the conversation with Nash, the more she was sure a die had been cast. Her question about the Fanta paintings had clearly shown both men that she was following a different agenda. A question born of frustration and impotence. An unforgivable lack of control. A rookie error. She screwed her hands into fists, closed her eyes. Famie Madden, you're losing it, she thought. Everything had just got more dangerous.

She drop-boxed the recording to Sam, adding, 'Call me soonest.' She thought about including her assessment of how she had handled the conversation but held back. Maybe it wasn't as bad as she thought. She listened back at double speed. Nash's annoyance at her suggestion the Foundation was his mother's legacy was curious. She played it back at normal speed. He certainly had a very high opinion of what his family had built and its contribution to the country.

And then those last exchanges. She gritted her teeth. Whether she should have asked the question or not, Nash certainly denied buying the Fanta images. He said he had lost no paintings in the fire, and that that was Michael's area. She thought again about her morning conversation with Michael Nash and the missing Thackeray art. If there was a connection

262

between the Fanta pictures and the Thackeray, it wasn't obvious to her.

Famie stopped the Uber two minutes from her house. She would walk the rest of the way. She stopped by the petrol station to buy bread and wine. In the queue to pay, she received three text messages in quick succession. First Lena: *How did it go?* Followed by *Suicide?* Before she could reply to either, the third arrived – from Howard Taylor. *The article is cancelled. Send all recordings, all notes to me by end of day.*

'Fuck!' she said. The woman at the front of the queue turned and frowned. 'Sorry,' Famie said. The woman turned back. Famie mouthed, 'Fuck,' again.

She paid, then stood on the forecourt. She'd been correct: she'd blown it. Nash and Taylor had heard enough. She rang Sam. He picked up immediately. 'It's off, Sam,' she said. 'The article is off. My own bloody fault. You heard why. Really, what a dumb bitch I am. Why mention the Fanta paintings and drop Lena in the shit? Why claim to have spoken to the London Fire Brigade when you're supposed to be writing a soft fluff piece? What the hell was I thinking?'

There was a brief silence.

'Where are you?' said Sam.

'Round the corner from my house,' said Famie. 'Why?'

'Because I agree with you,' said Sam. 'If these people are who we think they are, you aren't safe. Maybe Lena and Charlie too. I know you won't move out but I still had to say it.'

Famie stood watching an old woman fill her hatchback with petrol. Next pump was a motorbike, beyond that a Tesco food van. She quickly appraised each driver. 'It feels like we've been here before, Sam.'

'I'm coming round.'

'I don't need looking after, Sam.'

'I know that. That's not what I meant,' he said. 'Look. I've listened to both of the recordings you sent. Very interesting. Also, there's something else, which I'll mention when I'm there. We have to get ahead of this, Fames. Get Charlie to come over. We all need to talk.'

Famie stood with her shopping in one hand, phone in the other. What was done was done. She was still angry with herself but there was no doubting Sam's change in tone. He had heard enough to drop everything. She should take notice. She messaged Charlie, then walked home the long way round. She turned right out of the petrol station, right and right again. She paused at the top of her road. Cars parked on both sides, two wheels on the kerb, two in the road. No pedestrians. She crossed the road and walked down it with caution, eyes on her front door. Whatever the 'this' was that Sam thought they needed to stay ahead of, she'd take it seriously. Car by car, she approached her house.

When she was directly opposite, she studied the evidence in front of her. Three windows on the top floor, curtains drawn in two. Just as she had left them. Downstairs front room, shutters closed. Just as she had left them. And that was it, she thought. Enough already. She needed toast.

Famie looked both ways, twice, crossed the road and entered her house.

69

On the Regent's Canal, *Hilversum* hadn't moved from its mooring. Its curtains were still drawn. Its doors, should anyone have tried them, were still locked. Inside, City Boy sat cross-legged on the floor, reading a battered paperback. He wore gym shorts and a black vest. His phone and MR 73 revolver were by his side. Apart from page turning, he was motionless.

When his phone vibrated, he snatched it, hit accept. 'Yes,' he said. He listened for a few seconds. 'Understood.' He hung up, and replaced the phone next to the gun. He stayed sitting on the floor for a few minutes, eyes closed, breathing deeply. Eventually he stood, placed one foot on the chair, bent at the waist. After ninety seconds he swapped legs, bent again. When he was satisfied that his hamstrings were stretched enough, he dressed quickly. Blue suit and boots. White shirt. Black cap pulled low. He tucked the gun into the back of his waistband and slid the phone into his pocket. He stood by the door, listening intently. He waited. From the towpath, he heard slow footfall and conversation. He waited. A runner and a cyclist came next, faster steps and the whir of tyres on concrete. He waited. Silence. He unbolted the door, top and bottom, then resumed listening. More tyres, more runners. Still he waited, fingers on the door handle. He hunched slightly, like a marathon runner waiting for the off.

The noise faded away.

City Boy stepped outside.

70

Sam, Charlie and Famie sat at the kitchen table. The light of the day was fading, the sun already below the wall at the end of Famie's garden. The back door was open, the smell of cut grass filling the room. Famie had made tea for Sam and Charlie, coffee for herself. She was tempted by the last third of the Pinot Grigio in the door of the fridge, but she needed to be alert. Coffee would have to do.

'Before anyone says anything,' said Charlie, 'just before I left the flat Lena came storming in. Her eyes were red – she'd definitely been crying. I asked what had happened and she just shook her head. Said she couldn't talk about it. She looked as though she wanted to, but just when I thought she was going to say something, she ran to her room.'

Famie frowned. 'Poor Lena, but why are you—'

'Because she'd just been to see her dad,' said Charlie. 'That's why.'

'Is he okay?' said Sam. 'Has something happened?'

'That was my first thought,' said Charlie, 'but she said they'd had a big row. She wouldn't say what about. By this time she was in her bedroom, door closed. I tried to ask some more but she told me to fuck off. So I have. And I'm here.'

Famie let that settle. 'They don't argue normally, do they?' she said. 'They seem to get on pretty well, considering how totally screwed up the whole family is.'

'Never heard them argue once,' Charlie agreed.

'The list!' Sam leant forward, slopping his tea. 'It must be the list!'

Charlie looked confused. 'What?' she said.

Famie explained her surprise meeting with Michael Nash, the unveiling of the ten paintings and his horror at what he had seen. Charlie listened, astonished, eyes wide, mouth open. 'The wrong list?' she whispered. 'But that's impossible. It's also a catastrophe. But the wrong paintings?' She looked between Sam and Famie. 'All of them?'

'I asked him that,' said Famie. 'He wouldn't tell me. He was mainly shouting about the Thackeray. "Where is the Thackeray?" he kept saying. Then he left.'

'What's so special about the Thackeray? asked Sam.

Famie shrugged. 'I am, as you know, a massive expert in this art business. So all I can tell you is what's on the gallery's web-site. And that says it's on loan, and it is one of the best surviving examples of his art. Or was, obviously.' There was silence. Famie felt as though the story was racing away from her and disappearing over the horizon. 'What a bloody day,' she muttered.

'How many people know about this?' said Sam.

'Four,' said Famie. 'I assume anyway. Us three and Michael. That's it.' Another silence.

'That must have been what they were arguing about,' said Charlie. 'Michael must think it's Lena's fault somehow.'

'But it must have been his job to write the list, surely,' said Sam. 'He's the director of the gallery. Maybe the Fire Brigade messed up. Under the circumstances, it's amazing they saved anything at all.'

Charlie was out of her seat now. 'Unless all of them are wrong. Or most of them. The whole point of a grab list is to get these paintings.' She stabbed her right index finger into her left palm. 'Get this, get this, get this. Leave this, get this.'

'Can we see a copy?' said Famie. 'Is there a copy of the West End Gallery's grab list anywhere?'

Charlie thought about it. 'Lena had one,' she said. 'The fire-fighters had one. I can ask Lena but the fire brigade might be easier to deal with at the moment. Either of you still have contacts there?'

Sam put his hand up. 'I do, yeah,' he said. 'I'll make a call.'

Famie was getting agitated. She stood up. 'Meantime I fucked up at Robert's,' she said, 'and fucked up so badly they've cancelled the whole interview with the *Mail*. So we're back to your glossy glamour-photo parade, Charlie.'

Charlie looked astonished again, this time with added horror. 'What?' she managed. She sat down again. By the time Famie had finished explaining how the Robert Nash interview had concluded, Sam and Charlie both had their heads in their hands.

'So Taylor and Nash both know Lena told us about the Fanta paintings,' said Charlie, quietly. And, thought Famie, nervously.

'And Robert Nash says he hasn't lost any paintings,' says Sam. 'But let's assume he's lying. And that he and Taylor suspect we know about their significance. They'll want to shut that story down. Fast.'

Sam stood up, glanced at Famie. She recognized the hunch of his shoulders, the chewed lower lip, the narrowed eyes. Back at the agency it would have meant an editor had made a bad call, or management had announced another dumb-ass 'restructuring'. Since they had been working on the Howl website, it meant she had screwed up. She was used to it.

'Is your LFB contact at Euston Road?' she said. Sam nodded. 'You think we could both go there tomorrow morning?' He nodded again. Famie glanced at Charlie. 'Could Sam stay tonight as well?' she said.

Before Charlie could answer, Sam had his hand in the air. 'No, thanks, I'm fine,' he said. 'I'll call a cab. But all of us here – Lena too – need to be very, very cautious. We have made enemies of a very rich family. They will try to stop us.' He tapped at his phone. 'Uber in two minutes apparently,' he said. 'And, Famie, we need to write this story soon.'

'Before we're stopped, you mean?'

'Before we're stopped.'

71

Saturday

Famie waited for Sam at the Starbucks outside Euston station. A blanket of cloud and no discernible wind had kept the new day warm, the air stale. Six lanes of car fumes rolled over from Euston Road. She had slept badly, woken early. The coffee in her hand was her fourth of the morning. She paced the concourse. Sam was right. She had to write this story before the Nash lawyers stopped her. Of course, the fascist connections of the Nash family might be shown to be insignificant. The fascination with, and possibly the funding of, the far right in Germany might prove inconsequential. Helen Nash's choice of language might have been merely careless. Robert Nash's lies about the Fanta paintings could be seen as excusable. Understandable, even, under the circumstances.

But then there was Jamie Nelson. His photos, his travels, his evidence. She realized she was putting a lot of faith in someone she'd never met. Someone who had only ever been a wannabe journalist. Someone with a history of political activism and who had, at the very least, broken into and vandalized the West End Gallery. And then possibly, as the police suggested, had torched the place. She was always ferociously loyal to the registered users of Howl, but that had to have limits. What solid evidence had she that Jamie wasn't just a bad arsonist?

Sam appeared at her shoulder, and she handed him a coffee. 'You look like shit,' she said.

'Snap,' he said. 'But at least I slept in my own bed.'

'And, presumably, have fresh underwear on,' she said. 'So you win. Who's your guy here?' She waved her coffee cup in the direction of the fire station.

'Jon Goodall,' said Sam. 'He's the station manager at Euston. Used to be at Paddington, and we worked a few stories together. He said to text him when we're near. He'll come out.'

'Embarrassed to be seen with us?' Famie wondered.

'Possibly,' Sam said. 'The press office hasn't sanctioned the conversation, so maybe it's easier this way. Everything off the record.' They walked from the concourse, turned onto Euston Road and headed towards St Pancras.

'I'll record anyway,' said Famie. They waited to cross the road, Sam sent his text. Famie pressed record. She dropped her phone into her jacket pocket.

The fire station was a six-storey Edwardian building, terracotta and dirty limestone. 'LCC FIRE BRIGADE STATION 1902' was written in large black letters above three open garage doors. As they crossed the road, two gleaming fire engines came into view. A man in dark chinos and a grey sweatshirt walked from the first garage, raised a hand in salute. Mid-forties, broad-shouldered.

'Hey, Sam,' he said. The two men shook hands.

'Jon, this is Famie Madden. We're both working this story.'

Famie shook Goodall's hand. 'Hi,' she said, and smiled warmly.

He gave her the I-know-you-from-somewhere look that Famie had seen many times before. It was often followed with 'Aren't you that woman?' to which Famie normally replied, 'Probably not.' And that was that.

'Why don't we walk and talk?' he said.

They walked the block. There was no time for pleasantries. Famie was sure her mistake at the Robert Nash interview had lit a fuse on the story.

'You were at the gallery fire?' she asked.

'We all were,' said Goodall. 'It was a big one. It was a three-pump when we arrived and went straight to ten. It was thirteen by the end. Basement fires are the worst. Sometimes it's just a bin fire, five minutes and we're home. But this one, Jeez.' Famie and Sam said nothing. They waited for Goodall to pick up. They walked past the long sweep of a newly built school.

'It felt bad as soon as we arrived,' he said. 'You could sense how big the storm beneath us was. Hear it, smell it, see it.' He paused again.

'See it?' asked Famie.

'Yes,' Goodall said. 'The heat haze you get off a pavement sometimes on a summer day – it was like that. The air beneath us was being roasted. Normally we go into the basement first, then commence salvage. But we did them together or there wouldn't have been anything to salvage.'

'You'd been met at the gallery?' said Sam.

'Yes,' said Goodall, 'the owner's daughter. Bloody terrified she was. But she was our "responsible person", our point of contact.'

'What did she say?'

'That the gallery was empty. That it had been closed all day. Then she gave us the salvage list.'

'Did you have one?' asked Famie.

'We all did,' said Goodall. 'I had the iPad version, and there were embossed sheets too. It was a big list. Nine on the ground floor, eight on the first floor, ten on the second. We took everything from the ground floor, but just one from the first. It was way too dangerous by then. Shouldn't really have gone to the

272

first floor at all, to be honest.' He paused as they took a left turn, crossed the road. They now walked parallel with Euston Road and behind the fire station.

'Who did that?'asked Famie. 'Who went to the first floor?'

Goodall smiled. 'Mo Robbins,' he said. 'Young guy, fantastic firefighter.'

'Trustworthy, then,' said Famie. She had intended it as a statement, but it sounded more like a question, which was unfortunate.

'If he wasn't, he wouldn't be on the team,' said Goodall, clearly offended. Sam glanced at Famie.

'I'm sorry, that was clumsy,' she said. 'It's just because there's some dispute about whether the painting he saved was on the list.' Goodall stopped walking.

Famie and Sam spun round.

'I'm sorry?' said Goodall. The geniality had gone. He looked furiously at Famie.

Sam stepped up. 'It's the owner, Jon,' he said. 'It's Michael Nash. He says there was some art by William Thackeray that should have been saved. And it wasn't.'

'There was a lot that didn't get saved,' said Goodall,

'I was there when he saw the salvage,' said Famie, 'and he was shouting, "It's the wrong list. It's the wrong list."'

Goodall frowned now, stared at the pavement. 'But that's not possible,' he said. 'I mean, we didn't get much art out. That's certainly true.' He looked at Sam. 'Does he mean that? So we didn't save his favourite. Well, that's a shame but it's not the story here. A man died in there. The building is lost. That's the story. Has the bugger gone mad maybe?'

Famie shrugged. 'I don't know,' she said. 'It's possible, of course. But to pacify him, might it be possible to show him the list you were working from? Then this can all go away.'

273

Goodall's eyes narrowed. His voice dropped to a low hiss. 'His gallery gave us the bloody list in the first place. Get them to send it to you. Goodbye, Sam.' He turned on his heels and walked back.

Famie sat on a low wall in front of some council housing and put her head into her hands. Sam sat next to her. They were still there five minutes later, when Station Manager Jon Goodall emailed his grab list.

72

It was a twenty-one-page document, one painting per page. As Goodall had suggested, there were nine from the first floor, eight from the first and ten from the second. Sam checked it twice, passed Famie his phone. She checked it three times. The name William Makepeace Thackeray did not appear anywhere.

'Well, that's one question answered,' said Sam. 'Michael Nash was wrong and the brigade were right. Working from the list, they saved what they could. Salvage time was over very quickly, but even if they'd had another, what, five minutes? Even then the Thackeray art burns.'

'Yes,' Famie said slowly, cautiously. 'That has to be right. The idea that firefighters would save the wrong art always sounded a little unconvincing.' And yet, and yet, she thought. That tugging sensation again.

'Isn't that odd, Sam?' she said. 'The owner of the gallery went nuts because his favourite wasn't saved. But his own list doesn't mention it. His own list! So of course it wasn't saved. Also, Michael told me Lena had sent him images of all the saved art. And he seemed totally calm about it. Until he saw them for real.'

'And went crazy,' said Sam.

'And went crazy,' agreed Famie.

'So Lena sent him what he wanted to see,' said Sam, 'not what he should have seen.'

Famie let his words hang between them. 'Why would she do that?' she said eventually.

Sam carried on: 'So, two documents in play,' he said. 'One we have, one we don't. The grab list Jon Goodall sent us, which is here,' he waved his phone, 'and the document Lena sent her father, which we don't.'

Famie became aware of the rough brick of the wall pressing through the linen of her trousers. She stood, brushed herself down, then paced in front of Sam. 'Maybe both documents were altered,' she said. 'Might that have been possible? Lena changed hers so her father wouldn't go mad. And also someone altered the grab list to remove the Thackeray. And who knows what else? The gallery had lots of staff. Any one of them could have had access to the computer to change things around. Is there a date on the document?'

Sam scrolled. 'March the twenty-third this year,' he said. 'Maybe Lena altered this as well. Famie, we need to go to Gasholders. Lena might be upset and angry but we still need to talk to her.'

Famie's phone buzzed. 'Huh,' she said. 'It's a WhatsApp message from Brian Nelson in Jamaica. Jamie's father.'

'Don't tell me,' said Sam, 'you gave him one of your cards.'

'I did,' said Famie, ignoring the dig. 'He wants a phone call. Says it's urgent.' She frowned. What could possibly be urgent? 'Maybe the press are on to him again,' she said. 'Let's go back to mine, Sam. This is hardly the place for a transatlantic conversation.'

'And you get fresh underwear into the bargain,' said Sam.

They walked to Euston Road, turned left. 'I've told him fifteen minutes,' Famie said. 'It's a twelve-minute walk. Then I get a three-minute shower.' She set a fast pace. 'He's not an excitable man, Sam. Not at all. Dignified, I'd say. The quiet type. And I really didn't think I'd hear from him again.'

Sam smiled. 'What?' said Famie.

'You've got that look,' said Sam.

73

It was twenty-five minutes before Famie called. Back at her house, she had showered, changed, made coffee. Cropped cargo trousers, white shirt and trainers. Human again. She and Sam sat round her kitchen table. They both had notepads and pens. Famie's phone was between them, and on speaker.

'I'm sorry for keeping you waiting, Mr Nelson,' she said. 'London traffic,' she lied. 'As I'm sure you remember.'

'Good morning, Miss Madden, I hope you're well.' The line from Jamaica was clear, with just a hint of delay. 'Yes, I remember the traffic. Ten minutes is of no concern. I'm sorry if I alarmed you with my message.'

'Not at all,' Famie said. If there's something I can help with, do please ask. I'm here with my colleague. He can hear the conversation too.'

A slight pause.

'I can speak openly?' asked Nelson.

'You can.' Famie waved Sam in.

'Good morning, Mr Nelson,' said Sam. 'I'm Sam Carter. Famie and I run the website together. Please, if we can help you in any way . . .' He shrugged, sat back.

Famie gave him a thumbs-up.

'Did you work together at the news agency, Mr Carter?'

Sam, surprised, leant back in. 'Yes that's right,' he said.

'And were you at the cathedral when Miss Madden rescued that poor student?' said Nelson.

Sam mouthed, 'He's testing me!' Then he said, 'I was there, Mr Nelson. We worked the story together.'

I like Brian Nelson, thought Famie, but this doesn't sound very urgent to me. Unless what he's about to tell us actually is consequential, in which case . . .

'Very well,' said Nelson, as if he'd made up his mind up about something.

Famie scribbled, 'You passed!' and swivelled the pad. Sam grinned. They waited.

'So, as you know when I was with you, Miss Madden, at Jamie's house, I wanted just a few things of my son's. Photos mainly. Also a football top he had carefully folded.'

'I remember,' said Famie. 'It was claret and blue.'

'That is correct,' said Nelson. ' I took it because it was so neatly folded. Jamie was fastidious, Miss Nelson. It reminded me of him completely. I kept it folded, exactly as he had it in his drawer. I packed it into my case, wrapped in a bag so it stayed the way he had left it.' Famie fought back her impatience, made herself stay quiet. 'But the other day, when I was showing this shirt to a friend, another fabric appeared, just an inch or so of a khaki material. It slid from between the folds so I pulled it out.' Famie and Sam leant closer. 'It was a hat, Miss Madden. A floppy hat.' Famie didn't know what she was expecting but she was definitely disappointed. A hat for Chrissakes? She fidgeted in her seat, played with her pen. 'On the outside,' said Nelson, 'on the brim, were the words "Pamwe Chete".'

Sam jumped in. 'Can you spell that, please?' he said.

Nelson did so. 'It is the Shona language. From southern Africa. It means "Together only". It was the motto of the Selous Scouts who were from Rhodesia. Fought in the Bush War. Early 1970s. You can look them up, Mr Carter. Very brutal men.'

Sam had already looked them up, and nodded at Famie. She

sensed that her disappointment had been premature. 'Inside the hat were the initials HWN. And, in biro, "with thanks".'

'Harry fucking Nash,' muttered Famie.

'Actually, I think the middle name is William, Miss Madden,' said Nelson.

Famie and Sam stared at each other, mouths open. Famie spluttered. 'You know about Harry Nash?' she said.

'Of course,' said Nelson. 'I have made it my business since my son died to find out what I can about the Nash family. And as for your next question, no, I have no idea how Jamie came to be in possession of a Rhodesian special-forces hat.'

'You're ahead of us, Mr Nelson,' she said. Though I'm not sure where this takes us, she thought. It was certainly more evidence of the Nash family's long-running and deep support for the far right, now including Robert, Helen and Michael's father Harry. Whatever exposé she could write would not be short of shocks. That was for certain. Maybe that would be enough.

Sam had been reading rapidly from his phone. 'The Selous Scouts were involved in many atrocities, attacking and killing civilians. And, get this, they were involved in using poisons and biological agents in their operations.'

Famie tapped the table with her pen. 'How unsurprising that a Nash had been involved in some way,' she said. 'Wherever a white supremacist is in need, there's always a Nash on hand to help them. The world sees the arts centres and grants to the needy. But it's just chaff, distraction. A conjuror's trick.'

'Well, that's the reason I called,' said Nelson. 'That is why I said this was urgent.'

Famie frowned, leant in again. 'I'm sorry, Mr Nelson, I don't follow. The hat wasn't the reason you got in touch?'

There was a short laugh down the line. 'Of course not,' he said, 'though I hope you find the information useful.'

Sam pulled an exasperated face.

'Yes, very useful,' said Famie. 'Thank you. It fits a pattern. And I'll be sure to mention it in my piece. And the urgency you say is about something else?'

A longer pause. 'Yes.'

74

Famie stared at her phone, arms outstretched, willing Brian Nelson to speak. Sam had frozen, eyebrows raised, pen held in his right hand. A still life. Two people and a phone.

'Are you still there, Mr Nelson?' she said eventually.

'Yes, I am here,' he said. 'I was just making sure everything is switched on.'

Famie and Sam mouthed, 'What?' at the same time.

'Sorry,' said Famie, unable to contain herself any longer. 'I'm sorry, Mr Nelson. What needs to be switched on?'

'Location services,' said Nelson. 'Is my phone number stored in your phone, Miss Madden?'

'It is now,' Famie said.

'I have shared my location with you,' he said. 'If you wait one moment.'

Sam got up, walked round, stood over Famie's shoulder. Her phone buzzed. Words on her screen. Time sensitive. *Find My. Brian Nelson started sharing location with you.* 'I have it,' she said.

'Tap the button, what do you see?'

Famie's screen spun from London to a map of Jamaica, zooming in on its east coast. 'I see a town called Negril. You're on Archer Road, near Lexon Photography. Is that right?'

Nelson chuckled. 'If I ever get married again, Trevor there will sort me out. Not that he's ever there, these days. But he does a fine service. He has been there many years now. People seem to like what he does.'

Famie thought she was about to burst. 'Mr Nelson,' she said, 'what are we doing here? Can you explain? I am somewhat confused.' She hoped her exasperation hadn't been too obvious.

'Okay. Zoom out,' Nelson said. 'Go to the coast.'

Famie pinched her screen, directing the map eastwards. 'Okay, I'm on the coast,' she said. 'I see the Rockhouse Hotel and Spa.' Her heart had kicked up a notch. What was this game?

'South,' said Nelson.

Famie scrolled. 'The SOV Resorts,' she said.

'South again,' said Nelson.

Sam saw it first. He pointed at Famie's screen. She heard him gasp. Then she gasped. Long and loud.

'Ah. You have it,' Nelson said.

Famie enlarged her screen. And there it was. East coast of Jamaica. South-west of Negril. Due south from the Rockhouse Hotel and Spa and the SOV Resorts. Two words, positioned slightly inland.

West End.

75

Famie stared at the screen. West End. West End, Jamaica. The longer she stared, the faster her mind spun. Brian Nelson was speaking again. She realized she hadn't heard a word. 'Er, sorry, Mr Nelson. Say that again, please?' she said.

'I was just saying I don't know whether this is important or not,' he said. 'It didn't occur to me until yesterday when I was having a conversation with someone. They were telling me about West End. I checked on the old maps and West End has been there for a few hundred years. Since the bad old days, y'know?'

'Do you mean slavery, Mr Nelson?'

The briefest of transatlantic pauses. 'I do indeed mean slavery, Miss Madden.'

Famie and Sam ran from the house, slowing only when Sam couldn't keep up. A jog would have to do if they ran together. But she knew they now had to work terrifyingly fast. Every step was infuriating. She needed to press on. Famie turned to Sam. His face was red and perspiration poured from it. His shirt clung to his skin. He also understood her.

'You go on,' he managed, and waved her away.

'See you in the college reception,' she said.

Sam slowed to a walk and Famie accelerated away, hurdling the Agar Grove detritus. Within minutes she had taken the right turn and was running under the Eurostar bridge, St Pancras, Granary Square and Gasholders dead ahead. She needed to reach Charlie. She needed to speak to Lena. She needed to get to Kew. But first she needed to see the paintings again. The ten survivors that had made it onto the grab list, and out of the conflagration of the West End Gallery.

From Jamie Nelson's Instagram

And to answer your question, yes, I do wonder about my safety sometimes. But once I go there it's easy to feel paranoid. The guys in the house think that already. I keep suggesting new locks for the windows and doors but no one else is bothered. I thought I was being followed last week. Couple of times actually. Once near yours, then on the walk from the station to the house. Each one was nothing. But it's good to be nagged. Please continue!

Found these Blue Mountain coffee beans you must try. STUPID money but I've found the best I've had in England.

76

Famie ran into Granary Square, zigzagged through the lunch crowd, crashed into the art college. The receptionist looked up, startled. Famie took a moment to catch her breath, wipe her face. It was the same receptionist she had seen with Michael Nash – Daisy, her name was. I have a chance, Famie thought.

'I'm sorry, I look a state,' she said. She bent, put her hands on her knees. Her breathing slowed. 'You probably don't remember me but I was in here the other day with Michael Nash. He wanted to see the saved paintings from the gallery.' Famie used her best smile.

The receptionist smiled back. 'You're Famie Madden,' she said. 'I meant to say last time. I've read your book. Of course I remember. Can I help you?'

Famie had been going to lie her way in. Say she'd lost her purse, glasses, phone, whatever might work, but now, looking at the receptionist's wide eyes, she decided it was worth trying something different. 'Actually, yes, you can help,' Famie said. She lowered her voice, leant in. 'I'm working on a new story.'

The receptionist's jaw dropped. 'Like the Coventry one?' she whispered.

Famie didn't want to scare her needlessly. 'Not really,' she said. 'But just as important.'

'Will it be in the news?'

No question, Famie thought. One way or another. 'It might.'

'Am I in danger?'

'No, you're quite safe.' Christ, I hope so, she thought.

'Is it to do with the fire?'

Bingo. 'I think so,' said Famie. 'But I need to check something. I really, really need to have a quick look at the paintings that were saved. In the strong room. I know that should only be done by Michael or Lena Nash. But if there was any way you could let me in, just for a couple of minutes, it would be an enormous help.'

She could see Daisy struggle with her request. She chewed her lip, stared into the distance. 'You can stand with me the whole time,' said Famie. 'Two minutes?'

She nodded. 'Okay,' she said. 'I absolutely shouldn't.' She smiled coyly. 'But it's you, so that has to be okay. I couldn't live with myself if I said no and then . . .'

'And then bad things happened?' suggested Famie. God forgive me, she thought.

'Yes!' said Daisy, certain now of her decision. 'I'll get the keys. Probably better not sign for them, eh?'

Famie agreed. And let's get a move on now.

Daisy placed the keys in a tote bag and stepped from behind the desk. 'Follow me,' she muttered.

They walked the short distance to the strong room. Famie would have run, but didn't want to push her luck. They met no one on the way. When they stood in front of the steel door, Daisy handed the keys to her. 'I haven't done this before,' she whispered. 'You do it.' Famie took the keys, unlocked top and bottom, swung the door open. This time she knew where she was going. She strode to where the ten surviving pieces were lying against a wall. Ten shrouds but, she was sure, just two were of interest. She had replayed these paintings in her mind a number of times. And every time she cursed her ignorance. Classical music she knew. The books of Maggie O'Farrell and Michael Connelly she knew. Journalism she knew. But the fine-art world was lost to her. Too many posers and too much bullshit. But in her reruns of the grab-list art, she remembered the Ukrainian door, some metal work with words, a tomato and a scalpel, an exploding gun. The two she wanted to see again, as she remembered it, bookended the row. The first was a solitary Black figure on a bench and the second a Black family sitting in a room. Surely one held a secret.

She bent to begin the unveiling and heard Daisy take a deep breath. Then a sudden shout from Reception. Daisy jumped. She looked suddenly terrified.

'Don't worry, that's Sam Carter. He's a friend,' said Famie.

Daisy's hardworking eyebrows shot up again. 'He's here too?' she said. 'He was amazing in your book. I thought he was going to die in the cathedral.'

'Agreed,' said Famie, anxious not to embark on any more adulation. 'Could you bring him here? We really do work as a team.'

Daisy didn't hesitate this time. 'I'll get him,' she said, and bustled from the strong room.

Famie began removing the cotton cloth from each painting. Here they were, one more time. The sky and fields, the Black figure on the bench, the tomato and scalpel, the lined beige canvas, the small piece of metal with embossed words, the Black family in a room, the exploding gun, the orange clouds, the melting stripes and the vast Ukrainian door. Or whatever it was. She

289

had been wrong about the bookending paintings. The single figure on a bench was second, the many figures in a room was sixth. She stood back, stared at the ten.

Hurried footsteps from the corridor. Sam started speaking before he had entered the room.

'It's not just about what was lost, Famie, it's about what was saved.' He ran into view, scanned the saved paintings. He stabbed a finger at the painting with Black figures in a room. 'That's the one, Famie! That's the one!'

He couldn't contain his excitement. He stepped up to the painting. Stepped away. Bent down, stood up. 'When you ran on just now, I was reading some articles about Thackeray. His cousin Eyre Crowe painted that.' He glanced at his phone. 'It's called *Slaves Waiting for Sale* and was painted in 1861. Oil on canvas from an original sketch he did in 1853. It was . . .'

Famie raised a hand. 'Okay, wait, Sam' said Famie. 'Hold on. Begin again. Why this painting? What are you so excited about?'

Sam took a breath, scrolled and tapped his phone. 'So, as I understand it, based on what I've read in ten minutes, William Makepeace Thackeray and his cousin Eyre Crowe go to America in March 1853. Thackeray is famous because he had written *Vanity Fair* and *The Luck of Barry Lyndon*. He's basically considered number-two writer behind Charles Dickens at the time. So that's pretty big. Anyway, he embarks on a speaking tour. Crowe is basically his assistant, even though they're cousins.' Sam raised a finger. 'However, they fall out over slavery.' Sam glanced up at Famie, then back at the screen. 'Crowe is appalled and outraged at what he sees. Thackeray is more blasé. He doesn't exactly like it but he's no abolitionist. So when they're in Richmond, Virginia, Eyre Crowe visits a slave auction and sketches it. Later, he paints it and it's exhibited at the Royal

290

Academy in London.' He gestured at the painting. 'And now here it is.'

Famie crouched in front of the Crowe painting. It was about fifty centimetres by eighty in a heavy wooden frame. She picked it up, one hand at each end. It showed a nondescript, low-ceilinged room with, now she counted, five Black women sitting on a bench. They could be in their Sunday best, Famie thought. They wore colourful dresses, white aprons and red bow-ties. Three sported headscarves. One woman was nursing an infant. There were two other children. In the middle of the picture, a small girl, maybe three or four years old, sat on a knee. To her left, a boy, Famie guessed about ten years old, wore a smart blue jacket and matching peaked hat. To their left, an angry, sullen-looking Black man sat alone. Red waistcoat, brown trousers, folded arms and clenched fists. He was an image of suppressed rage.

Nine slaves. Waiting, Famie now knew, to be sold.

She checked around her. Sam was at her left shoulder. Daisy a few metres away. She looked agitated.

'Two minutes,' Famie said. 'If you like, we'll close up. You can go back to Reception.'

'No, I'll stay if that's all right,' she said. She looked at her phone. 'Two minutes, then.'

Famie took one last look at the painting. Behind the enslaved women there was a white slave trader. Black hat, brown suit. In a doorway on the far left of the painting, three men were talking – haggling, maybe. Potential buyers, Famie presumed. 'Not slaves being sold,' said Famie, 'but the anticipation of it.'

'And the white guys are like ghosts,' said Sam. 'It doesn't seem to be about them at all.' They were both transfixed, lost in a pre-civil-war Richmond waiting room until Daisy coughed.

'Very sorry, but we need to lock up now,' she said.

'Yes, of course,' said Famie. She placed the Crowe painting back on the floor, swathed it in its cotton sheet, then, with Sam, wrapped the others. 'That's it, we're done. Daisy, we love you. Thank you, thank you.' Daisy blushed. Famie and Sam ran from the room.

WEST END GALLERY
SALVAGE GRAB SHEET

ITEM
Slaves Waiting for Sale/Eyre Crowe

LOCATION/CLOSE-UP LOCATION, FLOOR PLAN
First floor. Stand 1

PRIORITY
One

DESCRIPTION
Oil on canvas. Interior.
Black women and a man, seated
53cms x 82cms

INVENTORY NUMBER
236

WEIGHT
1.1 kilos

ACCESS
Direct from first floor

REMOVAL
Gloves needed. One-/two-person removal

77

Outside the Gasholder flats, Famie pulled Sam onto a bench. She checked the time and texted Charlie. It was cloudier now, noticeably cooler, but Sam was still puffing.

Famie spoke first. 'So Michael Nash is the Thackeray fan,' she said. 'His art was on the grab list at one time. But wasn't on it when the gallery burnt. It had been removed. But the Crowe painting was saved. The only one from the first floor. It stayed on the list. You could say Crowe represents the abolitionists, Thackeray the status quo. That how you see it?' Sam nodded.

'And Thackeray versus Crowe is Michael versus Lena, surely,' he said. 'If they had a huge row that must have been what it was about, Michael furious that his list had been altered, Lena, as daughters are, furious at his reactionary politics.' He turned to Famie. 'Something like that?'

'Something like that, yes,' said Famie. 'That feels right anyway.' Her thoughts drifted back to the Crowe painting. 'That was some picture, wasn't it? That furious man, bottom right, with his jacket off and sleeves rolled up, looked like he was about to attack someone. Or run for it. Maybe both.'

'Maybe he did,' said Sam.

'And the women,' said Famie. 'They looked pretty smart to me. Even stylish. They had gold loop earrings too. Wasn't expecting that.'

'Apparently they would have been dressed up,' said Sam, 'to

look like "fancy girls". The greater the ornamentation, the higher the price.'

Famie closed her eyes. She needed to switch away from the horrors of the painting to the horror of the Nash family. And fast. 'I'm going to need your help writing this article, Sam,' she said. 'We need it legalled as we go. Get our guy on it. I'll start the document, share it with you, see how we go.'

'When do we start?' said Sam.

'I've started,' said Famie. She tapped her head. 'In here anyway. But we need to talk to Lena. And I want to go to Kew. ASAP. I'll write on the way.'

'I assume that's the National Archive you're visiting, not the gardens,' he said.

'You assume correctly. But first we need Lena. Come on. Charlie will let us in.'

They both stood, walked to the Gasholders entrance. Charlie was in the lobby and opened the door. She had no time for a greeting. 'Mum. I think Lena is missing.'

78

Charlie was pale, her hair wild. She beckoned them in. They took the stairs, single file. No one spoke till they were in the flat. Sam was last in and closed the door. Charlie leant against the kitchen table and folded her arms. 'As you know, yesterday Lena rowed with her dad, stormed back home, told me to fuck off. So I came to yours, Mum. When I got up this morning, she wasn't here. I've called her but she's not picking up. She's not replying to texts, WhatsApps and so on. That's never happened before.'

'The hospital?' said Sam.

Charlie shook her head. 'Apparently Michael's had no visitors today. I checked about an hour ago.'

Famie could tell Charlie was anxious and she wanted to help her daughter, but there were more important things to be concerned about. She rapidly explained their visit to the fire station, the emailed copy of the grab list, the call with Brian Nelson and their theory about Eyre Crowe's painting.

'That's one morning?' said Charlie. 'Jeez. It's not even eleven o'clock.' She walked around the table, stared out of the window. 'So. You have a grab list from the fire brigade. And it's different from the one Michael Nash wrote. Brian Nelson says that the original West End might be Jamaican. And the slavery painting was saved, instead of the Thackeray, because of an argument they had in the first part of the nineteenth century.' She turned, sat at the table. 'Is that right?'

Famie nodded. 'That's a fair summary of the morning.'

'Well, it works,' said Charlie. 'That absolutely would explain Lena's argument last night with her dad.'

'She never mentioned the painting to you?' said Famie.

'Don't think so,' said Charlie. 'What's it called again?'

'*Slaves Waiting for Sale*,' said Sam.

Charlie shook her head. 'I'd have remembered,' she said. 'For sure. We'd then have had a "You don't say slaves you say enslaved" conversation. And we didn't. So, no, she never mentioned it.'

'And the whole West End thing?' said Famie. 'Nothing there either?'

'I always assumed it was a London reference,' said Charlie. 'Why would anyone think differently?'

They all stared at each other. 'So what next?' said Sam.

'We need to find Lena,' said Famie. 'She holds the answers to so many questions.'

'Why don't I go to the hospital?' said Charlie. 'I think she'd want to make it up with her father. They're normally really close. I reckon she might go back, try to patch things up.'

Famie's head was buzzing now. 'Wait,' she said. 'Yes, it's a good idea but, Sam, you go too. Stay together. I'm scared of what these people can do. Have done. Let's assume they're responsible, in some way, for the fire and the death of Jamie Nelson. Keep that in mind. All the time.' She meant her words for both of them, but she was looking at Charlie.

'And what about you, Mum?' said Charlie. There was no mistaking the angst in Charlie's voice.

'I'll be in a taxi to Kew,' said Famie. 'A black cab chosen randomly. That's the way it has to be from now on. Don't trust Uber.'

Famie knew she had to go but was suddenly full of foreboding. She trusted Sam, and she loved Charlie. She couldn't think of two better people with whom to share her work and life. They had survived the attacks in Coventry together, set up Howl together, negotiated their way into the Nash story together. But this was suddenly a very dangerous inquiry, and she feared for both of them. She walked to Charlie's chair, put her arms out.

'Mum?' said Charlie, standing. They embraced. Famie held her daughter tight, felt her ribs hard against hers. Charlie and Sam exchanged looks of surprise. 'Mum, we'll be fine,' she said.

'Just take fucking care, that's all,' said Famie. She pulled away. They all grinned.

'Classic Famie parenting,' said Sam.

Famie pulled a face. Checked her watch. 'Gotta fly,' she said. 'Stay in touch. I'll message every fifteen minutes. Reply every time.' She strode for the door, then stopped. 'Agreed?'

'Yes, Mum.'

'Yes, Famie.'

She managed a smile, and ran for the stairs.

79

Famie found a cab near St Pancras. 'Is Kew okay?' she said to the driver. 'I know it's miles out.'

He looked into his mirror. 'If you're happy to pay the fare, love,' he said, 'I'll drive to you to Aberdeen.'

'Great,' she said. 'Thank you. And, no, just Kew. The National Archive, please.' She put on her headphones, chose the Mozart piano sonatas and accessed the National Archive website. It told her she had till four o'clock to order documents. She had till seven o'clock to read them. This will be tight, she thought.

She typed in her details, entered her reader's ticket number. If there were no slots available today, she'd have to blag her way in. She'd done it before, when she was suddenly posted to Pakistan and wanted to see documents about Partition with India, but it had been a tough negotiation to win.

The page loaded. There were five slots left. Famie took one, then searched the document database. Precision now would pay off later. Choose the wrong documents and she'd be out of time. She read the information carefully, then entered the appropriate catalogue codes. Sent the request.

The eighth sonata segued to the ninth. Famie started a new document. She titled it 'Nash' and started to write.

80

Michael Nash woke to find he had a visitor. He blinked a few times, then pushed himself up. Rearranged the pillows, found his glasses. His visitor was smartly dressed. Deep blue suit, white shirt, no tie. Mid-forties, white hair and beard. The man smiled, offered Nash a business card. 'Mr Nash, good afternoon,' he said. 'Paul Grayson. I'm the loss adjuster on your case.'

Nash took the card, read it. 'Okay,' he said. 'You need to talk now?'

The man smiled apologetically. 'I'm so sorry to trouble you here as you're recovering. Sorry, too, for the terrible fire you've suffered. I appreciate you must still be in shock.'

'Must I?' said Nash, sounding unimpressed. 'Well, maybe. I'll be out of here tomorrow, I think, so maybe we could talk then.' It wasn't a question, more of a dismissal.

The visitor nodded. 'No, I understand,' he said. 'But unfortunately time is of the essence. I have instructed the disaster-management company Shillings to assess the damage at the West End Gallery. I don't know if you've had any dealings with them, but they're thorough and discreet.'

'No, of course I haven't. Why would I? I've never lost anything before.'

'I understand, of course' said the visitor, 'but they're very concerned about the suggestion of arson in this case. They're making the point, and legally they're correct, that if one of your employees is responsible, all insurance cover you have may be null and void.'

Nash looked as though he had been punched in the stomach. He could barely speak. 'But that is preposterous,' he managed.

The visitor raised both hands, palms out. 'I know,' he said, 'quite preposterous. Totally agree. I have made reassuring noises but they need to hear it from you.'

'But it was the demonstrator!' said Nash. 'Everyone knows it was him! For Christ's sake, this is ridiculous.' Nash swung his legs off the bed. He was wearing chinos, shirt and jumper. He smoothed his jumper, and took a deep breath. 'You need to tell them, Mr Grayson, loud and clear, what I thought everyone had accepted. The arson was committed by the idiot who broke into the gallery. Your disaster people just need to talk to the police. You tell them that.'

Nash's visitor looked serious. 'If I may be so bold, Mr Nash,' he said, 'why don't you tell them? It would have so much more authority coming from you. And, you should know, they're about to view your surviving paintings. Maybe we could pay a quick visit.'

Nash frowned. 'They're doing what? he said. 'I haven't authorized that, what—'

'It's okay' said the visitor. 'Your daughter will be letting them in. Monitoring every move.'

Nash put his head into his hands. 'No, no, no, this is all wrong,' he said, through his fingers. 'All wrong. I should be there.' He slid off the bed and stood up. Grayson offered his hand. Nash pushed it away. 'I'm not a cripple,' he said. 'And I'm probably younger than you. Even if I don't feel it.' They faced each other, Nash the taller and thinner of the two.

'We could go there now, if you feel you can,' said Grayson. 'I'm sure the team from Shillings would find it reassuring.'

Nash continued to study Grayson, who put his hands into his jacket pockets and smiled. Eventually, Nash nodded. A mind made up. 'Very well,' he said. 'Then let's be quick about it. My coat is in the cupboard.' Grayson found it and helped him into it. The two men walked slowly from the ward, Grayson steadying Nash with a guiding hand.

81

Charlie and Sam spent their cab ride on their phones. Charlie called Lena again, Sam was reading about Eyre Crowe. Charlie left more messages, Sam made notes. Occasionally one looked up, then returned to their screen.

'I've just messaged Mum,' said Charlie, 'like she asked.'

Sam nodded, carried on scrolling.

'I think she's right to be worried,' she said, her voice barely audible above the engine noise. 'This is so unlike Lena.' She stared out of the window. They would be at the hospital in two minutes. 'If she hasn't visited her father, I'm going to wait,' she said. 'I'm sure she'd want to patch things up if she can.'

'Maybe,' Sam said.

'What do you mean, "maybe"?' she said.

'The saying is about burning bridges,' he said, 'but a burning gallery, and a dead man in its basement, might be the same. If their disagreement was in some way connected to the fire, then the relationship is in serious trouble. To say the least.'

Charlie said nothing. She blinked twice and cleared her throat. 'I'm scared, Sam,' she said at last. 'Scared for Lena. Scared for Mum.' Sam put down his phone, looked at her. 'I don't know where this is all heading,' Charlie continued, 'but it feels like we're on the edge of something. Did you ever get that feeling back at the agency? When you were on a story?'

The taxi pulled up at a red light. The hospital was a left turn. Sam pocketed his phone. 'Sure,' he said. 'You develop some kind of intuition over time. But sometimes it's wrong. I'm wrong. Wrong all the time, actually. Sometimes your feelings on a story are misplaced. You've been misled by your personal history and opinions. You make a snap judgement. You act on that judgement and you've called it wrong.' He shrugged.

'Don't think Mum would say that,' said Charlie.

Sam smiled. 'That's why she works faster than I do.'

A line of traffic edged its way in front of them, turning right. Two black cabs led the way, then a Range Rover. Both cabs were empty. The Range Rover had a passenger. Charlie grabbed Sam's arm.

'Fuck! That's him!' she yelled. 'Back of that car!' She pointed at the man sitting by the right rear window: swept-back hair, thick-rimmed black glasses, oversized coat. Unmistakably Michael Nash. And driving, a man with a white beard, white hair. Someone who looked like Kenny Rogers.

82

Charlie and Sam jumped from the cab. The driver had guessed there had been a change of plan and pulled up as soon as was safe. He had been making the turn anyway so stopped just a few metres from the hospital.

They ran back to Euston Road but the traffic heading east was lighter, and the cab was gone. Charlie tugged Sam's sleeve.

'Let's see if the hospital knows who Nash left with,' he said. They sprinted into the hospital reception. 'Bethlehem Ward?' he said, to a uniformed man behind a wide desk.

He stabbed a finger at some stairs. 'Up one, along two,' he said.

Charlie led the way, taking the steps three at a time. Signs on the first landing pointed them right. They ran along a corridor, zigzagging though visitors and medical staff, past double doors to the first ward on the right. At the double doors to Bethlehem Ward on the left, they crashed straight through to find an L-shaped counter with no one behind it, then rooms leading off a small waiting area with two sofas facing each other. A nurse emerged from the nearest room. Blue uniform, blonde hair piled high. Her badge said 'Deborah'.

'Can I help?' she said, eyes darting between Charlie and Sam.

'We were looking for Michael Nash,' said Sam, between breathless gasps.

'You've missed him,' said the nurse. 'Just popped out for a walk. He had a visitor.'

'Do you know who it was?' said Charlie.

'Said he was a colleague.'

'I see,' said Sam. 'Could we leave Michael a note? Would that be okay?'

'Of course,' said Deborah. 'Room six.' She pointed at a corner room, door open.

'Thanks,' said Charlie.

Inside room six, Sam closed the door. Charlie turned to him, frowning. 'Leave a note?'

He shrugged. 'Well, it got us in. And, actually, I will leave a note now we're here. Tell Nash we came to see him.' There was a medical pad at the foot of the bed. Sam began to write, while Charlie swept the room.

She noticed a small rectangle of card lying in the tangle of bedding. She picked it up, turned it over. 'Paul Grayson, loss adjuster,' she said, and reached for her phone. 'There's a number,' she said, stabbing the screen. She waited, listened. 'It's fake. Of course it bloody is. "Number not recognized".' She grabbed a handful of her hair, looked at the ceiling. 'Christ, what a mess!' She looked at Sam. 'He's in big trouble, isn't he?'

Sam nodded. 'I fear so,' he said. He sat on the bed. 'But on the off-chance this guy actually is the loss adjuster, we should get back to the square.'

They ran from the room.

83

The Range Rover had just turned into Regent's Park when it faltered, then jerked to a stop. Paul Grayson cursed, banged the steering-wheel. He fired the ignition. The car started. The engine ran long enough for him to ease the car to the kerb, where it died. He turned to his passenger. 'I'm so sorry, Mr Nash, both for my outburst and my car. The man at the garage assured me it was fixed. It would appear he was wrong.' He switched on the hazard lights, sighed deeply.

'This has happened before?' said Michael Nash.

'A couple of times,' said Grayson. 'There's a tube station around the corner. It's one stop. My apologies again. Can you manage that? I'll be right with you.' He checked his watch. 'If we go now, we'll just catch them. They know we're on the way.' He undid his seatbelt.

Nash stared out of the window. 'I don't think so. I'll just walk back to the hospital. It isn't far. If it's that important, they can come to me.'

Grayson nodded. 'Sure,' he said. 'That's fair. If they come to you, it'll be their B-team for sure. And we might not get the best hearing. But we can live with that maybe.' His hands went up and down, as though he was weighing fruit. 'It's fifty–fifty, I'd say.'

Nash said nothing, stared ahead. Grayson watched him.

Nash made up his mind. 'I don't like fifty–fifty,' he said, and released his seatbelt. 'If we see a cab, we take it.' Grayson stepped out of the car, walked round to Nash's side, opened the door and offered his arm. Nash waved him away.

The two men walked to Great Portland Street tube station. Nash was slow but speeded up as they got closer. Grayson bought two tickets, and they climbed down the stairs to the station. Michael Nash held on to the railing, took one step at a time. There was a minute until the next train for King's Cross St Pancras. Grayson stood just behind Nash, who was just behind the yellow safety line.

The air moved, displaced by the oncoming train. Grayson checked around him. The nearest passenger was ten metres away, studying his phone. He turned back. The train approached at speed. It started to brake. The train driver leant forward, staring straight ahead.

Five metres away, Grayson raised both arms.

Four metres away he placed them in the small of Nash's back.

Three metres away, he pushed.

84

Half an hour into her cab ride, Famie glanced up for the first time. The meter said £68.50. Left and right was the biggest cemetery Famie could remember seeing. 'The dead centre of Richmond,' said the driver, laughing at his own joke.

She removed one earbud. 'You've told that one before,' she said.

'That I have,' he said. 'There in a few minutes, love.' Famie nodded, replaced the earbud, returned to her phone. She hated writing with a screen so small. She cursed her thumb-to-letter accuracy. But she at least had a framework of an article to send to Sam. Starting with the fire, it was her account of what had happened to the West End Gallery, the discovery of Jamie Nelson's body and her visit to Dorking with Brian Nelson. That was as far as she had got. She pressed send, then gathered her thoughts.

The National Archive was not set up for people in a hurry. It was, by design, a place for deep research, carried out methodically, respectfully. It could not operate at the pace Famie needed. She steeled herself for a clash of cultures. Lena was still missing, and Sam had reported that Michael Nash had disappeared. Two ticking clocks, one painstaking, meticulous national institution.

Another glance up. The driver was slowing for sure. She needed ninety seconds to read one document she had accessed.

It was, she was sure, where the story started. She swiped twice. Text filled her screen. Modern font, ancient words.

'1833. An Act for the Abolition of Slavery throughout the British Colonies; for promoting the Industry of the manumitted Slaves; and for compensating the Persons hitherto entitled to the Services of such Slaves.'

This was, Famie knew, how abolition had been passed: with a massive payout to slave-owners. She looked at the driver. 'I'm going to read some weird stuff out loud. Ignore me. Just getting something clear in my head.'

'No worries, love. You carry on,' he said, and killed the intercom.

Famie read from the screen: ' "That the said Commissioners shall proceed to apportion the said sum into nineteen different shares, which shall be respectively assigned to the several British Colonies or Possessions herein-after mentioned; (that is to say,) the Bermuda Islands, the Bahama Islands, Jamaica, Honduras, the Virgin Islands, Antigua, Montserrat, Nevis, Saint Christopher's, Dominica, Barbados, Grenada, Saint Vincent's, Tobago, Saint Lucia, Trinidad, British Guiana, the Cape of Good Hope, and Mauritius." '

The taxi stopped. The driver checked his mirror. Famie held up a finger. 'One minute.' He gave a thumbs-up. She read on: ' "The said Commissioners shall have regard to the number of slaves belonging to or settled in each of such Colonies and are stated according to the latest returns made in the Office of the Registrar of Slaves in England." '

Famie closed the screen, pocketed the phone. 'Fuck me, this is grim,' she said.

The taxi dropped her in the National Archive's car park. Famie rounded up the fare to £100, happy to pay for the privacy. The air felt fresher away from central London. It had rained recently – she hadn't noticed. She jogged past artificial lakes, scattering pigeons and gulls as she ran. The National Archive, all glass and concrete, reminded Famie of a seventies campus university. Purpose-built, functional, sterile. According to their website, it had been voted Kew's ugliest building. It looked just fine to her. 'Public Record Office' had been carved, temple-like, in pale stone, high above the entrance. A more modest glass and metal sign said 'The National Archive', alongside their opening times. They closed at seven o'clock. She had six hours to get this story nailed.

She remembered the drill. Coats, bags and pens were all forbidden and to be left in a locker. She ran to the second floor 'map and large document reading room' with her notebook and pencil in a see-through plastic bag. She swiped her reader's card through the scanner; a guard checked the bag, nodded her through. She was in the middle of a long, low room. Grey carpet tiles, huge wooden desks in rows, and a maze of walls and partitions lined with files and books. A hushed academic silence. She guessed sixty desks, of which twenty were occupied. One was piled high with large grey foam wedges to support the more delicate volumes.

The collections and returns were in a side room, Famie presented herself at what appeared to be the front desk. A man, late thirties, in jeans and grey sweatshirt took her information, then smiled.

'What?' said Famie.

'You don't remember me, but I sure as hell remember you,' he said.

Then it clicked. 'Huh,' said Famie. 'You're the guy I saw when I was causing trouble last time. That was ages ago. You're still here.'

He pulled a face. 'My career advancement has been somewhat

been slower than I had expected,' he said. 'But I read your book. And I told everyone I'd helped you get the Partition of India documents back in the day. It's my claim to fame.'

Famie forgave him the precious time this was taking. 'I have a proper reader's card this time' she said. 'And I've ordered the documents upfront. Everything done properly.'

'Nice one. I'll just be a moment.' He wandered off.

'I'm in a slight rush,' she called after him, knowing it would make no difference. What was a 'slight rush' anyway? Famie forced herself to control her breathing. Nothing about what she was going to do could be hurried anyway. She was sure the information she needed was somewhere here. If this was, as someone had dubbed it, 'the nation's filing cabinet', all she had to do was ask the right questions. Find the right file. She checked her watch, then her phone. The man in the grey sweatshirt walked back, in his arms a thick cardboard box the size of a desktop. From his strained expression, this was going to hurt. It landed in front of her with a thump. She felt a dusty breeze on her face.

'This is the first,' he said. 'You get the next when you're done. Good luck,' he said.

Gingerly, she slid the box into her arms and adjusted her stance. She felt as if she was carrying two bags of soil out of a garden centre. No help was offered. She found her way to one of the vacant work desks and eased the box from her aching arms, relieved not to have dropped it. Her hands trembled. Famie steadied them on the desk. She lifted the lid.

85

Inside was a vast ledger: terracotta-coloured spine, light brown board and dark leather cover, with a white criss-cross stitch sewn into the hide. Scratchy black letters down the right side. Famie squinted. Two centuries old. Most of the words were intact, written in capitals. Each word on top of the next. She whispered the words as she read.'NO 1. WIC. JAMAICA.' Then a space. 'CAYMANAS, CLARENDON, HANOVER, MANCHESTER,WESTMORELAND.'

She ran a hand lightly over the cover. The white criss-cross stitching was flattened tape, used, Famie assumed, like a wire mesh to strengthen the cover. The board was battered and rough but the heavily inked lettering had survived .'Caymanas' must be the Cayman Islands. The other names she knew were four of the old counties of Jamaica. West End was in Westmoreland, the west coast just south of Hanover. If there were any Nashs in Jamaica who had received compensation for the loss of their slaves, this book would have recorded it. Her skin prickled. She wondered if anyone had opened this book in almost two hundred years. 'Here we go, then,' she muttered.

The cover creaked as she turned it over. Elaborate brown, red and blue marbled endpapers. A blank first page, stained with browns and yellows. The liver spots of ancient bookbinding. Famie wondered if she should be wearing the white gloves she had seen others using. She scanned the room. Some were, some weren't. There was no obvious dispensing point. She decided to press on, and wiped her her hands on her trousers.

She turned the heavy page. Intricate, elaborate handwriting filled the following spread. Twenty ledger entries written across eight columns. They were headed 'Compensation number', 'Signature', 'Date of Issue', 'Claimant', 'Date of Treasury Warrant'. Then three columns with cash amounts entered: 'Principal', 'Interest' and 'Total'. Printed across both in bold black type were the words 'Jamaica. Payments on account of West India Compensation, per Act 3&4 WmIV c73.'

'Bingo,' said Famie. This was precisely the book she needed. 'Act 3&4' was the Act of Parliament that abolished slavery, 'WmIV' was King William IV, who had signed the Act into law. She had no idea about the 'c73'. Assumed it didn't matter.

Famie leant forward to read some of the tangled letters more clearly. She smelt the dust and vanilla scent she associated with old-book shops. She ran her finger down the 'Claimant' column. A looped, italic, cursive hand had written each name. 'Joseph Stone Williams', John Pritchard', 'Anne Seivwright'. There seemed to be no order to the entries. They weren't alphabetical and they weren't in order of the settlement size. Williams had received £711 five shillings and threepence. Pritchard £88 and Seivwright £354 three shillings and eightpence.

Famie guessed there were around eighty pages. Twenty entries per page meant sixteen hundred claims for compensation. Westmoreland was the last county in the ledger. She needed to start there.

86

Famie ran her finger down the ancient pages of the ledger. Deep red index tabs had been added, dividing the records by county. Westmoreland was the last. She slid her finger into the thick papers, creating a break. Lifted slowly. When the pages were at ninety degrees, she used both hands to guide them down.

On the left, the names and signatures of the slave-owners. On the right, the amounts paid. Somewhere here, she thought, there must be a Nash.

The elaborate writing style, all loops and flourishes, made distinguishing names harder work than she'd expected. She scanned the first twenty entries, heart racing. King, Greaver, Appleby, Foucher. £25, £92, £711, £196 and seven shillings. Her finger ran down the column. No Nashs. She turned the page. McGibbon, Watt, Oliphant, Grant. £4,603, £20, £1,313 and seventeen shillings, £82 nine shillings and sevenpence. No Nashs. Page after page. More slave-owners, more payouts. With every column checked, her heart slowed, her mood soured.

The final page of Westmoreland entries took the total of parish claimants to 560. The last entry, Mary Golding, claimed £40 and eighteen shillings on 9 August 1836.

And that was that.

'Fuck,' said Famie. She sighed deeply. The next parish up was Hanover. She found the index tab, flipped back twenty pages. Repeated the search. No Nashs. Maybe she had this wrong. The Nashs might have lived in West End, Westmoreland, but their plantations could have been elsewhere on the island, recorded in another ledger, one she hadn't ordered and knew would take at least an hour to appear if she requested it now.

She didn't have that kind of time. Nowhere near.

She packed up the ledger, placed it back in its box, heaved it from her desk and staggered back to her fan at the document desk.

'Any good?' he said.

'Disappointing.'

'Second box of delights?' he asked.

'Yes, thank you,' she said. The man disappeared behind shelving and reappeared with a slightly smaller brown box, the size of a small suitcase. She took it, grateful it felt like just one bag of soil. Set it down on her desk, lifted the lid. It appeared to be a scrapbook. Bulging covers were stuffed with letters, newspapers, proclamations and petitions to the governor of Jamaica, Lord Sligo. One large white document folded out to A3 size. Under the royal coat of arms were the words 'To the negro population of the island of Jamaica'. Followed by 'Dear Friends. Our good King, who was himself in Jamaica a long time ago, still thinks and talks a great deal of the island. He has sent me out here to take care of you and protect your rights.'

Of course he did, thought Famie.

It concluded, 'I trust you will be good and diligent subjects to our good King so that he may never have cause to be sorry for all the good he has done for you. Your friend and well wisher, Sligo.'

Famie shook her head. What a fucking cheek, she thought. God forbid that the King might be disappointed in the behaviour of his previously enslaved population. The newspaper, the *Jamaica Dispatch* was dated 5 June 1834 and contained many adverts appealing for the capture of runaway slaves and offering great rewards in return.

'Seems some folk just didn't get your passive-aggressive message, Sligo,' Famie muttered.

The final pages were stuffed with letters headed 'Death certificates and marriage registers in relation to claims under the Slave Compensation Act'.

'Huh,' she said.

Famie looked up, spun in her chair. The other readers went by in a blur but she didn't register them. Two revolutions, then she spun the other way. Marriages and deaths. Of course marriages and deaths. Pay attention, woman, she thought. She stopped spinning. From her transparent plastic bag she removed her notebook, then wheeled her chair to a space on the desk and flicked through the pages till she found what she needed. She had taken two pages to draw a rough Nash family tree based on what she thought she knew.

The three Nash siblings were at the bottom. Robert, Helen, Michael. Their parents were Harry and Janet. Famie had written 'Suicide! Check!' by her name. Then Harry Nash's parents, James and Marion. The fascist fundraiser couple. And then it was a blank. A missing generation from, she presumed, the second half of the nineteenth century. Famie had no names to work on there but she knew where she was heading. If there was a Nash in Piccadilly in the first half of the nineteenth century, she might just have it.

She replaced the book in the box, returned it to her archive friend. She needed a favour.

87

Famie used her best smile. 'Hi, again,' she said. 'Bringing this back.' She pushed the box over the table. 'I assume you have the 1841 census here? That would be right?'

The man nodded. 'Of course. The censuses are always being asked for. You'd definitely need to book upfront. Best to go online. They're all digitized.'

'But all the terminals are taken,' said Famie, gesturing back into the study room.

'Do you know what you're looking for?'

Famie smiled again. 'I think I do.'

The man looked at his screen, tapped at a keyboard, glanced up at her. 'Okay,' he said. 'What are *we* looking for?'

'John Nash, living in Piccadilly somewhere,' she said.

The man typed, peered at his screen, beckoned Famie to his side of the desk. He pointed at the top of screen. 'You mean him?'

She leant in. A single white page, black-lined columns filled with more cursive handwriting. She looked to where he was pointing. In the 'Place' column, were the words 'Forty-one, Piccadilly'. Then 'Names of each person abode therein the preceding night'. The first name 'John William Nash'. Under the age and sex column, he had written '40' in the 'Male' box. As his 'Profession' he had entered 'Trader'.

'This what you wanted?' asked the archive man. Famie didn't reply. Her heart rate had kicked up again. Her finger traced the next name. This was what she needed. Everything, everything hinged on this woman.

She read across the page. A different hand. 'Forty-one, Piccadilly. Mary Nash (formerly Bennett). 36. Independent means.'

Famie felt her eyes brim. Mary Bennett. This was her. It must be her. 'Why would she have written "formerly" here?' she said. 'Wouldn't she have put "née" to indicate her maiden name?'

The archive man peered again at the screen and frowned. 'I'd say she was married before. Maybe her husband died. Or left her. She didn't have to give that information anyway. Not till the 1851 census. So she's making a point, I reckon. She is Mary Nash. But she was Mary Bennett.'

Famie turned to him. 'Sorry, what's your name?' she said.

The man looked surprised. 'Oh,' he said. 'It's Colin. Colin Slater.'

'Well, Colin Slater,' she said. 'I think I love you.' And she kissed his cheek.

He grinned sheepishly, blushing a livid scarlet. 'Oh,' he said.

'And now, if I may,' said Famie, 'I need that ledger again.'

88

Charlie had rung the hospital, rung Lena. She had hit the 'Find My Phone' icon constantly. She paced the flat, tidying, rearranging, fussing. She filled the kettle, let it boil and switch off. She stood staring through the steam as it evaporated around her. She reached for a mug, then stopped, fingers on the cupboard-door handle. She looked startled, then ran from the room.

She sprinted out of the building, swerved the shoppers and tourists, scanned Granary Square. Saw what she was looking for, took off again. Seb the coffee man had a small queue in front of his stall. Charlie joined it. Waited impatiently. He smiled when he saw her, whiskers twitching. The queue moved slowly, largely due to Seb having a conversation with every customer. Each coffee was a ritual. The tourists found his theatricality charming, Charlie found it profoundly irritating. By the time it was her turn, she was ready to burst.

'Seb, hi. Listen, I need your help. You always seem to know what's going on. Have you seen Lena? My flatmate. Only I think she's missing and . . .' Her eyes began to fill again. She shoved her hands into her dress pockets.

He ground some beans, scooped the powder into the portafilter. 'Sure I have,' he said. 'Few hours back.'

Charlie brightened. 'Did you see where she came from? Where she went? It's just I have no . . . She'd had an argument with her dad, you see, and . . .'

He pressed a button and the espresso machine hummed into

life. 'Didn't see where she came from, I have to be honest,' he said. 'She was thirsty. Bought water, said she'd been walking. But she went back to Gasholders. Three coffees. Cardboard tray.'

Charlie stared at him. 'Really? Are you sure?'

'Reckon so,' he said. 'That's just the direction she was walking, you understand. Never saw her go in.' He frothed milk.

'And three coffees?'

He nodded. 'Two cappuccinos and a double espresso.'

'How did she seem?'

He looked thoughtful. 'Awesome,' he said. 'And beautiful. Like always.'

'That's not what I asked.'

'No, but that's what I was thinking. Didn't notice much else, I'm afraid.' He poured the milk. 'I see her more than you, these days.'

Charlie frowned. 'Just think, please, Seb, if you can. This is really important. Was there anything about her that was different? Anything at all?'

He placed a plastic lid on the cup. 'Lena's always the same,' he said. 'Always. Rain or shine. Hadn't thought about it before, really. I like that. I think it's why that poor guy chatted her up that time.' Charlie's frown was back. He handed over the cup.

'I didn't ask for coffee.'

'I know. On the house.'

'Sorry, Seb. Who is "that poor guy"?'

'The guy that died in the fire. He was in my queue once. Started talking to Lena.' Charlie held the coffee, didn't move. A woman behind her leant forward.

'Have you . . . have you finished?' she said.

Still Charlie didn't move. 'Lena knew Jamie?' she said.

89

Lena, Robert and Helen Nash sat around a table. Each of them had a coffee and a switched-off phone in front of them. Lena pulled up the sleeves of her pink corduroy jacket and scowled. Robert and Helen tried smiles.

'So,' said Lena, '"an open and generous offer" is what you said you wanted to discuss. An offer about what? And why isn't my dad here?' She looked between them, eyebrows raised.

Helen leant in first. 'Well, we won't pretend this is easy, Lena, but we wanted to run a few things past you before we speak to your father. That's why we're doing it in this order.' She gave a little sigh. 'The offer is a settlement for you and your father to move away from the West End business. To leave completely. You'll be able to settle anywhere with anything. Just not as part of the family. To do that—'

Lena's hand was up. 'Woah, hang on. What is this shit? Move away from our family business? West End is as much my father's property as it's yours. So that's not a very promising start. But, hey, carry on, I'm all ears.'

Helen waited a beat. 'To do that,' she continued, 'we will pay your father his third of the business. Based on market value before the fire, paid wherever and however he wants. That's why it's generous.'

She sat back and Robert took over. 'There is a reason for this . . .' he waved a hand, looking for a phrase '. . . for this turn of events.' He looked away briefly. 'The loss adjuster has made, er, a somewhat informal approach to us. To me. Off the record, you know. He thinks your father grossly over-insured the gallery. To the tune of two or maybe three hundred per cent.'

Lena's cheeks flushed an angry red. She stared at her uncle. 'Bollocks,' she said. She dragged her chair up to the table and leant over as far as she could. Her face was barely a foot away from his. 'You're lying.' She turned to her aunt. 'And you're lying too.'

Robert Nash bent down, fished a document from a bag on the floor. He placed it on the table with a slap. 'A summary of his position,' he said. You'll see every painting's value is out.'

Lena reluctantly dragged her eyes to the file in front of her. A grey cover marked 'Private and Confidential'. Five sheets on headed paper, the seventy-three lost paintings listed in alphabetical order. There were two figures listed by every image. The amount it was insured for and the amount their expert assessed it was worth. In each case, the difference was remarkable. The Aphex and Steel painting, the first on the list, had been insured for a million pounds. Its true value, according to the document, was closer to three hundred and sixty pounds. Lena read through every page. Two fingers traced the figures in the two columns. She closed the file. 'Well, if that's true we have a problem. But, like I said, this family lies. Has always lied. It's a genetic weakness. And it afflicts some more than others. So . . .' she tossed the document onto the table '. . . who knows how you came by this? Do you want to explain?'

Robert checked his watch, walked to the fridge. 'You can, of course, talk with the team who put this together,' he said. 'I'll arrange it.' He removed a half-full bottle of rosé, poured three glasses, placed them on the table and sat down. 'But you see the problem. Just say for the moment the figures are right. If this became public knowledge . . .'

'Which, of course, you could arrange,' said Lena. Helen looked at Robert. Robert said nothing. Lena looked between them. 'Okay, then,' she said, 'which Howard Taylor could arrange.'

'Howard works in myriad different ways,' Robert said.

'So, that's a yes,' said Lena. Robert shrugged. Helen drank some wine. 'And the truth is, if you're being honest,' Lena continued, 'you've never liked my father being in the business. Probably never liked my father full stop. And you both think everything would be easier if he just wasn't part of everything. If he wasn't around. Yes?'

Helen shook her head. 'Not me. Michael is a sweetie. Very happy to have him around.'

Lena looked appalled. 'And there we have it,' she said. ' "Happy to have him around"? Really? Can you even hear yourself? You talk like he's some kind of fucking pet.' Her eyes narrowed. 'And tell me, because I've often wondered, is this all about your mother? That somehow my father is to blame for her suicide? Is that it?'

There was a silence. Robert shifted in his seat. 'Our mother wasn't well,' he said.

'And then something pushed her over the edge?' said Lena.

Helen's mouth dropped open. She glanced at Robert, who said nothing.

'My, God,' said Lena. 'That was Howard Taylor, too, wasn't it?' She sat back in her chair. She swallowed twice. She looked aghast. As though she was seeing them for the first time.

The expression of panic was unmistakable.

90

This time the box felt lighter. Famie's arms still shook with the effort, and she still grunted as she eased it onto the desk, but now she was in the zone. She heard nothing but her heartbeat, saw nothing apart from what was in front of her. The lid off, the ledger removed, her finger traced the index tabs to 'Westmoreland'. She lifted the pages. Eased them down.

Five hundred and sixty slave-owners. Five hundred and sixty claims. Five hundred and sixty payouts. One county, one island. Twenty-eight pages detailing who had claimed what. No mention of the enslaved, just the enslavers. As she stood over the names and numbers, Famie suddenly realized what she was looking at. 'Holy shit,' she whispered. Her eyes ran up and down the columns. The pounds, shillings and pence. 'It's another fucking grab list. That's what this is. Money offered, money grabbed.' Her head spun. She knew she was in a race, knew she was running out of time, but why hadn't she understood this before? She bent over the ledger, let her right index finger rest on the ancient paper. Slowly she traced her way down the 'Claimant' column, pausing occasionally to squint at a particularly indecipherable scribble. She spoke the names aloud: 'Maria Moore, Angela Foucher, William King, Sarah Greaves, Charles Chatfield.' She was surprised at the number of women making the claims, but wasn't sure why. She continued with her roll call: 'Bonella Stone, Margaret Young, Charles Braine.'

Twenty down, turn the page, another twenty, turn the page. Then, page three of the twenty-eight. Claim fifty-six. Famie's finger stopped. She stared at the writing, leant in and read it again. She felt her skin and scalp tingle.

Compensation Number 56. Date of Issue 9/3/35. Claimant Mary Bennett. Total £6,111 14 shillings.

And there she was. Mary Bennett, ex-slave-owner, wife of John Nash, soon to be in residence at 41 Piccadilly, London. From one West End to another. The start of the Nash empire and all of it based on slavery. Famie did a chair-spin of celebration, then took photographs on her phone. As she framed the image, her eyes fell down the page to compensation numbers 59 and 61. Same signature. Same name. Two more claims for Mary Bennett. One for £3,778 and another for £4,651 twelve shillings and threepence. Famie raced through the rest of the Westmoreland pages. Found nothing. A quick calculation gave her more than fourteen thousand pounds. She had no idea what that was worth today, but from what she had seen, Mary Bennett had been one of the biggest slave-owners on the island. And after abolition, once the enslaved had gone, doubtless to be the King's 'good and diligent subjects', it hadn't taken her long to return to England.

Famie straightened, paced the floor. That was it, surely. She had what she wanted. She had proof of the origins of the Nash wealth. And a clue as to why they were all such bastards. Her mind drifted to Jamie Nelson. 'It's all about the roots,' was his line and he was right. Is this what he had suspected? Is this why he had been in the Nash gallery? She walked around the tables while she thought.

As she arrived back at her desk, Colin Slater was hovering, both hands shoved deep into his hoodie's central pocket.

He looked awkward, still flushed. She gave him a quizzical smile. 'Hey, Colin,' she said. 'You need this back?' She pointed at the ledger. 'I think I've done with it.' Famie sat on her chair, began to pack up. Slater pulled up another chair, wheeled it until he sat next to her. Christ, what have I done? she thought.

'Is this, er, is this, a, you know . . .'

Famie waited.

'Is this a big, er, thing you're working on?' he managed.

Famie was puzzled. 'Kinda,' she said, 'but I'm just going. Why?'

'Well,' he said, 'someone else has been trying to book this box out.' He pointed at the ledger.

Famie sat bolt upright in her chair. It jerked forward a few inches. 'Someone is what?' she said.

'Trying to book the same documents as you. It's just that no one has ever asked for those documents before,' said Slater. 'Not for many years anyway.'

'And now there's a second,' she said.

'Well, there would be, but he's too late. Unless you're handing the ledger back?'

'He?'

'Yup. He's got a reader's card.'

'You know who it is?' said Famie, warning bells flashing in her head.

'I wrote it down,' said Slater. He passed a folded sheet to Famie. She unfolded it. Read the name. And shivered.

It was Howard Taylor. 'Oh, shit,' she said. 'How long ago was this?'

'The enquiry was ninety minutes ago,' said Slater. 'Is there a problem?'

Famie wondered what to say. 'No problem,' she said. 'Apart

from him being a vicious, vindictive piece of shit.' She smiled. 'Apart from that, we're fine.'

Slater wheeled back a few centimetres. He searched for words. 'Well, he's still too late,' he said. 'You're perfectly safe to keep the box till we shut.' A classic bureaucrat's response, she thought.

'And also,' said Slater, 'he's downstairs. In the document reading room.'

91

'Calm down, dear, you're fine with us,' said Helen Nash. 'We're on your side.' Robert Nash had finished his wine. Helen Nash had finished hers. Lena Nash hadn't touched hers. Robert had opened another bottle.

'No, you're not,' said Lena, standing up. 'And I'm late to realize this, but you're on your own side, Helen. And his.' She stabbed a finger at Robert. 'But you're not on mine, not on my father's and never have been.' Her hand rested on the grey cover of the loss adjuster's report. 'I still say bullshit,' she said.

'But you're not sure, are you?' said Robert.

'It's convincing,' said Lena. 'Of course it is. This is a Nash product after all. We've managed to be convincing for decades, haven't we? Centuries in fact.'

Robert played with an unlit cigarette, tapped the tobacco end on the table.'An interesting phrase,' he said. His voice was quieter now.

Lena frowned. 'What?' she said.

Robert kept tapping. 'Managed to be convincing,' he said. 'What did you mean by that?'

Lena took a mouthful of wine. She looked him in the eye. 'I think you know very well what I meant,' she said.

Now it was Helen's turn. 'I'm not sure I do, though,' she said. She glanced at Robert, then Lena. 'Am I part of this? Have I managed to be convincing too?'

Lena closed her eyes. 'Oh, please, spare me the whole innocent-abroad act. You know exactly what's what in this organization.'

'An organization that seems a long way from your heart, dear Lena,' Helen said. 'Even though we pay your salary, I believe.' She smiled briefly.

'You do,' said Lena. 'I'm very aware of that. And from my rather sad wage, I give generously to the German Greens. Just for the hell of it.'

Helen sat back in her chair. 'Really?' she said. 'Why the German Greens? What's wrong with the UK ones? Other than the obvious, I mean.'

Lena took more wine. 'Closer to power,' she said. 'And maybe, just maybe, the best way to fight the far right.'

'I see,' said Helen.

'Like the AfD,' said Lena.

'Yes, thank you,' said Helen. 'I know who the AfD are.'

'Of course you do,' said Lena. 'Silly me.'

She finished the wine.

Helen's mouth opened, then closed. Robert had left the table. He took a cup from a cupboard, poured himself some water, walked back to the table and sat next to Helen. He smiled. 'It seems we need to talk,' he said.

His phone buzzed. He glanced at its screen. A thumbs-up emoji from City Boy. He showed it to his sister. She stood, walked to a window.

330

92

Famie moved desks at speed. She packed up the ledger, heaved it to a new work station. The one furthest away from the entrance. The one partly obscured by pillars and a long, chest-high book-shelf. Back of the room. Right-hand corner window. She went back for the foam wedges. She made herself small and slid low in her chair. Both hands rested on the closed ledger. How the fuck did Taylor know she was here? She remembered the sense of threat she had felt in his company, of a malevolence that seemed to ooze from his overworked pores. She had him down as a rapist for sure, maybe worse. And now, somehow, he was in the National Archive, just one floor down.

Then a realization that made her flesh creep. These records were not digitized. The West Indies compensation payments to Bennett and all the other slave-owners existed in the pages of ledger No.1 WIC and nowhere else. If it was destroyed, the infor-mation was gone. The proof was gone. Famie had the photographs of the pages, of course, but she doubted that would be enough. She ran her hands over the two-hundred-year-old stitching that held the ledger together. She was certain Taylor would destroy it.

She knew she couldn't take it with her. Too heavy, too damn big. She knew, too, that she couldn't hand it back to Slater and his archive colleagues. Howard Taylor would doubtless find a way to access it, legally or illegally. And then it would be gone for ever.

She heard the reading-room door swing open. She stood, walked slowly, peered round the pillar. Two women, both in their sixties, rummaged for their reader's tickets. Famie walked back. She was certain it was only a matter of minutes before Taylor realized the first-floor documents didn't have what he needed. That he would have to heave himself to the second. That she needed a plan.

And that only one made sense.

She ran her finger to the Westmoreland tab, opened the ledger, heard the door. She paused. Checked again. A bearded man in his twenties. She sat back, turned three pages. Claimants forty-one to sixty. Names and numbers on the left page, payments on the right. She spread a hand over each page. It felt coarse and brittle. She looked around her. Three workstations were occupied, all men. They paid Famie no attention, lost in their own ancient worlds. The nearest man wore gloves. He was gingerly unrolling a scroll, bent to his task. The other two were reading.

The door again. This time it was Taylor.

Famie swallowed a gasp. Held her breath. Heart hammering, she watched as he swiped his reader's card. He carried no plastic bag, and the security woman just waved him through. He disappeared into the side room where Slater and his colleagues administered the requested documents. Famie had no time to fine-tune her thinking. No time to distract. No time to be discreet. At her desk, she stooped low. Her left hand held the edge of the left ledger page, her right hand flat on the right. She bit her lip. Pulled gently. It came away from the spine, tearing slightly from half-way down. She placed the loose page to one side. Now she held the right page and pulled. It tore a few millimetres from the spine but the pounds, shillings and pence were all safe. She glanced round. No one had seen her. She closed the ledger, placed both loose pages on the cover. She risked another glance around the pillar, saw no one. Taylor must be talking to Slater.

She'd have to fold the pages. Once, maybe twice. They felt fragile to the touch. They had survived well enough in a temperature-controlled environment but now they were out, might they crumble? Her breathing was short, her hands clammy. She wiped them on her jeans. She was out of time. She needed to leave.

She took both pages, placed the inked sides together, then folded them. Top over bottom. Then folded again, right over left. One hand pulled her shirt and T-shirt away from her skin, the other pushed both pages under her clothes. She tucked her T-shirt into her trousers, put her hands in her front pockets. Held the pages close. She felt the paper, girdle-like, flatten against her skin. Famie lifted the ledger back into its box, replaced the lid. She felt the dry roughness of the pages on her stomach. Hoped they'd survive intact. Hoped she'd survive intact.

She heard voices from the collections room. Slater and Taylor. She couldn't make out the words but guessed Taylor was being told he couldn't have the documents he wanted because they were out. And 'out' meant one of only thirty desks. It wouldn't take him long to find her.

Famie listened intently. More collection-room talk. More Slater, more Taylor. More to and fro. Then she realized what was happening. Slater was stalling. Keeping hold of Taylor while he could.

She had seconds.

93

While she could hear the rise and fall of Slater's words, Famie guessed she was safe. He had obviously guessed from her reaction to Taylor's name that she was frightened. And he was doing what he could to help her.

She heaved the box from the desk, walked to the table with the foam wedges. Twelve were neatly stacked in six interlocking pairs. It was a matter of seconds to hide the box. It wasn't a neat stack any more but to the casual eye at least, the ledger was gone.

Then the talking stopped.

Famie turned in time to see Taylor stride from the collections room, Slater following in his wake. She dropped to a crouch. Retied her laces in case anyone was watching her. She felt the ledger pages push and twist into her flesh.

If she had to, Famie knew she could sprint from here. That she could easily outrun a man who probably couldn't run at all. But where could she go? She had no transport, no knowledge of the area. And it was quite possible Taylor had help nearby. A driver maybe, some rent-a-thug he used when things got messy.

She tied her laces a second time.

Slater's voice was at the far end of the room. Famie had counted three rows of desks before the reading-room entrance, then three or four more. The voices were moving left, she scrambled right. A new desk, an occupied desk. A woman studying a scrolled map peered down at her, frowned.

'I'm fine,' Famie whispered. She needed her to stop looking

down. 'You carry on!' she said. The woman glared, then went back to her map. Famie scurried round the back of her chair, peered over her shoulder, like a child playing a game. Taylor was looking through an array of boxes, his back to Famie. Slater saw her, and found another box for Taylor to look in. His head was down but he was pointing. Out of Taylor's eye-line, his arm and finger were pointing at the fire exit. Opposite the entrance, window-side.

Now.

Famie stood up. She placed a hand on her stomach, felt the pages flatten, walked past the map woman to the window. If Taylor turned now, she would run. She was two desks and ten seconds from the fire exit. Eyes on Taylor. Slater wasn't looking. She didn't think anyone was looking. Longer strides. The pages felt clammy against her skin. One desk, five seconds. She saw Taylor straighten and turn. One more step. She pushed the metal bar on the fire door. It swung open. She stepped through, pushed it shut.

She jumped her way down the stairs. Two floors, four flights, twenty seconds. At the bottom of the stairwell, hand on the exit bar, she hesitated. Heart hammering in her chest, she forced herself to step back. If Taylor had traced her phone, he could trace her again. Wherever she ran, however she got back into the city, Taylor would know. Maybe he had one of the terrifying new phone-location apps she had read about. No permission needed, a precise geo-location provided.

Famie stared at her phone, cursing her lack of tech know-how. There was no way she could chuck it. She needed to write and post something very soon. Her phone was the only way to do that. She accessed the Find My Phone feature, hit 'me' then slid the 'share my location' button to 'off'. Is that it? she thought. Surely it'd be more complicated than that.

A bead of sweat dropped from her chin to her phone. How long could Slater distract Taylor? Ninety seconds, two minutes?

Her phone battery went red.

'Fuck it,' she said. The portable charger was in her bag. Which was in her locker.

Famie ran back up two flights to floor one, into the reading room. Head down, she marched to the exit. She felt every centimetre of the stolen pages around her waist. Christ, she could even hear them as she moved, the papers buckling and sliding. To mask the noise she spoke to the security man as he waved her through.

'Nothing to declare,' she said. 'And have a good evening.' The man nodded and she was through.

On the main staircase she took the steps two at time, almost crashing into two cleaners at the bottom. She apologized, stepped round their trolley. On her right the ground-floor café was quiet. To her left, the locker room was busy. She recovered her jacket and bag, plugged in the charger. From somewhere up the stairs, she heard voices. They were jumbled, incoherent. Then, clear as a bell, Colin Slater's voice calling down.

'Good luck, Mr Taylor!'

He might as well have shouted, 'Run, Famie, run!'

94

'If you remember,' said Robert, 'we're trying to provide your father with a way out. A path to leave all the crappiness and compromise of the corporate world. To walk away before any embarrassment from the lost gallery can stick.' Helen nodded, stared at Lena. 'So, of course,' he continued, 'we can engage with all your concerns about the family. Honestly and thoroughly.' Lena stood, arms folded, unimpressed. Half in, half out. Robert pulled deeply on his cigarette, blew the cloud to the ceiling. 'But, first, talk to your dad. Tell him about the deal. Isn't there a part of him that would love to be free of Helen and me?' He managed a modest smile. 'We can be horrible. We know that.'

Lena put her hands on the edge of the table. 'Wait. Wait,' she said. 'Will you stop with all this' – she slapped her hand on the table, punctuating each word – 'pathetic, mind-rotting, excruciating fuckery. You're doing it again!' She waggled her right forefinger between her aunt and uncle. 'But I know you! I've studied you! Your money funds two things. One everyone knows about. The philanthropy. The arts. The photos. We've all seen them. Bravo, aren't we great?' Lena slow-clapped, first at Robert, then Helen. 'The second? That's a different story, isn't it?'

Robert smiled. 'Well, you have a captive audience here. Your aunt and me. We're all ears.' He leant over the table, lost the smile. 'Tell me about the second.'

Lena hesitated, then made up her mind. She cleared her throat. 'The second is the funding of far-right groups across

337

Europe,' she said. 'MKN Global Fiduciaries. CitizenYes! Family First.' Robert sat back, swallowed hard. Lena leant in. 'You know it,' she said. 'That's the way the money goes.' She broke off, blinked twice. She looked around her. She appeared disoriented.

'You were saying?' said Robert.

Lena pushed herself up. She tried to turn. She made a surprised 'oh' sound as her legs folded beneath her. She keeled left, her eyes rolling back in her head. She hit the floor hard.

Robert and Helen didn't move.

'Christ,' said Robert.

'That's you, isn't it?' said Helen. Robert said nothing. 'You and your . . . pharmacy,' she said. 'That wasn't in the plan.'

Robert walked over to where Lena lay. 'I was improvising,' he said. He knelt down, stared at his niece. 'And I might need your help here, Helen.'

95

The obvious choice was the women's toilets. The archive's main doors were thirty metres away, the toilet was five. Six cubicles, all free. Famie took the last, bolted the door. Messaged Sam. *Photos on the way. Will call asap.* She selected all her recent images from her phone, posted them to Sam and Charlie.

Charlie messaged straight back. *Call me.*

Can't,

Urgent, Charlie messaged.

Famie gulped. Wrote again. *Can't speak.* She watched the cursor blinking. If Charlie said something was urgent, it was urgent. Maybe she'd found Lena. Or Michael. Or both. But there was no way she could have a conversation. Not when she was hiding in a public toilet cubicle. The two grey ticks next to her words turned blue. Her phone vibrated. Screen lit up. Just three words. *Lena knew Jamie.*

Famie read them over and over. She sat on the toilet seat. Lena knew Jamie. So was Lena the one follower on Instagram? Had they been working together? Did she know he was in the gallery when it burnt? Her head was still spinning when she heard the door to the toilets open. There was a long creaking sound from an old hinge or maybe an ancient door mechanism. Famie froze. She knew she had company. No one opened a toilet door slowly. Not unless they were checking who was inside.

She knew that all the cubicles were empty apart from hers. If it was Taylor, she'd know in seconds. She strained to hear.

Through the wall she heard clanking buckets but there were no footsteps. No one had come in. Just someone standing in the doorway.

So it was Taylor.

Famie stood up, stood still. She could hear her heart racing. Felt the sound reverberating around her cubicle. She placed her hands on the thin wooden walls, steadied herself. Breathed deeply. I am fucked, she thought. Two footsteps on the tiled floor. The sound of the door closing. More creaks, more steps. A darkening under the cubicle door. Famie held her breath. Two brown shoes appeared. The cubicle door rattled against its lock.

'You fucking pervert,' Famie hissed.

A chuckle. 'Ah, so it is you, Miss Madden. Now if you could just slide your stolen goods under the door, I won't report you to the police.'

He knows, she thought.

'I'm just having a shit,' she said. 'I'll be right with you.'

'Of course you are,' said Taylor. 'But you can multitask, I'm sure. Can you manage that for me? You could still slide the book under the door.'

Famie smiled. So he doesn't know. He's fishing.

'Then,' he continued 'and only then, I can promise to make sure the very lovely Charlie doesn't come to any harm.'

She stopped smiling. She knew he was provoking her. She could scream, of course, and she would if she had to, but she wasn't there yet. He pushed at the door again, harder this time. The lock strained in its bracket. She saw the screws shift.

'You know,' he said, 'if I were to lean against this door, my guess is it would fall on top of you. So if you have finished your business and pulled your knickers up, I would suggest—'

A loud clanking sound was followed by the rattle of a cleaning trolley crashing into the room. There was a brief silence, then a woman's voice: loud, Cockney: 'What the bloody hell do you think you're doing?'

Now Famie screamed. 'He attacked me! He's a pervert! I need help!' She heard the trolley rumble, then Taylor yell as it smashed into his legs. Famie unlocked the cubicle door, then charged at an already unbalanced Taylor. He fell to his right, arms flailing. He hit the floor, his head smacking the tiles hard. Famie stumbled, fell onto the trolley. Buckets and bleach spilt everywhere. She picked herself up, glanced at the two astonished cleaners.

'Don't let him escape!' she shouted. 'And call the police!' Taylor was trying to get to his feet, arms and legs flapping, like an upturned beetle's. Famie kicked him in the head and he stopped moving. She turned to the women who had retreated to the corner of the room, both clearly incredulous at what they had unleashed.

'Can you lock that toilet entrance door? Can you do that?' Famie said. They nodded, and one showed a bunch of keys on her belt. Famie smiled at them. 'Come with me,' she said.

96

Famie had ordered an Uber after all. She knew the rules. They were her rules. Black cabs or public transport: that was the choice. Proper knowledge, proper regulation, proper safety. She'd heard too many scary stories to stray too far from this path. But in an emergency? If you're out of London with a gangster on your heels and vital documents strapped to your waist? Well, you take your chances. Fifty metres from the National Archive, a nondescript block of flats was served by a nondescript car park. Famie was crouched, back to a low wall, shielded from view by a large Volvo. She had done this before, Berlin, Lahore and a service station off the M1. She felt safer. She felt invisible.

She called Sam. Jumped in before he'd said hello: 'Sam, did you get the photos?'

'Yes. Where are you?'

'We got them, Sam. It's Mary Bennett. She married John Nash in Jamaica. That's where the money comes from. *She* was the slave-owner. That's why there are no Nashs listed as slave-owners.'

Sam interrupted her flow. 'Famie, where are you?'

'And I've got the originals,' she said.

'Famie—' Sam broke off. 'You've – you've got what?'

'The ledger isn't digitized, Sam,' she said. 'It's where all this information comes from. Howard Taylor was after it. Somehow he was here. Howard fucking Taylor. If I hadn't taken it, he'd have destroyed it for sure.'

'Wait, what?' Sam was astonished. 'Taylor is at the Archive?'

'Yes,' said Famie. 'Hopefully still locked in a toilet with his head caved in. Or dented at least. I'll explain when I see you. But listen, Sam, you write the piece, okay? And it's this. This is the whole thing.' She knew she was speaking fast. Made herself slow down. 'The Nashs' wealth comes from slavery. We have the proof. And they use their money, all their accumulated wealth, to fund far-right parties all over Europe—'

'No,' interrupted Sam. 'We don't have the proof. Not for that.'

Famie closed her eyes. 'Okay. We – we suggest,' she said. 'We say what we know. That we understand. Use the photos. The fascist fundraiser, Helen Nash and the AfD man, old Harry's Rhodesia hat. All of them. If we have to pull back from saying they'd bankroll sodding Hitler if they could, then so be it.'

There was a brief silence.

'I can do that,' said Sam.

'I know you can,' said Famie. 'And you write better than me anyway.' Her knees were aching. She eased her way onto the tarmac.

Sam tried again. 'Famie. Where are you?'

'You remember when you found me and Charlie outside the Ramada? M1, junction two? We were on the way to Coventry. Well, I'm doing that again. Car park next to the Archive.' She flattened the documents under her T-shirt, stretched her legs under the car's boot. 'And Charlie says Lena knew Jamie.'

'Yes, she messaged me' said Sam. 'I'm annoyed it never even occurred to me. But it makes sense. Well played, Charlie. You spoken to her?'

'Sam, I haven't spoken to anyone. Not Charlie, not anyone. You?' She suddenly wanted to be back in her house. Or at Charlie and Lena's apartment. Somewhere that wasn't a car park. Somewhere she didn't have to sit on gravel.

'Michael's still quiet,' said Sam. 'And no word from Lena either. No one should be silent for this amount of time. Feels wrong, I have to say.'

'And Charlie?'

'In the flat, I think.'

Famie heard a car trundle into the car park, glanced around the Volvo's bumpers. A silver Prius. A lost driver. 'Sam, my ride's here. Call you back.'

Famie stood, hailed the driver.

97

The Gasholders flat was cooling, the afternoon sunlight curtained by billowing charcoal-grey clouds. Charlie had closed the balcony door against a squally wind and turned on the lights above the sink. She made tea. One eye on the kettle, the other on her phone. She flicked between WhatsApp, texts and Find My Phone. She poured the water, stirred, removed the teabag. She perched on a kitchen chair. Her phone rang. She snatched at it.

'Mum, are you all right?'

She let her mother talk. As Famie explained the escape from Taylor, Charlie stood up. All colour drained from her face. 'Jesus, Mum,' she whispered. 'Are you coming here? To the flat? It's just . . . Lena and Michael disappearing together isn't good.' She corrected herself. 'Disappearing at the same time is what I mean. They could be together, but it seems really unlikely.'

'I'll come to you,' said Famie. 'Sam is writing it all now. Sharing it as he goes. It'll be big, Charlie.'

'But what if it's killing Lena?' Charlie said, her voice trembling. 'The Nashs must know by now, Mum. You've said how dangerous they are. They'll come after all of us. I've double-locked here. What if this article is making everything worse for her?' Charlie's phone buzzed. 'Wait, hang on.' She swiped through her screen, put the phone on speaker. 'Okay, it's just Sam. Checking in.' She paced the room. 'I know we have to do

345

this, Mum, but what if it's Lena who pays the price? Is paying the price.'

'It's a fair point, Charlie, but we don't know anything. And until we do, Sam and I have to keep writing.' She paused briefly. 'And Lena knew Jamie. Might they have been working together?'

Charlie let the question hang between them. 'I guess they might have been,' she said. 'That has to be at least a possibility. That's why I'm worried about her.' She scrolled back to WhatsApp, texts and Find My Phone. 'You should call posh Sara in Dorking,' she said. 'She might know something.'

'I did ask her if she was the one he messaged,' said Famie. 'She said no. If she knew who it was, or whether it might have been Lena, that was the time to say.'

Charlie's screen showed the Find My Phone page. There was a change. As before it showed a map with the canal, Coal Drops Yard and the Gasholder flats. As before, Charlie's phone was a solid small blue dot. But now a blue circle with the letters LN had appeared, gently pulsing. Right next to Charlie's blue dot. Beneath the map it said 'Lena. Home. Live'.

Charlie held her breath, then gasped.

'Charlie?' said Famie.

'But that makes no sense,' muttered Charlie.

'What?' said Famie. 'What makes no sense?'

'Lena's phone has just appeared on my screen, Mum. And – and it's next to me. Like literally a few metres away. But I've been ringing it!' Charlie looked around her. 'I'll call you back Mum.'

She hung up, rang Lena. Walked around the flat, head darting left and right. Listening hard. Heard nothing. Turned over all the cushions she could see. In Lena's room she tore off the bedding, opened the cupboards, checked the shelves. In the kitchen she searched the larder, cupboards, fridge. Each sweep faster than the last. She found nothing. Charlie picked up her phone, walked till the pulsing 'LN' icon was right over her blue dot. She was standing by the kitchen table.

Then, slowly, she looked up at the ceiling.

'Of course,' she whispered. 'I'm so stupid.'

98

'How long will she be out?' Helen Nash hadn't moved from her seat at the table. Legs crossed, arms folded, she peered at her niece. Lena's mouth was open, lips flecked with dried spittle. Her eyes were closed, small traces of salt residue visible around the tear ducts. She appeared to be in a deep sleep. Her left arm was extended as though she was reaching for something, the right tucked under her body. Her hair was splayed over the thin rug she had fallen on. 'I assume it was Rohypnol you used on her. Or something similar. How long does it usually work for? In your extensive experience.'

Robert Nash fussed around Lena. 'We should put her in the bedroom, don't you think? While we work out what to do.'

'We?' said Helen. 'It's your bloody date-rape drug, not mine. You deal with her. I haven't had too much experience of sex with unwilling partners.'

Robert ignored her, picked up Lena's hands, let them drop.

Helen steepled her fingers, rested her head on them. 'You know,' she said, 'it really is scary how quickly you resorted to chemicals. A woman fights back. You knock her out. Just like that. Of course I knew you did this sort of thing but, Christ alive, now I've seen it in action. You really are one scary motherfucker.'

She stood as if to leave. 'Leave her there,' she said. 'A cushion, maybe. She'll be fine.' Helen threw one at Robert. He caught

348

it, lifted Lena's head, slid it between her and the floor, then returned to the table.

Helen sat down again. 'Could this ever have been different?' she said. 'Was this always how we were going to end up?' She stared at the ceiling.

'We're not "ending up" like anything,' said Robert, annoyed. 'Don't be pathetic. We're doing what needs to be done. Nothing more, nothing less. It's what we've always done.' He walked to his sister, sat alongside her.

'And now we have an hour to decide,' he said. 'It's a very tight window. So let's try again.'

'Really?' she said. 'Haven't you had enough? Michael's gone. And . . . I don't think I can. Really, Robert, this is all too much now.'

He shrugged. 'Okay, let's not try again. Let's give up. Let's lose the company. Let's lose everything we ever built. Everything the family has ever built.'

She squinted now, peering through the haze from her latest white and silver cigarette. 'Is that really the choice?' she said. 'I know we agreed but . . .' She pulled hard on her cigarette and exhaled through her nose. Twin smoke jets hit the table, then dispersed. 'We've held this together for so long, Robert. There has to be a different way. I totally agree about treasuring, about preserving the Nash name, but there must be alternatives.'

'Such as?' he said.

Helen shrugged. 'Legal agreements. Financial settlements. NDAs.' She waved her arms. 'You know the kind of thing. Let Taylor do what he does.'

'He does a lot of things' said Robert.

Helen closed her eyes. 'Christ.' She sighed. 'This is too close,

Robert. And you know it. She's too close.' She pointed her cigarette at Lena. 'And she seems to know the family history.'

'And that's why we take her down too,' said Robert. 'She and Michael had a row. Neither can live with the implications of what the fire has revealed. So, they decide to end it before the shame becomes known.' He lit up again. 'We take her down, Helen.'

'No, we take her *on*,' said Helen. 'If she still has the heart for it, which I doubt with her father gone. We deny, we dispute, and we leak all the mental-health, far-left stuff. Then we offer her another settlement.'

'And this?' Robert pointed at Lena. 'How does Sleeping Beauty here get explained?'

Helen reached for Lena's phone, turned it on. 'We text one of her friends,' she said, 'from her phone, anyone but that bloody annoying Charlie Madden, and say . . . say, "I'm feeling a bit woozy, just sleeping it off." That kind of thing.' Helen left the table, crouched next to Lena, held the phone's screen near her face, swiped up as it lit and unlocked. 'Then we carry her to the bed.' She looked up at her brother. 'That's the bit you're familiar with.'

He wagged a finger. 'No, we don't,' he said. 'We send nothing. She has to be off the radar for forty-eight hours. Until the drug's out of her system.' His head dropped. 'Christ, this is a mess!'

'Because you fucking drugged her! yelled Helen. 'That's why it's a mess. Now there are no good options.' Robert Nash moved to Lena's feet. Helen Nash stood at her head. Lena's phone burst into life. Screen lit, vibrating, silent. Helen held it as if it was suddenly radioactive. Arms-length, screen pointing at Robert.

'Turn it off, Helen,' he said, his voice controlled but failing to mask his anger. 'Just turn the fucking thing off. We're not answering. We're not messaging anyone.' He stabbed a finger at the phone. The screen said, 'Charlie'. 'Least of all that bitch.' They stared at each other. 'Come on, Helen, turn it off. We can sort this out.'

Helen switched off the phone and threw it onto the nearest chair. She jabbed a finger at her brother. 'And what would Dad say? What would "old Harry" do?'

Robert Nash squinted at his sister. 'You know very well what he'd do.' His voice was as low as hers was shrill. 'He'd throw her off the fucking balcony. That's what he'd do. Plus.' He pointed at his sister. 'He would know that we're a purer family without Michael. That he never understood, never got it. That he was always a mistake.' He shrugged. 'That he became an infection in the family.'

Helen Nash had just opened her mouth when there was a hammering sound from the front door. A hammering that didn't stop. Fist on wood. And behind the fist, a voice.

99

Charlie pounded on the door. Five hits with her left, then five with her right. 'Lena, it's me! Lena! Lena!' Five more with each hand. 'Lena! Lena!' She listened, leant in. Hooked loose hair behind her left ear, placed both hands flat on the painted wood. Put her ear to the door. She held her breath. Didn't move. On the second-floor landing, a carpeted silence.

She started again. Shouting, hammering. Shouting, hammering. Ear to the door. Shouting, hammering, ear to the door. Now she stepped back. 'Okay, Lena, if you can hear me, I know you're in there,' she called. 'And I know someone's in there with you because I heard them. Woman with a loud voice. I'm guessing that's your aunt Helen. She was either shouting at you or someone else is there too. Taylor is away chasing my mother, so my guess is it's your pervert uncle Robert. Or the bloke with a white beard. Either way, you should know Taylor is locked in a toilet in Kew. So I really wouldn't rely on him. And I am now calling the police. Hang on, Lena!'

Charlie jumped down the stairs, dived back into her flat and locked the front door. She slumped against it, breath coming in rapid gasps, and wiped her face with her sleeve. She kicked off her trainers and placed her phone on the floor. Hesitated. Then she called Famie, put her on speaker.

'Mum!' she said, immediately there was contact. 'No one answered the door. I could hear something inside. And I

352

certainly heard Helen Nash's voice when I was on the stairs. She's in there. With Lena, for sure. Probably that bastard Robert too.'

'Charlie' began Famie, 'I'm still thirty minutes away. Call the police, tell them what's happening.' Charlie hauled herself up, ran to her bedroom, found her DMs. She laced them fast. 'I will,' she called to the phone, 'but I need to do something this second, Mum. Like now!' She unlocked the door, hesitated, then ran back to the kitchen and poured herself some water.

'What are you going to do?' said Famie.

'Thought I'd kick the door,' said Charlie, 'Let them know we're on to them. Message me when you're close.'

'Don't take risks!' called Famie.

'You're hilarious,' said Charlie. She disconnected. Finished the water.

There was a thump, then yelling from upstairs. Charlie's head cocked, listening. Another thump. Yells. Her head swivelled. Someone was running down the stairs. She ran to the door, peered through the spyglass. A fisheye Helen Nash, hair flying, jumped out of sight. She would be gone in seconds. Charlie flew out in pursuit. She heard Nash crash through the main doors below. She was five, maybe six seconds ahead.

100

'Charlie, wait!' said Famie, but she was gone. 'Fuck!' she yelled. The Uber driver jumped, glanced round. 'Sorry,' she added.

The driver watched her in the mirror. 'Trouble at home?' he said.

'Yeah, kinda,' said Famie. 'It's complicated.'

He took the hint.

She untied, then retied her laces. 'How long do you think?' she said, trying not to sound too desperate.

The driver glanced at his satnav. 'Thirty-five minutes maybe,' he said. 'Everywhere is dug up. I am sorry.' He gesticulated around him. The two lanes of traffic, the lights, the roadworks. 'No one likes drivers any more. I've taken two detours already but it's thirty-five. At least.' Famie wanted to punch something.

'Nearest tube?' she asked. He glanced at his screen.

'Ladbroke Grove,' he said. 'You want to go there instead? It's about two minutes.'

Famie wasn't sure. She closed her eyes, rested a hand on the stolen pages of the Jamaican ledger, now flattened on the seat beside her. The stationary car was driving her mad. She felt caged, useless. For all the good she was doing, she might as well have been on the other side of the world. She opened her eyes. 'Yes,' she said, 'Ladbroke Grove, please.' She spied a supermarket bag on the front passenger seat. 'And if I tip you twenty pounds, could I have your bag?' He glanced at the bag, then Famie.

'What?'

'Twenty quid for your bag. Look, I'm adding it now.' She tapped her phone screen. Held it high. 'I'm serious. And, as you can tell, rather desperate.'

The driver shrugged, tipped biscuits and two bottles of water onto the seat, handed her the bag. 'Help yourself,' he said.

Famie slid the pages into the green and white plastic bag. She waited, coiled, as her driver inched his way forward. 'Give me strength,' she muttered. Two minutes later, the familiar London Underground logo appeared on a brightly coloured bridge. 'That's it,' she said. 'I'll jump out.' The driver stopped. Famie sprinted from the cab.

101

When Charlie crashed through the Gasholder main doors, Helen Nash was thirty metres in front and heading for Granary Square. Charlie was no runner but she was thirty years younger than Nash, didn't smoke, hadn't been drinking and wasn't carrying a small leather bag. She pursued Nash as she ran between the fountains, closing with every step. Nash threw a glance over her shoulder, saw her pursuer, ran faster. Charlie caught her a few metres from the canal-side taxi rank, grabbed her jacket collar and spun her round. 'Who's in the flat?' Charlie said.

Helen Nash was bathed in sweat, breathing hard. Charlie caught the fumes. 'Wow. You're pissed and you're old,' said Charlie. 'No wonder I caught you. Who is in the fucking flat?'

Nash struggled against her grip, ducked, pushed back. Passers-by slowed, a girl in a bucket hat started filming on her phone.

'Where is Lena?' yelled Charlie. She shook Helen Nash hard, hands gripping both sides of her jacket. Nash's head snapped forwards, catching Charlie's nose. Bone cracked bone. She cried out, hands instinctively to her face. Nash twisted away, ran a few steps. Charlie launched herself at her legs, catching her round the thighs. Both women crashed to the ground, Nash's bag spinning over the granite tiles. Blood poured from Charlie's broken nose. She scrambled, jumped on Nash's prone body. More people crowded round, two more started filming. Charlie straddled Nash. Blood dripped on Nash's face. Nash opened her eyes.

Tried to focus. Charlie slapped her face hard. Both sides. More blood splashed onto Nash's cheek and into her eyes and hair.

Two men stepped closer. 'You should back off now, don't you think?' one said.

Charlie was having none of it. She held up a bloodied hand, palm out. 'Wait! Stop!' she shouted. 'This woman is Helen Nash. Of the Nash family. That Nash family. She has a woman held against her will in a flat over there.' She pointed at Gasholders. 'I think she has a door key on her. I'm going to find it, then go and release my friend. You're all welcome to come along. Film as much as you like.'

The man stood his ground. 'You should call the police, then,' he said. 'You can't just attack someone like this.' Charlie ignored him, began searching Nash's pockets. She had two on her shirt, two on her jacket, three on her trousers. Charlie patted her down, felt in her pockets, found nothing.

Nash started to splutter, found her voice. 'This is a sexual assault,' she shouted.

'I'm calling the police,' said the man.

'This what you're looking for?' said the girl in the bucket hat. She stood next to Charlie, held out a small black handbag in one hand, a brass key on a leather fob in the other.

'Jesus, yes. Thank you,' said Charlie. She took both, threw the bag at Nash. 'Only need the key. To save my friend.' She was on her feet now. 'And when the police come,' she said to the man on the phone, 'tell them 302 Gasholders. Lena Nash, daughter of Michael, niece of Helen – this total bitch – is a hostage. Or a prisoner. Tell them that.'

Charlie held the key tightly in her hand. Glanced up at 302, pushed her way through the bystanders. The girl in the bucket hat filmed her all the way.

102

Lena Nash had been dropped just inside the second bedroom. She had stirred, then lost consciousness again. Robert Nash had studied her, then tugged her into the bedroom. He laid her on the floor, brushed her cheek with the back of his hand, hung his head and left the room.

In the lounge, he shut the blinds, turned on all the lights. He sat at the table and lit another cigarette. His first call was to Howard Taylor. 'Tell me you're not locked in a toilet,' he said to the answerphone. 'And call me. Immediately.' His second call was to City Boy, André Visser, who answered on the first ring. 'Come to the flat,' said Nash. 'I need you to deal with something.'

'I'm a way off,' came the reply. 'But I can be there in twenty.'

Nash sighed, irritated. 'No, Visser,' he said. 'I haven't got twenty minutes. Fifteen, maximum. *En my geweer.*'

'*Verstaan.*'

Robert Nash hung up. He rearranged the ash at the tip of his cigarette, poured a Scotch, made more calls. Three newspaper editors, two proprietors, four columnists. Each call followed a pattern, a routine. Bonhomie, flattery, a reminder of his largesse. Then the suggestion of an imminent breaking story. An incoming scandal with which he might need some help. Then a warm farewell. After each call, he walked to the bedroom, checked on his niece, left the door half open, returned to the table. The lights and smoke had turned the room a hazy shade of yellow.

Nash looked at his watch. His phone rang. Howard Taylor.

'What the fuck, Howard?' he said. 'I need you here. I needed you here an hour ago.'

'I have a driver arriving in five minutes,' said Taylor. 'I'm in Kew. I had a few difficulties with the journalist. We still do have a few difficulties with the journalist, actually.'

Behind Nash, movement in the darkened bedroom. A flash of pink, then it was gone.

'Which of the many difficulties with this fucking woman are you talking about, Taylor?' Nash was hunched over his phone, staring down at its screen, shouting into its microphone. 'Your trip to the Archive seems actually to have made everything worse. Am I wrong?'

More movement from the bedroom. A shadowed crescent of pink corduroy jerked forward.

Taylor's voice hesitated, briefly. 'That's not a correct summary, in my opinion,' he said. 'But it is true that the Madden woman now has the documentation she was looking for. She stole the pages she needed. Ripped them from the book in question. It was how I diverted some of the police activity. I made them realize she is the crook, not me.'

Nash leant even further in. His lips were almost touching the phone screen. 'You are a fucking imbecile,' he yelled.

Behind him, a shaft of light from the main room now lit Lena Nash as she peered out. Her skin was ash-grey, her hair wild. There was a pattern to her movements. It was as though she was voice-activated. When Robert Nash spoke, there was movement. When he was listening, there was stillness.

'This is existential,' said Nash, quieter now. 'You do realize that, don't you? Two hundred years of history. Of family history. *Our* family history. John and Mary Nash, Piccadilly 1837. Anthony and Caroline, 1865 . . .'

Ghost-like, Lena leant heavily against the door frame. She was slack-jawed, hollowed out by the drugs. There were ten metres between her and her uncle. Twenty steps, maybe more. It was unclear whether she could take any at all.

'Their son Thomas took it on,' Nash continued. 'Built everywhere for everyone. Around the world. So much of the empire came from this family, this blood. Rhodesia's best days came from Nash labour, Nash ingenuity. The trans-Canadian railroads, half the gold mines of South Africa and Australia . . . We made this world. You know this is true.'

Lena slid one bare foot forward. Then one more.

'This is what you're undermining, eroding, exposing with your failure to stop Madden. When my grandparents launched . . .'

Lena managed five steps, closed her eyes. She started to shake. Her head rolled, and her balance was gone.

Robert Nash's lecture continued.

Lena's knees bent. She eased herself to the floor. Dropped to all-fours. Her hair fell like a veil. She scuttled forward. Five metres away.

Nash stopped speaking. Lena stopped moving. Taylor's voice now. 'This is not lost,' he said. 'Far from it. City Boy is close by. He can tidy this up. You know he started the job already?'

'Of course. My brother.' Nash's voice was a monotone, matter-of-fact.

Lena blinked. Shuddered. Almost folded.

'And, yes, City Boy will be here in ten minutes,' said Nash. 'And we'll need to get this cleaned up quickly. A proper cleansing.' He smiled, lifted the phone to his lips. 'Just like the old days,' he said.

Lena crabbed two metres.

'Call me when you arrive,' said Nash, and hung up.

Lena eased back onto her haunches. Knelt just behind her uncle.

Nash finished the Scotch.

Lena stood up. Fumbled in her jacket pocket.

Nash spun round.

103

The only weapon Lena had found in the bedroom was a light bulb. She had unscrewed it, pocketed it. Now she palmed it, holding the metal base cap in the folds of her hand. Robert Nash, face to face with his death-white niece, jumped. Cried out in surprise. Lena swung her arm. With all the force she had left, she smashed the glass globe into his ear. The bulb shattered, thin shards lacerating the lobe. The filament and support wires penetrated deep into the auditory canal, piercing the eardrum.

Nash howled. He dropped to the floor, hands closed over his right ear, blood leaking through his fingers.

Lena lurched for the door.

104

Helen Nash had been helped to a bench, then left alone. She found wet wipes in her bag, cleaned as much of Charlie's blood from her face as she could, and placed them in a heap on the bench next to her. She took her phone from the bag, glanced at the screen, scrolled. She stared at her phone for a long time, then dropped it back into the bag. Her shoulders rolled forward and she rested her head in her hands. Congealed blood had matted her hair. Thick, sticky strands fell in front of her eyes. She didn't notice or didn't care. Any onlooker would assume she was either crying or praying, possibly both. An elderly man approached, looked at the space on the bench next to her. He saw the pyramid of bloody wipes, then walked on. For three minutes, she didn't move.

Eventually she uncurled and pushed herself to her feet. Holding the bag to her chest, Helen Nash walked slowly in the direction of what remained of the gallery. When she reached it, she paused. She glanced up at the criss-crossed layers of scaffolding and flapping tarpaulin. A slight shake of the head, and she moved on. She shuffled into the cavernous Waitrose. A uniformed security man looked up, followed her along three aisles. Nash stopped at the whisky shelves. She selected a £60 Japanese import and walked to the tills. The security man watched her pay, then left her alone.

Nash drifted out of the store, whisky and handbag both in a branded 'bag-for-life'. She returned to the gallery and walked round it twice. The entrance had disappeared behind a makeshift plywood door with a keypad lock. It featured ten digits and a small knob. She rummaged again in her bag and retrieved her phone. She scrolled for two minutes before finding what she had been looking for. She stepped up to the keypad, checked her phone, tapped four digits. She twisted the knob and tugged. The door creaked open and she stepped inside.

The entrance lobby still had a framed black and white photograph of the old Granary building on one wall: saved by a fire door. Nash pushed it open, stepped inside. The door swung shut behind her.

She stood quite still, waiting for her eyes to adjust. The gallery's grey tarpaulin shroud allowed barely any light to enter. Occasionally a gust found a loose seam or tear, and a sudden beam of sunshine would flash some light into the room. Then it was dark again. She found the torch on her phone, took a few steps. She was walking through rubble, clouds of ash billowing up. She stopped moving, slid the bag to the crook of her arm, covered her mouth and nose with a hand, then shone the torch around the room with the other.

There was nothing left. The room had been incinerated. Her torch picked out some unrecognizable chunks of twisted metal, walls burnt back to the brick, and fallen masonry everywhere. She swung the torch left to the staircase that led down to the basement.

'So that was where you died,' she said.

105

Famie stared at the information board at Ladbroke Grove underground station. Westbound, platform two. She estimated nearly two hundred people were doing the same: 'Train 1 Held. Train 2 Held. Train 3 Held.' Across the tracks, another teeming platform. Darkening skies, fast-moving charcoal clouds.

'Jesus . . .' she muttered.

Alongside her, two male students with backpacks. 'Passenger incident at Great Portland Street apparently,' said one. 'Does that mean what I think it does?'

The other nodded. 'Body on the tracks,' he said. 'Normally that's what it means anyway.'

Famie despaired. The roads were fucked, the tube was fucked, she was fucked.

More passengers arrived. She was jostled, squeezed. And she'd had enough. She pushed her way off the platform and out of the station. Google Maps said she was four point two miles away from King's Cross. She'd once run that sort of distance in twenty minutes but that was a couple of years back, it hadn't been through Portobello market and she hadn't been carrying stolen documents in a plastic bag.

But she was out of options. She messaged Sam. Told him to finish the article. Told him she was running it.

106

Lena glanced at the stairs, hesitated, then turned to the lift. She staggered the ten metres. Took two rests, one hand on the wall. Head down, rapid breaths. She reached the doors, stabbed at the button. She couldn't keep still. Her movements were manic, every muscle working. Her eyes snapped left and right between the door of 302 and the illuminated sign above the lift door. The '2' was lit, and she could hear the lift's approach. Lena had gambled on it being the best way out. In two seconds it would be there.

Way below her, doors crashed open. The sound of boots running up the spiral stairs rang loud in the stairwell. Lena froze. Someone was moving very fast. In front of her, the lift arrived and the doors trundled open. She stepped in, leant out. Waited for the climber. The door closed on her, she held out her hand. It pushed against her. She pushed back. The boots were louder, on the final twist of the spiral. She retreated inside the lift, hand still on the door. The runner's tread was now punctuated by gasps, like a mid-rally tennis player. A female tennis player. Lena took half a step out.

Charlie had reached the third-floor landing, turned right for 302. She held a key. Lena cried out, held up a hand. 'Here, Charlie!' Her voice was too thin and brittle to be heard. Charlie carried on, hand and key reaching for the lock of 302. She tried again, with more force: 'Charlie!' This time, Charlie turned, shock, then relief on her face. She sprinted to the lift, enveloped Lena in her arms. They cried briefly.

Lena wiped her eyes. She looked in horror at Charlie's bloodied face. Charlie grimaced. 'I'm fine. Your aunt's work' she said. 'Fucking witch.'

Lena held on to Charlie. She spoke fast, her words post-op rough. 'We have to go,' she said. Coughed heavily. 'We have seconds. We have to get out.'

'Lift?' said Charlie.

'Yes. Sorry,' said Lena. They stepped in and Lena let the door shut. Charlie pressed G, then held on to Lena.

'You'll still need to help me, I'm afraid,' said Lena. 'They drugged me, Charlie. And I feel really, really shit.'

Charlie took her arm. 'They actually drugged you?' she spluttered, incredulous.

Second floor.

'And – and I think they may have killed my dad.'

Charlie froze, struggled for words. 'But how . . . What? How can you . . . ?' she said. Her eyes brimmed.

'Just something my uncle said to Howard Taylor. On the phone. Talked about how a clear-up was needed. And that it had already started with his brother.'

First floor.

'Christ,' whispered Charlie. She tightened her grip on Lena. 'That can't be right.' She took a breath. 'Can you run?'

'I have to. He'll be out soon,' she said.

'Why is he not out already?' said Charlie.

Ground floor.

'I just glassed him with a light bulb,' said Lena. 'In the ear. An eye would have been better but it went . . .'

The doors opened. They froze. Listened intently. At first

silence, then the sound of running footsteps on the path outside. Getting louder.

Charlie reacted first. 'Let the door close,' she whispered. 'If you're in a hurry to get to the third floor you run it. They'll take the stairs, not the lift. I did.'

'My uncle ordered someone here,' said Lena. 'When he was on the phone. An Afrikaner, I think, from the language they were speaking but I was just coming round. Might be mistaken.'

Arms linked, they stood side by side. The doors closed. They tensed.

'What if he does take the lift?' whispered Lena. Charlie shook her head. They heard the runner crash the doors. Lena started to shake. Charlie pulled her close. They heard bounding footsteps on tiles, then bounding, receding footsteps on wood.

'Stairs,' whispered Charlie.

The lift doors opened again.

Charlie and Lena glanced at each other.

'Try to run?' said Charlie.

107

Helen Nash sat slowly on the bottom step. She flashed her phone's torch into the basement office. It was an impenetrable black hole.

She leant against the stair wall, placed the bag-for-life next to her, propped her phone one step up. She removed the whisky from the supermarket bag, twisted off the screw cap. Swigged a mouthful. Smiled. Drank some more. She raised the bottle above her head. A salute. 'Here's to you, Dad. You always said we'd fuck it all up. And you were absolutely right.' Another mouthful. 'And here's to you, Mum. Shit, we're the same.' She put the bottle between her legs, reached for her handbag and felt around inside. She produced a small white bottle with a screw cap. She rattled it, then emptied the contents into her hand. She pointed at each white pill as she counted.

'Seventeen,' she said. She counted again. 'Oh. Nineteen,' she said, her voice beginning to slur. She looked for a label, for dosage instructions, but there wasn't one. 'How many did you use on Lena, brother dearest?' she muttered. 'I wonder.' She stared at the pills in her hand. 'Oh, well,' she said.

108

Google Maps gave Famie the quickest route to the Gas-holder flats. It was simple enough. Ladbroke Grove, left onto Westbourne Park Road, then Gloucester Terrace, Bishop's Bridge Road, under the Westway and follow the Euston Road all the way to King's Cross. All residential, built-up and traffic-heavy.

Four point two miles.

She was on a fast pace already, switching between pavement and road. Trainers, cargos and shirt were far from ideal attire but it could have been worse. The carrier bag was an inconvenience but its contents were everything. The names, the signatures, the money. The evidence. The two pages from the ledger had survived being under her clothes, and now she had them rolled into a tube with the bag wrapped around them. She held it like an oversized relay-race baton. The other hand clutched her phone. An earbud in her left ear. She hated running and talking but this time she had no option.

Famie hadn't run for a personal best for more than a year but, with Charlie not answering her phone, Lena and Michael silent, she knew she had to produce one now. She couldn't afford to drop much below a five-minute-twenty-second mile but the first would be the slowest. She hopped, skipped and jumped through the detritus of Portobello market, grateful that most of the stalls and customers had been cleared away for the day. When pedestrians and shoppers saw her coming, they moved aside. If they didn't, she yelled. Famie realized she was being noticed. People dressed like her didn't run like her, unless something was wrong. Some looked around for the person chasing. Or the person she was chasing. It was crisis running and everyone instinctively recognized it.

While she was picking out a route along the next twenty metres of road or pavement, her head was clear. When she got an unobstructed stretch, the crisis she was running towards snapped into focus. She held up her phone, called Charlie. No reply. Find My Phone showed she was still at Gasholders. Famie's anxiety level kicked up a notch. She called DI Channing Hunter, started talking in breathless phrases as soon as she picked up.

'Channing, I'm running to Coal Drops. On the Westbourne Park Road. I can't find Charlie or Lena Nash. Or Michael Nash. Charlie told me she thinks Lena is being held captive. In room 302 at Gasholders. By her aunt and uncle. I'm writing a piece that'll show the Nash family to be funding far-right groups. And that the fire at the gallery was arson. And murder. They had Jamie Nelson murdered, Channing.' The vastness of the Westway flyover towered above her as she swung a hard right, then left into Gloucester Terrace. She ran on well-tended, manicured pavement slabs. 'You there, Channing?' she said.

'I'm here,' said Hunter. 'Just waiting for you to finish.'

'I've finished,' said Famie.

'You do know I'm not nine-nine-nine, don't you?' said Hunter. 'And I'm not on the arson team.'

'I do,' said Famie. 'Gotta go.' She ended the call, shoved the phone into a back pocket and swapped the document bag to her left hand.

Ran faster.

109

Outside Gasholders, hidden behind one of the gunmetal-grey cast-iron columns, Charlie and Lena hesitated, eyes darting left and right. The cafés and bars were extravagantly lit and teeming with life. At the end of their path, by the last wine bar on the left, the canal's footbridge. Two miles away, the LED screen at the top of the BT Tower glowed blue against the leaden sky.

'Hide or run?' Charlie had an arm hooked through Lena's.

'Both,' said Lena. 'If we can. I can't run far, I'm afraid.'

'Run, then hide,' said Charlie. 'Subway shops?'

Lena nodded. She took Charlie's hand. As they were about to step from behind the column they heard two gunshots in quick succession. Lena recoiled, pulled Charlie back to the metal. The precise location of the shots was impossible to judge but the women didn't need an acoustic engineer to tell them they were dangerously close. Back behind the column, they were hidden from the Gasholders entrance but a mere dozen paces away. With the most cursory of searches, their discovery would be inevitable.

'Forget the shops,' whispered Lena.

'Agreed' , muttered Charlie.

Thunderous footsteps from inside the flats pressed them tighter to the column. They heard the doors crash open. A man breathing heavily. Charlie held up her index finger. 'One,' she mouthed. Lena nodded, closed her eyes briefly. She nodded towards the next column, ten metres away. Charlie mouthed,

'Wait.' If the man ran left, it was over. If he ran straight ahead or right, they could move.

He ran straight ahead, towards the 'Welcome To Coal Drops Yard' sign and the steps that led down to the underground arcade. The women caught a glimpse of white hair disappearing and made their move. They ran to the next column, then, after an exchange of nods, the next. They pressed themselves against the cold iron.

'That was the Afrikaner presumably,' said Charlie. 'Your uncle might be right behind him, or bleeding out on the floor upstairs. Let's assume the worst and that he's on his way out too. We need to hide. When your fuckwitch of an aunt broke my nose, I slapped her face quite a lot. Told everyone to call the police. I guess no one did.'

'Call nine-nine-nine,' said Lena.

Charlie pulled a face. 'My phone is in the flat' she said. 'Left it there when I went after the fuckwitch. Don't suppose you've got yours?'

Lena shook her head. 'Mine's in three oh two, and yours in two oh two. But we're hardly going back in.'.

'So we need to hide,' said Charlie.

'Well, we still need a phone,' said Lena.

'A hiding place with a phone,' said Charlie. 'Right.' Her head darted left and right. The fourth gasholder, the one that had been turned into a park, was the next one round. Its six-teen cylindrical columns framed a lush circular lawn. An impromptu game of football was being played at one end; a few women were drinking on the grass at the other. Behind them, the lawn ran to the canal towpath. Two cyclists passed each other with helmeted nods. A line of ambling tourists in beanie hats looked lost.

'There are hedges and large bits of ironwork,' Charlie said, pointing at the park. 'We could hide there. Someone must have a phone.'

From behind them they heard raised voices. When the shouting stopped, all they heard was Robert Nash's voice. Only three columns away. Pained, but projecting clearly enough.

'I'm out, Visser. Which way did you go?' Nash said. Lena gasped, put a hand in front of her mouth. Both women leant closer and waited for Nash to speak again.

'Okay,' they heard him say. 'I'll go round the other way.'

110

Famie knew the Westway would take her there. As soon as she was running along its undercarriage, her route was set. When it came back to earth it was Marylebone Road, then Euston Road, and then she'd be at St Pancras. Above her, the thundering traffic saw a sprawling, high-rise cityscape. Famie's run-in was now a grimy dumping ground full of caravans, graffiti and scrap. There were tents too, rough sleepers making the most of the concrete ceiling provided by the elevated dual carriageway. No one paid her any attention.

Her time was slipping. She didn't need to check, she just knew. Dodging traffic and pedestrians had cost her. She was closer to a six-minute mile than the five twenty she needed. Fear was a great motor but it couldn't make her twenty-five again. Her lungs were tight, her feet blistering, and she had shin splints. The document baton switched hands again. Her phone sat heavy in her back pocket.

Famie ran alongside concrete pillars. Lengthened her stride. She counted her steps between them. Twenty-three for the first pair. She managed twenty-two for the next, then twenty. That felt better. This was the speed and rhythm she had to maintain. An agitated, panicked runner might be fast but they would burn out quickly. She'd be no use if she passed out at Baker Street.

Sam was writing the story, but as she ran she wrote a version in her head. She was pretty sure this had been Jamie Nelson's story all along. That he had discovered some or all of the Nash story, that he had recruited Lena, that he had died trying to discover evidence. She desperately needed to talk to Sam, but she wasn't sure she could speak at all. Even if she managed some breathless sentences, it would cost her in minutes. The end of the Westway was ahead, the elevation declining gradually until the road became just another jammed London thoroughfare. This wasn't the time to risk even a second. Whatever she was running towards would be the end of the story. She knew Charlie was in danger. She had to be there.

Famie guessed she had two miles to go. Eleven minutes.

This was going to hurt.

111

Charlie and Lena reached the Gasholders park, flung themselves between a large hedge and an elaborate piece of ironwork at the base of one of the columns. Nash had moved slowly. He missed their sprint and their dive. Flat on the ground, they scrambled to peer through the ornate cage-like metalwork. They watched Nash, handkerchief to his ear, study the area in front of him. He took a slow sweep from left to right, the canal, the towpath, the park, its footballers and its coffee drinkers. He seemed to see nothing of interest. Two of the women had looked up when Charlie and Lena crash-landed; none of the footballers had noticed. Charlie smiled at the women, one of whom smiled back.

'We can't move while he's there' ,said Lena. 'He's like a sniper. We're pinned down.'

'He should be in hospital. Sort that ear out,' said Charlie.

'And we can't borrow a phone without him seeing,' said Lena. 'So we're fucked. And that's even without the Afrikaans guy, whoever he is.' She hauled herself to a crouch and winced.

'Now he's looking straight at us,' said Charlie. 'Do. Not. Move. A. Thing.' They froze until his head moved slightly. 'And breathe',.she said. 'Actually he was looking straight through us.'

On the towpath behind them they heard raised voices. Foreign voices, maybe ten or more. Charlie turned her head. Chanced a one-eighty pivot. Through the hedge she saw the lost

377

tourists in beanie hats she had spied earlier. Evidently they were still lost.

Lena scurried round, lay next to her. 'South Korean,' she said. 'That's their flag on the beanie hat.' Twelve elderly men and women in white hats sporting the South Korean red and blue circle continued their argument. 'But they have phones and maps.' The Korean's cross words washed over them until one tried to say what Charlie and Lena recognized as 'nature reserve'. They stared at each other.

'Camley Street,' said Charlie. 'They want the Camley Street Nature Reserve.'

Lena got it straight away. 'We can do that' ,she hissed. 'Cross the bridge. Take them there!'

They saw Nash take a call and turn slightly. He waved his arm, shouting again.

'Now!' said Charlie. 'Move slowly.' She helped Lena up, they took six steps, moved out of the park. Walked to the Koreans, stood canal-side. Charlie smiled. Lena smiled.

'Nature reserve?' said Charlie. 'We can show you.' She pointed at herself and Lena. 'Shall we go?'

Three understood, translated rapidly. Smiles all round. 'I like your hats' ,said Charlie to one of the comprehending Koreans. He smiled, pulled the beanie from his head and offered it to her. He gave a thumbs-up, which Charlie returned. She pulled the hat down over her mass of curls, tucking what she could out of sight. She pointed at the canal's footbridge. 'We need to cross that bridge,' she said. Nods and understanding all round. A few clapped. The party of fourteen set off.

Charlie stooped as she walked, linked arms with Lena. They stayed parallel with the now hatless Korean and the woman at his side.

The footbridge was twenty metres away.

'I daren't look,' said Lena.

'He's still there' ,said Charlie, eyes hard left. 'Still on the phone. His Afrikaner guy will appear any minute, I'm sure. They'll hunt together. Stay tight.'

The first of the group had reached the top of the slender, sloping bridge. They hesitated. 'Go on over,' Charlie said. 'That's the nature reserve down there.' She pointed across the canal to floating reed beds and woodland.

Everyone smiled. They stepped onto the bridge. Two cyclists freewheeled past them. A group of runners approached in the opposite direction. The congestion made the tourists walk in ones and twos, stretched out like children on a school outing.

Charlie smiled and walked backwards, eyes flicking immediately left to the looming Gasholder flats. There were lights on in 32, darkness from 22. No sign of movement in either. The surrounding paths were all busy. Nash had disappeared. No sign of the Afrikaner. She turned, walked forwards. The bridge curved left. The runners clattered past.

Lena tugged at Charlie's arm. 'I hate this' ,she said. 'Can we go faster? Get off this bloody bridge?'

'Thirty metres,' said Charlie. 'Hang tight. It loops left and we're off.'

A few of the tourists stopped to take photographs. The nature park on the left, St Pancras Lock on the right.

'We can leave them here,' said Lena, tugging again. 'Please, Charlie, come on! They're so fucking slow. My uncle and his thug, they'll come here next.' She sounded increasingly frantic.

'Or they could go to the station,' said Charlie, 'or the *Guardian* building. Or the concert hall. Just as likely.'

'This is nearer' ,said Lena, pleading now. 'They're this side of the yard, Charlie. We need somewhere to hide till the police come'.

The end of the bridge was fifteen seconds away. There were many escape routes from there, south to St Pancras, north to Camden. From somewhere they heard sirens. They listened intently. There were multiple sirens from different directions. The wailing overlapped, converged. And was getting louder.

'Okay, let's go,' said Charlie.

112

For Famie, approaching Madame Tussaud's, everything was burning. Her feet, shins, groin and lungs were all screaming. The cargos had chafed enough to break the skin on her thighs and crotch. Blood and sweat seeped through the cotton. She ran on.

Her vision was blurred by the streams of sweat that poured from her forehead. She wiped her eyes every few steps. Waves of pain ran through her body. Her face was a rigid grimace.

She ran on.

The document-baton was slippery. She had dropped it twice, two heart-stopping moments, but each causing nothing more serious than a loss of rhythm. In her back pocket she could feel her phone vibrating but knew she wouldn't be able to hold it, operate it, speak into it. She was in the zone, the runners' 'flow state', moving by instinct. She anticipated each problem, saw obstacles early. The part of the brain that generated fear had been switched off. She had less cognitive processing, more neural power for what she knew she had to do. She skipped her way through the pedestrian maze, dropping into the gutter of Euston Road when she had to. She knew when she stopped, or even slowed, the pain would be overwhelming. But until then, she ran on.

The tight tangle of noise in her head was blood pumping, heart racing and feet pounding. Now, from somewhere she couldn't register, police sirens. A common sound, an everyday, every-hour sound. She took no notice. There was a pedestrian crossing in fifty metres. In the evening sky, the traffic lights glowed. The red man was lit for her, green light for cars. At forty metres, she still had the red man, flashing amber for cars. She kept her focus, kept her speed. At thirty metres, both lights were red. At twenty metres, the green man lit. Her stride was steady. She had this right. Famie hit the road as the green man flashed. She hit the pavement on the other side as the red man lit again. She ran on.

Another siren now, piercing and close. The three lanes of traffic tried to accommodate the demands of the wail and yelp. They pulled over, stopped, inched forward. Suddenly the ear-splitting howl wasn't on the road behind her: it was on the pavement. Still she ran on. It was only when a voice yelled her name that she was jolted back to the real world. 'Famie! Famie!'

The second time she managed to stop. She turned, chest heaving, waves of pain flooding her body. She wiped the sweat from her eyes. It was Channing Hunter. The DI was running towards her, beckoning her. 'Get in! Get in now!'

Famie couldn't speak, couldn't move. She bent over, held her knees. Her vision blurred. Lights popped. As Hunter reached her, she nodded. Allowed herself to be escorted to the back of the police car. She slumped inside. Still clutching the rolled documents, Famie vomited, then passed out.

113

Lena had been right, and Charlie had been wrong. Robert Nash hadn't run to the *Guardian* offices, the concert hall or the station. He'd followed in their wake. He found himself on the lower level of Coal Drops Yard, staggered into every shop and restaurant along one side, his henchman trawling the other. Drawing a blank, they climbed the metal stairs to ground level. They turned left, ran past the fish restaurant with outside tables and arrived at the top of the footbridge. Both men stopped. A group of runners pounded past them. At the curve of the bridge, a troop of tourists in silly hats were taking photos of the canal.

Nash was breathless, leant on a railing. 'Well?' he said.

Visser turned a three-sixty. 'Lights on in your apartment,' he said, glancing up at Gasholders. 'They were off before.'

'Fuck,' said Nash. City Boy pulled him away from the bridge. They took two recently vacated seats at the edge of the fish restaurant.

'This is too loose now,' said Visser, 'too many variables. You need to disappear.'

Nash drank water from a leftover glass, wiped his face with a napkin and stared at Visser. 'I have a few minutes,' he said. 'Just a few. To save everything.' He leant in. 'I want those girls. We find them and we find them first.'

'Police are here,' said Visser 'It's too late. Leave this to me.'

Nash smiled. 'This is the Met you're talking about. I know them. They know me. We get along.'

114

Charlie and Lena ran off the bridge, then hesitated. The nature park left, the short tunnel and the old church right.

'Hide!' said Lena. 'Please!' She pulled Charlie through the steel chairs and tables of the deserted café, into a small wood with landscaped paths. They jumped over a twisted hazel fence, threw themselves to the ground, crawled to some ivy-covered poplars. Charlie raised her head, peered though the leaves. She had a side view of the footbridge. 'Fine for now,' she said. 'No one on the bridge. The Koreans will be here soon but I don't think they'll see us.'

She lay down, her head a breath away from Lena's. Lena's eyes were closed and she was shaking again. Charlie wriggled over, put an arm around her and pulled her close. Lena calmed, the shaking subsided.

'The Afrikaner,' said Charlie. 'Your uncle called him Visser on the phone.'

'I haven't heard of him before,' said Lena. 'But my grand-father had plenty of dodgy friends. A lot of them seemed to speak Afrikaans. Like a code, you know?'

'What did your uncle say?'

'Something something *geweer*. I think it's the Dutch word for rifle. Or gun. We had a Dutch painting at the gallery with that in the title. A while back now.'

'Huh,' said Charlie. 'So, "bring a rifle"? "Bring a gun"? "Bring another gun"? Holy shit, we so need the police.' Lena started to shake again. 'Who will be here soon,' said Charlie, changing her tone. 'The sirens.'

'They're not closer,' said Lena.

'As soon as we see a police car,' Charlie persisted, 'we run. And it's over.'

Lena was crying now. 'I'm so sorry, Charlie,' she whispered. 'Really so sorry. What a fucking mess.' Her head was on the ground, hair in the soil. Tears pooled in her eyes, then dripped to the ground. 'All of this is my fault. All of it. Jamie. My dad.' She paused. 'And this.'

'You knew Jamie,' murmured Charlie. A statement and a question.

'He'd worked out who I was,' said Lena. 'Introduced himself at the coffee stall. He'd been waiting for the right moment. Said he'd been investigating his history. And that it overlapped considerably with mine.'

'Were you friends?'

'Yes.'

'Were you the only follow on his instagram?'

'Yes.'

'Were you seeing him?'

Lena sighed. 'It was complicated. Yes. Kind of. I thought we were but I'm pretty sure he'd been fucking Helen.'

Charlie inhaled sharply. 'Your aunt?' Lena nodded. 'No way.' Lena nodded again, wiped her eyes.

'How do you think he got the information he did?' she said. 'She was flattered. She got used. He stole her shit. I was flattered. I got used. He died stealing my shit. That's how I see it now.'

Charlie propped herself up. Checked the bridge. The pathways and Gasholders had lights. No sign of Nash. The chirping sirens were constant but sounded no closer. The Koreans were talking nearby but were out of sight. She dropped down. 'What was he doing in the gallery basement?'

Lena swallowed. 'He was trying to find some Nash history. The stuff I wouldn't tell him. He was writing a big piece on the family. He must have been on the demonstration, or watching it. Then, when it got criminal, he took his chance.'

'What wouldn't you tell him?' whispered Charlie. She heard voices, then the Koreans walking closer, still out of sight. She listened to their approach. Lena had caught them too.

'We should tell the police where we are,' she said. 'We have a few seconds here. Borrow one of the Koreans' phones. What do you think?' Lena pushed herself up to a squat. Soil and leaves stuck to her face.

'Lena, wait,' hissed Charlie. 'They can be seen from the bridge. Wait, wait, wait.' She crouched, peered through the leaves. Top of the bridge, two men. Nash and Visser. Looking straight at her. Charlie ducked. 'Shit, shit, shit,' she said. 'Top of the bridge. It's them.'

'Did they see you?'

'Don't think so.'

But the Koreans had. All of them seemed to notice Charlie and Lena at the same time. They called greetings, pointed, waved. Two bent to greet them.

'No, no, no!' said Charlie, horrified. She waved her hands, shooing them away. The two who had stooped stepped back, puzzled. 'Okay, this is bad,' she said. Hesitated, checked the bridge. This time she was seen. She recoiled, grabbed Lena's hand. 'Okay, we run,' she said.

They leapt the hazel fence, tore through the café's chairs to the road. They glanced left towards St Pancras and Euston Road. An open, empty road. Sirens, yes, police cars, no.

'Nope,' said Charlie.

'Church!' said Lena. They spun right for the tunnel. Lena freed her hand from Charlie's and ran in her slipstream. They were fast, quickly finding the darkness of the underpass. Lena chanced a look over her shoulder. Both men were off the bridge. Moving quickly. Closing fast. Thirty metres away.

And both with guns.

115

Helen Nash's phone's battery died and the torch went out. She sat in total darkness. There were eight tablets left and a third of the bottle of whisky. She had taken two tablets with each mouthful. Her movements were slowing fast. She placed two more tablets on her tongue, washed them down.

'This had better work,' she said, her words running into each other. 'Maybe I'd better hurry right along.' She took the final six tablets in her hand, held the whisky in the other. She saluted the darkness, and pointed the bottle into the basement.

'I'm not crying because of you,' she said. 'Just to be clear.'

The last of the tablets and the last of the whisky went down together.

116

Famie was only out for seconds. Hunter leant across, poured water over her face and wiped vomit from her cheeks and chin. Famie spluttered, then winced in pain as she registered the fire in her legs and feet. She heard the sirens, heard Hunter shout, 'Pavement. Tell them to use the pavement.'

Famie was in the back seat, passenger side, in the second of two police cars. The first was a BMW X5. In the seat in front of her, a police officer with an MP5 carbine resting between his boots, radio in his hand. In front of Hunter, a bearded driver waited for the car in front to move. Both men wore black baseball-style caps with black-and-white chequered bands around them and body armour. Neither man showed any frustration or impatience.

'Armed response vehicle?' croaked Famie. The siren drowned her words. Hunter leant closer. 'Armed response vehicle?' Famie said again.

'And armed response officers,' Hunter said. She looked as though she was going to say something else, but changed her mind.

'What aren't you telling me?' said Famie. The police car in front started to move. It swung onto the pavement. Famie's car followed right behind. Pedestrians flattened themselves against walls as they saw the cars coming.

Hunter looked at Famie. 'Michael Nash is dead' she said.

'Identified as the man who was on the tracks at Great Portland Street.'

Famie jolted up straight, the new adrenaline shot removing her pain and replacing it with terror. 'No, no, no,' she said. 'Really? They actually killed Michael?' She was incredulous. She pieced everything together. 'So we are . . .'

Hunter nodded. 'There are reports of shots fired in the Gasholder flats. Armed police are there now. No sign of Charlie. Or Lena. Or Robert Nash. Or Helen Nash.' She turned her eyes straight ahead. 'In summary,' she said, 'that's everything I know.'

Famie replayed the last conversation she'd had with Charlie. Lena's phone had just appeared on her screen. Charlie had said she was heading up to 32. Hunter anticipated Famie's next question. 'Charlie's phone was on the floor by the entrance of 22. Lena's phone on the kitchen table of 302. Unless they find someone else's, we can't communicate. I'm sorry, Famie.'

Famie nodded. She knew she shouldn't be there, knew that Hunter would have pulled rank or favours or both. She appreciated the gesture. She handed Hunter the plastic bag.

'Stolen goods?' said Hunter.

'For sure,' said Famie. 'It's another grab list. This one from 1837. Take care of it.' Hunter slid the bag under the driver's seat. 'That's all you have?' said Famie.

'Evidence bags are in the boot,' said Hunter. 'You want to stop?'

Famie's phone rang. It was Sam. She answered.

'Thank Christ!' he said. He registered the police sirens. 'Are you okay, Famie? What's happening?'

'Sorry, Sam. Robert Nash is armed. He's after Lena and Charlie. I'm with Hunter, heading to Gasholders.'

'And you have the documents?'

'I do.'

'Just as well,' said Sam. 'I published twenty minutes ago.'

'Hold tight!' shouted the driver. Famie hung up.

Both cars wove on and off the pavement. Cycle lane, bus lane, whatever opened up. Famie bounced hard against her seatbelt. She felt sick again. Closed her eyes. The British Library was ahead, left, she knew. Then St Pancras. Then King's Cross. It was the road between they wanted. Pancras Road. The taxi drop-off for the Eurostar, for King's Cross. Then the footbridge that would take them to Gasholders.

Famie opened her eyes. They were two vehicles from the bus lane with no buses ahead. Ten seconds to Pancras Road. One of the vehicles edged out of the way just far enough to let them through. One final blocking car: a battered Saab, its driver waving his arms in frustration. Unable to get out of the police's way and not wanting to use a bus lane, he found his car jolted by the BMW. Police bumper to Saab bumper.

'Take the fine,' muttered Channing. 'Use the bloody bus lane.'

The Saab driver got the message and drove straight on, slowly to start with, then, the BMW still pushing, accelerated away. The two police vehicles, millimetres apart and now off the leash, tore past the Gothic towers and turrets of St Pancras station. From where Famie sat, the two police cars were locked together. They took the left turn at more than forty miles per hour, tyre screech and burn briefly louder than the siren.

The car radio squawked. Famie missed the words. Hunter's radio squawked. Famie leant in close. She heard everything.

'Two suspects crossing footbridge. Both armed. Both running. Heading your way, Hunter.'

Forty miles an hour became forty-five. Both police vehicles slalomed through taxis and Eurostar passengers. Famie held her seatbelt with both hands. The police officer with the machine gun stabbed a finger at the windscreen. 'There,' he said, his voice raised. He spoke into his radio. 'We see them,' he said.

117

Twenty metres beyond the tunnel, Charlie and Lena reached steps marked 'St Pancras Gardens'. Charlie grabbed Lena's hand again, hauled her up. There was a manic desperation to their movements. The sirens were closing but their pursuers were closer. One stumble, one trip and they would be on them. The path to the church ran through a vast leafy graveyard with well-spaced ancient, elaborate graves on all sides. It was obvious to both women that the church was too far away. They had seconds to choose a hiding place. The beech trees weren't wide enough, the bushes too sparse. Which left a choice of two, maybe three gravestones. Charlie was leading. She chose the biggest. A long sarcophagus in battered, wordless Portland stone. They had both walked this graveyard many times, taken photos of J. C. Bach's grave, Mary Wollstonecraft's too. Hers was one along from their blank monument but too small for two people to hide behind.

They hit the ground hard, then scrambled to a crouch. Their breath came in short, shallow gasps. Charlie eyed the distance to the small church, shook her head. Their next move would have to be soon, but it couldn't be that. Lena, beside her, pointed to the far end of the path nearest the church porch. A family of four had emerged. Man, woman, two boys aged around eight and six. The woman had a map in her hand. She paused to read it, then appeared to point straight at Charlie. All four started to walk towards them.

'It's the Wollstonecraft grave,' said Lena. 'Shit. They're going to take a photo or something.'

'With their phone,' whispered Charlie. 'We need their phone.'

'We can't talk to them!' hissed Lena. 'How can we do that?'

The sirens were very close now, piercing the air. The family of four stopped, pointed. Two men had just run into the graveyard.

118

Despite their speed, the two police vehicles were just metres from each other, Famie's car tucked in right behind the BMW. She assumed Robert Nash and his muscle were after Charlie and Lena but maybe Helen was involved here somewhere. She recognized the familiar knot in her stomach. All parents worried about their kids, but only she got hers into mortal danger. She was grateful for Hunter and the armed police officers in front of her. For now, the fear was overriding her pain and exhaustion.

The cars hurtled through the tunnel, then braked hard, throwing Famie and Hunter against their seatbelts. They had stopped just shy of the garden's steps, the BMW twenty metres beyond. Sirens switched off, lights still flashing. The policeman in front of Famie slipped out of the car, crouched by the wall, his MP5 held across his chest. Their driver ran to the back, popped the boot, grabbed his gun and crouched behind his colleague. Both had holstered Glocks strapped to their thighs, yellow Tasers attached to their body armour

'You stay here,' said Hunter. 'Obviously.' She held Famie's gaze.

Famie said nothing. What could she say anyway? She knew Hunter had had to say it, knew also that Hunter assumed she'd ignore the instruction at the first opportunity. So she shrugged. Hunter left the car.

Famie undid her seatbelt, watching the two officers by the

steps. The first was gesturing, presumably to colleagues in the BMW, then to the man behind him. Both men scuttled up the steps and out of sight.

Famie lasted seven seconds before opening her door. She leant out. Saw no one. Got out of the car.

119

Charlie and Lena watched the family watching Nash and whoever was with him. They couldn't see the police cars but the
flashing blue lights sent their urgency all through the graveyard.
The family looked startled, uncertain, knew something was
wrong. Both parents reached for their sons. Their raised voices
weren't English.

'They're German, I think,' hissed Lena.

The father noticed Charlie and Lena. Both women mimed
a phone call, pointed back at him. Then the two boys pointed
at Charlie. Lena's mime changed to frantically waving both
hands, palms out. Charlie joined in. The family understood.
They backed away. Then the woman yelled, *'Sie haben Waffen!'*
She wrapped an arm around the shorter boy, pushed him back
into the church. The man grabbed the taller boy, followed her
inside.

Charlie and Lena shrank back against the tomb. Eyes
everywhere.

'Shall we run?' said Charlie. Lena seemed unable to speak.
She took Charlie's hand, pulled her close. She was shaking again.
Behind them, the sound of running boots on grass. Getting
closer. Charlie tensed. He was coming from her left. She leant in
front of Lena – a human shield – just as a tall muscular man with
white hair ran in front of them. Lena screamed. He raised a
pistol.

'No!' yelled Charlie, throwing herself on Lena, covering her head and body.

'Fucking move or I'll just shoot both of you!' yelled the man. The women held each other. More yelling.

Two shots.

120

Famie was sprawled across the entrance steps, peering over the top, Channing Hunter next to her. Their car's two policemen were ten metres in front, crouched on the path, weapons raised. Halfway to the church, beyond some graves, a tall man with white hair had a gun drawn.

Charlie, she thought. Charlie's there. Charlie and Lena. He's aiming at them.

'Armed police!' The shout was from elsewhere in the grave-yard. White-hair Man raised his gun in response. The shots took the top of his head off.

There was more shouting. Famie fought the urge to run to Charlie. Hunter placed a hand on her shoulder.

'Not yet,' she said.

Two more shots. From two different directions. An exchange of fire. The police on the path circled left, keeping low. They used every tree and gravestone to pause, gesture with fingers and hands, move on. Now she saw the BMW police. They were mirroring their colleagues, circling right. Pausing, taking aim, moving on.

More sirens. From everywhere now.

Famie felt useless and ridiculous in equal measure. She knew the shooter was dead, assumed Robert Nash was alive. That it was he who was firing at the police. But the action had moved to the edges of the graveyard. In front of her, centre stage, just behind that ridiculous white tomb, her daughter and best friend were hidden. Were they injured? What had Robert Nash done to Lena? What might he do now? Her mind was made up. She'd explain to Hunter later. Assuming there was one. Hunter's hand still rested on her shoulder but she could power through that.

She tensed against the steps, lifted her right foot to the fourth step, her left to the third. Hands on the first. A starting block. She felt her trainers cut her again. Her heart raced. She could hear the blood pulsing in her head.

Between her and the mausoleum, one beech tree, then two gravestones. She would do this in three stages. Tree, gravestone, then Charlie. She breathed deeply. Hunter lifted her hand to scratch her nose. Famie powered from the steps.

She was at the tree in five seconds. If Hunter had called out, she'd missed it. She leant against the trunk, peered round. The BMW police had disappeared again. The bearded officer who had driven her car was hunkered down by a circle of gravestones. She wanted him to see her, wanted him to know what she was doing. But he didn't look up.

Famie was at the gravestones in four seconds, diving into their cover, hitting her head and shoulder on the limestone. She was ten metres from the mausoleum. Wanted to call out but knew it would be stupid. She gathered herself. Crouched with her hands on the ground. Flashing blue lights now seemed to surround the graveyard. There were shouts and slammed doors but Famie wasn't waiting for any of them.

Just as she raised her head she heard a small voice say, 'Go!' Charlie and Lena sprinted away from her. Famie swallowed a cry, watched as they ran into the church. She slumped back down. 'What the fuck are they doing?' she whispered. Why would they run into the church when there are police every-where? Weirdly she felt reassured to see them both, and clearly they were okay. But they must know something. There must be a reason to be in there and not out here.

Famie followed. She ran past the dead man. He was on his back, arms splayed like he was sunbathing. Eyes open. Head bleeding into the ground. Twenty metres from the church porch she lengthened her stride. Now she saw the BMW policemen and they saw her. One was lying just on the dip, where the grave-yard sloped to trees and a main road. The other was crouched by a particularly sturdy beech tree. One waved her away. The other spoke into his radio.

Famie ran inside the church.

121

Robert Nash sat on a wooden chair, legs crossed. His arms rested on his right knee. His right hand held a gun. It was aimed at six people who stood against a cracked, whitewashed wall. Charlie and Lena were first, then the German family. The father shielded the younger boy, the mother shielded the elder. Both boys were crying. When Famie burst in, Nash jumped to his feet. He waved the gun between her and and the six.

'My favourite journalist' he said, wheezing heavily. 'Who knew there'd be so many of us?' He gestured with the gun barrel. 'Go on then, join your miserable daughter.' Charlie's look of desperation cut Famie to the quick.

'Sorry,' she whispered. She joined the line, took Charlie's hand and faced Nash. 'Why keep the family?' She nodded at the Germans. 'Let them go. Now you have us, what's the point of keeping them?'

Nash had sat down again. Congealed blood encased his ear and half of his cheek. It looked as though he was having trouble breathing. 'Do you ever shut up?' he said. 'Because you seem to speak all the fucking time. You've only been here a minute, and already I'm fed up with hearing your voice. And, yes, it had actually occurred to me to let them go. But I decided against it. For the moment.'

Famie glanced left and right. Above the entrance there was a small gallery, all of which was filled with a grand pipe organ. The ground floor was filled with chairs, the walls covered with elaborate plaques, statues and icons. A roped-off altar held six enormous candles and a flamboyant gold triptych. He saw her looking. 'Do you pray, Miss Madden?' he said.

'No,' she said.

'Not even in a place like this?'

'Especially not in a place like this.'

'You should try it sometime,' said Nash. 'Now might be a good time, actually.'

'I'm good,' said Famie. 'Thanks for your concern, but I'm a lost cause, I'm afraid. As, I suspect, are you.'

Nash smiled. 'Maybe so, maybe so,' he said.

'Although,' said Famie, 'my entire life hasn't been funded by the proceeds of slavery. So I suppose there is that.'

Nash stopped smiling. 'Is that what this is?' he said. 'All of this because of some trading traditions in the early nineteenth century? My family did well, that's true. We then invested everything in Britain. In its infrastructure, in its backbone. But people like you don't appreciate success, do you, Miss Madden? You don't really like Britain at all, do you?'

Charlie was growing increasingly agitated, tugging Famie's hand every few seconds. Lena had remained motionless, eyes closed. The German family was still and quiet. Outside, sirens seem to encircle the church. Flashing lights flooded through every window, turning the whitewashed walls blue and silver.

Famie smiled. 'Your analysis is, to no one's great surprise, totally fucked. I love living here as much as anyone because it gives me the freedom to investigate shit families like yours.'

Charlie pulled at her hand.

'When you say, "My family did well," ' said Famie, 'what you mean is, "We grew fat on the profits of a barbaric enslavement. An enslavement of millions. We then kept all of that money.

403

That is what we invested. We invested our blood money."'
Another, firmer, tug. ' "Oh, and occasionally we gave some to
fascists when we felt like it, but mainly we kept it."'

'For Christ's sake, Mum,' muttered Charlie. Lena was silent,
motionless. The German children had started to cry again.

Nash pushed himself up from the chair. He walked to Famie,
gun in his right hand. 'This word "slave",' he said. 'Do you where
it comes from? Your business is words, Miss Madden, so I'm sure
you do.'

'No,' said Famie, 'I don't. Does it matter?'

Nash walked down his line of hostages. 'Yes, it does. And
once I've told you, our German friends can leave us.' The father
whispered his translation to his family. The boys stopped crying.
Nash walked back, stood opposite Lena. 'And you, my dear
niece, need to hear this, I think.' Lena's eyes stayed closed. She
seemed to Famie to be in some kind of trance state.

' "Slave",' said Nash, 'comes from "Slav". It's from around the
early fourteenth century. So many Slavs were sold to conquering
tribes, they actually named slavery after them. Not black people,
not brown people, not any colour people. White people. White
Slavs. You see? They were the most prized human goods. They
filled the slave markets of Europe, Asia and Africa.'

Famie heard heavy boots running outside. Nash seemed to
hear nothing other than his own voice, perhaps enjoyed hearing
his words amplified around the ancient walls.

'So, you see, the slavery you speak of, Miss Madden, the slavery that enrages you, Lena, is just the way trade used to work. It
was the natural order of things. The anti-slavery organizations
were always a front for the commercial interests of India and the
like. 'Les Amis des Noirs', I believe was the phrase. They always
intended to destroy the natural energies of the West to favour
those of the East. My family fought against this.' Nash paused,

held up a hand. 'Mistakes were made, of course. But we learn, we improve ourselves. Slavery is a crime now, but then? Of course not. The idea is absurd. Are we really to say the Spanish, the Dutch, the French, the Swedes, the Danes, Norwegians, Russians, Portuguese and the Germans . . .' here Nash swept his hand in the direction of the terrified family '. . . are we really to say they had it all wrong? These mighty nations? I think not. My family thinks not.'

He walked to the German end and addressed the father. 'Now you may go. The rest of us will stay for a while.'

The father and mother muttered thanks and, heads down, shepherded their boys to the door. They walked as quickly as they could, glancing at Famie, Charlie and Lena as they passed. The father nodded and mouthed, 'Thank you.' The mother clasped her hands together, held them in front of her. Famie watched them hesitate before pushing the door open. The father went first, the family behind in single file. They all heard him shout, in slow deliberate words. 'We are a family from Düsseldorf, Germany. My name is Karl Schneider. My wife is Gabriele Schneider. Our sons are Georg and Thomas. We are coming out, okay?' There were muffled shouts in return. Then it was only sirens.

'So just us, then,' said Nash. 'Now we begin.'

Lena opened her eyes.

From inside her shirt, she produced a gun.

A Manurhin MR 73 revolver.

She shot Nash in the stomach.

122

The crack of the gunshot bounced around the church. Many seconds after Lena had pulled the trigger, the sound still reverberated around its walls. Nash staggered back into a row of chairs, fell to the floor, blood ballooning across his belly. No one else moved. Frozen in horror. Then Charlie yelled at Lena. Famie pulled her away. Ears ringing, she ran in front of Lena. She spoke words but heard only a muffled rumble. Held out her hand. Tried to say, 'Give me the gun,' but Lena pushed past her. Aimed the gun again.

The church doors crashed open. Four police, weapons raised. 'Armed police! Armed police! Drop your fucking weapon!'

Famie heard those words just fine. She raised her hands, backed away. Charlie copied her. Lena dropped to the floor alongside her uncle.

'Lena, stop, throw it away!' Charlie screamed.

'Lena, back away now,' yelled Famie. 'For the love of Christ . . .'. She noticed Nash's gun at her feet. Turned to the police. 'There's a gun here,' she shouted. 'On the floor. It was his, Nash's.' She pointed to where he lay, writhing.

'Leave it. Step away. Step away.' It was the bearded driver from her car. Surely he knew who she was. Who they all were. She spoke fast.

'I'm Famie Madden. This is my daughter Charlie. This is her friend Lena Nash. She was held prisoner by him.' More pointing. 'Her uncle. Robert Nash. We had no idea she had a gun. I think she got it from that guy you killed outside.'

The bearded policeman took a step forward, weapon raised. He spoke slowly and loudly. His words rang through the church.

'Lena Nash, drop your fucking weapon. Stand up. Step away. Show me your fucking hands.' He walked nearer.

'Lena, please!' screamed Charlie.

Then there was silence. Lena had not stood up, stepped away or dropped her weapon. She was kneeling by her uncle. She leant to whisper into his ear. The marble and granite reflected her every word.

'Sixty years of Nash slavery. Two centuries of Nash profits. Now it all stops. And I found out. I changed the list. It was me.' She licked her lips. 'I saved the slave painting. It was an atonement. An act of atonement.' Lena wiped her face with her hand. 'The rest of it burnt. The slaves survived.' Robert Nash opened his mouth, no words came out.

'My dad told me some,' said Lena. 'Jamie Nelson told me the rest. That was his name. The man who died when the gallery burnt. He was my friend. You didn't know him. But he knew you. He told me that back in Jamaica when slaves rebelled, often they executed their enslavers. Well. You are a monster. Our family are monsters. Now it stops.'

Lena flicked her eyes to the police. She raised her gun.

Two shots fired simultaneously. One from Lena's gun killed Robert Nash. The other from a policeman's gun killed Lena Nash.

123

There was no pecking order to the funerals. Famie had hoped there might be but she also knew it never worked like that. Helen Nash was buried first. Today had been Lena, tomorrow was Robert. She didn't know about the Afrikaner. Didn't care.

She had been to so many funerals. She wondered if anyone aged forty-five had attended as many. Today's had been the worst. It wasn't how it had been run or what had been said – Famie had barely noticed either – but the howling, rage-inducing injustice of it all. She stood at her sink, ran the water cold, filled a glass. Her only job at the crematorium had been to support Charlie, hold her up, be stronger than her. She had managed that but, Christ, it had been hard. She drank the water, filled the glass again. She had been so proud of Charlie. From somewhere her daughter had managed to find some words to say about her best friend, words that had made everyone in the chapel sob. Famie couldn't recall any of them. She had just been willing her to get to the end without collapsing. When Charlie had returned to her seat she was shaking. She had rested her head on Famie's shoulder for the rest of the service.

Famie finished her second glass, then filled a jug. She watched the post-funeral exhaustion play out in her remaining guests. Sam and his police officer wife, Jo, sat with posh Sara on garden chairs, Charlie was walking by the far wall with Brian Nelson, who had surprised everyone by flying back for Lena's funeral. Benoit had come from Paris by Eurostar and was sitting on a blanket with two of the Nash Fund women. Half-full wine glasses stood on the garden table alongside what had been a bowl of rice salad, some bread and a cheeseboard. In the late-afternoon sunshine, it all looked like the remains of a slightly chaotic family picnic.

Famie took the water jug and some stacked tumblers outside. She placed them on the table and sat with Sam, Jo and Sara. Sara's hair had been cut messily short, with purple highlights added. It gave her the look of an anime character, Famie thought. A disguise, maybe. Benoit walked over, took a cup and filled it.

'I've sort of just offered Sara a job, I think,' said Sam, smiling. A Chablis smile. It suited him.

Sara grimaced. 'That's not quite true,' she said, 'but he was being very generous for sure.'

'Which job were you offering?' asked Famie. 'Not yours, I hope?' She glanced at Jo to gauge her reaction but she just smiled and looked away.

Sara was clearly puzzled. 'You're not leaving Howl, are you?' she said. 'Not after your extraordinary takedown of the Nash family?' She looked between Famie, Jo and Sam. 'Oh,' she said, 'unless I've stumbled into something. In which case, I withdraw.' She sat back.

Jo Carter, black dress, shoulder-length black hair, put her hand on Sam's knee. 'It's under discussion, that's all,' she said. 'We have a lot to talk about over the summer.' That doesn't sound good, thought Famie. She let Sara pick up.

'Okay, well, from where I sit, for what it's worth, Howl is extraordinary. It was where Jamie went when he wanted inspiration. The standard of journalism he aspired to was the standard Howl set. He would have loved what you guys did with the Nash story.' She pointed between Famie and Sam. 'Fearless. Absolutely bloody fearless.'

'Actually,' said Sam, 'there was loads of fear. Publishing that piece was terrifying.'

'I can attest to that,' said Jo.

'Were you always like this, Famie?' asked Sara.

'Like what?' said Famie.

Sara thought for a moment. 'Brilliantly, relentlessly ferocious. Totally focused.' She smiled. 'I don't know. On edge twenty-four seven.'

'*Rien à foutre*,' said Benoit, raising his cup to Famie. 'Zero fucks given.' He wandered back to the Nash Fund women.

Sara laughed. 'Yeah, maybe that,' she said.

Sam raised his hand. 'For the first and last time in my life, I will answer for Famie,' he said. Jo looked alarmed.

'This'll be interesting,' said Famie.

'Famie has always been the best journalist in the room,' he said. 'Any newsroom you could name. Her instincts. Her understanding. Her attitude. Always the best. But the "*rien à foutre*" bit, to quote Benoit, she got from her ex-husband.' Famie frowned, surprised. She was reasonably sure Sam would make this work. She said nothing. 'Or maybe I should say,' he continued, 'because of her ex-husband. And she has warned me not to mention him ever again but when you've been messed around as much as Jacob messed Famie and Charlie around, you can either go off the rails and into rehab or you become a team. And that was what happened. They became an incredible team.'

Famie felt her eyes prickle. 'And you can stop now,' she said. 'Thanks and everything but stop. Anyway, it was you who pressed "Go" on this story, Sam. You're on the team.' They exchanged smiles.

'And as it turns out, we were right to publish,' said Sam.

'Jamie did the groundwork. We could never have done it without him. That's why his name was on the piece.'

The Howl article had been headlined 'Empire of Shame: Nash Fortune Built by Slavery' and given the byline 'Famie Madden, Sam Carter, Jamie Nelson.' After publication, all West End companies had ceased trading, then folded altogether. The death of the Nash siblings and the collapse of their business had made headlines around the world. Brian Nelson, doorstepped back home in Jamaica, had been pleased to restore some family pride. He approached Famie now, arm in arm with Charlie. They had both been crying.

Nelson, black suit, black tie, sat next to Famie on one of the plastic kitchen chairs that had been dragged outside. Charlie sat cross-legged on the grass, watching spiralling, screeching swifts high in the sky above her.

'Remind me when your flight is, Mr Nelson,' said Sam. 'I can run you to the station.'

Jo shook her head. 'You're not driving anyone anywhere,' she said.

Nelson smiled. 'No one should be driving now,' he said. 'A taxi will be fine. I must to leave in twenty minutes. And I need to thank you again.' He looked at each of them in turn. 'My wife would have been proud today. Alice would have been so proud. She would have liked you all so much.' He wiped away more tears. 'I am more familiar with the Nash family tree than is good for me, of course. I hope to forget them all in time but maybe I won't manage that. My family tree will be rejoicing for sure. Not at the deaths, I don't think I wish that on anyone. But the truth is out.' He managed a sad smile. 'And, as Alice would have said, the truth will set you free.'

Famie watched Charlie, whose attention was still on the

swifts. She hadn't spoken much. The funeral was the most Famie had heard from her since Lena's death. She was sure that witnessing her best friend being killed was a trauma Charlie would never escape. Not really. She would try, and Famie would help her, but the brightness of Lena's blood on the marble, and the volume of gunfire made for an unshakeable and vivid memory.

They had gone back to Gasholders together, grabbed a few clothes, her phone and laptop, then hurried out again. She had moved into Famie's spare room, knowing the flat would be sold. Lena had left no will and had no relatives. The state would take the proceeds. A government minister had already pledged to donate an equivalent sum to an anti-slavery charity.

Jo Carter placed her drink on the table. She leant forward in her chair and looked between Nelson and Famie. 'Why didn't they just admit it all years ago?' she said. 'When they found out what had happened, why didn't they just admit it, pay over some money and move on? Loads of companies have done that. Why didn't they?'

'I've been thinking about that,' said Famie. 'Best guess? No one was asking questions for a long, long time. Family secrets. But old Harry Nash, Lena's grandfather, he knew for certain. I think his wife knew too. Or found out somehow. And that is, I think, one of the reasons behind her suicide. It had all gone too far by then. To admit to anything would have invited ruin.'

'And also invited attention to what they were spending money on,' said Sam. 'Their family history of funding far-right parties suggests they were hardly bothered with human decency or democratic norms. James and Marion, old Harry's parents, were hanging out with Mosley's fascists. So we know where their sympathies lay.'

'And if I may,' said Nelson, tugging on a grey cap against the afternoon sun, 'you only go back two generations from James

412

and Marion Nash to reach Mary Bennett, slave-owner. Formerly of West End, Jamaica. Wife of John Nash. Grandparents to James and Marion.' He spread his arms. 'It's not so far back. Not really.'

Charlie stirred, and looked away from the aerobatic display, which continued above her. 'We heard him, though,' she said. She spoke softly, her voice troubled. Everyone turned, leant in. 'We heard Robert Nash in the church. Me and Mum. We heard. "It's just the way trade used to work," he said. "It was the natural order of things," he said.' She was facing everyone, but her eyes were on Brian Nelson. 'They aren't the words of some-one struggling with his family history. I think he was actually proud.'

There was silence.

'He said that?' said Nelson, his words almost a whisper.

'He did,' confirmed Famie. She looked at Charlie. Had she had seen Lena's glance to the police before she shot her uncle? She had replayed that moment so many times. It had looked to her as if it might have been an SbC. Suicide by Cop. That Lena knew what would happen if she pulled the trigger, but fired anyway. If Charlie had missed it, she wasn't about to tell her. Not yet. Maybe it would come out in time.

Famie was happy to let that news wait. She had something else to mention. 'I'm sure Lena knew everything,' she said, 'but needed us to tell the story, not her. She steered conversations. I didn't realize at the time. Down at the canal, it was her who mentioned the Fanta modern art her uncle had bought. When we hadn't found the second steganography image, she was the one who suggested there might be something else in the tree roots.'

'Needed us to tell the story,' said Charlie, 'because she was afraid of her family.' The rest didn't need saying. So no one said it.

Famie's phone buzzed. She excused herself.

Channing Hunter grimaced as Famie opened the front door. 'Apologies,' she said. 'Is everyone still here? I got caught up with something.'

Famie smiled, beckoned her inside. Locked and bolted. 'No, you're fine,' she said. 'Brian Nelson is leaving soon but if by "everyone" you mean our very small team, then, yes, we're all here. Come on through.'

Hunter hesitated, and put a hand on Famie's arm. 'Just before we go outside,' she said.

Famie raised an eyebrow. 'Don't tell me,' she said. 'Howard Taylor's confessed to being a gangster, sexual predator and killer?'

Hunter didn't smile. 'Not exactly. But he's been refused bail. So he isn't going anywhere. No, it's the graffiti on your wall and the car you reported. The black Range Rover. Remember?'

'Of course.'

'It's a diplomatic car,' said Hunter.

'Surprise me,' said Famie.

'Saudi Arabia,' said Hunter.

Famie wasn't that surprised. There had been a lot of critical reporting on Howl from journalists in and around Saudi. 'I'd been hoping for Canada, obviously,' she said, 'but Saudi is interesting. A bit flash for a spying mission, though.'

'Maybe they were just lost,' said Hunter.

'Of course,' said Famie. 'Just "lost" outside my home. And just shortly after we had run some pieces on human rights and corruption there.'

'One other thing,' Hunter said. She selected photos on her phone and held up the screen. 'Six months ago,' she said. Her screen held a photo of the same Range Rover with a Palestinian

414

flag flying from the passenger window.' It was on a drive-through of Jewish areas of north London.'

Famie shrugged. 'Well, he's an idiot then, whoever he is. What about the graffiti?'

'We spoke to the Turkish Embassy' said Hunter. 'All they said was that they know the Grey Wolves have a handful of enthusiastic supporters in the UK. But "enthusiastic" paramilitaries are dangerous people.'

'A lone wolf and a grey wolf,' Famie said.

Hunter acknowledged the point. 'Probably,' she said.

'What am I supposed to do with this information?' she said. 'I know I'm a target, Channing. I take precautions.'

Hunter pulled a face.

'Okay, sometimes I take precautions,' said Famie. 'Now come outside, for Christ's sake. Get a drink.'

The two women emerged, blinking, into the sunshine. They both produced sunglasses. Sam handed them each a glass of white wine. 'We were about to make a toast,' he said. Everyone was standing. A rough semicircle, with Brian Nelson in the middle. Famie caught Charlie's eye, smiled. Charlie smiled back. Sam raised his glass towards Brian Nelson. 'To Jamie,' he said. The glasses were raised.

'To Jamie,' they chorused.

Brian Nelson held his glass higher, longer. 'Duppy conqueror,' he said.

From Jamie Nelson's Instagram

I love it. You're a revolutionary after all. Walked round your gallery this morning. Yes, I waited till you were gone. Thought it might be easier that way. Anyway. To see *Slaves Waiting for Sale* in a Nash gallery is the most radical thing ever. A Nash gallery! I took a seat, watched it for an hour. Every minute was a privilege. I intend to come back. The man with the rolled-up sleeves in the bottom corner is my new hero. He is SCORN. He is DEFIANCE. Have crossed arms and slouched shoulders ever looked so MIGHTY? That man is DANGEROUS. It's my new look, for sure.

To sit in a building I am still convinced was funded by slave money and see such things made me weep. Yes, I did. And it's because of you. So I know I've done some bad things, said some bad things, made you feel bad (sorry again), but this painting, Lena, is something else.

Back when the compensation was paid to the slave-owners it was a FEEDING FRENZY in the UK. It was CASH FOR CHATTELS. More than £6 million was paid to Jamaican slave-owners. SIX MILLION.

Average price in Jamaica, £22 nine shillings per enslaved man woman or child. Suddenly everyone was a slave-owner. Your family laughed and danced all the way to all of their many banks. And they have been laughing and dancing ever since.

I am nearly there with the proof. We are nearly there. Are you sure you can't get me over the line? (I'm doing that smile you like if it helps.) If you change your mind, I'll be up for the demonstration this weekend. See you there?

Prayer of
St Pancras Old Church, London

Saint Pancras, our patron, pray for us;
and may the souls of the faithful,
through the mercy of God,
rest in peace.

Amen

Acknowledgements

[2 pp To Come]

About the Author

Simon Mayo MBE is the author of three previous novels, *Mad Blood Stirring, Knife Edge* and *Tick Tock.*

He worked as a radio broadcaster for the BBC for forty years and now presents on Greatest Hits Radio.